Players in Paradise . . .

Meredith Courtney. The stunning, young newscaster. Her widely acclaimed charms were dazzling . . . and her beauty bright enough to capture the world's most eligible man.

Alexander Kirakis. The passionate tycoon. His vast display of wealth was matched only by his hidden treasure of dark secrets.

Nick Holliday. The hot young film director. His smoldering romance with Meredith Courtney opened the door to the biggest story of her career.

Tom and Elizabeth Ryan. Hollywood's greatest director and his beautiful actress wife. The shocking tragedy of their past could destroy Meredith's newfound love . . . and Alexander's empire.

DANCE OF THE GODS

For my husband Tony, with all my love—
yesterday, today, tomorrow and always

DANCE

OF THE

GODS

NORMA BEISHIR

B
BERKLEY BOOKS, NEW YORK

Of the Good in you I can speak, but not of the Evil,
For what is Evil but Good—tortured by its own hunger
and thirst?
Verily, when Good is hungry, it seeks food, even in dark
caves;
And when it thirsts, it drinks even of dead waters. . . .

Kahlil Gibran
The Prophet

DANCE OF THE GODS

A Berkley Book / published by arrangement with
the author

PRINTING HISTORY
Berkley edition / May 1988

ISBN: 0-425-10839-2

A BERKLEY BOOK ® TM 757,375
Berkley Books are published by The Berkley Publishing Group,
200 Madison Avenue, New York, N.Y. 10016.
The name "BERKLEY" and the "B" logo
are trademarks belonging to Berkley Publishing Corporation

PRINTED IN THE UNITED STATES OF AMERICA.

10 9 8 7

AUTHOR'S NOTE

No book is the product of the author's efforts alone, and I wish to express my deepest gratitude to those who helped to color the mosaic of this novel with the many tiles of their expertise, their knowledge, and their memories—and thank those who gave me their support and encouragement when it was needed most:

My editor, Damaris Rowland, for her guidance, support, and patience above and beyond the call of duty . . .

My agent, Maria Carvainis, for her enthusiasm, encouragement, and personal commitment . . .

The team at Camp Berkley for making the dream a reality: Roger Cooper, Ed Breslin, Sabra Elliott, Leigh Haber, Diane Ekblad, Frank Kozelek, Joni Friedman, Rick Surmacz, and Geanine Thompson.

Sybil Pincus, for her fine-tooth comb copyediting . . .

Nancy Coffey, for her initial support . . .

For their assistance in research: Louis Danos and Achilles Papersenos of the Greek Embassy in Washington; Tony Hatch of Atlantic Richfield, Los Angeles; Earl Zimmerman of GA Technologies in San Diego; Bill Thomes, for a crash course in business administration; and Pam Thomas and Jerry Koch for info on filmmaking . . .

For their overall support and encouragement: Karyn Witmer-Gow, Kitty Glenn Doyle, Joan Treloar, Boni Heck, Jake and Lolly Beishir, Jim and Audrey Relling, Kay Schlesinger, Donna Tyson, Jan Dierkes, Mary Miller, Betty Stewart, and Loretta Raney . . .

And for inspiration, my son, Collin, the eighth wonder of the world . . .

Norma L. Beishir
St. Louis, Missouri
October 20, 1987

PROLOGUE

᠊᠊᠊᠊᠊᠊᠊᠊᠊᠊᠊᠊᠊᠊᠊᠊᠊᠊

New York City, December 1986.

A light snow was falling. Up and down Fifth Avenue the windows of all the fabulous shops—Cartier, Saks, Tiffany & Co., Van Cleef & Arpels, Harry Winston, Gucci, Bergdorf Goodman, Steuben Glass—glittered with magnificent holiday treasures that beckoned shoppers to come inside. The sounds of honking horns filled the air as a river of pedestrians—shoppers laden with brightly wrapped Christmas packages, office workers gratefully calling it a day, wide-eyed tourists eagerly taking in the sights, and the usual assortment of street vendors—flooded the streets, resembling a scene from the Exodus. Traffic was bumper to bumper as buses, taxis, and chauffeured limousines jockeyed for positions along the thoroughfare.

Huddled in the back of one of those limousines, Meredith drew her Russian lynx coat around herself for warmth, but it did no good. The chill was deep within her bones, and it had nothing to do with the weather. Inside the limousine it was warm . . . but Meredith was numb with a fear she could not put into words. Normally, she would have been glad the day was over, glad to be going home, but tonight nothing gave her comfort. She felt as though her whole world was about to come crashing down around her, and there was nothing she could do to prevent it.

Tonight Meredith was oblivious of the pulsing excitement that was so much a part of life in Manhattan. She glanced absently at the shop windows, having suddenly lost her Christmas spirit. She peered through the window as the limo inched its way toward its destination. On the west side of the avenue, nestled between Forty-eighth and Fiftieth streets, was the sprawling community of skyscrapers, plazas, stores, and cafés known as Rockefeller Center. "As solid as seven million dollars," Alexander had once told her. Alexander. Meredith was usually eager to get home and spend a quiet evening with her husband, but now she found herself glad he was not going to be there when she arrived. Alexander was in Paris on business, and Meredith was grateful. He knew her too well; he would have recognized her tension immediately. He would have known that something was wrong. Meredith wasn't sure that this was something she could share with him. Not yet.

The limousine slowed to a stop in front of the Olympic Tower at the corner of Fifth Avenue and Fifty-first Street. The chauffeur opened the door for her, and as Meredith stepped out into the cold night air, the wind whipped her long blond hair around her face. She paused for a moment to gaze up at the building, a magnificent bronze jewel rising into the twilight sky. Fifty-two stories of pure opulence, fit for a king. As she made her way toward it, the liveried doorman, poised at the entrance like a member of the Praetorian Guard, smiled and held the door for her. She nodded absently to him and headed across the red-carpeted lobby toward the elevators. She rang for the elevator impatiently, repeatedly. Hurry, she thought anxiously. Please . . . hurry.

"Is something wrong, Mrs. Kirakis?"

She turned, startled. One of the concierges, easily recognized by his familiar dress uniform—brown slacks, blue-gray jacket, waistcoat, and white satin bow tie—stood behind her, a look of concern on his face. "Are you all right, Mrs. Kirakis?" he asked, trying to be helpful.

She managed a weak smile. "Yes . . . I'm just a bit tired,

that's all," she assured him. "It's been a long day. I'm glad to finally be home."

He smiled. "Your husband arrived about an hour ago," he told her as he held the elevator for her.

Meredith swung around to face him, unable to hide her surprise. "My husband? Are you sure?"

He nodded. "Yes, ma'am," he said. "No mistake. I went up in the elevator with him myself."

"Thank you," she said as the doors closed slowly and the car began its ascent. She leaned back against the wall, trembling. She wondered why Alexander was back from Paris so soon. What could have happened? What else could possibly go wrong now?

He was waiting for her when she let herself into their apartment. He came to her and embraced her gently. "I hoped you would not be late," he said as he released her.

"Did everything go all right in Paris?" she asked as she took off her coat.

"Of course. Why do you ask?"

"I don't know. It's just that lately we seem to be living in the eye of a hurricane. I can't help wondering what's going to happen next," she admitted wearily. "I thought maybe whatever you went there for fell through or something . . ."

"It could not have turned out better." He studied her for a moment, his black eyes narrowing suspiciously. "Perhaps you should tell me what is bothering you."

"Me?" Her laugh was mirthless. "Overwork, that's all. Nobody's told Harv Petersen that slavery's been abolished."

"Your work? You are sure that's all?"

"Scout's honor," she said, making her voice light. "I've got a splitting headache. I think I might lie down for a while before dinner. Do you mind?"

He shook his head. He didn't believe her for a minute and she knew it. She was grateful that he was not pressing her to tell him more than she had already. She had not been lying about the headache, however, feeling the familiar throbbing pain in her right temple. She kissed Alexander again and retreated to their bedroom before he decided to question her further.

As she lay in the darkness, she tried not to think about it,

but it was impossible. She had thought of nothing else since
the special messenger had arrived at her office with it that
morning. There had been no letter, nothing to identify its
sender—just a photocopy of a legal document that needed
no explanation. Its message had been only too clear. Not
knowing who sent it bothered Meredith most. It meant that
someone knew the truth, someone who could turn it into a
dangerous weapon. Meredith sat up and switched on the
bedside lamp. She removed the envelope from her oversize
shoulder bag as carefully as if she were defusing a bomb. A
bomb would not have frightened her as much. She removed
the paper from the envelope and stared at it for a long time.
How was she going to break this to Alexander? she asked
herself for the hundredth time that day. How could she ever
make him understand? Would he believe her when she told
him that she had no idea who had sent this?

That single piece of paper, in the wrong hands, could
destroy them.

ONE

ℝℝℝℝℝℝℝℝℝ

Los Angeles, July 1979.

Meredith Courtney, a newscaster for television station KXLA, parked her car across the street from the Beverly Wilshire Hotel and glanced at her watch. Nine forty-five. Good. She was early. She peered into her rearview mirror and ran a comb through her thick, ash-blond hair. She checked her makeup automatically, a habit she'd picked up after a fellow newscaster once told her she looked overdone on camera. She twisted around in her seat and noticed that the KXLA mobile production van was pulling up behind her. Her cameraman had arrived. She got out of the car and waved to Brian as he began unloading his equipment. He grinned when he saw her.

"Hi, lady," he greeted her cheerfully. "They got you workin' early today. It ain't even noon yet!"

She smiled. "We can't all be night owls, now, can we?" she teased. "You've been spoiled, doing the nightside spot with Harry Jacobs."

"Who is this guy, anyway?" Brian asked as they crossed Wilshire Boulevard together. "A foreign diplomat or something?"

"Constantine Kirakis?" Meredith laughed aloud at the

thought. ''Where have you been, Brian? He's only one of the richest men in the world. You've really never heard of him?''

The cameraman shrugged. ''I guess I've led a pretty sheltered life up until now.''

''You must have,'' Meredith agreed, amused. ''For the record, Constantine Kirakis is an honest-to-goodness Greek tycoon—ships, oil, diamond mines, the whole package. His is a classic rags-to-riches story if there ever was one: the poor boy from the wrong side of the tracks who built an empire with nothing but his own ambitions.''

''So he *is* news.''

''Definitely.'' Heads turned as Meredith crossed the lobby of the Beverly Wilshire, but she did not notice. She was accustomed to being recognized on her home turf. After all, she knew she was in a highly visible profession. It had never occurred to her that she would have been noticed regardless of her profession. Meredith was a striking woman, slender, bronzed, with the kind of delicate, perfect features and wide blue eyes that made magazine covers, and a magnificent long mane of tousled blond hair. She was a genuine California golden girl.

Meredith maneuvered her way into the jammed banquet room and found a seat, while Brian looked for a suitable location that would give him a clear, unobstructed view of the podium from which Kirakis would be speaking. While Brian knew nothing of Constantine Kirakis, he knew that this tape was important to Meredith, and that was all he needed to know. Meredith Courtney, he knew from past experience, was a perfectionist who insisted upon total commitment and professionalism from all who worked with her. Brian knew she would be hell to get along with if this latest project turned out to be less than perfect. He made some minor adjustments and waited for her signal.

As Constantine Kirakis was introduced, Meredith dug into her shoulder bag for a thick steno pad and a handful of pencils. She took notes in rapid shorthand, thankful she'd taken the time to learn it. Her notes would help her later, when she prepared the material for broadcast. She had already thought of different things she wanted to mention about her subject on the air, and this assured her that nothing would be forgotten. She motioned to Brian, indicating that she wanted a closeup. Constantine Kirakis was an impressive man, something she wanted to convey to the viewers who would see this tape on the eleven o'clock news. She wanted them to feel the power and authority behind his forceful gestures, in his strong voice speaking heavily accented English. She wanted them to sense everything she experienced as she sat there in the crowded banquet room. He was a giant of a man, she noticed now—tall and powerfully built, an imposing figure in his black suit, which created a sharp contrast to his reddened, windburned face and his shockingly white hair and mustache.

He must have been handsome as a younger man, Meredith thought.

As the conference dragged on, Meredith began to feel as though she had wasted her time in coming. She was annoyed by the way the reporters from *Shipping News* were dominating the conference, obviously viewing this as the perfect opportunity to question Kirakis about tonnage, cargo rates, sea routes, and the issue of shipping versus air freight. Her viewers would not be interested in those topics; they would want to know about the Kirakis Corporation's many projects now under way in the United States, projects that would mean hundreds, even thousands of jobs. They were interested in the fabulous diamond and emerald choker, reportedly worth over two million dollars, that Kirakis had given his wife Melina for their fiftieth wedding anniversary. They wanted to know about Kirakis's son, Alexander, the heir apparent to the Kirakis empire, the Casanova of the jet set, whose romantic adventures made gossip columns all over the world. At the rate things were going now, Meredith thought dismally, she might have to scrap the idea of showing the Kirakis tape at all.

At eleven forty-five, a Kirakis PR aide interrupted the conference, suggesting they all adjourn to La Bella Fontana, the hotel's restaurant, for lunch. Maybe if she could manage to be seated next to him at lunch . . . that would be perfect! As the group filed out of the banquet room, she stopped to give Brian some last-minute instructions before sending him back to the station. They would not be allowed to tape in La

Bella Fontana—she wouldn't even ask—but if she could just talk to Kirakis, maybe they could return later and tape an interview in his suite.

Much to her disappointment, the reporters from *Shipping News* beat her to it. They're like a bunch of hungry vultures, she thought irritably as she headed for an empty table. Distracted by this latest upset, she collided with a man headed in the same direction. "I'm sorry, I didn't—" The man she'd bumped into was not one of her fellow reporters. He was tall, at least six feet two, dressed in a suit that probably cost a small fortune. He was dark, with sharp, symmetrical features and the most incredible eyes she had ever seen. They were so dark they appeared to have no pupils. His hair was also dark, neatly styled, falling in a deep wave across his forehead. When he smiled at her, his eyes glowed like polished onyx.

"I'm Alexander Kirakis," he introduced himself. His voice was deep, resonant, with only a slight accent—not at all like his father's.

"I'm Meredith Courtney—KXLA News," she said. She stared at him like an idiot, unable to stop herself.

"A reporter?" he asked, somewhat amused. "I would never have guessed. You are far too lovely to be anything except perhaps a model or an actress."

She smiled. "Do I detect a bit of chauvinism?" she asked.

"On my part? Never!" He laughed, a deep, husky laugh. "You must forgive me . . . I have been brought up to observe certain old-world traditions—"

She raised a hand. "No need to explain. Apology accepted, Mr. Kirakis."

"Alexander," he corrected.

"Alexander," she repeated slowly.

Alexander Kirakis glanced back at the table where his father sat with four men from *Shipping News*. "You were hoping to join my father, were you not?"

She nodded. "Unfortunately, the sharks got there ahead of me."

"This is most unfortunate for my father," Alexander commented as he turned back to her. "He does not often have the opportunity to dine with a beautiful woman on these trips," he said with a dazzling smile that made Meredith blush unexpectedly.

"Thank you, but—"

"I, on the other hand, never pass up such a promising opportunity," he continued. "I would be honored if you would consider joining me, Meredith."

"I'd like that," she said without hesitation.

"Excellent." He took her arm, and she felt an involuntary shudder course through her body. "Come, we'll take one of the booths." He guided her across the room to one of the curtained booths that afforded total privacy. "I prefer privacy whenever it can be found. It's such a rarity for me these days," he explained as they seated themselves. "I hope you do not object."

"Not at all," she said quickly. Meredith looked around. She had not been there in some time, and she'd forgotten just how splendid it was. The red velvet wall covering and the trickling fountain in the center of the room gave it an elegant atmosphere. There were flowers everywhere, literally everywhere. It felt as though they had been transported by magic to some artfully contrived hideaway in Europe, perhaps in Vienna or Budapest.

"It reminds me of a place I once stayed at in Austria," Alexander commented, almost as if he had read her mind. "Tell me—have you eaten here before?"

"Once or twice—it's been a while," Meredith admitted.

"The food—how is it?"

"Oh, it's excellent," she assured him. "There's no place close by that can compare."

"I'll trust your judgment," he said promptly.

She smiled. "I hope you're not disappointed, then." Maybe she would get that interview after all; surely no one could be closer to Kirakis than his own son. She glanced at the menu absently, aware that he was watching her. "I hope you're enjoying your stay here in L.A.," she said. The way he looked at her, she felt like a schoolgirl again.

"Definitely," he answered with a suggestive smile. "Everything I've seen here so far is quite beautiful."

Meredith blushed once more. "I'd think our smog would be hard to take. Where you come from—"

"Where I come from?" He laughed aloud. "I live in New York City!"

"But didn't you grow up in Greece?"

"I did." He paused. "I take it you've never been there."

"No. No, I haven't."

"Athens is very much like Los Angeles," he told her. "As a matter of fact, it has often been referred to as Los Angeles with ruins. It has the smog, the same traffic tie-ups, the same throngs of tourists. It was once a lovely old city, but in recent years it has become very commercial."

"I take it you don't approve," she concluded, suppressing a smile.

"No, I don't," he answered truthfully. "Athens has always been a city rich with history, with tradition. As it becomes more and more a tourist attraction, it loses its specialness. I find it quite sad."

"Then life in New York hasn't caused you to sever your ties with your Greek heritage?"

He looked at her, surprised. "Where would you get an idea like that?" he asked.

"Well, everybody knows you've lived in the States for almost thirteen years. And everybody knows your father is against it. Wouldn't you say you've become somewhat Americanized?"

He smiled. "In some ways, perhaps. Though I tend to feel that one never completely escapes the influence of one's family traditions. I have found that I still observe many of the customs I grew up with, no matter where I happen to be."

The waiter came and took their order. Over lunch, Alexander talked about his parents and his childhood in Greece. He entertained her with anecdotes about the people and situations he had encountered in his travels as a senior vice-president of the Kirakis Corporation. Meredith found herself wondering if this could be the same man she'd read so much about. She saw none of the arrogant, self-centered playboy in this bright, witty, exceedingly charming man who now sat across from her, going out of his way to be cordial. But then, she reminded herself, that had to be part of his charm, part of the fascination he held for some of the most beautiful women in the world. Just this morning, she'd seen a photograph of him in the *Los Angeles Times* with his woman of the moment, Italian film star Francesca Correnti.

Alexander was honest with her when she asked about the possibility of getting an interview with his father. "We are leaving immediately after this press conference," he told her. "Our jet is waiting for us at the airport. We will be flying back to New York this afternoon. I *am* sorry—I think Father might have enjoyed it tremendously."

I guess it would be asking too much to pray for a heavy fog at the airport, Meredith thought dismally. "Maybe next time," she said optimistically.

"If there is a next time," Alexander said slowly. "Father does not come to the States often—not since I've taken over as head of our North American operations. In the past few years he has seldom traveled outside Greece. He's becoming a bit of a recluse in his twilight years, I think."

"Then maybe I could interview *you* the next time we meet," she suggested.

He flashed her an easy grin. "You have my word on it," he promised. "If and when we meet again, I'll give you an interview."

"I intend to hold you to it," she warned him. As if I'm ever going to run into him like this again, she thought.

Alexander and Constantine Kirakis left the Beverly Wilshire that afternoon, flanked by the security guards the elder Kirakis insisted upon having wherever he went. A limousine waited to take them to the airport where their private jet was standing by. "You are sure you will not come back to Greece with me, Alexander?" Kirakis asked as the limo traveled south on the San Diego Freeway. "Your mother would be so pleased to see you."

"You know it's impossible for me to get away just now, Father," Alexander said. "There's so much I'm involved in at the moment, so many meetings—"

Kirakis looked at him crossly. "You are sure it is business that prevents you from coming home?" He shoved a copy of the *Los Angeles Times* at his son, folded back to show a photograph of Alexander with Francesca Correnti. "Or perhaps this lady is your reason?"

"Hardly," Alexander responded indifferently. He knew that Francesca would be there, waiting for him, whenever he returned, no matter how long he stayed away. She was always there, always ready for him. There were times he found her devotion a bit suffocating, times he felt the need to get away from her for a while. He would have liked nothing better than to return to Greece for a week or two. He had not seen his mother in months, and he missed her terribly. She had not been well lately, and her doctors had advised her against making long trips, even by air. This had prevented her from visiting Alexander in New York as she'd done frequently in the past.

Kirakis scowled at the newspaper photograph. "I think you could have been more discreet, Alexander," he said finally.

"That photograph was taken—"

"As you and the lady were entering the lobby of the Plaza—where she is presently staying," Kirakis finished. "You could not be more blatant about this—arrangement —if you had taken out a full-page advertisement in *The New York Times*."

"It is most difficult to be discreet, Father, when the paparazzi follow me everywhere," Alexander said defensively. "I have almost no privacy these days."

"That is because you have made yourself such a good target for these people," Kirakis insisted, his displeasure apparent. "They know if they stay with you long enough, sooner or later you will do something worth photographing. Today it is Signorina Correnti. Who will it be next week—or next month? You have become a media celebrity, my son. Unfortunately, the publicity you have been getting is most unfavorable."

"Am I being reprimanded, Father?" Alexander asked icily.

"Your mother and I do not approve of the way in which you conduct your private affairs, Alexander—we have made no secret of our feelings about that—but we are aware that we cannot live your life for you," Kirakis said, choosing his words carefully. "We ask only that you try to be discreet about it. Your mother is quite sensitive about airing the family laundry, so to speak, in public."

Alexander drew in his breath. "Very well. I shall try to honor your wishes," he promised. "Now—may we discuss something else? I'm weary of the subject."

"I am sure that you are," Kirakis agreed. "But tell me one thing, Alexander—do you not ever give serious consideration to the prospect of getting married? Do you not ever contemplate having a family of your own—children?" There was genuine concern in his voice.

Alexander's laugh was weak. "I'm not ready for marriage, Father—and I am certainly not ready to become a father," he said. "And even if I were, I have yet to meet a woman I could consider a suitable wife."

"When *I* was your age—" Kirakis began, annoyed.

"When you were my age, Father, you and Mother had been married for almost ten years. You had already established the Athena Shipping Company—which later became Athena Maritime—the flagship company of the Kirakis Corporation. Mother had had two miscarriages and was warned that she could die if she attempted a third pregnancy," Alexander finished, ticking off the facts on the fingers of his left hand. "Yes, Father—I know our illustrious history by heart. I should. I memorized it as a child, much in the same way that other children memorize fairy tales."

"You make light of it, Alexander, but it is your heritage —your legacy. When I am gone, you will be the sole heir to all that I have fought so hard to achieve," Kirakis reminded him. "And like all empires, it must have heirs if it is to endure."

Alexander turned to look at his father. "So this is why people have children, is it?" he asked with a touch of bitterness in his voice. "Tell me, Father—why do poor people have them? They have nothing to leave to them."

"I am trying to be patient with you, Alexander, but you do not make it easy," Kirakis said quietly, staring absently into the traffic as they approached the Los Angeles International Airport. "I assumed that you, above all, would understand. The corporation must always be run by a Kirakis. A Kirakis must always be its majority stockholder."

"And where is this written, Father?" Alexander asked coldly.

"Ah, it is no use trying to talk to you!" Kirakis growled.

Alexander could be so unreasonable sometimes, he thought. Would he ever *really* be ready to fulfill his destiny as sole heir to the Kirakis empire?

In her small office at the KXLA building, Meredith related the events of the afternoon to Kay Wilson, one of KXLA's technical directors. Meredith expressed disappointment at not having gotten the interview she wanted, but told Kay that she found Constantine Kirakis's son most impressive. "I sat down expecting Bluebeard, and he turned out to be Prince Charming," she confided to her colleague. "He was really a pleasant surprise."

"Apparently," Kay said as she poured herself a cup of coffee from a coffee machine in one corner of Meredith's office. She took two sugar cubes from the small covered bowl next to it and hunted through the drawer for the jar of creamer she knew Meredith kept there. "Tell me, is he really as good-looking as his pictures?"

"Better," Meredith responded without hesitation. "It's funny . . . he didn't seem conceited at all. But a man who looks like that has to know it—unless he's never been in front of a mirror in his life."

"Hmmm . . . he's made quite an impression on you, I see," Kay said with a wicked grin.

"It's not what you've got going through that suspicious little mind of yours at all," Meredith said. "He seemed like a very nice man. Of course, it's hard to tell much about anyone after spending little more than an hour with him in a crowded restaurant."

"Of course," Kay agreed readily. "Tell me something. He obviously scored Brownie points with you. Why didn't you interview *him*?"

"I thought about it," Meredith admitted. "He seemed so open at first. I thought it would be simple to get him to talk to me. But the longer we were together, the more I felt I'd be wasting my time asking him. It was all on the surface. He was pleasant and charming, but he didn't discuss anything of any importance. I came away with the feeling that he's actually quite guarded."

"Ah-hah, a man of mystery!" Kay declared triumphantly.

"Sounds intriguing." She perched on one corner of Meredith's desk and peeked at her notes. "Who're you interviewing tomorrow—or shouldn't I ask?"

"Nick Holliday—better known to the moviegoing public-at-large as this year's hottest new director. The studio's words, I might add, not mine." Meredith's tone was skeptical. "Probably has an ego as big as all outdoors."

"You never can tell," Kay said.

Meredith made a wry face. "The way *my* luck's been running, I'd be willing to bet a week's salary on it."

Kay laughed heartily. "You've just had a rough day, that's all. It's called the I-don't-have-a-tape-for-tonight's-broadcast syndrome," she diagnosed. "Just wait and see. The tide will change. It always does."

New York City.

"You are sure you will not change your mind and come back to Greece with me?" Constantine Kirakis asked his son as they crossed the airstrip at Kennedy International Airport together, heading for the familiar blue and white corporate jet. "It would make your mother so very happy."

"Father, nothing would make *me* happier than to be able to go home and spend some time with her, but as I've already told you, it's impossible for me to get away just now," Alexander said wearily. "So much is going on right now—"

Pausing at the bottom of the ramp, Kirakis held up a hand to silence his son. "Ah, yes, business as usual," he sighed. "I suppose I should be pleased that you are taking such an interest in the business. Very well, I shall try to explain to your mother. But I warn you—she will be most disappointed."

"No more disappointed than I am at this moment," Alexander insisted. "You will relay my regrets?"

Kirakis hesitated for a moment, regarding Alexander with an odd look in his eye. "Of course. Come home as soon as you are able." Impulsively, he reached out to embrace his son tightly—something he had not done since Alexander was a child. "I will miss you also, my son."

"And I you." Alexander returned his embrace, silently wishing he could erase the friction that had existed between himself and his father in the years since he'd elected to live in New York. He loved his father deeply and wanted his love and respect in return. If only he could make him understand. But there were times when even Alexander himself did not understand why he behaved as he did. "Have a safe journey, Papa," he said softly. He had not called his father "Papa" in many years. "I'll come home as soon as I can."

"A promise I shall expect you to keep," the older man said as he released his son. He turned and climbed the steps to the waiting jet, pausing at the top to wave to Alexander one last time. Alexander waved too, then turned abruptly and headed back to the waiting limo.

Kirakis seated himself in the passenger section and fastened his seat belt. Through the window, he could see the limousine drive away. Again, he wished he could have persuaded Alexander to come with him. It had been a long time since Alexander had been home, too long. And Constantine Kirakis was worried about his son.

More so than he had been willing to admit.

"Alex, *caro,* you must learn to relax." Francesca Correnti sat up in bed. The sheet fell to her waist, exposing her magnificent breasts, but Alexander took no notice of it. "You must learn to forget business sometimes and concentrate on pleasure," she told him.

Alexander stood naked by the window, staring absently at the sprawling panorama of Central Park. He has such a splendid body, Francesca thought. Like the statues she'd often admired in the world's great museums. Perfect —absolutely perfect. It seemed to Francesca Correnti, who had made love with some of the most magnificent men in the world, that this one most certainly had to have been designed by some incredible act of sorcery. Surely, she told herself, such absolute perfection could not have been the product of a genetic accident, that chance matching of genes and chromosomes that could produce either a disaster or a perfect specimen such as Alexander Kirakis.

She got out of bed, nude, and crossed the room with

graceful determination. She wrapped her arms around his neck and began to nibble softly at his earlobes. "Come back to bed, *caro mio*," she whispered. "Come back to me, and we will make love again and again—"

He chuckled softly. "And you will teach me to make more time for pleasure?" he asked as his hands roamed over her flesh.

"Ah . . . you could not have a better tutor, *diletto mio*." She ran her fingers through his hair. "You see, *carissimo*, I am expert in the art of giving pleasure."

"Oh?" He drew back his head and looked at her, his grin wicked. "This expertise you speak of—it can be proven?"

She smiled. "It is proof that you need?" Francesca rose to the challenge, as he'd known she would. She kissed him hungrily as she traced his lean, muscular chest with her fingertips. She withdrew slowly, deliberately, and dropped to her knees in front of him. She took his penis in one hand and with the other began to stroke it slowly, gently, all the while murmuring Italian love words.

"Take it in your mouth, Francesca," he urged.

"Yes, *carissimo*, in time. You must learn to be patient," she cooed. "You must learn to control yourself, or it will all be over much too quickly." She took the tip of his organ into her mouth and sucked at it lazily as the shaft began to swell. She drew it further into her mouth, taking as much of it as she could. Her fingertips lightly stroked his testicles. Alexander could feel his desire rising and ebbing like a great tidal wave, threatening to engulf him. With his hands on her head, he held her firmly as he began to thrust his hips. The things she was doing to him with her mouth, her tongue . . . he could barely control himself, could barely keep from exploding.

He closed his eyes. No, he thought, summoning up all of his strength to maintain control. Not yet, not yet. He was weakening, losing control. He had to have her now, or. . . . He withdrew abruptly and pushed her onto her back on the carpet. Falling on top of her, he entered her in one quick motion, thrusting himself inside her with an urgency that made Francesca cry out. "You don't misrepresent yourself, *cara mia*," he gasped breathlessly. "You are indeed an expert at giving pleasure.'' He continued to thrust, moving deeper, faster inside her. She began to move with him, her hips rising off the floor to meet him, digging her nails into the flesh of his shoulders.

"I try to please you, *diletto mio,* because I love you," she breathed. "I have loved you from the moment I met you."

He looked down at her oddly, as if seeing her for the first time. His mouth came down on hers, hard and demanding. "No," he muttered. "No, you keep saying that. You say that you love me, but you lie!"

She looked up at him, bewildered, not understanding why he doubted her. "I do not understand, *caro.* I *do* love you! You are my life! Why do you doubt me?"

He shook his head furiously, either unable or unwilling to accept it. "No—don't lie to me!" he roared, his thrusts more frantic than ever as he approached his orgasm. There was a pain in his eyes that was always there when they made love, but Francesca had never understood why. "Don't lie to me. . . ."

"I *do* love you!" she cried out, caught up in the frenzy of his excitement. "I loved you enough to offer to give up all that was important to me just to be with you."

"No!" His face was dark with anger. "Lies! Always lies! Don't say that!" Suddenly his whole body shuddered violently. It seemed as though he were suspended in time and space for an eternity. Finally he went limp on top of her, burying his face in her breasts.

She stroked his head tenderly. "I *do* love you, *caro mio,*" she murmured. "If only I could make you believe me."

When he finally pulled away from her, his eyes were red and moist with tears. He tried to keep his voice light. "Well, your talents have not been overrated."

She forced a smile. "I have no reason to profess to be what I am not," she said simply.

He was frowning as he got to his feet and collected his clothes. He went into the bathroom, took a quick shower, and dressed in silence. It had happened again, he thought dismally. When she tried to tell him she loved him, it was as if a fog had clouded his brain, and everything that had followed was now a blur in his memory. Catching sight of his own reflection in the mirrors, he paused, staring at himself as though he were looking into the face of a stranger, someone he'd never seen before.

And what about *you*? he asked himself, troubled. Do you profess to be what you are not, or are you simply hiding what you really are?

Alexander stood at the windows of his study in his apartment in the Olympic Tower, staring thoughtfully at the Manhattan skyline before him, the millions of twinkling lights sparkling like a sea of precious gems as far as the eye could see. He felt oddly relieved that Francesca had left earlier that evening aboard an Alitalia flight to Rome. In two days, she was to begin work on her latest picture. She'd offered to turn it down, to stay in New York with him, but he had insisted she take the part. He'd never been comfortable with Francesca for long periods of time. She was far too possessive. There were times he felt as though she were trying to swallow him whole. He knew she wanted to marry him. She'd certainly made no secret of it. She felt they had a good relationship. He'd never told her that his interest in her did not go beyond the intense sexual attraction that had brought them together. None of his past relationships, he realized now with a mixture of concern and regret, had ever grown beyond that initial physical attraction. They'd all cooled off after a few weeks or less, and he had always gone off to find himself a new lover without a passing thought for the woman who had just departed from his life.

Though Alexander had known Francesca Correnti for more than a year now, they'd never been together for more than a week or two at a time. Even when they first met, that summer in Rome when she'd invited him to share her home at Olgiata, he had insisted upon taking a suite at the Excelsior on the Via Veneto. In New York, he'd always reserved a suite for her at the Plaza, though she'd made it clear that she expected to stay with him at his apartment. It had been necessary, he thought now. He'd needed to keep her at arm's length. He'd insisted upon it.

Francesca had never understood, but she'd accepted it because she had no choice. Alexander never met anyone halfway. Compromise was not a part of his nature. He was a man who lived by his own rules.

Alexander Kirakis had never been able to care enough for any woman to put her feelings and needs above his own.

The clock on the antique nightstand read two-fifteen. Alone in bed, Alexander thrashed about as if he were being tortured, mumbling incoherently. "No!" he shouted suddenly. He sat bolt upright, eyes wide open, his lips parted in a silent scream as he trembled violently. His entire body was drenched in perspiration. He sat still for a few seconds, struggling to catch his breath. He knew he'd been having a nightmare, but now that he was awake, he could not remember what it had been about. He knew only that it was terrifying. Running one hand through his hair nervously, he fumbled in the darkness for the switch that would turn on the lamp. As the light came on, he drew in a sharp breath and slumped over, relieved. What had he been dreaming about? he wondered. What could have been so frightening that it could do this to him?

He got out of bed and stumbled into the bathroom, switching on the bulbs on either side of the gilt-framed oval mirror over the Italian marble sink. Bending over the sink, he turned one of the large gold knobs and cold water instantly surged forth from the faucet. Cupping his hands to catch it, he began splashing it on his face until he stopped shaking. He turned the water off and reached for a towel. As he straightened up, he caught sight of his own reflection in the mirror. It was an odd feeling, as though the face looking back at him were that of a stranger. He looked drawn; his eyes had a haunted quality. He stared at the image in the mirror for a long moment, then threw down the towel and went back into the bedroom.

Realizing sleep was impossible now, he put on his robe and went to his study. There was a stack of reports on the desk that needed his attention. He decided he might as well make good use of the time as long as he would not be going back to bed. Settling down in his high-backed chair, he took a report off the top of the stack and attempted to review it, but he found he was unable to concentrate. His mind was on the nightmare that had disrupted his sleep so violently.

He threw the report down on the desk in frustration. This was not the first time. It had happened before, more often than Alexander cared to recall, and it was always the same. He would awaken abruptly in the middle of the night, shaken from a sound sleep by a dream so terrifying he could not go back to sleep afterward. Yet he was never able to remember the dream once he was awake.

He leaned back in his chair and breathed deeply. Though there had been many women in his life, though he'd enjoyed an active sex life over the past ten years, he'd never spent an entire night in any woman's bed, and had never brought any of his lovers here to spend the night. He'd always told himself he needed to maintain an emotional distance between himself and his women, needed to be able to turn away from them once he'd satisfied himself. But the truth was he could never allow himself to fall asleep after having sex because the dream might come, and they might see him in a moment of weakness.

He saw himself riding Francesca with the fury of a man possessed on the floor of her suite at the Plaza. Even now, he wasn't sure what had happened. Francesca's declaration of love had triggered something in his mind that summoned up a violence so fierce it had stunned him. He had not wanted her to say she loved him.

Why? he wondered.

TWO

𒊹𒊹𒊹𒊹𒊹𒊹𒊹𒊹𒊹

Burbank, California.

Meredith brought her blue MG convertible to a slow stop at the front gates of Centurion Studios, waiting patiently while the security guard searched his pass list for her name. He directed her to Nick Holliday's office, which turned out to be nothing at all like what she had expected. She was ushered into a small, untidy room not much larger than a walk-in closet by a pretty, redheaded girl who couldn't have been more than eighteen, dressed in faded jeans, T-shirt, and sneakers.

"Nick's expecting you," the girl said in a shrill, high-pitched voice. "He should be right back . . . probably just ran to the john."

Meredith managed a slight smile. "Thank you." After the girl had gone, Meredith looked around. The place was a mess. The desk was covered with scripts, unopened mail, and newspaper clippings that Meredith guessed to be movie reviews. On the walls were framed movie posters of the films he had directed. On the few chairs in the room were cardboard boxes filled with miscellaneous props from some of those pictures. A well-worn denim jacket hung on a hook on one wall, and a stack of back issues of *Variety* sat atop a filing cabinet in one corner of the room. The man who occupies this office is either very busy or an incurable slob, Meredith thought. Or both.

He burst through the door quite suddenly, his nose buried in a script, a pencil tucked behind one ear. He looked younger than Meredith had expected—maybe twenty-nine or thirty—and was dressed in jeans and a blue work shirt. His hair was dark, thick and unruly, but his beard was neatly trimmed. She couldn't see his eyes behind his dark aviator glasses. "Sorry I'm late," he apologized. "This place has been a real zoo today. Been waiting long?"

"No." Meredith shook her head. "Ten minutes—fifteen at the most."

He took the pencil from behind his ear and made some rapid notations on the dog-eared pages of the script, then tossed it aside and removed a box of toys from his chair and sat down. "They're for the picture," he explained, gesturing toward the box.

She nodded, smiling.

"Oh—I'm sorry. I forgot to introduce myself. I'm Nick Holliday." He grinned as he removed the glasses, revealing twinkling blue eyes. "Like I said, it's been crazy around here today."

"I can imagine," she said agreeably. "I'm Meredith Courtney, KXLA News."

He raised an eyebrow in mock surprise. "Oh, yeah. So I'm news now, am I?"

"You're news as far as the moviegoing public is concerned," she told him. "Someone from the station spoke to you about this, didn't they?"

"Oh, sure. When and where?" he asked. "You know, I can use all the publicity I can get." His voice dropped to a low, conspiratorial whisper. "Business ain't been too good lately."

She laughed. "Uh-huh," she said slowly. "I have a list of questions, and if everything meets with your approval, I'd like to bring a cameraman out here this afternoon and tape the interview."

He looked over the list she gave him, then up at Meredith again. "This stuff looks pretty tame," he said approvingly. "Nothing here about me getting busted for possession of drugs, nothing about the orgies out at Malibu, nothing about the casting couch. Yeah, I guess this afternoon would be okay. You could bring your man over to the set, and we can do this between takes—okay with you?''

"Great," she agreed. "If you have time now, I'd really like to go over some things with you before the taping."

He nodded. "That sounds reasonable." He looked at his watch. "It's almost noon. Have you eaten yet?"

"No," she said.

"Are you hungry?"

"Well, yes," she admitted.

"Good! What do you say to grabbing a bite at the studio commissary? The food's not the greatest, but they haven't had a case of ptomainē in over a week, so I guess we're safe."

"Sure—why not?"

"So—you *do* take chances! A girl after my own heart," he told her. "I've got to stop by the set for a minute, but I promise it won't take long." He got to his feet. "Shall we?"

As they walked together through a maze of large buildings that all seemed to look alike, Meredith observed Nick Holliday with mild amusement. He seemed to be in a perpetual hurry and spoke with exaggerated hand gestures. His enthusiasm for his work bordered on manic excitement.

They visited the sound stage where he would be filming that afternoon, and he gave the technical crew some last-minute instructions before taking Meredith on to the commissary for lunch. Over a meal that was much better than he'd led her to believe it would be, they discussed her plans for the interview, and he made some suggestions. He offered to allow her to tape a segment of the afternoon's filming to use with the interview, and Meredith became enthusiastic. He certainly was the most accommodating subject she'd ever encountered. Maybe Kay was right, she thought. Maybe the tide's about to change.

Nick Holliday talked openly about his background and his days as a film student at UCLA. He told her about the man who'd given him his first big break. "I used to hang around the front gates—got to know a lot of people who worked here that way," he recalled. "Then one day I got lucky. Tom Ryan noticed me—you've heard of him, I'm sure."

Meredith nodded. Who hadn't? Tom Ryan was practically a Hollywood legend, regarded by many as one of the most successful producers in motion picture history.

"Anyway, Ryan took pity on me and offered to look at samples of my work. He liked what he saw, and here I am." Nick grinned. "Of course, mine was hardly the first career he'd launched. He was the driving force behind some of the biggest names in Hollywood—Sarah Gallison, Grant Mallory, Elizabeth Weldon, Tara Spencer—"

"He was married to Elizabeth Weldon, wasn't he?" Meredith recalled.

It was the first time she saw Nick frown. "Yeah, for almost five years, until she died in '53," he said quietly. "But that's a closed subject. Nobody dares to even ask him about it these days."

"Did you ever dream you'd be as successful as you are now?" Meredith asked, sensing that he wanted to change the subject. "Even with Tom Ryan's reputation as a starmaker behind you, did you have any idea you'd be so successful so soon?"

Nick grinned. "The truth?"

"Of course."

"No, I have to admit that I didn't," he said honestly. "It's been an overwhelming experience. I mean, I always knew I'd make it somehow. I'd still be camped out at the gates if Tom hadn't come along when he did. They'd have had to look at my stuff just to get rid of me. No, my career has outstripped even my own wild imagination. I never expected to become a household word or anything like that."

Meredith paused. "How do you account for the astonishing success of all three of your films?" she asked. "They are, after all, among the greatest box-office hits of all time."

"Oh, I can't really say for sure." He ran his fingers through his hair. "Except maybe . . . I grew up in the most typical middle-class American tradition you can imagine. Before Dad died, well, we were as average as hot dogs at the ball park. Maybe I just have an inborn rapport with Mr. Average Moviegoer. Maybe the public likes my movies because *I* like them—and I've always been one of them."

She smiled. At first she'd thought it was all a front, a carefully cultivated image. She hadn't been able to imagine a man as successful as Nick Holliday being even a little self-deprecating. But maybe he was right. Maybe his incredible success *did* come from his rapport with the moviegoing public, his self-proclaimed middle-class upbringing. Maybe he *was* everything he appeared to be after all, Meredith thought.

The taping that afternoon went well, better than Meredith had anticipated. Nick insisted upon walking her to her car afterward, and she thanked him for his cooperation in doing the interview. "It's nothing," he insisted. "Like I said before, I can use all the free publicity I can get. Besides, I think I'm in love."

She laughed, not taking him seriously. "Are you always on?" she asked, curious.

"No—not always." He reached out and took her hand. "Listen—what are you doing tonight?"

"Probably overtime," she said, keeping her voice light.

"I'm being serious, Meredith," he said solemnly. "What are you doing for dinner?"

"Most likely having takeout Chinese at my desk at the station." She knew what he was leading up to, and she was trying to avoid it.

"How about taking the time to have dinner with me?" he asked. "I know a great little Italian place in Glendale . . ."

"I can't. Really," she insisted.

"How about tomorrow?" he pursued.

"I work late just about every night." She started to get into the car, but he was still holding her hand.

Nick was undaunted. "Then we'll make it breakfast," he said promptly. "There's a little café near the beach—we can eat outdoors and watch the sun come up."

"I can't. I really can't." She finally withdrew her hand and slid in behind the wheel. "But thank you for asking."

"I know you're not married or anything like that because I called the station and asked," he said then. "Have I offended you or something?"

"No, it's not you. I . . . I just never mix business with pleasure. I don't go out with anyone I'm interviewing," she said feebly. He was making it almost impossible for her to refuse. She started the engine, then she thanked him again and drove away, thinking she'd seen the last of him.

She had no way of knowing the second secret of Nick Holliday's success: he never gave up on anything he really wanted.

"Flowers for Meredith Courtney," the mail clerk sang out loudly as he carried a large white box through the newsroom to her small office. "Third time this week," he said with a grin as he handed the box to her. "You must have some guy real hung up on you."

"I wish you wouldn't broadcast it all over the place," she said sullenly as she opened the box. She did not have to look at the card. She already knew who had sent them.

The young man let out a low whistle. "Roses this time. Nice going," he told her. "Take my advice—hold out for marriage."

Meredith scowled, waving a letter opener at him menacingly. "Out—before I make tonight's evening news for killing you in front of all these witnesses!"

He retreated, laughing.

Meredith opened the card and stared at it blankly. The message was always the same: *How about giving me a chance to prove I'm a nice guy? Love, Nick.* Love! Infatuation, maybe, but certainly not love, she told herself. He didn't even *know* her! Maybe that's one way to get him to lay off, she thought. I could go out with him once. The fantasy probably wouldn't match the reality, and—

"More flowers?"

Meredith looked up. Kay was standing in the doorway. "More flowers," she said with a nod. "He doesn't seem willing to take no for an answer."

"Maybe you should go out with him." Kay entered the office and closed the door.

"What?" Meredith looked genuinely surprised. "You've got to be kidding!"

Kay's face was serious. "Why do I have to be kidding?" she asked. "Obviously he likes you—or he owns a flower shop. He's going to a great deal of trouble to impress you."

"Sure." Meredith's face was grim. "You know how those movie guys operate. They tell every girl they meet they love her just to get her into bed and then—"

"Wow! You must really have been burned by some guy once upon a time!" Kay concluded.

"What makes you say that?" Meredith asked warily.

"You're really down on men. They're not all ogres, you know." Kay proceeded to peel an orange. "If you ask me—"

"I *didn't*," Meredith cut in sharply.

"If you ask *me*," Kay repeated, "I think you're being unreasonably prejudiced."

"Prejudiced?" Meredith looked insulted.

"Yeah, prejudiced. You've got it in your head that because Holliday's a hotshot director, he's a lech. Apparently it's never occurred to you that there are some very nice people in the motion picture industry who do *not* do drugs of any kind, who do *not* change spouses like we change our clothes, and who do *not* participate in the decadent Hollywood scene. Some of them," she added smugly, "even go to church on Sundays and have long and happy marriages."

"Okay. You've made your point," Meredith said resignedly. "Now, could you *please* close the door on your way out?"

"I'm not leaving yet."

"That's what I was afraid of," Meredith groaned.

Kay pulled up a chair. "Look, I've never met the guy, but from what you've told me, he must be okay. He's obviously got it bad for you, because the flowers and the phone calls have been coming nonstop for almost two weeks. I think the least you could do is give him a chance. You don't have to marry him or anything. Just have dinner with him. You *might* find yourself pleasantly surprised, you know."

"I've been so busy lately—"

"Poor excuse," Kay said promptly. "You can't spend your whole life working."

"You *can*—and you'd *better*—if you want to get ahead in this business. Especially if you're a woman," Meredith insisted.

"Caryn Hammond just got married, and she's our lead anchor."

"What are you trying to tell me?" Meredith asked, putting down her pencil. She hadn't had much of a social life since she'd come to work at KXLA, it was true, but it had been her own choice. She wanted to give her career her full concentration now. A serious relationship could only get in the way. Besides, how could it have any chance of survival under these circumstances? Kay knew that better than anyone; her own marriage had ended in divorce last year.

"Ambition's great," Kay said, "but success can get pretty lonely if you've got nobody to share it with. You know what they say—it's damned lonely at the top."

Meredith smiled for the first time. "Okay, okay. You win. The next time I see Nick Holliday, I'm going to accept his invitation—and while I'm at it, I think I'll tell him what a champion he has in you."

Kay grinned. "Good. You can tell him right now. He's out in the reception area."

"Do you come here often?" Meredith sat across from Nick Holliday at a corner table in a small, cozy, dimly lit Italian restaurant in Glendale, sipping a glass of white wine.

He nodded. "I discovered Angelino's right after I was hired by Centurion, a few years back," he recalled. "I liked it right away—mainly because it's nothing at all like the so-called 'in' restaurants. Nobody comes here to see or be seen." He grinned. "If they did, they'd be out of luck."

Meredith glanced around the small, nearly deserted dining room. "Obviously," she commented with mild amusement in her voice.

"Personally, I hope it stays this way," Nick said as he put down his fork.

Meredith smiled. "If it does, it'll be out of business within a year," she predicted, brushing a strand of hair back over her left shoulder.

Nick shook his head. "It's not always this slow." He paused, admiring her in the flattering light. She wore a simple green linen dress, cut low with pencil-thin straps over her shoulders, and little jewelry, just a single strand of pearls and small, simple earrings. Her hair hung unadorned about her shoulders. "You look especially beautiful tonight," he told her.

She accepted the compliment graciously. "Thank you." Then she took a bite of the lasagna. It was just the way she liked it—lots of thick, gooey cheese. "I take it you're not exactly fond of the Hollywood social scene," she said finally.

He shrugged. "I just lock my door to it," he said simply. "It's just not my style."

"When I interviewed you at the studio, you made a rather offhand remark about your middle-class background," she remembered as the waiter refilled her glass. "Where are you from? Originally, I mean."

"L.A.," he answered. "I grew up out in the San Fernando Valley." He took a forkful of pasta. "What about you?"

Meredith hesitated for a moment. "I'm from one of those small midwestern towns that nobody's ever heard of," she said, reaching for her wine. "One of those towns that's so small it doesn't show up on any maps and where everybody knows everything about everyone else."

"Sort of like Hollywood, right?" he quipped.

She laughed. "Not exactly—but you get the picture."

He studied her for a moment. "Why'd you leave?" he asked, hoping he wasn't out of line. "What made you want to join the rat race?"

She thought about it for a moment. "I don't know. I suppose I always felt the need to get away—as if I didn't really belong there. I wanted to be somebody, and I knew it wasn't going to happen for me there." Her tone made it clear she didn't want to discuss it further. "What about you? Ever get the urge to get away from the rat race, as you call it?"

He shrugged. "Not so much as I wanted to get away from my own background," he admitted. "I always had the feeling my life got off on the wrong foot. Dad was Catholic and Mom was Jewish, and neither of their families ever accepted their marriage—let alone the fact that they had a child. Needless to say, I didn't see much of any of them while I was growing up."

Meredith looked at him expectantly, waiting for him to go on. God, she thought, he'd known the same kind of emotional isolation she'd felt as a child!

"Dad died when I was seven," Nick recalled with a

frown. "He was a salesman, out on the road most of the time. One day he just didn't come back—or that's how it seemed to me at the time, anyway."

Meredith looked down at her plate. "I'm sorry," she said softly. And to herself: I know the feeling.

"I missed him. And I hated him for dying, for leaving us like that—no warning, nothing. Just one day he was there, the next day he wasn't," Nick remembered. "I had a hard time coping for a while. It was just Mom and me, and here I was, the only Jewish kid in school—and I got picked on a lot. I took to spending most of my time at home—alone—or at the movies. The movies were my salvation, my escape from the real world, where I never really belonged."

Meredith was silent for a moment. She would never have guessed that anyone as cheerful and optimistic as Nick could have been the product of such a lonely, troubled childhood. "Is that when you became interested in making movies?" she asked.

He nodded. "I had this little cheapo Brownie camera. I was always taking pictures, always in sequence. Then I'd arrange them appropriately in a scrapbook with captions under each one so they told a story," he recalled, pressing his fingertips together pyramid-fashion on the table. "When I was fourteen, I'd saved enough to buy an ancient movie camera from the local pawnshop, and I made all kinds of movies about all sorts of things—traffic on the freeway, kids at the beach, sporting events—experimenting with different angles and stuff." He paused. "When I told my mother what I wanted to do with my life, she was behind me one hundred percent. She held down two jobs for over five years to put me through UCLA. I'm just glad I'm able to take care of her now."

"Where is she now?" Meredith asked as the waiter arrived with dessert.

"Israel," Nick replied. "She always wanted to go there, so I sent her. She's been there almost four months now, and from her letters, I get the feeling she's in no hurry to come home."

"Not too many successful people think of their families once they've made it," Meredith commented. She hadn't seen her own family in years.

"I wouldn't have it any other way." He looked at his watch. "Listen—the night's still young. After we leave here, I know a great little place—"

She shook her head. "I can't. I have to be at the station at five tomorrow morning."

"What about tomorrow, then?"

She reached across the table and took his hand affectionately. "I've really enjoyed tonight, Nick," she said softly, "but let's take it one day at a time, all right?"

Athens, September 1979.

Constantine Kirakis stared at the papers on the desk in front of him until he was bleary-eyed. It had been a long day, but he'd accomplished a great deal and was satisfied with the results. That day, he had signed contracts that would mean billions of dollars' worth of new business for the Kirakis Corporation. The majority of those deals were connected with the North American offices, and he was pleased. Alexander was doing a marvelous job in New York. Still, Kirakis wished his son had not elected to go there. He would have been much happier if Alexander had wanted to stay in Greece, to work side by side with him at the corporation's world headquarters. It had always been his dream to have his son in Athens, at the hub of the corporation's international affairs. He had hoped to be the one to prepare Alexander for the time when *he* would become chairman of the board. One day, Kirakis would become the world's largest multinational corporation—and Alexander would be at the center of that global operation. He had to be ready for it.

"It is so late, Costa. Why do you not put your work aside for tonight and come to bed?"

Kirakis looked up. His wife Melina stood in the doorway of the study, wearing a pale blue velvet robe. Her heavy blond hair, normally worn in a tight chignon, now hung loosely about her shoulders, and Kirakis thought to himself that it made her look ten years younger. Even at sixty-seven, she was still a handsome woman. The years had been kind to her. He stood up and extended his arms to her. "I am sorry, *matia mou*," he said as she came forward. "I did not realize the hour.'' He embraced her gently. She seemed so fragile now.

"Apparently." She looked up at him and smiled. "You are no longer a young man, Costa. You must learn to relax more often."

He smiled too. "You sound exactly like that old scoundrel Karamanlis," he said reproachfully. "You two have perhaps been conspiring to retire me again?"

"There has been no conspiracy," Melina told him, taking a seat in one of the dark blue velvet chairs near his desk. "We simply worry about you. You push yourself too hard."

"Nonsense! I do what must be done, that is all."

"It must be done, I agree, but must you be the one to do everything? I was under the impression that Alexander would be given more control over corporate affairs," she said quietly. "Is he not capable—"

"Alexander is more than capable," Kirakis said quickly. "He is brilliant and he shows great potential. Unfortunately, there are other factors that prevent me from allowing him the authority I would like to give him now."

"What other factors?" Melina wanted to know. "Do you still hold it against him because he has chosen to make a life for himself in New York?"

Kirakis shook his head. He stood at the windows, watching a ship in the distance. Moonlight illuminated the shimmering, calm Aegean. "It has nothing to do with his choice to stay in the States, although I am the first to admit that I am disappointed by that choice. No, Melina, it is the life-style he has chosen for himself." He took a folded newspaper clipping from his pocket and passed it to her. "This turned up while I was in Los Angeles."

Melina unfolded it carefully and stared at it for a moment. It was a photograph from an American newspaper, a photograph of Alexander and a woman whose face was all too familiar to Melina Kirakis. "Francesca Correnti," she said. "So she is back in his life again, is she?"

"Apparently," Kirakis said tightly. His disapproval was clear in his voice. "It would seem that this one has outlasted the others."

"Perhaps we should be encouraged by this," Melina began slowly, still looking at the picture.

"Encouraged?" Kirakis turned to look at her in disbelief. "I cannot believe you would say such a thing. You are telling me you would like to see our son married to this woman?"

"No, of course not." Melina folded the clipping again and returned it to him. "I am not suggesting that Alexander marry this woman—or even that he may be considering such a thing. I am only pointing out that he may finally be learning to maintain a relationship. It is a step in the right direction, is it not? In the past he has never continued to see the same woman for more than a few weeks."

"You are right. It is encouraging—*if* he is not serious about this particular woman," Kirakis agreed. "But of all the choices he could have made . . . Francesca Correnti is an actress, a woman who has had many lovers. She is hardly a suitable consort for Alexander—at least not for a permanent arrangement."

"Arrangement?" Melina's laugh was light. "My God, Costa, you sound as if you live in the Dark Ages! I am surprised you have not tried to arrange a marriage for him yourself!"

"You know perfectly well that arranged marriages still take place in our social circles," Kirakis reminded her as he poured himself an ouzo. "Would you like one?" he asked, raising his glass.

Melina shook her head. "And *you* know, my husband, that Alexander would never stand for such a thing."

"No, our son definitely has a will of his own," he conceded. "I think, however, having seen some of his 'choices,' that I might be able to select a better wife for him than he could choose for himself—if he would choose a wife at all."

"I would like to think that he is almost ready to give up his cherished bachelor status and settle down," Melina said.

"I would like to believe it as well," Kirakis said with a sigh. "But it is not something I expect to happen soon."

Melina was silent for a few seconds. "This is what you meant by other factors that had influenced your decision not to grant Alexander more responsibility within the corporation?" she asked finally. "You feel that his private affairs will interfere with his ability to handle those responsibilities?'' Melina knew her husband well; she could almost read his mind.

Kirakis frowned as he sipped his ouzo. "Let us just say that Alexander has never been wise in his dealings with women,'' he said quietly. "He has gained a notoriety for himself as far as the media is concerned. I think not a day passes that his name or photograph does not appear in a newspaper or magazine somewhere in the world. The publicity has not been good for the corporation's image.''

"That is what you are most concerned with? The corporation's image?'' There was anger in Melina's voice. She had never approved of the way he'd begun grooming Alexander for the succession since childhood, always tying Alexander's future to the corporation's, as though he would have no other life but that which Kirakis had mapped out for him.

Kirakis shook his head. "Melina, it is more complicated than you may think,'' he told her. "We do business with some of the largest banks in the world. From time to time we take out loans—large loans—to finance projects for the corporation in various parts of the world. We are on good terms with those banks—now. The fact that Kirakis is a solid, conservative corporation is in no small way responsible for the security those bankers feel when they do business with us.''

"And you think the bad press Alexander has been getting in recent years will make those conservative bankers reluctant to do business with him?'' Melina asked.

Kirakis turned to look at her, and she could see the answer in his eyes. "Yes, *matia mou*, I do,'' he said slowly. "They read about him, they hear all the stories about the shallow, jet-setting life-style he lives, and they are cautious by nature. They question his ability to make sound business decisions. They see him as irresponsible.''

"I think it is unfair to judge him by his private life,'' Melina said then. "If Papa had judged you by *his* first impressions—''

"If your father had not taken the time to look beneath the surface, you and I would never have been married—and he would never have financed the start of the Kirakis fleet,''

Kirakis finished with a slight smile. "But Alexander may not be so fortunate. Times are different now, and our son has not had the good sense to fall in love with a banker's daughter as I did."

"So he is to be judged on his personal conduct as much as he will be on his track record as a businessman?" Melina concluded.

"I am afraid so." Kirakis paused. "And if he continues as he has . . ."

Melina turned to face him. "Costa, I know how important it is to you—has always been to you—that Alexander fulfill his destiny as your heir apparent," she said. "God knows you've been planning for this day since he was five years old. I know this is hard for you to accept, but Alexander is young. There is time—"

"He is thirty-one years old as of November seventeenth," Kirakis reminded her. "When *I* was thirty-one, we had already been married for several years. I was quite settled, both as a husband and a businessman."

"But as you have said yourself, times have changed since you and I were Alexander's age."

"Not that much," Kirakis insisted stubbornly.

She looked up at him and smiled. "More than you would like to believe, I am afraid."

He shook his head again. "Sometimes I think you are blind where Alexander is concerned."

"And sometimes I have exactly the same feeling about you," she admitted. She kissed his cheek affectionately. "We are both hopeless, are we not?"

He smiled. "So it would seem."

"Come to bed," she urged. "It is late, and there is nothing you can do about Alexander's love life tonight."

He put his glass down on the desk. "You go ahead," he told her. "I will join you shortly."

"You are not going to work—"

"No. I will be with you in no more than a few minutes."

She nodded. "Very well."

He watched her climb the staircase with the grace of a duchess, a grace he knew that one could only be born with. He was filled now with a deep, ever-growing concern, for Melina as well as for Alexander. He went back into the study and poured himself another drink. Standing at the windows, pondering the great, silent calm of the Aegean at night, he thought about the conversation they'd just had. Though Melina was quick to come to Alexander's defense, he knew that his wife was just as concerned about their son as he was, perhaps more so. Kirakis smiled to himself. Melina's devotion to Alexander was stronger than her disapproval of the shallow, superficial life-style he had chosen for himself. Melina, Kirakis had realized long ago, would forgive Alexander anything.

The question was, Kirakis thought as he switched off the lights and made his way up the staircase, would *he* be able to forgive his son if Alexander's reputation were to jeopardize the future of the Kirakis Corporation?

Los Angeles, October 1979.

"You always change the subject whenever I ask you about your childhood. Why?" Nick wanted to know. He and Meredith walked barefoot in the sand along the beach at Santa Monica, their pants rolled up almost to their knees. Meredith wore a loose cotton shirt and no jewelry except a simple silver ring on her right hand, and with her long hair blowing in the soft wind, Nick thought she'd never looked more appealing.

She laughed. "Holliday, I thought you invited me out here to watch you shoot, not to be interrogated," she teased, taking his hand and giving it an affectionate squeeze.

"Why *do* you avoid discussing it?" he pursued.

"I'm not avoiding anything," she insisted, brushing her hair away from her face with one hand. "There's just nothing to tell, that's all. I have a very dull past."

He looked skeptical. "Surely there must be something to tell," he said in a disbelieving tone.

Meredith shook her head, amused by his persistence. "I come from a small town, remember?"

"Peyton Place was a small town too—and we all know what went on *there*," he pointed out, pushing his dark glasses up into his hair.

She nodded. "Okay, you win." Her voice took on a dramatic note as she spoke. "I might as well confess everything. I don't come from a small town at all. I was born in London. My father was the ambassador to the Court of St. James. I grew up on the Continent—private schools in Switzerland, the Sorbonne in Paris. I had my first important affair at the age of fifteen with the very worldly son of a French vintner. Then there was the race car driver in Monte Carlo, the Italian actor in Rome—and, oh, yes, the Arab prince who tried to buy me from my father for a dozen camels. There was very nearly an international incident over *that* one!''

"Be serious!" Nick scolded.

"I *am* serious!" she maintained with mock indignation. "You wanted to hear all the sordid details of my past."

"I'm trying to get to know you," he said, "but you sure as hell aren't making it easy."

"I'm sorry," she said, suddenly serious. "But if you really want to get close to me, Nick, don't pressure me about the past. I put it behind me a long time ago—and I'd like to keep it that way."

I'd like to forget it ever happened, she thought.

New York City.

A steady rain was falling. Because of the weather and the late hour, relatively few people were out walking on the streets of Manhattan. It hadn't had any noticeable effect on the traffic; taxis, buses, and limousines passed Alexander as he walked along Central Park South, oblivious of both the traffic and the weather. Alexander was not afraid to walk alone in New York at night, and in fact did so often. His hands shoved deep into the pockets of his overcoat, he strode along briskly, turning the corner at Fifth Avenue. A taxi driver shooting past him as he crossed the street—against the light—shouted a profanity at him, but Alexander didn't respond. His mind was on other things.

It had been a long and exceptionally difficult day. He'd left his office with a throbbing sensation centered at the base of his skull that had been the beginning of a monumental headache. He'd dismissed his driver and had taken off walking, trying to relax. Now, pausing to look at his watch, he realized he'd been walking for the better part of four and a half hours. Fortunately, the pounding in his head had finally subsided. He'd been troubled by those damned headaches on a regular basis for as long as he could remember. When he was a small child, his mother had told him, he'd had a serious accident—a head injury—and had almost died. At that time, the doctors in Athens had been afraid he might have suffered permanent brain damage. He'd been lucky; the only lasting aftereffects were the frequent headaches.

He rubbed the back of his neck absently as he turned the corner at Fifty-first Street and entered the red-carpeted lobby of the Olympic Tower. The new concierge, recognizing him immediately, greeted him with a smile and held the elevator for him. Alexander acknowledged the man with a nod but did not speak. As the elevator doors closed, his mind was on a deal he'd been working on for the past six months. It was at last ready to be finalized.

If he could sell his father on it.

Los Angeles.

Immediately after the eleven o'clock broadcast, Meredith hurried back to her office and collected her things. Eager to leave, she rushed for the exit, only to be stopped by one of the cameramen. "Hey, Meredith!" he called after her. "Where's the fire?"

"No fire, Hank," she said, laughing. "Just an important engagement."

"With whom—as if I didn't know . . ."

"I'm meeting Nick—and I'm already late!" He knew all right, she thought as she crossed the parking lot to her car. *Everybody* at KXLA knew. As she sped off without regard for the posted speed limit, she glanced at her watch. Nick was probably wondering what had happened to her. She should have phoned, but Nick would understand.

It was after midnight when she reached the exclusive Malibu Colony where Nick lived. Nick was waiting for her, and she suspected that he'd gone to a great deal of trouble to make the night a perfect one: there was a fire roaring in the huge stone fireplace, wine chilling in an ice bucket on the bar, dim lights, soft music. "You're making a real production of this, Holliday," she observed wryly. "I hope you're not going to be disappointed."

He took her in his arms and kissed her. "I won't be disappointed," he muttered in her ear. "I'm sure of it."

He took her suitcase and carried it upstairs to the master bedroom. Meredith followed behind, silently taking in everything around her. When he'd said he lived in a beach house, she'd pictured something entirely different. This place was magnificent, like a castle by the sea. Everything about it was unmistakably masculine. "I bought this little place with the money I made from my first picture," he told her as they entered the bedroom. He put the suitcase on the large brass bed and pulled back the drapes to reveal a panoramic view of the Pacific Ocean. "How's this for a backyard·pool?"

"Do you do everything in such a big way?" she asked, extending her arms through his.

He grinned. "Everything. Absolutely everything." He embraced her, kissing her longingly. His lips moved down her neck, his hands under her blouse, gently squeezing her breasts. "God, I want you, baby," he whispered.

"Yes, Nick . . ." Her voice was low, but there was an urgency in her tone that was unmistakable. "Oh, yes . . ."

He lowered her to the bed and hovered over her, kissing her as he started unbuttoning her blouse. She wrapped her arms around his neck, offering herself up to him as he nuzzled her breasts, now fully exposed. She shivered as he began to suck at her nipples, moving from one to the other, arousing her. She unbuttoned his shirt and ran her fingers lightly through the thick dark curls that covered his chest. With her fingertips, she played lightly with his nipples, making them erect. He rolled over on his back, and now she was on top of him. She raked her fingers through his hair as he unzipped her slacks and pushed them down around her knees. His fingers played between her legs, fondling her, exciting her as she squirmed out of the remainder of her clothes. His body was lean and strong, even better than she'd imagined. "You've got the advantage," she told Nick as she caressed his shoulders. "You're still partially dressed. How am I supposed to make love to you with your pants on?''

He pulled away from her and sat up. ''The situation can be remedied in no time at all,'' he said as he unbuckled his belt. Meredith reached for his zipper, but he stopped her. ''I know how eager you are, babe, but you'll just have to be patient for a minute, okay?'' he chuckled. He wriggled out of his jeans and took her in his arms again. ''Now—where were we?''

''Right here.'' She rolled him over on his back again and began kissing him playfully, her lips moving down his neck, over his chest and his belly, down to his stiff, swollen penis, rising from the thick patch of dark hair covering his groin. How long had it been? she wondered. How long had it been since she'd wanted anyone like this, since she'd even cared? She took him into her mouth and began to suck gently as she cupped his testicles in her hand, caressing them lightly. He trembled at her touch. She could feel his excitement growing. Then, abruptly, he withdrew, quickly pushing her over onto her back. ''Not so fast,'' he whispered. ''It's my turn.'' He slid down until his head was directly above the delta of soft golden hair covering her pubis. As he bent his head, he parted the lips of her vulva and she felt his tongue, moist against her clitoris. He began to lick and suck at it like a starving man who was having his first meal in weeks. A delicious warmth spread through Meredith's groin as he kept at it, bringing her sharply to an orgasm. As her body convulsed with pleasure, he pulled away and rose up over her again, and she felt the force of his thrust as he entered her suddenly, urgently. His hips began to move rhythmically as she wrapped her legs around his body, then she began to move with him, thrusting her hips to meet his, begging him to go faster, moaning with pleasure as he reached his orgasm, his body tensing for one long moment before going limp.

He buried his face in her blond mane, and his breathing was labored as he lay silently on top of her, trying to catch his breath. Finally, he raised up and smiled at her, and his hair was damp with perspiration. ''Well, well . . . I'd say it was definitely worth waiting for, wouldn't you?'' he asked.

''Definitely,'' she breathed, deliciously satisfied.

They made love three times that night, and each time was

better than before. Afterward, when they were both too exhausted to move, they lay in each other's arms in the darkness, and Nick held Meredith as though he were never going to let her go. Never, she thought, had she felt happier or more secure.

"Can't sleep?" Nick whispered.

Meredith shook her head, not trusting her voice.

He hugged her. "Looks like we've both got the same problem," he said.

"What do you suggest we do about it?" she asked.

He pressed his index finger to her lips. "Sssh," he said softly, kissing the tip of her nose. "I've got something to say to you, and I've got to do it now. Don't say anything until I've finished, okay?"

She nodded, looking at him questioningly.

"I've been lying here thinking about us, about what we ought to do," he began. "After tonight, I'm convinced that there's no way I can ever let you go. I want you here with me, all the time. I want to wake up with you every morning and fall asleep with you in my arms every night." He sat up. "I want you to move in. I want you to live with me."

"Yes," she said softly, unable to imagine *not* being with him now.

He kissed her again. "God help me, I think I'm falling in love with you," he said, stroking her hair.

She looked at him. "Does that upset you?" she asked.

"It scares the hell out of me," he admitted.

"Why?"

He shrugged. "I've always been afraid to love anyone, afraid of being burned," he said slowly.

She studied him for a moment. "Who hurt you, Nick?" she asked finally.

He frowned. "Nobody. Why?"

"Anyone who's afraid to love has usually been hurt before," she reasoned. "Were you?"

"It's a long story," he said quietly.

"I've got time, if you want to talk about it."

He shook his head. "Maybe some other time, okay? I don't want anything to spoil what we've got right now."

And he pulled back the sheets and made love to her again.

THREE

༄༅༄༅༄༅༄༅༄

New York City.

"I think my father is being terribly narrow-minded about this," Alexander complained, pacing the length of the room like a caged animal. "Surely he realizes the many advantages of moving the corporation's world headquarters here to New York." He stood at the windows of his Olympic Tower office, staring thoughtfully at the Manhattan skyline. He turned suddenly. "You have not had much to say, George. What do you think?"

George Prescott, one of the senior vice-presidents of the corporation and Alexander's only real confidant, sat in one of the black leather chairs in front of Alexander's desk, his feet propped up on one corner of the desk, his arms folded behind his head. "You know I agree with you," he began, "but regardless of how either of us feels, he still has control. His vote is the one that counts."

"And his word is final," Alexander said grimly.

"Absolutely. Unless you know of a way to bring him around to our way of thinking, the headquarters office will remain in Athens as long as he's still breathing and able to fight us on it."

Alexander frowned. "I'm afraid you're right. I have tried

to talk to him, to reason with him, but my father is a stubborn man," he admitted. "I had hoped that I could rally the board members to pressure him a bit, but if it came down to a vote . . ." His voice trailed off.

"You'd still lose," George concluded, running one hand through his thick blond hair. "Fifty-one percent gives him the deciding vote, unfortunately. Either way you go, you're going to lose."

Alexander sat down, thoughtful for a few seconds. "He will be flying in for a meeting this week. Perhaps I should approach him again."

George smiled but said nothing. He knew that Alexander was not about to give up, not when he thought he was right. George knew his friend well. He and Alexander had forged their alliance while both were attending the Harvard Business School, and it was a solid friendship built upon mutual respect and admiration. George Prescott was the only executive within the upper echelons of the Kirakis Corporation aside from Constantine Kirakis himself who dared to speak his mind to Alexander without fear of immediate dismissal. He alone could tell Alexander when he thought his friend was wrong or behaving irrationally. Alexander, who normally discouraged anyone who tried to get close to him, regarded George as the brother he had never known. Those who wanted to get Alexander's attention knew that the key to reaching him was George Prescott, for George had the ear of Alexander Kirakis himself.

Unfortunately, George realized now, Alexander was very much like his father, perhaps too much like his father. Constantine Kirakis, like Alexander, was a man who refused to change his mind when he believed he was right. The two were the proverbial irresistible force and immovable object, George thought, amused. It was going to be interesting to see who won this time. "Maybe you ought to just give him a little more time," he said after a while, reaching for his gold cigarette case. "You said yourself he's really impressed with the growth of the North American operations. The figures speak for themselves. He can't go on denying the obvious much longer: the future of Kirakis is right here in the Big Apple."

"Perhaps you're right," Alexander said slowly. He

paused for a moment. "Have you made plans for your winter vacation yet? I've rented a chalet near Gstaad . . . "

Gstaad, Switzerland.

Alexander arrived in Switzerland at the end of the first week in December, planning to stay for at least two weeks. He'd rented the chalet for the season, certain that a number of corporate executives would take advantage of its availability over the next three months. Certainly George could be counted on to seize the opportunity. George, who had grown up in Colorado, had been an Olympic hopeful in his youth and had practically grown up on the slopes of Aspen, Vail, Keystone, and Steamboat Springs. Even today, seventeen years after he had abandoned his dreams of Olympic gold, skiing had remained an important part of his life. George had always taken the sport more seriously than Alexander ever could.

Alexander discovered that he'd arrived at the time of the Gstaad-Château d'Oex cross-country ski run. Skiing enthusiasts from all over the Continent had turned out in record numbers on the slopes, eager to compete with the finest athletes in Europe. Alexander, however, did not share their excitement. Though he was a natural athlete who excelled at many sports, including skiing, he'd never been interested in competition. Polo was his sport, the only one he took seriously. Skiing was only for recreation. In the years he had been growing up in Greece, he'd spent his winter holidays at some of the most glamorous resorts in Europe: Gstaad, St. Moritz, Chamonix, Kitzbühel. He'd quickly discovered that those elegant winter paradises provided a splendid backdrop for the most sensuous of romantic interludes, as well as a wide range of willing and eager partners. While the days on the slopes were exhilarating, he invariably found the nights to be even more so.

He met Marianne Hauptmann during the afternoon of his second day at Gstaad. He'd seen her for the first time that morning on the slopes, and decided then that she was, without a doubt, the most beautiful sight Gstaad had to offer. She was slim but full-figured, with a heavy mane of dark hair that framed her exquisite oval face. Her features were

delicate and as close to perfection as could possibly be, her
eyes large and dark, almost as dark as his own. When she
smiled at him, they seemed to glow. He'd wasted no time in
introducing himself to her, inviting her to join him for lunch
at an inn nearby.

"I've seen you out there," he said in French, gesturing
toward the slopes. "You ski quite well."

"So do you," she said in a voice that was soft, her French
fluent but with a strong German accent. "I have been
watching you as well—out there, on the Hahnenkamm."

"Hahnenkamm?" Alexander understood very little
German.

She smiled. "The steep racing slope," she explained.
"You handle yourself like a professional. Do you ski often?"

"Not as often as I would like," he admitted as they
walked together through the crowded streets in the village.
"You're from Gstaad?"

She shook her head. "No, it would only seem so, since I
spend so much time here," she said with a little laugh. "I
am originally from Zürich. My father is an officer with the
Schweizerischer Bankverein. He was transferred to Neuchâtel when I was eight, and that is where I grew up. Now I am
studying at the Université de Genève."

He held the door for her as they entered the inn. "You
come to Gstaad often, you said?" he asked as they made
their way across the crowded café.

"I ski whenever I can," she replied. She was younger than
he would have liked, Alexander realized as he listened to her
speak with the unrestrained enthusiasm of a university
student, but she *was* a woman. A woman he wanted and
intended to have.

Over lunch, they talked—mostly about skiing. Marianne
had a ravenous appetite, he observed with amusement as he
watched her devour her lunch. "I always eat too much—and
too fast—when I am nervous," she admitted as she popped
the last bite into her mouth. "It's a very bad habit, but one I
have found difficult to break."

"And why might you be nervous?"

"I am not sure," she confessed, dabbing the corners of
her mouth with her napkin. "Perhaps because I like you so
very much. I have never known anyone like you before, and I

want so very much for you to like me.'' Her dark eyes were eager.

He reached across the table and took her hand. "You have nothing to worry about," he assured her. "I like you very much, Marianne."

He'd had no trouble convincing her to go with him that night. He thought about it as they drove up to the magnificent chalet overlooking the village in the hills surrounding Gstaad. There had never been any doubt in his mind that he would end up in bed with her. He'd known it from the moment he saw her on the slopes.

When they arrived, Alexander immediately built a fire in the fireplace and chilled a bottle of wine. Marianne explored the chalet, taking in the splendid interior with the awe of a child on Christmas morning. "This is beautiful!" she exclaimed, her eyes shining as she turned to face him. "Do you own it?"

"Unfortunately, no," he said as he took two glasses from the cupboard. "It is rather nice, isn't it."

"Nice?" She laughed aloud. "It is like a small castle!"

"Then it is fitting that I have brought you here," he said, settling down in front of the fire, motioning for her to join him. "After all, a castle is the only place for a princess."

She blushed. "You are too kind."

He looked at her for a moment. "Kind?" he asked. "No, Marianne, kindness has nothing to do with it." He took her in his arms. "I don't think you realize what a beautiful, desirable woman you are. Tonight I intend to show you." He kissed her hungrily.

"Oh, yes, Alexander," she whispered, her nails digging into his shoulders. "Yes . . . love me . . . please . . . love me . . ."

He held her close, kissing her and stroking her hair, caressing her through her clothing. He sensed her shyness, her reluctance to give herself to him. He'd known it would be no simple matter to seduce her. She probably had not had much experience with men. The wine would release her inhibitions, he thought confidently. He released her abruptly and reached for the bottle. Opening it, he poured her a glass and insisted she drink all of it. "It will help you relax," he told her.

"I will be all right," she insisted. "I do not need—"

"Drink it, Marianne," he said firmly. "I want you completely relaxed. I want you to enjoy what's going to happen between us tonight."

She nodded slowly. More than anything, she wanted to please him. She finished the wine and allowed him to pour her another. She could feel a delicious warmth coursing through her body. They sat by the fire for a long time talking, until they had finished the entire bottle. Then he took her in his arms again. He kissed her, his lips moving slowly, searchingly down her neck as he lowered her to the floor. He slid one hand under her sweater and his fingers squeezed one of her nipples gently. "I want you, Marianne," he whispered hoarsely. "I want to make love to you."

"Yes . . ." she moaned.

He pulled her sweater up and lowered his head to her breasts, nuzzling each of them as she trembled nervously at his touch. "Let yourself go," he whispered. "Relax and enjoy what I'm going to do to you." He began to suck at her nipples as he unzipped her wool slacks and pulled them off. His fingers explored the dampness between her thighs as she began to relax under his manipulations. "Soon, Marianne," he whispered as he unbuckled his belt and unzipped his pants. He struggled out of his clothes and returned to her, pressing himself into her. "Feel how much I want you," he breathed. "Feel it, Marianne . . ."

"Oh, yes," she cried as he pushed himself into her, taking possession of her flesh, fulfilling the promise he'd made to himself the first time he saw her. His breath came in harsh gasps and he moved powerfully, taking her with that same urgency he did not completely understand himself. His orgasm came quickly, explosively, before he could satisfy her needs, and he fell off her in gratified exhaustion.

He lay beside her, staring up at the ceiling for a long time. Eventually he turned to her and broke the silence. "Come with me—we'll go up to the bedroom," he told her. "We'll make love again and again, until we have *both* been satisfied."

Marianne was not disappointed. Alexander did make love to her again and again that night under the eiderdown quilts in the master bedroom. Though Marianne had been to bed with other men before Alexander, she'd never had an orgasm. Alexander, with his mouth and his hands and his splendid body, had enabled her to experience a kaleidoscope of exquisite sensations she'd never dreamed possible.

Later, in the darkness, Marianne lay beside him in silence, thinking about what had happened between them, and she was filled with a joy so complete she could not believe it was real. This is just the beginning for us, she told herself. He was all she had ever wanted in a man. She finally drifted off to sleep, to happy dreams of a future with Alexander.

When she woke the next morning, he was gone.

Alexander was downstairs, where he'd spent most of the night. Slumped in an armchair, he stared into the dim glow of the dying fire in the huge stone fireplace, trying to rationalize what he'd done. He knew it was wrong. Marianne had the ripe, appealing body of a woman, but she was in reality not much more than a child. A child, dammit! He ran one hand through his hair in frustration. He should never have brought her here—yet when he saw her out on the slopes, he hadn't been able to help himself. He had to have her.

Had to have her. Unable to resist the temptation. It was always the same story. Certain women affected him that way, but he had no idea why. He saw them, he wanted them, and that was all that mattered to him. Yet after he'd satisfied himself, he always felt as though he'd suddenly found himself in bed with another man, a boy, someone he shouldn't have been in bed with. He felt physically ill, as if he might vomit. Why do I keep doing it? he asked himself. Why do I do it when I know how I'm going to feel later?

And why, knowing this, would he most likely take Marianne to bed again?

"You are returning to New York so soon?" Marianne sat cross-legged on the bed, wearing only a sheer, pink silk peignoir, frowning as she watched him dress. "I thought you would be staying on for at least another week—"

"It can't be avoided." There was an unmistakable tension

in Alexander's voice. He stood in front of the mirror, knotting his tie. "It is business and I am needed there."

"I see." She toyed with the delicate gold bracelet on her wrist, the bracelet Alexander had given her the day before. "This is so beautiful," she said softly. "I shall cherish it always."

But Alexander wasn't listening. His mind was on the cable that had arrived from George that morning. His father was flying to New York and expected to meet with him. It was most unexpected news, but Alexander was optimistic. Perhaps he had reconsidered Alexander's proposal to relocate the corporation's world headquarters. Perhaps now he was ready to listen to reason.

"You have not heard a word I have said, have you, *Liebchen?*" Marianne asked, a mild note of reproach in her voice.

"No," he admitted. "I am sorry. I have a great deal on my mind right now."

She smiled. "I am a banker's daughter. I am accustomed to such distractions," she said. "I was only trying to tell you how very much I love the bracelet."

"Oh—I'm pleased that you like it," he said tonelessly.

She rose from the bed and went to the window. Down below, Alexander's valet was piling his luggage into the trunk of the car. She frowned. He really was leaving. "What I love most about it," she began slowly, turning back to face him, "is that every time I look at it, I am reminded of you."

Alexander did not respond. His mind was still on the meeting with his father.

"I will miss you," Marianne was saying.

"What? . . . I have no idea," he said absently.

She was silent for a moment. "Alexander, why do you always leave me after we make love?" she asked finally. "Every night I fall asleep in your arms, but when I wake, you are always gone."

Alexander shrugged. "I'm often restless at night. I didn't want to disturb you."

"Insomnia?" she asked. "It is apparently a common complaint among businessmen. My father has had many sleepless nights as well."

He reached into his pocket and brought out the keys to the

chalet. "How long before you have to return to the university?" he asked.

Her heart skipped a beat. "Two weeks. Why do you ask?"

He gave her the keys. "I've leased this place for the season. Stay on as long as you like," he told her.

"Oh, no, I could not—"

"Of course you can. Stay here and enjoy it," he said, smiling. He scribbled an address on the back of one of his business cards and gave it to her. "Leave the keys with this gentleman when you're ready to leave, all right?"

She nodded silently. She had hoped he was going to ask her to go with him to New York.

The valet appeared in the doorway. "The car is ready, sir," he announced.

Alexander nodded. He put on his coat, kissed Marianne lightly on the forehead, and left without a backward glance. He did not see the tears in her eyes, and she did not begin to weep until she heard the front door slam.

He looked back only once as he climbed into the waiting car. She stood at the window, waving to him. It was just as well he'd had to cut his vacation short, he thought as the car pulled away. Marianne was behaving like a lovesick schoolgirl. It was best to end it now, before the situation got out of hand. He had no way of knowing that it had already gone too far, that it had gotten out of hand the night he'd brought her there.

Marianne was in love with him.

Los Angeles.

Meredith met Tom Ryan, Nick's mentor and possibly one of the most successful film directors of all time, on the set of Nick's latest picture. Ryan was taller than Meredith had imagined, lean and athletic-looking, with a rugged, masculine face and thick blond hair that he combed straight back, away from his face. There was a melancholy air about this reclusive Hollywood legend who so seldom appeared in public, a deep, ineffable sadness that Meredith could sense in just the few minutes she'd spent with him.

"He seems so distant, as if he's living in another world," she told Nick that night in bed. "There was such an overwhelming emptiness about him—I could actually feel it!''

Nick stared up at the ceiling. "The man's seen a lot of heartache in his time, babe," he answered quietly.

Meredith propped herself up on one elbow. "Nick, what actually happened? I mean, how did his wife and child die?"

"I don't know all of the details," Nick said, turning over to face her. "Nobody does, really—except Tom himself, of course, and he's not talking."

"He's never told anyone?"

"Not as far as I know."

"But so much has been written on it—it's a story that's fascinated movie fans for decades, one that still fascinates them—" she began.

"Yeah, I know," Nick said, nodding. "But Tom's never been willing to discuss it with anybody, and certainly not with the media. He's got a lot of bitterness locked up inside himself, and he's never come to grips with it."

"He's never even talked to you about it?"

"Like I said before, he doesn't like to talk about it—and I've never asked," Nick said, stroking her arm. "I figure if he wanted to tell me, he would. All he's ever told anybody was that they were filming on location—they didn't do much of that back then, but it was a big picture, the exception rather than the rule—and there was an accident of some kind and the boy was killed. Elizabeth couldn't cope with her son's death. She just collapsed. I think she must've had a stroke or something."

"And after all these years, he's still not talking?" Meredith was openly intrigued.

"No, and I can't really say that I blame him. Once you've been to hell and back, you don't like to relive the unpleasant memories," he said grimly.

"You know, if someone could get him to talk . . ."

Nick sat up. "Look, I think I know what you've got in mind, and I'm telling you now that it won't work. He's not going to talk to you or anybody else about it—especially not someone from the media. He's kept it quiet all these years—why would he suddenly come out with the whole story now?"

"Maybe if you were to ask him—" she started.

"No. I'm not getting involved," Nick said firmly, clearly annoyed. "I told you before, Meredith, the guy's been like a father to me. The way I see it, he's got the right to let his wife and son rest in peace if that's what he wants. He has the right to bear his pain alone if that's his choice."

"Rumor has it that Tom Ryan's on his way out," Meredith said then. "To revive this story now could revive his entire career."

"I don't think he really gives a damn if his career is revived or not," Nick said quietly. "I don't think he's cared about much of anything since that accident."

"You don't want me to do the story at all, do you?" she said flatly. "With or without your help."

"I'd be lying if I said I did," Nick said. "I care a lot about Tom. I don't like the idea of exploiting him —especially when you would be the one doing it."

"Exploiting him?" Meredith looked at him, surprised.

"Yeah, exploiting him. He doesn't want the story to go public, that's obvious, or he would have come out with it a long time ago. And he certainly wouldn't think of doing it now just to save his career." He paused. "So you tell me—is it exploitation or isn't it?"

"I've never thought of it that way . . ."

"You thought about the station's ratings, right?"

"Of course, but—"

"An exclusive like this could mean a big boost to your career, couldn't it?" He looked at her. "I'm not faulting you for being ambitious, babe. God knows I've got my share of it. But not at the other guy's expense. Tom's been dying a slow death ever since the accident. To start hounding him about it all over again could push him over the edge."

"So it is true?" Meredith asked.

"What's true?"

"I've heard that Tom Ryan's developed a drinking problem, that he spends a lot of time at the local bars and usually gets pretty well smashed. They say that most of the time he can't even drive himself home."

"I wouldn't know about that," Nick said tightly. "I've never seen him drunk myself. All I know is that I can't see putting him through that all over again." He got out of bed and put on his robe.

"Where are you going?" Meredith asked, switching on the bedside lamp.

"I was having trouble sleeping anyway. I think I'll go downstairs and go over the script. I've got a few bugs to work out of it before we shoot tomorrow." He turned and left the room.

The morning air was cold. A group of gulls flew over as a red-gold sunrise blazed against the eastern sky. On the western horizon, a small boat with brightly colored sails headed for land, the sails billowing in the breeze. Down the beach, two runners in shorts and bare feet ran in the sand. Meredith smiled wearily as she drew her sweater around herself tightly. At least she wasn't the only idiot out at this ungodly hour, she thought.

She hadn't slept well. She couldn't stop thinking about what Nick had said to her. He was dead set against her even asking Tom Ryan for an interview. She wasn't completely sure herself she wanted to do it. Her brief meeting with the man had left her with a haunting mental image of a man who'd carried a deep, unspeakable pain within the depths of his soul for too many years. Still, the journalist in her wanted the story, wanted to find out what it was he'd kept from the rest of the world for the past twenty-six years, and it was that part of her that resented Nick for trying to stand in her way.

In the beginning, Meredith had been afraid to let herself get involved with Nick. She'd been sure that his swiftly rising star would eclipse her own, that the relationship that had developed between them did not fit into the plans she'd made, did not fit into her carefully mapped-out future in broadcasting. Nick had convinced her that it would work, that their lives could complement each other's. She had believed him, until now. Now she found herself wondering if she could allow Nick's friendship with Tom Ryan to stand in the way of her pursuit of the story she knew could open doors for her.

"Meredith—wait!" a voice called out from behind her. She turned to see Nick running toward her. She stopped and waited for him to catch up.

"I thought you'd still be asleep," she told him.

He paused to catch his breath. "I was—until I woke up and found you gone."

She nodded. "I couldn't sleep," she admitted. "Are you still mad at me?"

He looked at her. "Mad?" he asked. "I was never mad at you."

"Come on, Nick. Do you think I really believed you wanted to get up in the middle of the night just to go over a script?" She looked down at her feet as she walked.

"I've done it before."

"Sure you have, but last night was for a different reason."

He was silent for a moment. "Okay," he said finally. "I was a little upset. Tom's been good to me. I don't want to see him go through that unpleasantness again. I figured if I excused myself, I wouldn't end up saying something stupid that I'd regret later."

"I thought so."

"Are you still set on doing the interview?"

"I don't know," she admitted. "I have to think about it for a while. I don't want to make a decision I might be sorry for."

They walked along in silence. Nick picked up a piece of driftwood and threw it into the air. It landed on the sand several yards in front of them. "It really means a lot to you, doesn't it?" he said finally. It wasn't a question.

"I think it could be important, yes." She kicked the sand absently.

"Okay," he said slowly. "Suppose I take you to see Tom. Maybe this weekend?"

She looked at him. "You'd actually help me get the interview?" she asked, surprised. "After last night, I thought—"

"Wait a minute," he cut in, shaking his head. "I didn't say I'd ask him. That's your job, and I want no part of it. I said I'd take you to see him. If you can persuade him to talk to you, fine. I hope you get the story, if it means that much to you."

She hugged him. "Nick, I don't know what to say," she admitted. "I know how you feel about this, and, well—"

"Yeah, I feel pretty strongly about it, but I feel strongly about you, too." He paused. "There's just one thing."

"What?"

"If he turns you down, if he won't have any part of it, will you drop it?" Nick asked. "He's been through enough. The press has been hounding him for years. It's got to end somewhere."

Meredith kissed him. "It's a deal."

New York City.

Alexander was surprised by the arrival of his mother at his Olympic Tower apartment the week before Christmas. "Why didn't you let me know you were coming?" he asked as he embraced her gently. She seemed so small now, so frail.

"If I had phoned, it would not have been a surprise now, would it," Melina Kirakis said as she removed her fur coat. "I simply could not bear the thought of not having my family together at Christmas." Until recent years, Christmas had never been celebrated in Greece on December twenty-fifth, but Melina, whose own mother had been British, had always insisted upon such a celebration in her home as a tribute to the mother she'd never known. Looking back now, Alexander could not recall a time when they had not been together for the holidays, but as hectic as his schedule was now, especially after having taken that week's vacation, he had not felt able to leave his office for any length of time. He hadn't reckoned with his mother's determination to follow tradition, even if it meant defying her doctor's orders by making the trip.

"I thought Dr. Karamanlis forbade you to travel," he said.

"That quack!" Melina scoffed. "What does he know?"

"Come now, *manna mou*," he said, amused. "You know perfectly well that he's one of the finest physicians in all of Greece. When he tells you that it is not advisable for you to travel, I think that you should listen to him."

"And sacrifice spending Christmas with my only child? I would not hear of it," she insisted stubbornly. "If I have to return to Greece on a stretcher, then so be it—but I will not have my family scattered to the four winds for the holidays!"

"For one so fragile, you certainly have a will of iron, Mother," Alexander observed lovingly. She was classically beautiful—flawless porcelain skin, regal bearing, a totally elegant woman. If only he could find a woman exactly like her . . . but he was convinced that such a woman did not exist. His mother was truly one of a kind. "You've come a long way," he said finally. "You must be tired. Why don't you take a nap before dinner?"

"A nap? Is that all you and your father ever think about?" she asked indignantly. "You sound exactly like him! I will have you know that I am not as ill as the two of you seem to think I am!"

"Mother—" Alexander began.

She patted his cheek affectionately. "You are such a handsome man, Alexander. Tell me—when do you suppose you will take a wife and make me a proud grandmother?"

He smiled. "I doubt that that will ever happen, *manna mou*. You see, I've given up on ever finding a woman who measures up to you."

Her smile was sad. "I am not the saint you think I am, Alexi," she said quietly. "I am far from perfect."

"You're perfect as far as I'm concerned."

"You are biased," she said accusingly. "I worry about you, my son. You are thirty-one years old now, and you have yet to have a serious romance. That is not good. When your father was your age—"

"When Father was thirty-one, the two of you had been married several years," Alexander finished. "We've been through this before, but as I've told both you *and* Father many times, I've not yet met a woman I'd want for my wife. It's not so simple . . ."

She settled down on the couch and motioned for him to join her. "Tell me, Alexander—do you not *ever* seriously consider settling down with a wife and children of your own?"

"I've thought about it," he said tightly, avoiding her eyes.

"Seriously? Remember, Alexander, I have always been able to tell when you are lying to me."

He was tempted to lie to her for a moment, but he knew that she was right: he had never been able to fool her. "Not as seriously as you would like me to, I am sure,'' he said finally.

"Perhaps you have doubts?'' she suggested. "Something you would like to talk about? I am always here for you, my son, you know that.''

"I know that, yes,'' he responded, nodding slowly.

"You say you have not yet met a woman you would want for a wife,'' Melina continued. "But it would seem to me that you always choose women who are a great deal alike, women who have much in common. A deliberate attempt to involve yourself with women who are unsuitable, perhaps?''

His smile was weak. "You've taken up psychoanalysis now?'' he asked.

"One would not have to be a professional to recognize the problem here, Alexander,'' she told him. "You tell me one moment that you will not marry unless you can find a woman who is like me. Then you turn around and involve yourself with women who are as unlike me as can possibly be. That would suggest to me that you avoid involvement—serious emotional involvement—by always choosing women you know you will not be able to fall in love with.''

He smiled. "I think you worry too much.''

"I worry because I love you,'' she insisted. "Your father and I, all we both want is for you to be happy.''

"And to be happy, you think I must be married and have children,'' he concluded.

"It made us very happy,'' she said simply.

"Did it make you happy when Damian died?'' he wanted to know. "Did it make you happy to have to go through so many miscarriages?'' He saw the look on her face and lowered his voice. "I'm sorry, Mother. I didn't mean to—''

Melina shook her head. "It is all right,'' she told him. "After a time, the pain becomes more bearable.''

"Do you ever really get over it?'' he questioned. "Does the pain ever go away completely?''

"One learns to live with it—to cope, to go on living—but no, the pain never really goes away.'' Melina looked at him. "This is what troubles you, Alexander?'' she asked. "You are afraid to care because you may lose that person?''

He paused thoughtfully. "I'm not sure,'' he said slowly.

"I've never really thought about it. It is simply something I've always felt, something I cannot explain . . ."

Melina smiled patiently. "You must not be afraid to care," she told him. "You cannot continue to hide, to keep the world at arm's length out of fear. To find happiness of this kind, there are risks one must take."

He frowned. "I would like nothing better than to have the kind of marriage you and Father have always had, but . . ." His voice trailed off.

"Then you must not continue to hide behind that wall you have erected around yourself. You must be willing to put forth the effort to make it happen," Melina insisted. "It is true that your father and I have had a good marriage, a very strong one, but ours has not been a union without its problems. We have suffered many losses over the years, fought many battles. Our marriage has endured because we have not allowed tragedy to drive us apart. We have faced our problems together and become stronger as a couple for it."

Alexander looked away from her, contemplating the Manhattan skyline. "Not all marriages fare as well as yours has, I'm afraid," he said carefully.

"That is because they have not been given the chance," Melina said as she took his hands in hers. When she spoke again, it was in an urgent, passionate voice. "Ah, Alexander, in so many ways you are so very much like your father. You are both so strong-willed. Both of you are unyielding, ambitious men. Neither of you, unfortunately, has the ability to forgive or forget." She paused. "Over the years, your father has mellowed. The years have mellowed him; the tragedies he has endured have tempered the steel. You are still young. I would hope that you will not have to go through all he has before you open your eyes. I hope that you will learn to bend on your own. More than anything, I wish for you to find happiness."

He reached out for her then, clinging to her as he had not done since he was a small boy. "Mother," he whispered. "I am so very glad you've come."

"I would not have had it any other way, my son," she told him, holding him close. "You will see. It will happen for you one day . . ."

Los Angeles.

The Ryan mansion, located high in the hills now known as Bel-Air, had been built long before Bel-Air became a fashionable address for celebrities. It was an English Tudor-style home perched high atop a hill of rolling lawns and carefully tended trees that lined the long, circular drive leading up to the main house. A high stone wall surrounded the entire ten-acre estate, and Nick explained to Meredith that Tom Ryan had had the wall built when he and his wife first bought the property in 1948. "They wanted privacy more than anything else," Nick told her as they drove up to the house. "They worried about their child's safety. They were afraid someone might try to kidnap him."

Meredith was silent, still taking in the splendor of the mansion itself. "It's like something out of a fairy tale. I've never seen anything so beautiful."

"They knew how to live in style back then," Nick said as he held the car door for her. "Tom reached the zenith of his career back in the forties—Hollywood's golden era. The really big stars lived like royalty."

"Times have changed, haven't they," she commented.

"For some of us, anyway," he agreed as he rang the doorbell. They were admitted to the house by Tom Ryan's Mexican housekeeper and taken to his study, where he was waiting for them.

Tom Ryan greeted Nick warmly. "It's been a long time since you've been here, Nick," Ryan told him. "Too long."

"You know how it is, Tom," Nick said with a grin. "You don't get to the studio very often, either."

The older man frowned. "There's not much for me to do around there these days."

"Nothing in the works?"

Tom's laugh was hollow. "I haven't had anything 'in the works' for a good many years. You know that."

Meredith was eyeing the glass on his desk. Bourbon. Probably straight. The bottle—which was almost empty —sat beside it.

"What brings you here?" Tom asked. "Problems with the new picture—or with Ed Goldman?" Ed Goldman was the new studio boss at Centurion.

"Neither," Nick said, slightly embarrassed. "Actually, it's Meredith who wanted to see you this time."

Tom turned to look at her. He saw her staring at the bottle and walked over and put it away quickly. "Well, then—what can I do for you?" he asked, trying to keep his voice light.

"I'm with the news department of KXLA—"

"I know," he said. "I've seen you on the late news many times. I'm a bit of a night owl."

"I'd like to discuss the possibility of doing an interview with you," she began, "on you and your late wife—"

"No," he said tightly, his mood changing abruptly. He turned to Nick. "You knew about this?"

Nick nodded. "Yeah. I knew. I know how you feel about this, Tom, but Meredith thinks—"

"It's out of the question," Tom said flatly. "Liz and David have been dead almost twenty-seven years now. Let them rest in peace."

Meredith rose from her chair to face him. "Mr. Ryan, hundreds of articles and features have been done about you and your family over the years," she reminded him. "There have been dozens of stories published, all different versions of the story. There's been more speculation over it than there has been over the Kennedy assassination! If I wanted to just cash in on it, I could just put together a film and draw my own conclusions."

"So what's stopping you?" There was bitterness in his voice.

"I don't want to do it that way. I don't want to do what everybody else has been doing. I want a film that will move people, that will touch them. I want the truth. I want to tell the story as it really happened."

"What good would it do now?" Tom Ryan asked.

Meredith took from her briefcase a thick manila folder containing photocopies of newspaper clippings she'd collected at the public library and newspaper morgues. "Look at some of these—here's one. It tells how your wife died in a hospital in Europe after your son's accident. It says she was pregnant at the time and went out of her mind, then tried to abort the baby by using a wire coat hanger—"

"Meredith—" Nick was touching her arm.

"He has a right to know what they've been saying, Nick,"

she insisted. She turned back to Tom. "Here's another one. They claim that neither Elizabeth nor David is really dead at all, that she caught you with another woman and refused to come back to the States with you. Some people will do anything to sell a story, Mr. Ryan! Look at this one—this writer claims that your wife suffered a breakdown after the death of your child and is still alive in a mental institution somewhere—"

"*Enough!*" Tom Ryan screamed at her, his face twisted with rage.

Nick took Meredith by the arm. "I think we'd better go now," he said quietly.

"No, Nick. Not yet," she protested.

He was firm. "We had a deal, remember?"

She looked at him for a moment. There was disapproval in his eyes. "I—oh, all right." She extended her hand to Tom, offering him the file. He wouldn't take it, so she put it on the corner of the desk. "Please, Mr. Ryan, read it," she urged. "Think about it, and if you change your mind, let me know." She turned and left with Nick, but Tom Ryan didn't notice.

He was staring at one of the clippings she had given him.

"Okay, I got carried away. I admit it," Meredith said sullenly as they drove back to Malibu. "I got carried away and I blew it."

"We had an agreement," Nick said quietly.

"I know," she said, turning to look at him. "But dammit, Nick, I—"

"You went too far, Meredith," he told her. "I told you how he felt about this whole business."

"Doesn't he care about the things that have been written about him, about his family?" she asked. "Doesn't it bother him that so many stories have been told?"

"I really don't think he gives a damn about anything anymore," Nick said truthfully. "It's all been downhill for him since the accident. He's dead inside. Nothing much matters to him these days."

"Not even his wife's memory?"

Nick looked at her. "I think you made your point there," he said tightly.

"Do you think there's a chance he might change his mind?"

"I don't know. I doubt it. But if he doesn't, just remember our agreement."

She nodded. "I will. If he doesn't come around, I'll drop it. Much as I hate to, I *will* drop it," she promised.

He was silent for a few blocks. "Look, I know how much this story means to you, okay? But keeping it quiet is as important to Tom—maybe more so—as exposing it is to you."

"You're telling me I have to respect his right to privacy."

"Something like that, yeah."

"I told you I would. If he doesn't change his mind, I'll leave him alone," she said. "Now, could we please drop it?"

Meredith had almost given up on ever hearing from Tom Ryan, when he phoned her at the station a week later, asking to see her. As she drove through Bel-Air, she wondered if she could possibly have reconsidered. When she arrived, he was waiting for her in the library and was considerably more pleasant than he had been at their last meeting.

"I've had a chance to think about the things you said to me the last time you were here," he said.

"Have you changed your mind about the documentary?" she asked as the housekeeper poured her a glass of iced tea.

He smiled, and Meredith realized it was the first time she had ever seen him smile. Even in his photographs, he always looked so somber, so unhappy. "Let's just say that I'm considering it for now," he responded. "After you and Nick left last week, I looked over the clippings." He gestured toward the file lying on the coffee table in the center of the room. "I had stopped reading anything the press reported about Liz and me right after I came back to the States, after—" He stopped short.

"After the accident?" she asked carefully.

He nodded. "I hadn't realized how distorted the reports had become. I've thought it over, and decided that I'll give you a chance. I'm willing to talk with you, to cooperate with you, to an extent," he explained. "Then, if I could see that it was being done properly—"

"Then you might be persuaded to tell me everything? Including what really happened to your wife and child?"

"Yes."

"Great," she said promptly. She glanced up at the mantel. Over it hung a huge oil painting of a woman and child. The woman was exquisite, with long, luxuriant black hair and fine, aristocratic features. She had the most extraordinary eyes Meredith had ever seen, dark and oddly mysterious. The child looked remarkably like his mother, with the same coloring and delicate features.

"Elizabeth and David," Tom Ryan told her. "It was completed just three months before . . . "

She nodded, turning back to the painting. "She was beautiful."

He smiled sadly. "The real beauty of Elizabeth couldn't be captured on canvas," he said, staring up at the painting. "She was special in every way. I've never known anyone quite like her, so uniquely and totally herself. I always thought David would have grown up to look like her. As you can see, the resemblance was striking."

"It certainly was," Meredith agreed.

"I don't think I'll ever forget the first time I saw her," Tom said then. "Words just couldn't describe her. She was a rare combination of innocence and sensuality. Alluring but so very vulnerable. I suppose that was the real secret of her success: she was like a dozen different women in one beautiful package. In the five years we were together, she never ceased to be a surprise to me. I could never be sure what to expect from her next."

"A lot of people think you 'made' Elizabeth Weldon," Meredith said.

"I think Liz would have been a big star even if we had never met," Ryan said truthfully. "She had a magic about her when she was performing that's hard to find, even in the best actresses. She had star quality—she was a presence, even off-screen."

Meredith looked at the shimmering gold statuette on the mantel. The Oscar Elizabeth had won—posthumously—for her last picture. If it could talk, imagine what kind of tales it would tell, Meredith thought.

"She was from Texas," Ryan was saying. "Her father

was one of those rich, hotshot oil barons, and Liz grew up in San Angelo. She ran away from home when she was eighteen. Even then she wanted to act, but her parents saw actresses as being one step above prostitutes. They had her future all mapped out for her, so she decided she'd just have to run away. She'd been planning it for months. She came out here on a Greyhound bus during the war, took drama classes, and damned near worked herself to death at some little drive-in hamburger place out in West Hollywood until she started getting parts on a regular basis. I spotted her quite by accident one day. An agent I knew wanted me to see a client of his who had done a walk-on in the same picture. His client stank, but Elizabeth was so incredible—she just seemed to leap out at me.''

"She was that good?"

He laughed for the first time. "No, that's not what I meant at all," he said. "Her inexperience was apparent in every move, every gesture. But I'd been in the business long enough to know potential when I saw it. There was definitely something special about her. She was beautiful, yes, but it was more than that, much more. It's hard to define, really. She wasn't just an actress playing a role. She became, in the most complete way I've ever seen, the character she was playing.''

"You met her after you saw the film?"

His smile was sad. "Almost a week later. It took me that long to track her down, to find out who she was and how to contact her," he recalled. "I had my secretary call her and ask her to meet me for lunch. She'd never been to the Brown Derby before—that was the 'in' place back then. She walked in the door, looked around, and I thought she was going to faint.''

"Was that when you fell in love with her?" Meredith hoped she sounded civil.

"I think so, yes, but I didn't realize it until several months later," he admitted. "She was so beautiful that day. It was hot, right in the middle of summer. She was wearing a white summer dress with ruffles and flowers embroidered on it, and a huge, wide-brimmed white hat. I remember thinking to myself that it was a damned shame she'd been born too late to play Scarlett O'Hara. She was a real southern belle. In a town that's notorious for its beautiful women, she was extraordinary.''

"Did she ever resent having to give up making movies after your son was born?" Meredith asked cautiously.

"Resent it?" He laughed at the suggestion. "No, definitely not. Liz knew she didn't have to sacrifice anything she didn't want to give up. Her retirement was her own idea. After David was born, she couldn't bear to be parted from him. I suppose it would have been better for all concerned if she had been willing to leave him behind, just once . . .''

"You're referring to Europe?"

He nodded, not trusting his voice.

"How did it happen?" Meredith asked softly.

"We were filming on location," he recalled, the pain in his voice clear. "David was there with us. We'd tried to impress upon him the importance of staying close to the rest of us. We didn't know the area well, and we were in a strange country where there weren't too many people who spoke English. But how can you really reason with a child that young? He wasn't quite five years old! He wandered away, not very far, but far enough to . . .''

Meredith said nothing, waiting for him to go on.

Ryan finally found his voice. "He fell into some old well that had been abandoned years before. It was a narrow shaft, very deep—at least three hundred feet, I think. For four days we tried to get to him, but we were too late . . .'' He began to weep openly. "He died there." Ryan looked at Meredith, his eyes filled with tears. "Can you imagine how horrible it must have been for him? How could he know how hard we tried to save him? What must he have been thinking when he died?''

FOUR

〰〰〰〰〰〰〰〰〰〰

Kennedy International Airport.

Marianne Hauptmann was both impatient and excited, impatient because the flight from Geneva had taken so long, and excited because she had never been to New York before—and because she was about to be reunited with the man she loved.

She had not cabled Alexander from Europe to let him know she was coming, nor did she intend to phone him from the airport. No, she wanted to surprise him. It had been such a long time, but she just knew he would be as happy to see her as she would be to see him again. How long had it been? He had not written or phoned her since he'd left Switzerland, but she told herself that many men were not good at letter-writing, and Alexander was probably one of them. As for his not calling, she was sure he had been terribly busy and had not had the time. None of that mattered now. Soon they would be together again, and that was the important thing.

Marianne knew her father would be furious when he discovered that she'd left the university at the beginning of the semester, but he would understand—after she and Alexander were married. She no longer needed a formal education. She wanted only to learn to be a good wife for Alexander. What good was a degree in history anyway? she asked herself as the customs official opened her hand luggage and inspected it thoroughly.

She took Alexander's business card from her handbag and read it carefully. Her English was passable, but far from perfect. At least she would be able to give a taxi driver the address of Alexander's office in Manhattan. She knew that he lived at the Olympic Tower, that his offices were at the corner of Fifth Avenue and Fifty-first Street. She would have no trouble in finding him. She collected her luggage and headed for the exit.

Sitting in the back of a taxi headed toward Manhattan, Marianne leaned back in her seat and drew a deep breath. She looked out the window as the taxi crossed the Queensboro Bridge. The sky was clear and she could see the magnificent skyline of lower Manhattan glittering in the midmorning sunlight. It is like another world, Marianne thought, exhilarated. Exactly the kind of place she would expect Alexander to call home. It was unlike any city she had ever seen, larger by far than Zürich or Basle, the largest cities in Switzerland. She recalled reading somewhere, a long time ago, that New York was the largest city in the world. She didn't know if that was still true or not, but looking at it now, she could believe it.

"Here we are, miss," the taxi driver announced as he slowed the car to a stop in front of the Olympic Tower.

Marianne nodded. "Thank you," she said, double-checking the address on the card. She paid him, gave him a generous tip, then waited as he took her luggage from the trunk, leaving it with the doorman.

She took the elevator up to the floor occupied by the Kirakis Corporation's executive offices. As she stepped out of the elevator, the first thing she noticed was the receptionist's desk: it was modern in design, semicircular, made of polished mahogany. The receptionist was a smartly dressed blonde who looked to be about Marianne's age, busy with an elaborate telephone console that never seemed to stop buzzing. On the wall behind her was a gigantic world map encased in Plexiglas. At its center was the corporation's logo, and below that, in silver block letters, the words

KIRAKIS CORPORATION—NORTH AMERICAN HEADQUAR-TERS. Between calls, the receptionist directed Marianne to Alexander's office, which she found with no difficulty, but his secretary was unwilling to allow her to enter without identifying herself.

"I am Marianne Hauptmann, and I have come from Geneva to see him," Marianne said in her halting English. The stupid girl—didn't she know that the future Mrs. Kirakis stood before her? "Is he in or not?"

"He's in, yes, but he's—" the secretary began.

Marianne smiled, relieved. "Do not announce me. I wish to surprise him." Before the secretary could stop her, she barged into Alexander's office. He was on the phone when she entered, but ended his call quickly and jumped to his feet. He did not look at all pleased to see her.

"Stacey, I told you I was not to be interrupted for any reason!" he snapped as his secretary rushed into the room, looking quite distraught.

"I tried to stop her, Mr. Kirakis," the woman said helplessly.

He turned to Marianne. "What are you doing here?" he asked crossly.

"*Liebchen*—I thought you would be happy to see me," she answered, not understanding his behavior. "I came all the way from Geneva to surprise you!"

He stared at her for a moment, then turned to his secretary again. "You may leave us alone now, Stacey," he said quietly.

She nodded. "Yes, sir." She closed the door as she left the room.

Alexander turned back to Marianne. "I was under the impression that you would be returning to the university when you left Gstaad," he said, his voice hard.

"I did," she said, looking down at the floor. "But when I did not hear from you, I missed you so that I had to come . . ."

He turned away from her. "That was a very stupid thing to do," he said finally.

She did not understand why he was acting so strangely. "I thought you would be happy to see me. I thought you expected me to come here . . ."

He turned to look at her again. "Where on earth did you get an idea like that?"

"In Gstaad . . . we were so happy," she said, dangerously close to tears. "I could tell that you loved me. I knew that once we were married . . ."

"Married?" Alexander looked genuinely surprised. "I never asked you to marry me!"

"Of course you never said the words, but I could tell . . ." she began nervously.

He came around the desk and grasped her shoulders. "You *assumed*, Marianne. If I want to marry a woman, I think *I* should have the opportunity to ask her, don't you agree?"

She was sobbing openly now. "But in Gstaad—"

"In Gstaad we had a most enjoyable interlude. That's all it was, Marianne. A pleasant interlude—for both of us," he said, lowering his voice. He was beginning to feel sorry for her. "If you misunderstood anything I said, I am sorry."

"Sorry?" She pulled away from him, her face red and distorted from crying. "I have been such a fool—a blind, stupid fool! I actually thought you loved me! All I was to you was someone to take to bed!"

"We barely know one another," he said quietly. "How could we have fallen in love?"

"I did! I love you!" she cried. "I have given up everything I hold dear—my father, my education, everything—to come here, to be with you! I have made you the most important part of my life, and I find I am nothing to you! Very well, Alexander, I shall remove myself from your life as quickly as I can!"

"If I loved you," Alexander began slowly, "didn't it seem odd to you that I never once contacted you after we parted in Gstaad? It has been more than two months, Marianne. I do not know how you feel about such things, but if I were in love, I would not be able to be parted for the lady for that long without at least a telephone call."

She nodded. "I have been so foolish . . ." she said in a choked voice.

"What will you do now?" he asked, not sure he'd made her understand. He had not led her on. Her belief that he was in love with her had sprung from her own imagination.

She wiped the tears from her eyes. "That is no concern of yours now," she said tightly.

"Do you need money to return to Geneva? I will help you in any way—"

"No!" she exclaimed. "It is bad enough that I have allowed myself to be used by you. It is enough that I have foolishly believed that you could really have wanted me for your wife. I will not take your money. I feel very cheap and dirty right now, Alexander. To take your money would make me feel like a common whore!" She looked up at him, and there was pain in her eyes. "I will leave you as you wish. I shall go home to Switzerland. I promise not to bother you again."

She ran out of the office before Alexander could stop her.

Los Angeles.

Normally, Meredith enjoyed the drive from L.A. to Malibu, never tiring of the magnificent Southern California coastline, but today she didn't even notice it. She was thinking about her most recent meeting with Tom Ryan, wondering if Nick had been right. Had she gone too far in her search for a story? In the past few weeks, she had observed a change in Ryan's personality that disturbed her. He was moody and withdrawn and often uncommunicative. When she was there, he drank too much, and she often found herself cutting the sessions short because he was unable to go on. She'd confided to Nick that there were times she considered dropping the project.

She looked over at the two thick scrapbooks lying on the seat beside her. Ryan had loaned them to her. They were the scrapbooks Elizabeth had kept while she was still alive, scrapbooks filled with pictures and clippings and reviews of her performances, reviews Ryan had said he'd often urged her to ignore, insisting that only box office receipts counted. Meredith wondered if Tom himself had added anything to those books after her death. Probably not. She had the feeling he had not been able to bring himself to look at them since Elizabeth's death. He hadn't even opened them when he handed them over to her.

Nick was away, filming on location in Mexico, so Mere-

dith knew she would be alone all evening. She would have
plenty of time to look through each of the books thoroughly,
to examine every photograph, every clipping. When she
reached the beach house, she remembered it was the
housekeeper's night off, so she showered, made herself a
light dinner of scrambled eggs and toast, and settled down in
bed to look at the scrapbooks. In the first she found photos
of the young Elizabeth, just arrived in Hollywood from
Texas, eager to realize her dreams. She looked so young—so
vulnerable—in those pictures. Meredith tried to imagine
what it must have been like for her. Had she ever been afraid
she wouldn't make it? Had she ever thought of giving up?
Had she ever known discouragement or disappointment?

"What was it like for you back then, Elizabeth?" Meredith asked aloud. "Did you ever feel you'd made a mistake?
Did you ever consider packing up and going back to Texas?"

She found a studio publicity shot of Elizabeth as she had
appeared in her first major role. Indeed there was a magic, a
specialness that seemed to come across even in the photographs. No wonder she became a star, Meredith thought as
she studied the photo.

She read the reviews. Some of them were good, which did
not surprise Meredith at all. As a rule, reviewers had a
tendency to pan anything that had been a great commercial
success. It was almost as if they resented an actor or a writer
or an artist who achieved any degree of success in his or her
chosen medium. They must've been eating their hearts out,
Meredith thought wryly.

It was almost three in the morning when Meredith reached
the end of the second book. On the last page was a yellowed
newspaper clipping featuring a photograph of Tom, Elizabeth, and their son David at the airport the morning they left
for Europe. The child did look incredibly like his mother. If
he had lived, he'd be a grown man now. Probably a real
heartbreaker, too, Meredith thought as she put the books
aside and switched off the lamp.

She wished Nick were there. Suddenly she felt unbearably
lonely.

Nick returned to Malibu on Friday evening, filled with
enthusiasm for the new picture he was working on. "I think

it's going to be my best to date," he told Meredith as she helped him unpack. "In fact, I wouldn't be at all surprised if it turns out to be the biggest box-office hit of the year."

She smiled. "That good?"

"Better," he said confidently. "Wait'll you see the rushes."

"I can't wait."

He took one of the empty suitcases and stored it at the back of his closet. "With a little luck, I won't be needing these for a long time to come."

"I hope not. I was beginning to feel like I was living here alone," she admitted.

He grinned, taking her in his arms. "Not a chance, babe," he said as he kissed her. "I'd take you with me if you were ever free to go."

"Sometimes I wish I were." She stopped short. "You really look tired. Maybe we ought to skip dinner and go straight to bed."

"I'm all for that, honey, but remember—I've been away for a couple of weeks. We go to bed, I probably won't get to sleep." He winked at her. "Know what I mean?"

She made a face. "I meant go to bed—you know, to *sleep*." She kissed the tip of his nose playfully. "You know, sometimes I wonder about you, Holliday."

"Oh, yeah? Why?"

"Look at yourself. Every time you go away on location, you come back looking like you've lost ten pounds and haven't slept in weeks. Don't you take time for minor things like eating and sleeping?"

"Nope," he confessed. "I try to get the filming out of the way as fast as I can so I can get home to you."

"You're hopeless!" she said, laughing.

"Tell you what. Since neither of us has to work over the weekend, why don't we take advantage of it?"

"What have you got in mind?" she asked suspiciously.

"Well, how would you feel about taking a long walk on the beach in the morning, first thing? Then maybe we could go out for lunch, take in a movie, and make reservations for dinner at the Hungry Tiger downtown?" He started kissing her neck, and his beard tickled.

Meredith laughed as she wriggled away from him.

"Sounds great to me, but lately it seems like it rains every time we both have a free weekend. I think we may be jinxed," she said.

"Nonsense!" he snorted. "I happen to have it on good authority that this weekend is going to be unseasonably warm, sunny, without a cloud in sight." He started to unbutton her shirt. "It wouldn't dare rain. Not this time."

It rained all weekend. "That's what you get for making threats, Holliday," Meredith said, standing at the bedroom windows, observing the downpour. "It's not nice to mess around with Mother Nature, you know."

"I don't think that's how the expression goes, honey, but I get the message anyway." Nick was sprawled out on the bed, leafing through the weekend newspaper. "We could still take in a movie if you want."

"No, thanks. I think I'd rather stay home and stay dry," she said morosely.

"Well, I guess we could think of other things to do here," he drawled, leering at her.

Meredith turned to look at him. "You've got a real one-track mind, mister," she said, giggling.

"So I've been told." He sat up. On the floor beside the bed, he noticed a large stack of old movie magazines. He picked up the one on top and leafed through it. "What's this for?" he asked.

"Research."

He looked up at her. "You've been to see Tom again," he guessed.

She nodded. "Yesterday. He's saved those old magazines all these years—can you believe it?" she asked. "He told me they were Elizabeth's. She apparently kept every issue she was featured in."

Nick found a feature on the Ryans and studied it for a moment. "She was really a knockout, wasn't she."

"She was beautiful," Meredith agreed. "It's a shame. She was only twenty-eight when she died."

"I take it Tom hasn't told you everything that happened on the picture location," Nick said as he returned the magazine to the stack.

Meredith shook her head. "I think it's going to take a while to win him over," she sighed. "After all he's been through, he still sees the press as the enemy."

"Maybe."

"You don't sound too optimistic," she said.

"Look, babe, I know the guy, and probably know him better than most people around here. He never confides in anybody. I just can't see him doing a hundred-eighty-degree turn now," he told her. "I think you're headed for a big letdown."

"You let me worry about that, okay?" She crossed the room and put her arms around his neck. "I'm a big girl. I can take it—if it happens."

"Uh-huh." He pulled her down on the bed beside him. "You know what? It seems like all we talk about these days is Tom Ryan and his deepest, darkest secrets."

"I thought you liked Tom," Meredith said as she rumpled his hair playfully.

"I do. But I can think of better things to talk about in the rare time we have alone." He kissed her lightly. "And I can certainly think of better things to do."

"Like what?" she asked innocently.

His grin was wicked. "Like this . . ."

New York City.

Alexander looked over the papers spread out on the desk in front of him. "The reports are excellent," he said slowly. "Your people are quite thorough."

George, seated across the desk, nodded. "That's why I picked them."

"So what do you think?" Alexander asked, looking up at him.

George shrugged. "Any one of these companies would make an excellent acquisition," he answered without hesitation. "Any or all of them would be a wise investment."

"But if it were your decision to make, which of them would you choose?" Alexander wanted to know.

"Well, since you're asking for my opinion," George began with a grin, "National Technologies gets my vote.

Their record is impressive. Right now they're getting a large number of government contracts.''

Alexander nodded. ''You're absolutely right. But what about the Empire Hills Development Company? It appears they're also growing in leaps and bounds.''

George shook his head. ''They're in over their heads,'' he said. ''Big financial problems. I'd only take it if I were looking for a tax write-off.''

''Perhaps we could acquire the company and turn it around,'' Alexander suggested. He was interested in expanding the corporation's real estate holdings, and in spite of the obvious difficulties the Oregon-based development company was facing, it looked promising to him.

''I'd think about it long and hard,'' George said honestly. ''I'd check it out very carefully first.''

Alexander nodded. ''Perhaps you're right,'' he said at last. He put the folders for the two companies aside. ''The oil company looks like a winner.''

George nodded. ''They just had a big strike in the Gulf,'' he said, remembering a conversation he'd had with one of the corporation's executives in Corpus Christi that morning. ''I think—'' Both men turned at the sound of voices raised in anger on the other side of the door. Suddenly the door flew open and Constantine Kirakis burst into the office, waving a folded newspaper in his hand. His face was dark with rage.

Alexander got to his feet. ''Father—I was not expecting you—'' he began.

''I know you were not expecting me!'' Kirakis snapped. He turned to George. ''You will excuse us?''

George took one look at his face and got to his feet quickly. ''Alexander—call me when you're free, okay?''

Alexander nodded. George left the room, and Alexander turned back to his father. ''What's wrong?'' he wanted to know. ''It isn't Mother, is it?''

''Your mother is all right—under the circumstances.'' Kirakis thrust the newspaper into Alexander's hands and stabbed at it angrily with his index finger. ''Read it!'' he ordered sharply.

Alexander scanned the brief article quickly. He sank into

his chair and looked up at his father. "I had no idea," he began slowly.

"You knew this young woman, did you not?" Kirakis demanded.

Alexander nodded. "Marianne? Yes, I met her two months ago, at Gstaad," he said quietly. "But—"

"You had an affair with her?" Kirakis's tone was uncompromising.

"Yes," Alexander admitted. The newspaper report said she had committed suicide. "I had no idea she was so disturbed," he began. "I certainly never thought she was capable of taking her own life."

Kirakis's eyes were cold. "She took her own life because of you," he growled. "Does that not mean anything to you?"

Alexander looked surprised. "Because of me? Father, I barely knew her!" he protested. "We spent a week together at Gstaad—"

"And she came to New York looking for you, expecting you to marry her," Kirakis finished.

"How did you know about that?" Alexander asked.

"Word travels fast in our business, Alexander, even as far off the beaten track as you think we are in Greece," his father snapped irritably. "I know all about that little episode that took place right here in this office. It was just last week, was it not?"

Alexander nodded. "My name isn't mentioned in the article," he said. "Why do you think she took her life because of me?"

Kirakis's jaw tightened visibly. "Over the past ten years I have spent a great deal of time—and money—keeping your name out of the headlines," he said grimly. "Sometimes my efforts have failed. At any rate, I leave nothing to chance. My contacts, particularly in Switzerland, are excellent. Fortunately, several of them are in the Geneva police department." He took a small piece of paper from his breast pocket and gave it to Alexander. "The young woman left a note. One of my people managed to get it, luckily before the press got wind of the story."

Alexander read it three times. When he looked up at his

father again, his face was pale. "I had no idea she was so—troubled," he said again. "I certainly never thought—"

"That is your problem in a nutshell, Alexander. You have never stopped to consider the possible consequences of your actions!"

"She seemed, well, she seemed perfectly normal to me," Alexander said slowly, remembering how cheerful and animated she had been the morning he met her out on the slopes. "Nothing about her would have indicated that she was in any way unbalanced. We were together all week, and I had no idea . . ."

"And what about when she came to New York?"

Alexander frowned. "Then I wasn't so sure. I didn't have the faintest idea how she could have misinterpreted anything I might have said, how she could have gotten the idea that I wanted to marry her," he said. "When she left, she was obviously quite upset."

"You tried to stop her?" Kirakis asked.

"No," Alexander admitted. "I thought it could only make matters worse. When she said she was returning to Switzerland, I assumed she was going back to the university. Nothing she said gave any indication she planned to kill herself."

"You have gone too far this time, Alexander." There was a warning note in Kirakis's voice. "This is a serious matter. It is no longer just a game, with you proving yourself a stud with every woman you meet. This is suicide. A woman has taken her life because of you. There could be repercussions if this should be leaked to the media. Do you have any idea what it could do to your future in the business world—and to the future of the corporation?" he asked.

"This has nothing to do with—"

"This has *everything* to do with it!" Kirakis roared. "Kirakis has always been regarded as a solid company. A good risk financially. Someday you will be controlling it—and you will be at the mercy of the same bankers who now see you as irresponsible! If they regard you as a bad risk when you need their assistance, when you seek loans from them, then what will become of you? What will become of the corporation?"

Alexander fell silent. He had never thought about it.

"This is the last straw, Alexander," Kirakis told him. "I have had it with you and this unacceptable life-style of yours! Things are going to have to change, and change quickly, or I will make you very sorry you have not heeded my warnings. You have my word on that!"

"Father, you must believe me," Alexander said finally. "I never led her on. I never made any promises. I never told her I would marry her. I never even said that I loved her!"

"All of that is irrelevant now, Alexander," Kirakis said sharply. "She is dead, and that note links her suicide to you. Regardless of what did or did not happen between the two of you at Gstaad is unimportant now." He started for the door, then paused. "I suggest you give serious thought to what I have said."

"Wait, Father," Alexander said quickly. "The newspaper account says only that she killed herself in a hotel room in Geneva."

"What of it?"

"How? How did she die?" he asked.

Kirakis frowned. "She hanged herself."

FIVE

Though Alexander would have liked to believe that the worst was over, that his father had said all he intended to say on the subject of Marianne's suicide before his unceremonious departure from Alexander's office that afternoon, he knew that in all likelihood it was just the beginning. His father was not normally given to discussing private matters, particularly those of such a scandalous nature, in public places. Unfortunately, the incident in Alexander's office proved to be the exception to that rule; his father's rage had been such that he had not been able to control his anger. Now that they were alone, Alexander was filled with an uncomfortable certainty that the worst was yet to come.

"I can no longer tolerate such blatantly irresponsible conduct on your part, Alexander." Constantine Kirakis stood across the room, his back turned to his son as if he could not stand to look at him. "In the past I have overlooked a great deal, or, to be more precise, tried to overlook it. When I could not overlook it I paid handsomely to keep it out of the headlines. At first I told myself that it was to be expected. You were young and such sexual experimentation was normal. I told your mother it was nothing to be alarmed about, that it would pass in time. I assured her that it was only a matter of time before you would take a wife and settle down." Kirakis turned to look at his son. "But this latest development is inexcusable, Alexander. It makes me doubt your suitability as my successor. It makes me doubt your ability to assume that responsibility."

Alexander, seated at his desk, looked up at his father warily. "What are you saying?" he asked cautiously.

"Have I not made myself clear? I have doubts about you as a suitable successor to the board of directors. I find myself questioning your ability to one day take my place," Kirakis answered honestly.

Alexander rose to his feet. He stared at his father, thunderstruck. "This is unfair, Father," he protested. "You hold me responsible for the actions of a woman who was clearly quite disturbed, a woman who died by her own hand!"

"After you rejected her!" Kirakis turned to his son in anger. "You took advantage—unfair advantage—of an impressionable, troubled young woman. You used her. You seduced her and used her for your own pleasure—and then you destroyed her!"

"I had no way of knowing!" Alexander shouted defensively. "We were together only for that one week in Gstaad! I didn't realize—"

Kirakis raised a hand to silence him. His face was dark with anger. When he spoke again, his voice was low, but it was filled with a deadly seriousness. "I think you should be aware that I am giving serious consideration to changing my will."

Alexander looked up, stunned by his father's words. "Changing your will? You can't be serious! Over this?"

"I am serious, Alexander," Kirakis said gravely. "If I cannot be certain that you are able to control your private life, I cannot have confidence in you as my successor. I will not allow the corporation to be ruined, but I am sure you are well aware of my feelings on that subject."

"But who—" Alexander began, visibly upset.

"Who will inherit the controlling stock in the corporation?" Kirakis shook his head. "I have no idea—yet. I have not had the opportunity to consider my options. I am afraid that you, my son, have placed me at a grave disadvantage. This is one problem I never expected to face. There was never any doubt in my mind, until now, that is, that you would one day succeed me.''

Alexander's face was ashen. "I cannot believe you would really do this," he said slowly, gripping the edge of the desk until his knuckles went white.

"Believe it, because I most certainly would," Kirakis said quietly. "It is not something I want to do. But if you leave me no other choice, it is what I must do. If you do not exhibit a more responsible attitude in the future, I will have no choice but to place the controlling stock of the corporation in the hands of someone who can run it as it must be run if it is to endure." He turned back to the window again. "Consider this your final warning, Alexander. You are a Kirakis. The last of the line, my sole heir—for the moment. Start living up to your responsibilities before it is too late." He turned abruptly and left the room.

Alexander remained in the study long after his father had gone, thinking about the ultimatum Kirakis had delivered. Knowing his father as he did, Alexander did not doubt for a moment that he would do exactly what he had threatened to do. Constantine Kirakis did not make idle threats. No one knew that better than Alexander. Even if his father did not want to refuse Alexander control of the corporation, he would still do just that if he felt it were absolutely necessary.

Alexander took a deep breath and reached for a stack of reports lying on the desk in front of him. After a few minutes that seemed like an eternity, he gave up trying to review them, unable to concentrate. He tossed the papers aside and massaged his temples in an attempt to release the tension. It felt like a vise that was closing in on his skull. He got to his feet slowly and moved around the desk. The strong smell of his father's Egyptian cigarettes still filled the air.

He stood at the windows, staring into the darkness without really seeing anything. He could not help wondering if things would ever be the same between himself and his father again. By taking her own life, by specifically naming him in her note, Marianne had succeeded in driving a wedge between Alexander and his father that might prove irrevocable. It was ironic, Alexander thought now, that so many women had passed through his life, each of them vowing to "get even" with him, and Marianne, who had probably never given a thought to revenge when she killed herself, had managed to strike a blow from which he might never recover. Her death had threatened the one thing in the world that mattered most to Alexander: his birthright. The Kirakis Corporation was his one consuming passion, his tempestuous, demanding mistress, arousing powerful emotions from some wellspring deep within his soul as no mortal woman had ever been able to do. For Alexander, the possibility of losing that was more frightening than the prospect of death itself.

Somehow he had to find a way to prevent it from ever happening.

Los Angeles.

"It would make a fantastic documentary," Meredith told Chuck Willard, the station manager at KXLA. "People have been fascinated by this story for years, probably because Tom Ryan's always refused to talk about it. No one's ever been able to learn the truth—until now, that is."

"What makes you think you can get Ryan to talk when no other reporter's been able to get through to him?" Willard asked skeptically.

"I don't *think* I can, Chuck—I *know* I can," Meredith responded confidently.

"I've heard that before." He wasn't convinced. "You know, Meredith, I was just starting out in this business when all that took place. I remember how much I wanted to be the one to get to Ryan, to get the whole story from him the minute he stepped off the plane—me and every other reporter in this town, that is. He wouldn't talk to anybody then, and as far as I know, he never has."

"He'll talk to me. In fact, he already has."

He looked at her for a moment. "You've already talked to him?" There was disbelief in his voice. "How is it that you've been able to talk to him when no one else can get him to even return a phone call?"

Meredith smiled. "None of those other reporters is living with Nick Holliday, Chuck," she said simply.

"Oh, I get it," he said, nodding slowly. "You can get to

him when no one else can because of his close relationship with Holliday. I should have guessed.''

''Now, wait a minute,'' she said quickly, her body tensing visibly at the implication that Nick had engineered her interviews with Ryan. ''I want to make one thing very clear: Nick's against the whole idea. He wouldn't have any part of it. I couldn't have gotten him to talk Ryan into this if I'd wanted him to. He introduced me to Ryan—that's *all*.''

''But of course Ryan's going to look upon you more favorably because of your relationship with his protégé,'' Willard concluded.

''Maybe, maybe not. But the way I see it, if that gives me an edge, why not use it?'' Meredith asked. ''I wouldn't be the first reporter to pull a few strings to get a story, I'm sure.''

Willard shook his head. ''No, you wouldn't,'' he conceded. ''Tell me—just what did you say to him to convince him to talk to you?''

''It wasn't so much what I said as what I was able to show him.'' Meredith told him about the clippings she'd left with Tom Ryan. ''I knew he wasn't going to change his mind about it overnight. I figured he wouldn't even look at the clippings for a day or two. He'd need time to muster his courage—it's been a long time since he's read anything about himself or his family in the press—but once he'd had a chance to think about it, I was sure he'd come around.''

''That was all it took? A little pep talk and some old newspaper clippings?'' Willard asked in amazement.

''Hardly,'' she said with a wry smile. ''I've had to practically move heaven and earth to win his trust, to convince him that I don't intend to exploit him or his ordeal.'' She explained the conditions of her agreement with Ryan.

''And you think he meant it?'' Willard asked.

Meredith was confident. ''I don't think he would have bothered to call me at all if he didn't intend to at least give me a chance,'' she replied. ''That would be pointless, don't you think?''

Willard nodded. ''I guess you're right.''

''I think it's worth the gamble,'' Meredith said then.

"The way I see it, I've got nothing to lose and everything to gain by sticking it out. If I win him over, this could turn out to be the biggest thing that's happened to me since I've been at KXLA. If not, I'm back where I started, but at least I'll know I've given it my best shot."

He was thoughtful for a moment. "Sure, but what if I make a firm commitment to this project and Ryan decides to back out? We've got no program, and my ass is in a sling!"

"Not necessarily."

He looked at her. "How do you figure?"

"Suppose I were to pursue the story just like I'd handle any other story for the station," she proposed. "If it doesn't pan out, we just scrap the project and forget about it. But if I *do* get him to talk, you agree to give me a time slot and we air it as a special. This could be a real ratings winner—not just locally, but possibly nationally as well. We could sell the network on it, you know."

"We could at that," he said slowly.

"I'll keep after Ryan and drag the story out of him any way I can," she promised. "If I don't come through, you lose nothing."

He paused. "Okay. You have yourself a deal—with those few strings attached, of course," he finally agreed. "Go ahead and give it your best shot."

Meredith extended her hand. "Deal."

Tom Ryan poured himself another drink. Realizing the bottle was empty, he dropped it into the wastebasket next to his desk. He went over to the bar for another, but the two bottles he found there were also empty. He checked the liquor cabinet, but the shelves were bare. Where had it all gone? he wondered. The liquor store had just made their regular delivery last week. That damned housekeeper again; she'd probably done away with it. It wouldn't be the first time. She was forever preaching to him about drinking too much. He knew she was just trying to be helpful, trying to look out for him, but it didn't stop him from feeling annoyed with her.

He looked up at the painting hanging over the fireplace. Even now, after more than twenty-five years, the sight of that painting made him feel as though his heart were being ripped from his body. Even now he found himself unable to accept the reality that they had been lost to him forever. How could it have happened to them? he asked himself again. How? They had been so supremely happy. They'd had everything they could ever want: a happy marriage, a beautiful child, totally compatible careers, incredible successes and triumphs. Their future could not have looked brighter. Then, in one hellish night, it had all been abruptly, cruelly taken away. David was gone, Liz was gone, and Tom Ryan wished he were dead.

He stared at the painting for a long time, recalling the day it was completed. David, a typical, active four-year-old, had been impatient and restless during the long hours of sittings with the artist—until that last day. He'd been a perfect angel, in Liz's words. He had posed patiently and without complaint, and the artist had captured the true spirit of the child in his mother's arms. Liz had laughed, insisting that this had to be a good omen. Her laugh . . . God, he wished he could hear it now! That beautiful, magical laugh that could weave its spell on anyone coming within its range. Tom Ryan recalled now how happy his wife had been that morning. She'd just learned that she'd won the role half the actresses in Hollywood were ready to kill for, the role she'd been certain would get her an Oscar nomination. At the time of her retirement in 1948, she had told reporters that she was not going to miss acting because, while she was unquestionably a star, no one in the business took her seriously as an actress. She was tired of being billed as a sex goddess. But that picture, she felt certain, would change all that. It was destined to become a classic. It would prove her to be an actress of the first magnitude.

She'd been so optimistic about the role. Even the morning they left for Europe, she'd told the press at large that it was the best thing to happen to her professionally. Tom Ryan buried his face in his hands as he recalled her words to that group of reporters at the airport. Her early prophecy about the picture had come true: it had become a classic, it had proven her to be a brilliant actress, the actress he had always known she could become, and it had earned her an Oscar.

But the price for ultimate stardom had proven to be too high, even for Elizabeth. It had cost them all the things in the world that mattered to both of them: their child, their love, their wonderful life together. If only they could have foreseen what was going to happen. If only they'd had some kind of warning.

He looked up at the portrait again and blinked back his tears. On the mantel, just to the right of the painting, stood her Oscar. Looking at it now, he was filled with a rage so strong, he could barely keep himself from hurling the damned thing through the picture window. Why had he ever agreed to talk to Meredith Courtney at all? he asked himself. Her probing had stirred up all those painful memories he'd spent the past twenty-six years trying to bury.

He thought about it for a moment, then reached for the telephone on the desk and dialed the familiar number of the Swissair reservations office in Los Angeles, the number he'd dialed so many times over the years that he no longer needed to look it up. "I'd like to make a reservation . . . yes. On your first available flight to Lausanne. Tonight? That would be perfect, yes . . ."

"We're going to celebrate tonight," Meredith told Nick when he phoned her at the station that afternoon. "I just talked to Chuck Willard this morning and he's given me a green light on the Ryan documentary."

"That's great, babe," Nick told her. "But you're not the only one with good news today. It looks like we've both got something to celebrate."

"Oh?" she asked. Nick liked to make a big production of everything, she thought with amusement. "Don't keep me in suspense, Holliday. What's your good news?"

"I got the word this morning: *Reflections* has been nominated for Best Picture by the Academy. And yours truly has been nominated for the Best Director award," he announced. Meredith could almost feel his excitement coming through the phone at her.

"That's wonderful!" she declared. "But level with me —didn't you really expect to get the nomination?"

"I wasn't sure," he admitted. "I thought the picture was

good enough, of course, but everybody knows that the nominations are more a matter of Hollywood politics than film quality. I mean, look at some of the past winners.''

"Maybe, but you really deserve to win," Meredith insisted, "and I'm not just speaking as a biased critic who happens to be in love with the director. *Reflections* is a great picture.''

"Let's hope the Academy agrees with you," Nick said lightly. "Where do you want to go to celebrate?"

"Oh, I don't know. How do you feel about a certain little Italian place up in Glendale?''

"Angelino's?" Nick laughed. "God, how long has it been since we've been there?''

"Too long, if you ask me," Meredith said. "What do you say, Nick—is it a date?''

"I wouldn't miss it for anything," he told her. "You know, I had no idea you were so sentimental.''

Meredith paused for a moment. "I was just thinking . . . how would you feel about asking Tom Ryan to join us?" she asked. "It seems to me that neither of us would have anything to celebrate tonight if it weren't for him.''

"If you really want to," Nick said slowly, without much enthusiasm.

"You don't sound too thrilled about the idea.''

"I just had a more private kind of celebration in mind.''

Meredith laughed. "Don't worry, we'll have our private celebration after we get home. You have my word on that," she assured him. "What do you say? Shall I call Tom and see if he's free?''

Nick paused for a moment. "Sure—why not?" he agreed finally. "As long as you remember, when we get home . . .''

"You're impossible, Holliday," she teased. "But I guess I'm stuck with you. I'll call Tom before I leave here this afternoon.''

"Why don't you try him right now?" Nick suggested. "I've got to run anyway. We've been having problems on the set all day. I didn't even get a break for lunch.''

"Poor baby," she said lightly.

The receiver clicked in her ear. She waited for a moment,

then dialed Tom Ryan's number. It rang several times before he finally came on the line. "Tom, it's Meredith Courtney."

"Hello, Meredith," he responded in an odd voice. "I'm afraid you've caught me at a bad time. I was just on my way out the door—"

"I'll only keep you a minute," she promised. "Nick and I are going out to celebrate tonight. He just found out that *Reflections* has been nominated for an Academy Award, and I have a green light on my documentary idea. We'd really like you to join us."

"I'm afraid I can't." There was a tension in Ryan's voice that Meredith found puzzling. "I'm going out of town for a few days."

"I'm sorry. I mean I'm sorry you aren't free to join us. But—"

"Tell you what," he said then. "Why don't I give you a call when I get back? If all goes well on this trip, we'll have a long talk—and I'll tell you everything you want to know."

"Sure, Tom," she said breathlessly, hardly able to believe what she was hearing. Was he serious? Was he really going to tell her exactly what had happened to his wife and son? "I won't keep you. See you when you get back."

There was a pause. "Yeah. I'll call you." The receiver went dead.

Meredith sat staring at it for a long time. She pressed the receiver to her lips thoughtfully. Where could he be going? she wondered. And why did the fate of her documentary hinge on the outcome of this trip?

Who could he be going to see?

"At the risk of sounding cliché, I'm willing to pay a penny for your thoughts, pretty lady," Nick said in a teasing voice, holding up a coin. He smiled at Meredith, and his blue eyes seemed to dance. "You've been sitting there for the past few minutes with your fork in your hand and a faraway look in your eyes, and you haven't touched your plate."

Meredith smiled too. Her face, her thick, blond hair now falling loosely about her shoulders, even the rose-colored silk of her dress seemed to take on a golden glow in the candlelight. "I was just thinking about the last time we were here," she said slowly, her eyes drifting around the crowded restaurant. "Do you remember?"

He let out a groan of mock anguish as his eyes rolled upward. "How could I forget?" he asked. "I was trying so hard to impress you that night. I did everything but balance a ball on my nose!"

Meredith gave a little laugh. "And I was trying just as hard not to be impressed." She paused, looking down at her plate. "You know, it's nothing short of a miracle that we ever got together."

He reached across the table and took her hand in his. "I'm not sure exactly how it happened, but I'm glad it did," he said in a low voice.

She looked up at him, and her pale blue eyes were shining in the flickering light of the candle. She reached out and placed her free hand over his. "So am I," she said softly.

"I know you wanted Tom to join us tonight," he said, "but I'm just as glad he wasn't available. I really wanted to be alone with you."

Meredith smiled, glancing around the room. "I'd hardly say we're alone."

"You know what I mean."

She nodded. The tiny diamonds adorning her earlobes shimmered with the movement, catching the light brilliantly. "I know exactly what you mean." She reached for her glass. "What about a toast? We did come here for a celebration."

He nodded and released her other hand, picking up his own glass. "You're absolutely right." He raised his glass in a toast. "To us—to my getting the Oscar nomination and to your success with the documentary. May our winning streak go on forever."

Meredith touched her glass to his. "At least," she added. She sipped the wine. "You know, it hasn't been all that long since the last time we were here, but they've made a lot of changes."

Nick looked around the room and scratched his beard thoughtfully. "They've expanded," he said slowly. "The dance floor wasn't here. The place was so small we could barely walk around the tables. Dancing would have been out of the question, not that it ever bothered me."

"You don't like to dance?" Meredith asked, realizing

now that they'd never been dancing in all the months they'd been together.

He grinned. "You wouldn't want to dance with me, babe," he told her. "I'm notorious for my two left feet."

"You always underrate yourself," she said accusingly. "Sometimes I wonder if you do it just to get me to protest."

"Hardly," he said as his eyes met hers. "But I won't say I don't enjoy it when you tell me how wonderful I am."

She laughed. "You don't need me to tell you. Just keep reading *Variety*."

"It means more to me coming from you."

The band members took their places up on the bandstand and began to play. Meredith looked at Nick. "Well, are you going to ask me to dance or not?" she wanted to know.

He grinned. "You do enjoy living dangerously, don't you." Then he stood up and held out his hands to her. "Your wish is my command, princess," he said gallantly.

Meredith stood up. They held hands for a moment, then he led her onto the dance floor and took her in his arms. She put her hands on his shoulders and relaxed against him as they began to move with the music. She smiled up at him. "Two left feet, indeed!" she exclaimed softly. "You dance much better than you claim."

He grinned. "Wait and see."

She put her head on his shoulder as they danced. How long had it been? she asked herself. How long since they'd gone out like this, just the two of them? How long since they'd been able to enjoy their time together, without intrusion?

"We should do this more often," she whispered.

"Go dancing?" he asked.

"Do anything—as long as we do it together," she said.

"Sounds good to me." Nick looked down at her, and he was moved by the reflection of love he saw in her eyes. As he guided her around the crowded dance floor, their bodies pressed together in movement with the slow, sensuous music, he felt the stirrings of a desire he was not sure he could control. Meredith, feeling it too, was overcome by a feeling so powerful it threatened to engulf her. Both of them were becoming more and more aroused by the moment. Finally, unable to stand it any longer, Nick bent his head and kissed her behind the ear. "Let's get out of here," he whispered. "Let's go home."

She looked up and smiled knowingly. "The celebration's over already?"

"No," he said in a low, husky voice. "It's just beginning."

Waiting for Chuck Willard in his office, Meredith asked herself how many times she had been in this office in the past two years without ever really taking notice of the surroundings. Usually, whenever she went there, it was in the midst of a crisis, but today she could appreciate the totally modern decor he had chosen, sleek and contemporary from the chrome and glass tables to the plain, uncluttered desk and credenza, from the simple gray leather chairs to the potted palms arranged near the gigantic windows. When the drapes were not drawn, he was able to observe the chaos of the newsroom through the glass wall that separated him from his staff. Nobody gets away with anything around here, Meredith thought wryly. She glanced at her watch. Nine-thirty. Where was he? she wondered. It wasn't like him to be late. Not Willard. When he'd phoned her at home the previous evening to tell her he wanted to see her in his office first thing in the morning, he had made it sound so important that Meredith had made it a point to arrive early. She smoothed her skirt over her knees. The gray suit she wore was one of her favorites, similar in style to those designed by Dior in the late 1940s. The jacket tapered at the waist, the shoulders were only slightly exaggerated, and the lapels were black velvet, set off by a small diamond pin Nick had bought for her while he was on location in Rome. Meredith liked the suit for its look of sophistication and its subtle elegance.

At that moment, Chuck Willard barged through the door like a bull on the rampage, briefcase in hand and a look of frustration on his face. "Sorry I'm late," he growled as he closed the door. "It's been one hell of a morning. Been waiting long?"

"A while," Meredith replied honestly.

Willard took off his overcoat and hung it up. He seated himself at his desk and buzzed his secretary on the intercom. "Hold all my calls until further notice, Sally," he instructed. Then he turned back to Meredith. "I originally arranged this meeting to ask you if you'd be interested in taking over as co-anchor while Dana's in the hospital," he announced without preamble. Dana Welles was the present anchorwoman on KXLA's evening news broadcasts. She had entered the hospital last week for a breast biopsy, and was now recovering from a double mastectomy. For the past week, her spot had been taken over by Roy McAllister, a veteran anchorman from Seattle who had recently joined the KXLA staff. Why was Chuck looking for a replacement for Roy? Meredith wondered.

"As I was leaving this morning, I got a call from Dana. She's still in the hospital, but she thought she should let me know as soon as possible that she's resigning. She and her husband talked it over—this cancer scare really shook them up—and they decided she would not be coming back after she's released from the hospital," Willard explained. "I'd like you to replace her—permanently—if you're interested."

"Of course I'm interested," Meredith said carefully. "But what about Roy? I thought he was doing an excellent job."

"He was—is." Willard shook his head. "Unfortunately, the viewers aren't warming up to him. They like the idea of a woman on the anchor team. I happen to think you're the best woman for the job."

Meredith thought about it for a moment. "How soon do you want me to take over?" she asked.

"Today. Right now."

Lausanne, Switzerland.

From the outside, the Clinique de Lausanne did not look like a hospital at all, let alone the finest psychiatric institution in all of Europe. At first glance, it might have been mistaken for a deluxe hotel. It was situated on acres of perfectly manicured lawn, all the grounds surrounded by a high wall. At the only entrance heavy, wrought-iron gates opened to a long, tree-lined drive that led up to the main building, an enormous seventeenth-century château. Inside, the rooms were elegant suites, affording each patient total

privacy. Security at the clinic was tight, since its patients
most often included luminaries from the worlds of international society, politics, entertainment, and the arts, or, even
more frequently, the spouses or children of those celebrities.
The medical staff included leading psychiatrists and psycho-
analysts from all over the Continent. The clinic offered its
patients and their families the very best that money could
buy.

The staff of the Clinique de Lausanne, from the nurses
and orderlies down to the maintenance personnel, prided
themselves on their dedication to confidentiality as much as
on the first-rate care they provided. Though staff members
had been approached on occasion by reporters and photographers trying to gain access to a given patient, they always
refused, no matter how much money they were offered. They
were not impressed by the promise of wealth any more than
they were by the familiar—and often famous—faces of their
patients, having been as accustomed to these realities as they
were to the many sad faces of mental illness.

"I wish I could offer you hope, monsieur, but to do so
now would be cruel on my part," said Dr. Henri Goudron,
chief of staff of the clinic. "You see, in a case such as this
one, the trauma has been more than the mind is able to deal
with. When it cannot cope, it retreats—a defense mecha-
nism of sorts."

Tom Ryan frowned. "You're telling me there's no hope
—not now, not ever?" he asked.

"I am telling you nothing I have not told you many times
before," Dr. Goudron said quietly. "Twenty-six years,
monsieur—it is a very long time. The longer she separates
herself from reality . . ." He shrugged helplessly.

Tom Ryan lit a cigarette. "What you're saying is that
there's no chance she'll ever come out of this."

"Ah, monsieur, there is always a chance," Goudron said
quickly. "But in madame's case it is a slim one, a very slim
one indeed. Virtually nonexistent. It is so remote that"—he
gestured emphatically—"I cannot be optimistic."

"I see," Ryan said softly.

"As I have told you before, I think it is a waste of your
time and money to continue to visit her every month as you

have been doing over the years. She does not recognize you. She does not know that you are even here.''

"But *I* know I'm here," Ryan replied.

Dr. Goudron drew in a deep breath. "I see. Well, then, if it somehow gives you peace of mind to see her, then I suppose it must be a matter between you and your conscience, monsieur,'' he said slowly. "But for madame's part, it will do her no good.''

"May I see her now?" Ryan asked impatiently.

Dr. Goudron nodded. "Of course." Both men rose from their seats and left the psychiatrist's office. They walked in silence along the deserted corridors of the clinic and climbed the wide, ornately carved staircase to the second floor. The doctor opened the door to her suite and motioned to Tom Ryan to enter. As Ryan went into the room he saw her, seated in a large velvet chair near the windows, her beautiful face bathed in the warm glow of the afternoon sunlight. It seemed so incredible; she had changed very little in the past twenty-six years. She was still as beautiful as she had been years ago, before this happened to her, before their lives had been turned into a living hell. Her face seemed untouched by time. Her luxuriant dark hair was still as shining and well tended as she had always kept it. It was as if in this room, time had stood still. He knelt down beside the chair and took her hand. As always, she just stared ahead blankly, not blinking, not even acknowledging his presence. He took a deep breath, then said softly, "Hello, Liz."

The flight from Lausanne to New York City took thirteen hours. Halfway across the Atlantic the 747 encountered turbulence, but the pilot came on the PA system immediately and announced that this was a minor problem, nothing to be alarmed about. Tom Ryan had not been worried about it at all. Nothing would have made him happier just then than to see the plane plunge into the ocean or explode in midair, ending his life as quickly as possible. I've been dead for more than a quarter of a century, he thought dismally. They just haven't buried me yet.

The flight attendant offered him a pillow, but he waved her off. He was not tired, nor was he hungry or even thirsty. He only wanted to be left alone with his thoughts, with the painful memories that always surfaced in full force after he visited Elizabeth. Memories of the night their child had been taken from them. Memories of the night he'd told Liz there was no longer any hope, that David was dead. Memories of the way she had fallen apart, first screaming hysterically, then collapsing in his arms in a deathlike silence that would entomb her for the rest of her life. He blinked back a tear. God, it *was* going to be for the rest of her life! Goudron had as much as admitted it. The doctor's words still echoed through his mind: slim hope . . . virtually nonexistent . . . so remote I cannot be optimistic . . . twenty-six years is a very long time. . . . Tom Ryan closed his eyes tightly. He was torn between his need to share his agony with someone —anyone—and his long-standing commitment to protect Elizabeth from the outside world for the rest of his days. Though he had thought about ending his own life more than once, he knew it was out of the question as long as Liz was still alive. He had to be here for her. Who would look after her, make sure she was properly cared for, if he were gone? Who could he trust with that most sacred duty? He thought of Meredith Courtney, of the conversation he'd had with her the day he left for Lausanne. He'd promised to tell her everything. He wanted to tell her. Ryan not only liked Meredith, he trusted her. He felt confident that she would not try to exploit Liz and her illness as others had over the years. Still, what would happen to Liz if he were to let the truth come out? Even now, after so many years had passed, Elizabeth Weldon-Ryan was still news, especially in Hollywood. Would he still be able to protect her, keep the wolves away from her?

He remembered the morning he had left her at the clinic, that beautiful, late-summer morning in September 1953, when he had forced himself to say good-bye. Returning to the States without her had been almost as hard as telling her their son was dead. But Tom Ryan told himself over and over that he'd had no choice, that it was the only way he could protect her from the media onslaught that would have awaited her had he taken her home. He'd chosen to place her in an institution in Switzerland because he'd known that to take her to a hospital anywhere in the States would sooner or later be revealed by one of the more insensitive members of the press, and her life as it was would become a sideshow. At the Clinique de Lausanne she would be safe. No one would bother her there. Dr. Goudron had offered his personal assurance that she would have complete privacy for as long as she was a patient there and that, in the end, had decided him. Liz had been through enough, he told himself. If he could do nothing else for her, he could certainly make sure that she was comfortable and well cared for for the rest of her life.

When the plane landed at Kennedy Airport, he discovered there would be an hour's delay before his flight to Los Angeles could take off. He went into the airport lounge and ordered a martini. By the time his connecting flight was called, he had had four drinks and was about to order another. He had deliberated the issue until he could no longer think straight.

But he still had not made up his mind as to what he was going to tell Meredith.

Los Angeles.

Meredith cursed under her breath as she negotiated the sharp curves and turns along the treacherous Pacific Coast Highway in her blue MG convertible. She hated having to use Route 1 at all, but until someone came up with a better way to reach Malibu Colony, she knew she was stuck with it. It had been a long, grueling day and Meredith was exhausted. She reached over and switched on the car radio, fiddling with the dial in search of an album station. The sound of the music and the salty smell of the ocean several hundred feet below were relaxing, a welcome change from the hectic pace she'd maintained all week. She slipped on a pair of dark glasses to block out the glare of the late-afternoon sun. She decided to make it an early night, a light dinner and bed by nine. She had nothing urgent to work on tonight, and Nick was up in Carmel on location and wouldn't be back until Friday.

It was funny, she thought as she got off the highway and headed down into the Colony. A year ago, if anyone had told her she'd be in this position, she would have laughed. She'd long ago resolved never to become dependent upon another person, either financially or emotionally. To do so, she reasoned, would mean allowing that person a degree of control over her life—and she'd always been dead set against allowing that to happen. Until she met Nick. Nick had changed everything for Meredith. He'd made her reconsider her plans for the future, both professional and personal. Falling in love with him made her realize that her career, important as it was to her, was no longer enough. Ambitious as she was, she'd discovered that her work alone was not enough to keep her satisfied. She wanted Nick, wanted the life they had found together.

Her thoughts returned abruptly to the present as she brought the car to a stop in front of the beach house. Noticing the ominous-looking clouds coming from the east, she decided to put the top up on the car. The forecast called for rain, and it looked as though they would definitely get it that night. She let herself into the house and descended the stairs to the sunken, oval-shaped living room. She put her briefcase on the blue upholstered couch and took off her trench coat, then walked to the panels of floor-to-ceiling windows overlooking the ocean. The spectacular view was interrupted at the center of the room by the massive stone fireplace that was surrounded by tall, shaggy, but carefully tended plants. The plants had been her idea. Since she'd redecorated, the place did not look as strictly masculine as it had when she first moved in, but with its oak-paneled walls, beamed ceilings, and stone accents throughout, it still had a definite rustic look about it.

Meredith checked the answering machine for messages. Whenever Nick was out of town, he called every day and left messages on the tape. She switched on the machine and listened as she dropped her bag on the couch and kicked off her shoes. A smile came to her lips as Nick's latest message came on. He was still coming home on Friday—no delays so far. He loved her, he missed her, and he couldn't wait to get home to her.

The next message was from Kay. She knew Meredith was alone this week and called to find out if she wanted to join her for dinner tonight. Why hadn't Kay asked her at the station? Meredith shook her head. How like Kay to think of these things on the spur of the moment. She'd have to call Kay back and tell her she appreciated the offer, but she was tired and planned to get to bed early for a change.

Then another familiar voice came on: Tom Ryan's. "Meredith, I just wanted to let you know I'm back in town. I've given a great deal of thought to what we've been discussing and I've decided I'm going to trust you. Don't try to call me. I'll be out most of the afternoon. I'll come to your place around eight." Meredith's heart skipped a beat. That message could mean only one thing: he was finally going to open up to her. He was going to tell her everything. So much for calling it a night, she thought as she switched the machine off. She no longer cared. She'd be willing to stay up all night for this.

She looked at her watch. Six-thirty. She'd have enough time to shower and change before he arrived. She'd have the housekeeper make something light; maybe she'd ask Tom to stay for dinner. She called Kay, then went into the kitchen to talk to Pilar about dinner. As she hurried upstairs to shower, she suddenly realized she wasn't tired anymore. She felt like singing. She couldn't wait to see the look on Chuck Willard's face when she delivered her exclusive. She was about to solve a mystery that had baffled movie fans for over a quarter century.

This one was going to open doors for her professionally.

At a small tavern in Santa Monica, Tom Ryan sat alone at the bar, nursing a lukewarm Scotch. He had no idea how long he'd been there. What difference did it make? he asked himself. He sipped the drink and made a wry face. God, it was awful! He signaled the bartender. "Bring me a fresh Scotch, Smit," he called out. "This stuff tastes like gasoline!"

"Don't you think you've had enough, friend?" the young man behind the bar asked, eyeing him carefully.

"I'll tell *you* when I've had enough," Ryan said crossly. "Now, how about that drink?"

Smitty shook his head. "Sure thing," he said as he reached for a clean glass. It was always the same old routine:

he came into the bar two or three times a week, drank himself into a stupor, then allowed Smitty to send him home in a cab. But tonight, somehow, he seemed different. He was in a strange mood. Smitty was curious but knew better than to ask him about it.

Tom Ryan twisted on the stool and looked toward the window. He wondered when it had started to rain. It had been cloudy when he'd arrived at the Los Angeles International Airport that morning. He hated rainy nights. They made him think of the nights before Liz. . . . He closed his eyes tightly. He thought about what he was going to do, and he hoped it was the right thing.

"Looks like it's gonna be a real downpour this time," Smitty commented as he put the glass of Scotch down on the bar in front of Ryan. "You live far from here?"

"Up in the hills," Ryan answered absently. "I'm not going straight home tonight, though. I've got important business to take care of first, something I should have done a long time ago."

"Sure," Smitty said with a nod. Every time the tall blond man came in, he rambled on and on about the wife and child he'd lost years ago. He never made much sense, but Smitty always figured the wife had walked and taken the kid with her. "You want me to call you a cab now?" he asked.

Ryan shook his head. "Not tonight," he said blankly.

"It's no trouble—"

Ryan turned to look at him. "Like I said, I've got business to take care of tonight." He picked up the glass and downed its contents in one long swallow. "Got to do it alone."

The bartender shrugged and went on about his business. He tried to look out for innocent motorists as well as his regular patrons, but it wasn't always possible.

Tom Ryan glanced at his watch. Six forty-five. He'd have to get going if he intended to make it up to Malibu by eight. He thought about calling Meredith, just to make sure she was home, but changed his mind. He had to just go on up there and face her before he lost his nerve. He took a gold money clip from his pocket and removed a fifty-dollar bill, tossing it down on the bar in front of Smitty. "Keep the change, chum," he said as he got to his feet and started for the door.

Smitty picked it up and looked at Ryan in disbelief. "This is a fifty, friend," he said finally.

Ryan nodded. "Keep it," he said with a tired smile. "Sometimes, Smit—sometimes I think you're the only friend I've got."

Smitty just stared at him, not sure what to say.

"I'll see you next week—unless we end up having to build an ark," Ryan said as he opened the door. "Damn, it's raining hard!"

"You sure you won't change your mind about that cab?" Smitty gave it one last try.

"Not tonight."

"Okay," Smitty surrendered reluctantly. "Thanks for the tip, friend."

"You earned it, Smit." Ryan closed the door as he left the tavern. Smitty stepped out from behind the bar and went to the window. He watched Tom Ryan get into the Rolls-Royce, and once again he wondered why a guy like that spent most of his time in a dive like this, drinking himself half blind. He didn't know the man's name, but he knew he must have money. He spent it as if he had loads to burn. He drove a car that probably set him back a small fortune.

Once in the car, Ryan fished through his pockets for his keys. He selected the right one, put it in the ignition, and the engine came to life. He listened to its low hum for a moment, then glanced over at the large manila envelope lying next to him on the seat, the clippings Meredith had given him the first time Nick brought her to the house. He was going to return them to her tonight. He could no longer stand to have them around. He couldn't bear to look at them one more time. It disgusted him, the way they'd all tried to capitalize on his pain. Tonight, he promised himself, he would put an end to the rumors and speculation once and for all.

The Pacific Coast Highway, with its treacherous twists and turns, was considered dangerous for a competent driver on a good day, but on a dark, rainy night when visibility was near zero, for a man who had been drinking heavily and found it difficult to keep his thoughts on the task at hand, it was suicide. Behind the wheel of the Rolls-Royce, Ryan strained to see the road, but his mind was thousands of miles away. He was thinking of Elizabeth as he clumsily negotiated the sharp curves. When he left her at the clinic, it was because he knew she would be safe there; she would be protected from the outside world. But what would happen to her now? How would she be affected by his decision to reveal his story—their story—to Meredith? Would the shallow semblance of a life she now had in Switzerland be destroyed by what he was about to do? He had to believe it would not. He had to believe he was doing the right thing, because after years of secrecy, he felt the need to relieve himself of his burden. He needed to tell his story, needed to put an end to the lies and the rumors once and for all.

Preoccupied with his troubled thoughts, he did not see the semi approaching from the opposite direction. The big truck swung wide as it took the turn, and its headlights were blinding. Ryan released the wheel as he tried to cover his eyes. The car swerved crazily as it smashed through the guardrail sideways, hurtling downward, into the ocean. It all happened so quickly that there had been no time to think, to react. There had only been that single, blinding flash of light, followed by the sounds of glass breaking and metal smashing, then a loud, deafening roar.

And finally, the darkness of oblivion.

Meredith stood at the windows, watching the rain as it beat against the glass, wondering what could have happened to Tom Ryan. His message said he'd come by around eight, she thought as she checked the time again. It was now ten-thirty. Where could he be? she asked herself. Had he changed his mind—again? She'd lost track of how many times he'd agreed to see her, then abruptly canceled or been conveniently absent when she arrived at his home in Bel-Air. She wished she knew what he could have been thinking, what was going through his mind. What was he hiding? And what did it have to do with the deaths of his wife and child?

She went to the telephone and dialed his number. After the fifth ring, his housekeeper came on the line. "This is Meredith Courtney," she said. "Is Mr. Ryan in?"

"No," the housekeeper answered in a heavy Spanish accent. "Mr. Ryan, he left here early this afternoon, and I have not seen him since. He tell me he was coming to see you.''

''He was supposed to be here two and a half hours ago,'' Meredith told her. ''Was he going anywhere else?''

''No, not as far as I know. Perhaps he went—'' The woman stopped short.

''Where?'' Meredith asked. ''You were going to say something. What? Where do you think he went?''

''Nowhere,'' the housekeeper insisted nervously. ''It is not my place to say. Mr. Ryan—he would be furious with me if I say anything at all.''

''Something could have happened to him,'' Meredith reminded her. ''It could be important.''

''No,'' the woman insisted. ''If he does not come home, if you do not hear from him soon, perhaps then—but I cannot say right now. Really—I must not.''

Meredith took a deep breath. ''Okay. I understand,'' she said finally. ''If he comes in, will you please ask him to give me a call, no matter what time it is?''

''*Si*, I will do that.'' The receiver clicked in Meredith's ear. She lowered it slowly, placing it back on its cradle. It did not take much of a guess to know what the housekeeper was thinking. She thought Ryan was in some bar, drinking his brains out.

Meredith went back to the window. She wished he would call and at least let her know whether or not he was coming. He could be so damned exasperating sometimes. If this documentary were not so important to her career, if she did not care so much about doing this story, about following it through to its conclusion, she'd forget the whole thing and tell him what she thought of these games he seemed to be playing. One minute he was willing to open up to her, to tell her anything she wanted to know, and the next he was avoiding her as if she were an IRS agent. Why?

The telephone rang. Startled, she snatched up the receiver. ''Hello?'' she responded with anxiety in her voice.

''Meredith?'' It was Kay. ''I wasn't sure I'd find you at home.''

''Where would I go?'' Meredith asked irritably. ''I told you earlier, I'm expecting Tom Ryan—''

"Then you don't know!"

"Know what, for chrissake?" A faint sense of unease brushed Meredith.

"It's been on the radio, on TV . . ."

"I haven't had the television on all evening," Meredith said as she found her way to a nearby chair. "What's happened?"

"Tom Ryan—he had an accident out on Route One. I guess he was on his way to see you. The road was slick from the rain. Some guy in a semi swung wide and cut him off. He went through the guardrail. He's dead, Meredith."

Meredith sat staring at the receiver as if it were some strange object she had never seen before. Tom Ryan . . . dead? She couldn't believe it.

"Meredith?" Kay was calling her name. "Are you all right?"

Meredith finally found her voice as she put the receiver to her ear again. "I will be," she said slowly. "I'll talk to you in the morning, okay?" She replaced the receiver slowly and turned back to the windows. Staring blankly into the darkness, into the pouring rain, she suddenly felt cold inside. This is just a bad dream, she told herself. A horrible nightmare. Any minute now, Tom's going to be knocking at the door, ready to tell me everything. But the rational part of her knew that was not going to happen. Ryan was dead. He was never going to be able to tell her what really happened to Elizabeth after David's fatal accident. She would never be able to do the documentary now.

She blinked back tears. She had truly liked Tom Ryan, liked him as much as he would allow her to like him. Others saw him as cold, aloof, often abrasive, but in the time she'd spent with him, she had found him to be a deeply tormented man carrying a terrible burden deep within his soul.

"Why?" she whispered. "Why?"

SIX

〰〰〰〰〰〰〰〰〰〰

It rained the morning Tom Ryan was buried. Under a gray, gloomy sky, a large group of mourners gathered at Forest Lawn to pay their last respects to their friend and colleague. Those familiar faces clustered around the open grave, sheltered beneath their somber black umbrellas, looked like a congregation of Hollywood royalty—big-name stars, well-known producers and directors, leading columnists, studio executives—many of whom had known Ryan since his earliest days in the business. They'd known Elizabeth as well, Meredith thought now. She stood at Nick's side, dressed in a simple black suit with a wide-brimmed black hat, eyes cast downward as the service began. It struck her as odd that Ryan owned plots here—and probably had for several years, according to Nick—but Elizabeth and David were not buried here. Why? she wondered. What possible reason could he have had for not burying them in the same place he knew he would eventually be put to rest?

Stop it! she scolded herself. Stop trying to unravel those loose threads! It's all pointless now. Tom's dead, and so is your documentary. But even now, as she looked down at the flower-strewn coffin, she found herself thinking of her last conversation with him, wondering once again what could have been so urgent that he'd had to leave town suddenly just before his death, and what could have taken place during that time to make him decide to tell her everything.

She turned to look at Nick. She could see the pain in his eyes. He was taking this much harder than she had expected him to. He and Ryan had been close, but even so, she had not anticipated his reaction to the news that his friend and mentor was dead. She'd expected him to be upset, yes, but he had been totally devastated. It was like losing his father all over again, he had told her. She hesitated for a moment, then reached out and took his hand. He glanced sideways at her, and his smile was sad. She gave his hand a reassuring squeeze.

The coroner's report indicated that there had been a high level of alcohol in Ryan's blood at the time of his death. This did not surprise Meredith. Though Nick, who probably knew him better than anyone else, refused to discuss it, Meredith had always suspected that Ryan had been fighting a losing battle with the bottle for many years now. The driver of the semi had told police at the scene of the accident that Ryan appeared to have lost control of his car on the slippery pavement and that he himself had barely escaped a head-on collision with the Rolls-Royce. First he had lost control of himself, then his car, Meredith thought dismally. Though everyone was carefully avoiding the word "drunk," she suspected he was probably in a pretty bad way at the time of the accident. He'd know that what he was about to do would take courage, courage he simply did not have. He'd probably been drinking to get up his nerve . . . or to kill the pain.

As the service came to an end, the crowd began to break up. Meredith stood silently at Nick's side as he spoke briefly with two of his colleagues. She glanced over at the coffin again. Soon it would be lowered into the ground. Soon Tom Ryan's body would be buried, and his fiercely guarded secret would be buried with him. After twenty-six years, his torment had finally come to an end. *I hope you've finally found the peace that's eluded you for so long,* she thought sadly.

She and Nick walked arm in arm back to their car, neither of them speaking. She had the feeling that Nick was not ready to talk about it, to tell her how he felt. She decided to leave him alone with his grief for a while. As he unlocked the door on the passenger side and opened it for her, she paused to look up at the dark clouds filling the sky. The rain had almost stopped. The dreary weather had made the already depressing scene at the funeral worse, but now it looked as if it were passing over.

"I'm glad this day's finally over," Nick said as he came into their bedroom. Unbuttoning his shirt, he took it off and threw it across the back of a chair. He walked over to the windows and opened them, inhaling the cool evening air. "You know," he said softly, "I still can't quite believe it. I can't believe he's really dead."

Meredith, wearing only a sheer, emerald-green silk teddy, sat cross-legged in the middle of the bed, brushing her long blond hair. She stopped what she was doing and studied him for a moment. The emotional pain he felt was evident in his eyes, in the dark circles beneath them, in the lines in his face that made him look ten years older. "I know," she said quietly. "I feel the same way."

Meredith put down her brush. "Nick, I've been thinking. Maybe we should both consider taking a couple of days off. We could stay here, or we could get away somewhere, just the two of us. I think we both need it."

He hesitated at first. "I don't know. I keep thinking if I work, if I keep busy, I won't think about it as much." He sank down onto the edge of the bed and slumped over in exhaustion.

Meredith knelt behind him, massaging his neck and shoulders. "Don't you think I could take your mind off it?" she asked, trying to keep her voice light.

He twisted around to look at her. "If anyone could do it, it would be you," he said with a weary smile as he planted a kiss on her cheek.

"Well, then—are you willing?"

"What do you have in mind?"

"Something restful," she said, kneading the taut muscles in his shoulders and upper back. "Maybe we could just stay here. Go to bed early and sleep late. Breakfast in bed and long walks on the beach. We've had so little time alone together in the past few weeks. This is exactly what we both need right now—time alone to talk, to share things the way we did when I first moved in.''

He paused thoughtfully. ''We haven't had a hell of a lot of time together, have we,'' he said, as if realizing it for the first time. ''If I'm not off on location, you're dashing across the state on assignment. We only seem to see each other in passing these days.''

Meredith managed a slight smile. ''It *has* made the little time we've had together more exciting,'' she conceded, ''but if I had a choice, I'd like more time with you.''

''Me, too.'' He stood up, unzipped his pants, and pulled them off. ''We should start thinking about taking a vacation —a real vacation. Just you and me, as far from Los Angeles as we can get.'' He turned to look at her again. ''You've always wanted to go back to Paris. Maybe we could go there for a couple of weeks.''

Meredith smiled. ''I'm going to hold you to that, you know,'' she said as she moved to one side of the bed and switched off the lamp.

Nick got into bed and Meredith snuggled against him in the darkness. She felt his arms around her, holding her close. She desperately needed that closeness now. Tom Ryan's death had left her shaken, much more so than she was willing to admit. It had made her stop and think about things she'd never considered before. She and Nick had been so sure of each other, of their relationship, that they had begun to take each other for granted. They'd been so busy, so wrapped up in their individual careers, that lately there had been precious little time to nurture the romance in their relationship. Later . . . it was always later. Neither of them had stopped to think that there might not be a later. They had never considered the possibility that an accident, a serious illness, even a drastic career conflict could bring their life together to a screeching halt. They'd never thought about what might happen if one of them were to leave one day and never come back.

Meredith looked up at him for a moment, lightly tracing the planes of his face with her fingertips. He lay silent, unmoving, gazing upward at the ceiling. She touched his lips with her index finger. She knew what he was thinking about. "Want to talk about it?" she asked.

Nick frowned, still staring ahead blankly. "What's the point?" he asked dismally.

"It might help to get it off your chest."

"I doubt it."

She studied him for a moment. "Don't shut me out, Nick," she said softly. "I know I wasn't as close to Tom as you were, but I cared about him too. I understand how you feel. I know what you're going through. I want to be here for you—if you'll let me."

He stroked her hair. "I'm sorry, babe," he said, turning over to look at her. "It's not that I'm trying to shut you out. I'm just not quite sure how to put what I'm feeling into words."

"Why don't you just say what you feel?" she suggested.

He sighed deeply. "When I first met Tom, when I first got to know him, he told me I was almost the same age his own son would be if he were alive today. He said he'd always had high hopes for David, hopes he'd end up in the business one day. I guess that's why we were so close: I filled the void left by his son's death, and he took the place of my father," he said quietly.

Meredith looked at him. "You miss him, don't you—your own father, I mean. You almost never talk about him."

He nodded. "Yeah," he said finally. "I guess I never really stopped missing him."

"What was he like?"

Nick hesitated. "He was a good man who worked too hard and was almost never home," he recalled. "When he was there, he was always tired, but he was a good father. He always had time for me, no matter how tired he was."

"It bothered you, didn't it—him being gone so much," she said.

"Yeah, it did." Nick frowned. "I understood why, but it didn't make it hurt any less. I needed him. A kid needs two parents who are *there*—absentee parents are like not having any. When we have kids, we're going to both have to make some major changes in our life-style, you know."

Meredith was surprised by this last remark. It was the first time he'd ever even hinted at the possibility of making a real commitment to her, to their relationship. She said nothing, but rested her head on his shoulder and held him as tightly as she could.

At this moment, she could not imagine a future for herself that did not include him.

A cameraman and technician waited outside the KXLA building in Mobile Production Unit 9, one of fifteen such vehicles deployed by the station's news department. Meredith, who had gone back to the assignment desk for directions, emerged from the building and raced across the parking lot. "Hey, Meredith, where are we going?" asked the technician, seated behind the wheel, as she climbed into the back of the van and closed the door.

"A fire in North Hollywood—an old warehouse full of movie props and costumes." Meredith claimed a swivel-mounted chair sandwiched between the driver's seat and all the high-tech equipment—videotape editing machines, videocassette recorders and players, mixers, monitors, tape recorders, power packs, lights, and a microwave transmitter that would enable them to transmit live if necessary—packed into the back of the vehicle. "Wouldn't you know I'd end up drawing a fire the one day I wear a dress?"

The cameraman grinned. "Them's the breaks," he teased. "Frankly, I'm surprised to see you out on the streets at all. I thought once you'd been moved up to the anchor desk, we'd seen the last of you here."

Meredith laughed. "Heaven help me if I ever decide to give up live reporting altogether," she declared. "I don't think I'd ever want to be chained to an anchor desk and do nothing else. How would I ever be able to keep up with what's going on out here?" She hung on to her seat as the technician maneuvered through the unusually heavy traffic on the Santa Monica Freeway as if he were doing time trials for the Indianapolis 500.

"Hey, Bernie—watch it, will you?" the cameraman snapped irritably. "I'm not ready to let my wife cash in my life insurance yet—*if* you don't mind!"

"Do you want to get there before they put out the fire—or after?" Bernie shot back at him.

"Listen, you two." Meredith was straining to hear a transmission coming in over the van's CB radio. The competition was also sending someone over to cover the fire. She wasn't surprised, considering that the warehouse contained a lot of priceless memorabilia from some of Hollywood's greatest classics. "For the record, guys, *I* would like to get there in one piece *before* they get the fire out. Settle your differences on the way back, okay?"

Bernie laughed. "Don't mind us, Meredith," he said as he headed down the exit ramp. "It's just our brand of gallows humor."

"Yeah," the cameraman chimed in. "Sometimes we get sent out to cover some pretty grim events—like that accident up on Route One."

Meredith, who had been rummaging through her large shoulder bag, looked up. "Tom Ryan's accident?" she asked.

"Yeah—we went up with Julie Morgan to get a tape when they recovered his body from the water," the cameraman recalled. "He was a friend of yours, wasn't he?"

"In a way," Meredith answered. "I wanted to be there myself, but . . ." Her voice trailed off.

"Be glad you weren't," he told her. "It got pretty messy. They practically had to cut him out of the car."

"Mission accomplished," Bernie announced as he braked the van to a stop behind one of the fire engines. Meredith leaned forward, craning her neck to get a better look at the flames shooting upward from the top of the building. She opened the door and climbed out of the van. The sky was filled with black smoke. She took a thick steno pad and a felt-tipped pen from her bag and lit out ahead of her crew, picking her way through the maze of fire trucks and spectators. Her mind was already on the story behind the tragedy: the human cost, if any; the possibility of having to evacuate adjacent buildings; the potential loss of jobs resulting from the fire. Past experience told her that the basic information—how the fire started, when and where—would be easy to obtain. She would question the fire department officials, detectives from Bomb and Arson, eyewitnesses. No problem there.

Her two crewmen, linked by a heavy cable and encum-

bered by all their equipment, struggled to keep up with
Meredith as she dodged puddles and drifts of smoldering
debris and stepped over uncoiled hoses in her dogged pursuit
of eyewitnesses and bewildered warehouse employees. She
sought out those willing to be interviewed on camera, people
who could provide her with the information she needed to
reveal the human element, the human interest story behind
the incident—the angle that had become her professional
trademark.

Spotting the opened doors of the warehouse's loading
dock, Meredith quickly decided that this would make a
perfect visual. She positioned herself in front of the smoking
maw to tape her tease, that one-line condensation to be aired
at the start of the evening broadcast, a summary of the story
to follow. From the moment she stepped out of the van, the
story she was covering had been the only thing on her mind.
Everything else was forgotten. Now, as she stood before the
cameras, her professional instincts took over once again.
Microphone in hand, she looked directly into the camera and
spoke in a clear, strong voice: "A million-dollar fire destroys
three decades of Hollywood history and leaves ten jobless.
I'm Meredith Courtney, and I'll have a report."

Her crew called away on another assignment, Meredith was
met by a station courier who drove her back to the KXLA
building. She spent the afternoon viewing the exposed tape,
approximately a half hour's worth of footage, with Dan
Bellamy, a skilled videotape editor who would assist her in
winnowing it down to the polished three minutes for the five
o'clock broadcast. Meredith liked Bellamy and enjoyed
working with him. He was totally professional and easy to
work with. Since they generally saw eye to eye on how the
tapes should be edited, she was usually quite satisfied with
the results.

"No doubt about it," Bellamy commented as they viewed
the videotape. "The camera loves you."

Meredith smiled but did not respond. Her eyes were on the
monitor, watching the tape intently. She was constantly
viewing her own material, looking for mistakes, for ways to
improve her performance. She was only too aware that a

great deal of her early success had come from what Chuck Willard referred to as her "screen presence." He felt that the secret of her overwhelming popularity was directly related to her appearance. How many times had he told her how photogenic she was? He felt the high cheekbones, the pale blue eyes making direct contact with the camera, and the thick blond hair were a turn-on, particularly to the male viewers. Meredith told herself she was fortunate to photograph well, but she was determined not to rely solely on her physical assets. She was a serious journalist, not a fashion model, and she wanted to be taken seriously in her profession not only by her viewers but by her colleagues as well. She wanted to be known as a hard-hitting reporter, not just a pretty face. She still remembered the resentment she'd encountered from the other women on the KXLA news team when Willard decided to make her co-anchor. Most of the others had been with the station longer and had more experience. Behind her back they made snide remarks about how Chuck Willard had promoted her because of her looks. Meredith had ignored them all, determined to prove them wrong.

Chuck Willard appeared in the doorway. "Meredith, I need to talk to you as soon as you're finished here. It's important," he told her. "I'll be in my office."

She nodded. "Give me another twenty minutes, okay? We're almost through here." She tucked a pencil behind her ear.

Willard signaled his approval. "You know where to find me."

Meredith turned her attention back to the monitor as Willard went on his way. She wondered idly why he wanted to see her. If he intended to let her know the documentary was officially being scrapped, he needn't have bothered. She had known it from the moment Kay broke the news of Tom Ryan's death to her. Without Ryan, there was no definite conclusion to the story, and without a conclusion, there was no documentary.

When she and Dan Bellamy were finished, she excused herself and headed down to Chuck Willard's office. He was on the phone when she entered, and motioned to her to sit down. She took a chair across the desk from him and waited for him to end the call. He grinned at her as he put the receiver back on its cradle. "Well, as the saying goes, I've got both good news and bad news for you."

"Skip the bad news, Chuck," she said wearily. "I already know—the documentary's off." She leaned on one arm of the chair.

He looked at her for a moment, then nodded. "Yeah, it is. But that's not why I wanted to talk to you," he said. "The good news I have for you is going to more than make up for the disappointment I know you're feeling over that."

"Great. I can use some good news right now," she admitted, resting her chin on her hand.

He leaned back in his chair. "A few months ago I got a memo from New York," he began. "The network brass was interested in seeing some tapes of local talent. I figured they were looking for possible replacements for some of the people on the network news team. I sent them tapes of some of your interviews."

"And?" Meredith knew there had to be more.

"They liked what they saw. As I've told you many times before, you have screen presence. The cameras adore you, Meredith. You photograph like an angel and you have a good, strong voice. But the network people saw something else: honesty." He paused. "The people in New York feel that nothing has more impact on an anchor's popularity with the viewers than perceived honesty—the way they come across on the screen. They gave you *very* high marks in that category." He was smiling like a proud father.

"Have they made an offer?" she wanted to know. He was driving her crazy, telling her what they had to say but still withholding the bottom line.

"You might call it that," Willard said, pulling himself upright in his chair. "Carla Granelli, their anchorwoman on the network evening news program, is leaving for Europe next week to tape a series of interviews with political leaders there. They need someone to fill in at the anchor desk while she's away. They want you—if you're interested."

"Of course I'm interested!" She did not bother to restrain her enthusiasm.

"Then you're accepting the offer?"

"Did you doubt it for a minute?" she asked incredulously. "How soon will I have to leave for New York?"

"Well, they want you by Friday, though you don't go on the air until next Monday. You'll need time to prepare for it—it's a world apart from doing local news—and of course you'll be meeting with network executives and news department people."

"Why don't I plan to leave immediately after Thursday's broadcast?" she suggested. "That should allow me plenty of time for everything I'll have to do."

"That's fine with me," he said. "I'll give them a call this afternoon to let them know."

"Let me take care of that, too," she said quickly.

He shrugged. "If you want."

She stood up and walked to the door. "I suppose my feelings should be hurt," she said in a teasing voice. "It would appear you're trying to get rid of me." She winked and closed the door as she walked out.

Meredith was elated. Driving home that evening, the whole world seemed to be colored by her euphoria. Even the heavy traffic did not bother her. The billboards, the advertising signs, and the telephone poles along that winding nine-mile stretch of highway between Los Angeles and Malibu, which she normally considered a blight on the otherwise picturesque landscape, seemed almost beautiful somehow. She started humming to herself. She tried to imagine the next three weeks, and eagerly looked forward to doing the network news. This was something she'd dreamed about ever since she made the decision to pursue a career in broadcast journalism. In the beginning, it was a goal that seemed as far away as Mars, but Meredith had worked hard, and her dedication and determination had finally paid off. True, it was only a temporary position, but she was confident that this was just the beginning for her, the first of many exciting challenging things to come.

She couldn't wait to share her news with Nick. She would have liked to celebrate with him over a romantic candlelight dinner, but it wasn't possible. Nick was away on location again, this time in San Francisco. He was due back late that night, but she would probably be asleep by the time he got

home. She'd have to tell him over breakfast tomorrow
morning. Maybe she'd tell Pilar to make something special.
They could eat out on the sundeck, and she would tell him
her fabulous news then.

As she approached the sharp curve where Tom Ryan's
fatal accident had taken place, she noticed workmen from
the California Highway Department installing a new, stronger guardrail. She wondered if it would have saved Ryan's life
had they installed it sooner. It was too late for speculation
now, she told herself.

She brought the car to a stop at the Malibu Canyon traffic
light. No point in brooding over it now, she decided. She
was disappointed that she would never be able to do that
documentary, but her career certainly wasn't suffering for it.
This offer from the network was the perfect opportunity for
her to show them what she could do. If she played her cards
right, if she made all the right moves at the right times, she
felt reasonably certain that she could turn this temporary
anchor position into something permanent.

She had every intention of giving it her best shot.

When she woke the next morning, Meredith was surprised to
find herself alone in bed. She sat up and pushed her hair
away from her face, wondering if there had been a last-
minute delay, if Nick was still in San Francisco. Then she
saw his luggage next to the open closet door. His jeans and
shirt were draped across the back of a chair. Meredith smiled
to herself, drawing her legs up and hugging them to her
chest. Nick was up early as usual. Why did that surprise her?
He was probably out running on the beach. He liked to run
every morning, no matter where he was or what the weather
conditions happened to be. He claimed it was the best way
he'd found of blowing off steam. When he was in the middle
of doing a picture, particularly when he encountered difficulties, he was tense, and running provided him with a means
of both physical and emotional release.

Meredith got out of bed and went over to the windows
overlooking the beach. No sign of him. She dressed and ran
a comb through her hair. She was glad Chuck Willard had
suggested she take the day off. The next few days were going
to be hectic as she prepared for her trip to New York, and

this would give her a chance to spend an entire day with Nick, hopefully uninterrupted by the outside world, before she left. It was, she told herself, long overdue. She knew Nick would not be going to the studio today. When he called last night, he'd left a message on the answering machine to let her know he was wrapping up the picture, right on schedule, and planned to "do nothing" for at least a couple of days. Today was going to be perfect, Meredith promised herself. They would make every second count.

She went downstairs and found Nick seated at the red-wood table on the sundeck. He looked up and grinned as she pushed open the sliding glass doors and came out onto the sundeck. "Good morning, sleepyhead," he greeted her, extending his arms.

"Good morning yourself," she said as she bent down to kiss him. "You're up bright and early. Why didn't you wake me?"

"Didn't see any reason to. I found your note, saying you were taking the day off, so I figured I'd let you sleep as long as you wanted." He put down the copy of *Variety* he'd been reading. "You'll need the rest. Tonight we're going to celebrate."

She looked at him, surprised. How did he know? Of course—he'd called the station after she left last night and someone had told him. Probably Kay. "Who's the snitch?" she asked.

He gave her a puzzled look. "Snitch?"

"You don't have to protect anybody. I know you talked to somebody at the station," she said, taking a seat across the table from him. "I'm not mad—I just wish they had let me tell you myself."

"I don't have the faintest idea what you're talking about, Meredith."

"Come on, Nick—"

"I'm serious. I don't know anything about what's going on at the station. I haven't talked to anybody there since the last time Kay Wilson came up here for dinner," he insisted.

"Then you really don't know?"

"Know *what*, for crying out loud?"

"I'm going to be in New York for the next three weeks—co-anchoring the network news." She saw the strange look on his face. "Carla Granelli's going to be in Europe on special assignment. They needed a replacement, and Chuck Willard said I was their first choice. He sent them some of my tapes a while ago, and apparently they were impressed. That's why I took the day off. I wanted to spend some time alone with you before I leave."

"When do you leave?" he asked carefully.

"Thursday, right after the evening broadcast," she answered. "Chuck tells me they were very enthusiastic about my work. This could just be the beginning. If they like my performance in New York, it could lead to a permanent position with the network. Isn't that wonderful?"

"That's great. That's just great," he said in an irritated tone, looking away from her, gazing distractedly out at the ocean.

She looked at his face now as if seeing it for the first time. He looked like an impaled animal. "What's wrong, Nick?" she asked. "I thought you'd be happy for me."

"Oh, sure—I'm thrilled! Can't you tell?" he demanded sarcastically. "Why shouldn't I be happy? You're running off to New York for three weeks—"

"I'm not just running off, as you put it," Meredith said as she reached for the coffee. "This is a part of my job—a very important part."

"A part that could take you to New York for good," he concluded.

She stared at him for a moment. "This shouldn't surprise you, Nick," she said quietly. "You've known, right from the beginning, how important my work is to me. You've known all along that I never wanted to be a local newscaster for the rest of my life."

"Right. What I didn't know is that you seem to care a hell of a lot more about advancing your career than you do about me, about us," he snapped. "I never realized—until now —that you'd leave me in a minute if the network made you a better offer." He raised his hand abruptly, then scratched the back of his head in a gesture of frustration.

"That's not true, I—" she started, surprised by his response.

"Isn't it?" His blue eyes were cold. "Are you going to sit there and tell me that if you went to New York and they offered you a permanent spot on the network news staff, you'd turn it down?''

"No—of course not," Meredith answered truthfully.

"I didn't think so," Nick said, frowning. "You never were able to get away with a lie. You're too transparent. You wear your emotions like a neon sign." His stare was like ice.

"Then how can you doubt my feelings for you?" she asked.

"How can I *not*—when your career always seems to take priority over us?" he demanded.

"That's not fair, Nick," she said quickly. "I've never stood in the way of anything you've had to do in order to further your career. I've never complained when you've gone off on location for weeks at a time. I've always accepted it because I know how important it is to you and I understand it. Why can't you show me the same consideration?" She was both hurt and annoyed.

He shook his head. "Can't you see what's happening to us?" he asked. "We're already drifting off in opposite directions. When I'm not on location, you're doing triple time to follow up on some story. We have so little time together now, what do you think it's going to be like when you go to New York?"

"This is pointless, Nick," Meredith said wearily. "I'm only going to be in New York for three weeks. They haven't offered me anything permanent. Maybe they will, maybe they won't—it's too soon to tell."

"Come on," he said coldly. "We both know you're good enough to be on the network team, and unless they're all blind, they're going to see it too."

Meredith looked at him. "What if they do make me an offer?" she asked. "We've been faced with long separations before. We can deal with it, if and when it happens—if we're both willing to try."

"Sure we can." There was sarcasm in his voice. "At first we'll have maybe two weekends every month together. Once in a while I'll fly to New York for a day or two, or you'll come back to the Coast to cover a story. You and I might get together for a night—two if we're lucky—unless I'm off on location. In the beginning we'll make the best of every minute we can grab, but after a while we'll both be so busy that we'll get tired of trying. You'll make a new life for yourself in New York, maybe even get involved with someone else. Maybe we both will.''

''You certainly don't have much faith in the strength of our love,'' she said quietly, looking down at the table.

''I don't seem to be able to compete with your career,'' he said crossly. ''Whenever it comes down to a choice, your work always comes first with you. I'm just getting tired of playing second fiddle.''

''So what you're saying is that I have to choose. It's either you or my career?'' she asked carefully. Now she was angry.

''The way things stand now, I'd say there's no way to avoid it.''

''I see.'' Meredith was trying to control herself. ''It doesn't matter at all to you how hard I've worked for this chance, does it? Well, I couldn't—wouldn't—turn it down now! I've never stood in the way of things you've had to do that took you away from me for long periods of time. I've never asked you not to do things I knew you had to do.'' She paused, afraid she might explode. ''I've never interfered with your career, and I don't think you should try to stand in the way of mine.''

He looked at her coldly. ''Then you still plan to go to New York?''

''Of course I do,'' she said, growing angrier by the minute. ''An opportunity like this doesn't come along every day. I'm sorry you don't understand that.''

''I'm sorry too.'' He threw down his napkin and got to his feet abruptly, spilling his coffee on the yellow linen tablecloth. His eyes were blazing with anger. He disappeared into the house, slamming the glass door so hard that it cracked. Meredith stared after him, still astonished by his reaction to her news.

Please, Nick, she thought sadly. Don't force me to make a choice.

Meredith walked alone on the beach at sunset, lost in thought. Nick had walked out on her that morning and had not yet returned. She'd never seen him so angry before. In the five months they'd been living together, they'd had their share of disagreements—even arguments—but never anything like this. Never had she been faced with the possibility of having to choose between her love for him and her dedication to her career. She understood how he felt; why couldn't he understand *her* position? If she gave in to his wishes, if she turned down the network's offer, she would be passing up a rare opportunity. If she went to New York, she ran the risk of losing Nick for good. He was so outraged by her decision to go ahead with her plans that she had the feeling she would return to L.A. to find she and Nick no longer had a relationship. Why don't you understand? Why can't you be as supportive of my ambitions as I've tried to be of yours? she thought resentfully.

The confrontation between them that morning made Meredith stop and think about their chances of having a future together. Now, as she walked along the beach in the darkness, she realized something she'd never even thought about before: as much as she loved Nick, as much as she wanted to hold on to what they had together, she knew in her heart that if he ever forced her to choose, she would choose her career without hesitation.

It was late when Meredith finally returned to the beach house. She turned out the lights in the den and the living room, then double-checked the front door to make sure it was locked. Nick had his key if he did decide to come home during the night, she thought as she climbed the stairs. That didn't seem likely, though. She wondered if he intended to return at all before she left, or if he would stay away until he was sure she was gone.

She went into the bedroom and switched on the lamp beside the bed, then turned down the sheets and undressed. There was no point in waiting up for him, she thought as she went into the bathroom to run her bath. Besides, she was bone-tired and had a long, busy day ahead of her tomorrow. It's not fair, she thought, piling her hair up on top of her head and securing it with several large clips. Nick's poor attitude had put a damper on her high spirits. She was determined not to let it get to her. She stepped into the tub and sank down into the cloud of fragrant bubbles. The warm water, scented with jasmine bath oil, felt silky against her skin. Relaxing. She needed to relax, to unwind, to forget, if only for a little while, the choice Nick was forcing her to make.

She thought she heard sounds coming from the bedroom but decided it was probably her imagination. She lay there for a while, then decided she'd better get to bed before she fell asleep in the tub. She stood up and stepped out of the water. Reaching for a large bath sheet hanging nearby, she dried herself carefully, then wrapped the towel around herself and went into the bedroom. Nick was stretched out on the bed, arms folded behind his head, staring ahead blankly as if he did not see her. "I was beginning to think you weren't coming back," she said as she crossed the room.

"Would it really have mattered to you if I hadn't?" he asked in an acid tone.

Meredith looked at him. "Of course it would," she replied, removing the towel. She slipped into a sheer silk nightgown, then sat down on the bed. He turned over on his side, his back to her. "I think you're being unreasonable, Nick," she said quietly. "This isn't going to solve anything."

He turned back to face her again. "You think I'm being unreasonable because I love you, because I don't want to lose you?"

She looked at him, puzzled. "What makes you think you're losing me?" she asked.

"Come on, Meredith," he said coldly. "Do you think I'm blind? Do you think I haven't seen it coming?"

"I don't know what you're talking about," she said tightly.

"I knew from day one how ambitious you were," he said. "I just kept hoping what we'd found together had come to mean more to you than your career."

"What about you?" she asked. "Does it mean more to you than yours?"

He stared at her for a moment. "I don't know how you can even ask."

"Does it?" she asked again.

"Of course it does!" Even in the darkness, she could see the tension in his face.

"Then explain something to me, because I'm really confused. Why is it that you think I should automatically know you care more about me than you do about your work—yet you feel I don't care because I've accepted an offer to work out of New York for three weeks? You've spent more time away than that . . . God, you've spent as much as a month away on location!'' she reminded him.

"If it were just the three weeks, I wouldn't give it a second thought,'' he said, pulling himself up and resting on his elbows. "But we both know this is just the beginning, don't we? You've got talent and you've always had more than your share of drive. You've put a lot into your career. Those network people are going to see that right away. In no time, they're going to offer you something more permanent, and where will that leave us?''

"We'd still have each other, Nick," she said softly. "We wouldn't have much time together, that's true, but we've always managed to make the best of what time we did have.''

"Meredith, how long do you think that's going to last?" he asked. "I told you this morning—with you off in New York for weeks at a time and me going off on location so often, we'd find it harder and harder to manage even a day together. We'd end up just drifting apart without even realizing it.''

"If it were that easy to split us up, I'd say we didn't have a chance to begin with," she said evenly.

"It's happened to couples who've been together longer than we have," he said.

"But we've stayed together so far, and there have been a good many separations," Meredith pointed out.

"Not as many—or as prolonged—as they would be if you were to land a permanent spot with the network," he insisted. "I just don't see how it can work.''

"We could give it a try.''

He turned to look at her. "Why is this so important to you?" he wanted to know, his expression a mixture of irritation and concern.

Meredith drew back as if she'd been struck. "Don't you see, Nick? I want my career. I want my financial independence. I don't want to ever be dependent upon anyone but myself. I don't want to have to look to anyone—lover, husband, *anyone*—for support. I don't want to find myself in the position of having to stay with a man—you or anyone else—just because he happens to be paying the bills." She turned on him in anger. "I can't imagine myself spending my days at the beauty salon or shopping on Rodeo Drive! I could never be satisfied organizing fund raisers and smiling at charity functions until my face cracks! I happen to enjoy my work! I like the excitement, being recognized for myself and not for the man I happen to be living with! Is that so wrong?"

"If independence is so damned important to you, why did you ever move in with me to begin with?" he asked irritably.

Her face was serious. "Because I fell in love with you, because I wanted to share my life with you, *not* because of your bank balance! Don't you see, Nick? I'm here because I want to be! Would you have it any other way?"

"I don't want to lose you," he said sullenly. "That's all I care about right now."

"And I don't want to lose you, either," she said, touching his arm gently, her expression softening with the realization that he was more afraid than angry. "But you've got to realize that my career is as important to me as yours is to you, and you have to accept it, because it's not going to change."

"I don't want to lose you," he repeated tensely.

She studied him for a few seconds. "What are you afraid of, Nick?" she asked finally. "For as long as I've known you, I've had this feeling. . . . At first it seemed as if you were reluctant to care, to let me get too close to you. Then you finally did let yourself get really involved—but even then, you wouldn't make a real commitment. And now it's as if you regard my career as a threat to our relationship. Why?"

He shook his head. "That should be obvious, under the circumstances," he said crossly.

"Why, Nick?" Meredith pursued. "Anyone who's afraid of serious involvement has usually been burned. Who burned you?"

"Nobody," he snapped, annoyed. "I just figured our careers would eventually get in the way—and apparently I was right. Then, after I got to know you and fell in love with you, I started to think maybe I'd been wrong. I thought we had something special, that nothing could ever come between us—not your career, not mine, nothing," he said as he got to his feet. "Now, though, I'm not so sure—about anything."

"It doesn't have to come between us," she insisted. "We can make it work—if you can accept the demands of my career as I've come to accept yours."

"It would seem I don't have much choice," he said grimly.

"I want *you*, Nick," she told him. "I want you like I never thought I'd ever want anybody. I'd like to think we have a future together."

"Then at least we agree on one thing," he said with bitterness in his voice.

"I love you, but you can't expect me to give up everything I've worked so hard to accomplish," she said.

He looked at her. "I've never asked you to give up anything before."

"You want me to turn down the best offer I've had since I've been in this business."

"Only because I'm afraid you'll make such a good impression on those network VIPs that they'll want to keep you up there." Nick frowned. "I know that sounds incredibly selfish on my part, but I can't help how I feel. I can't stand the thought of losing you. I want you here—with me. I want us to have a good life—together."

Meredith crossed the room and put her arms around him. "I do love you, Nick, and I want us to be together too," she assured him. "But I can never, ever give up what I have as a newscaster. If you can live with that, we can work it out." She kissed him, but as he held her close, she found herself wondering if anything had been resolved at all.

Would he ever really accept her decision?

There was an uncomfortable silence between Meredith and Nick as they ate breakfast on the sundeck the next morning. Though they'd talked some more last night and agreed to make a real effort to work out their problems, Meredith knew Nick would never really be able to accept her fierce dedication to her career. She glanced at the large crack in the glass door. Until now, she'd forgotten all about it. She'd have to get someone out to replace the panel today.

Too bad she couldn't take care of the steadily widening gap between herself and Nick as easily.

"When I came home the other day a crew from the highway department was putting up a new guardrail on that curve where Tom was killed," she said, trying to make conversation.

Nick looked up from his Spanish omelet. "Yeah, I know," he said quietly.

"It's about time they replaced it."

"Yeah. Too bad it took Tom's death to get it done," Nick said darkly as he turned his attention back to his plate. A soft breeze blowing in from the ocean ruffled his hair gently.

Meredith sprinkled cinnamon in her coffee and stirred it slowly with a faraway look in her eyes. "What do you think will become of the estate now?" she asked. "There's no one left to inherit on either side, is there?"

"Not as far as I know." Nick shook his head, rubbing his beard thoughtfully. "Tom never mentioned any relatives, and knowing him, I'd be willing to bet he didn't leave a will."

"So it will probably go to the state."

"Probably," Nick agreed. "Unless somebody comes forward and can prove they're a blood relative." He scooped up the last bite and popped it into his mouth. "That's not likely, though."

Meredith sipped her coffee. "I can't help wondering what's going to become of the mansion. I suppose it'll be put up for sale."

"I would think so," Nick said with a grin. "Are you thinking of buying it, maybe?"

She smiled. "Don't think I wouldn't like to," she said, taking a forkful of hash browns. "No, I was just wondering what will happen to it, to all of his things—the painting of Elizabeth and David, her Oscar, all the old photographs and memories. Tom tried so hard to keep everything just as she left it. It was almost as though he expected her to come back to it one day."

Nick shrugged. "Everything will probably be put up for auction. Most likely collectors will get the biggest part of the stuff," he guessed.

"It seems like such a shame." Meredith paused for a

moment. "Tom was so concerned about preserving her memory. Did you ever see the rooms upstairs?"

He shook his head. "He never offered to show me around, and I never asked."

"It was unlike anything I've ever seen before. It was as if it were still 1953 in those rooms," she said, remembering the day he had shown her around. "Her dressing room was like something from the old movies on the Late Show."

Nick grinned. "Maybe you should go to the auction—if there is one—and buy everything. Just to keep the memory intact, of course."

"Don't think I haven't considered it," she said quickly, taking another bite. Her blue eyes were bright with excitement.

"Oh, come on, Meredith—I was only kidding!"

"Well, I wasn't," she told him. "Maybe we could go—you know, I'd really love to own that portrait."

"What for?" He looked at her for a moment. "Somehow I never thought of you as a collector."

"I can't explain it," she admitted. "I've just been fascinated by it since the first time I saw it. I would love to own it."

He shrugged. "Makes no difference to me, if you really want it," he told her. He got to his feet. "I think I'd better get going. I've got a meeting at the studio."

"I thought you were taking a few days off."

"I'd planned on it, but since you're going to be in New York, I think I'd rather be working, keeping busy. I'm meeting with studio execs to discuss backing for my next picture."

She caught his hand as he started to pass her. She looked up at him, her expression one of concern as she pressed his hand to her lips. "We can work it all out," she said confidently. "You'll see."

He hesitated for a moment, then bent down and kissed her. "I still don't like it, but I think I'd rather have you part of the time than not at all."

"You do understand, don't you?" She wanted reassurance.

"I'm trying." He pulled away and went into the house. Meredith frowned. Was Nick right? she wondered. Was it only a matter of time before these long separations finally caused their love to disintegrate?

New York City.

The three weeks Meredith served as a substitute anchorwoman on the network news was the most hectic period in her professional life. She found herself putting in long hours at Intercontinental Broadcasting's massive Broadcast Center complex on West Fifty-second Street, either in front of the cameras or in the office she'd been assigned for the length of her tenure there, writing or reviewing material for the evening broadcast. Her free time—what little of it there was—was spent socializing with network executives and others she felt could help her reach her goal. Though she would never have admitted it to Nick, she was positioning herself for a more permanent spot on the network team in the future. Though Nick had promised to fly east and spend the weekends with her, his own hectic schedule had made it impossible for him to do so. On top of everything else he had in the works, he had received an unexpected shock shortly after Meredith left for New York: the attorneys handling Tom Ryan's estate informed him that Ryan had left a will and had named him in it, leaving Nick the estate in Bel-Air and everything in it. "It's the damnedest thing," a confused Nick told Meredith over the phone. "Everyone in the law office was so tight-lipped about the will itself. I never saw the actual document—they wouldn't let me—but they told me Tom wanted me to have the house and its contents because I was the closest thing he had to a son still living."

For a moment, Meredith wondered if she might still have a chance to revive her documentary, but she quickly dismissed the thought. Tom Ryan had guarded his past—and his wife's—fiercely during his life. She doubted there was much chance of finding anything revealing in the house.

During her last week in New York, she accepted an invitation from Sam Clifford, the executive producer of the IBS evening news program, to join a group from the news department for dinner at the Rainbow Room. Meredith accepted without hesitation.

The Rainbow Room, sixty-five floors above Fifth Avenue,

offered a spectacular view both inside and out, and she found herself as taken with the splendid 1930s Art Deco interior as she was with the stunning view of the glittering skyscrapers of midtown Manhattan. Over a delicious entree of beef Wellington, Meredith had the feeling that she was being scrutinized and evaluated by the network people, but this knowledge did not bother her. She was confident in her ability and in the way she presented herself to them. She'd worked hard for this opportunity, had planned carefully for it, and she knew she was ready. More than ready.

"I must say, you've done a marvelous job, Meredith," Clifford told her over dessert. "You've been a—" He stopped short as Meredith became vaguely aware of someone approaching her from behind.

"Would any of you mind if I borrow Miss Courtney for a few minutes?" The voice that had interrupted their conversation was unmistakably familiar to Meredith. Everyone at the table had stopped talking. They were all looking up at Alexander Kirakis, who now stood at Meredith's side, smiling down at her. Her heart was beating wildly as she struggled to maintain her composure. She took a deep breath and looked up at him. He was still the most devastatingly handsome man she'd ever seen. Why does he affect me this way? she asked herself. "It's been a long time," she said evenly.

"Too long." He extended his hand as the band began to play. "May I have this dance?" he asked politely.

She hesitated for a moment, aware that everyone at the table was staring at her. Let them stare! she thought defiantly. "Of course," she said, smiling, as she rose to her feet gracefully. She could almost feel the eyes of everyone in the room on her as he took her hand and led her onto the dance floor. Her heart was still racing, and as he took her in his arms, she wondered if he could feel it. I hope not, she thought.

"You're full of surprises, aren't you, Mr. Kirakis?"

"Alexander," he corrected.

"Alexander."

"It has been a long time, has it not?" he asked as they began to move with the music.

"Six months, at least," she responded, keeping her voice

light. "I'm surprised that you remembered me." She'd always had the feeling that he wouldn't recognize a woman an hour after they'd met—unless he was sleeping with her.

"I never forget a beautiful woman," he assured her. "Certainly not one as lovely as yourself."

Meredith looked over his shoulder. She could see the group at her table staring at them openly, and she remembered her first meeting with Alexander in Los Angeles. "If you remember me," she began carefully, "then you must also recall the promise you made to me at La Bella Fontana."

"Promise?" he asked innocently.

"You told me that if and when we met again, you'd give me an exclusive interview."

"So I did." He held her a little closer as he whirled her across the dance floor. "It wouldn't be proper to go back on one's word now, would it?"

"Certainly not," she agreed.

"I will definitely consider it." His hand caressed her bare back imperceptibly. "Do you live in Manhattan now?"

She shook her head. "I'm on assignment. Temporarily. This is my last week here." She felt his hand lightly stroking her back, but she had no desire to stop him. Why? she asked herself.

"I see." He studied her face. "Then perhaps we should get together to discuss it before you leave. Dinner, tomorrow night?"

She thought about it for a moment, remembering she'd made other plans. She shook her head. "I'm not free tomorrow night," she told him.

"Make yourself free," he said simply.

Meredith looked up at him, and she saw something in that disarming smile, in those incredible black eyes, that she did not quite understand. "It's not that simple," she said finally.

"Of course it is."

She hesitated. Getting an interview with Alexander Kirakis, who almost never gave interviews, would impress the network people. "I'll see what I can do," she told him.

"Do that." He leaned closer, and she could feel his breath, warm against her neck. "You look lovely tonight," he whispered huskily. "Even more so than the first time I saw you."

Meredith felt his lips brush lightly against her neck, and she drew back and looked at him suspiciously. "Your dinner invitation—it has nothing to do with my request for an interview, does it."

"What do you think?" The black eyes glittered wickedly.

"I think you should tell me why you really want to see me," she insisted.

"I think that's obvious."

"You're wasting your time."

"Am I?" he asked, unconvinced.

"Yes." She tried to make her voice firm. He was still rubbing her lower back gently.

"One never knows unless one tries, yes? The first time we met, we had only a brief time together and I had to rush off to the airport with my father. I promised myself I would rectify that situation if I ever found you again. And now . . ." He let his voice trail off, but the message was clear.

She managed a slight smile. Six months ago, she might have been tempted. "You're just a little bit too late," she told him.

"Oh?" He raised an eyebrow questioningly. "Husband or lover?"

"That's none of your business."

The black eyes flickered with amusement. "Have I struck a nerve?"

"No. It's just that I don't like being questioned about my private life."

"I see." There was a taunting note in his deep, resonant voice. "But it's all right for you and your colleagues to continually pry into my private affairs?"

"That's different and you know it."

"So I'm fair game and you're not, is that it?"

"You're news," she pointed out. "The public cares about what you do, who you see."

"And I care about what you do and who you see," he countered. "I should have stayed on in L.A. last summer. I should never have let you slip away from me then."

"There was nothing to let slip away," she reminded him.

"There could have been, given the opportunity."

"We met on strictly professional terms, if you'll recall."

"Not my fault," he insisted.

"I have to maintain my professional distance."

"Why?" he asked. "Why is that so important to you?"

"Not important," she said. "Necessary."

"You *do* have someone waiting for you at home," he concluded.

She hesitated for a moment. She wanted the interview, and she did not want to antagonize him when she was this close to getting it, but she had to make it clear that their relationship could never be anything more than a professional one. "Yes," she said finally. "Someone who's very important to me—and I will not risk losing that for anything. Not even a story."

He smiled. "I admire your loyalty," he said. "But you cannot blame me for trying—or continuing to try. I'm not accustomed to not getting whatever I go after."

"Are you still willing to consider the interview?" she asked.

"I will *consider* it."

Meredith changed the subject. "You dance very well," she observed.

"I'm accustomed to leading," he said simply.

The band stopped playing. Meredith pulled away from him slowly, breaking his embrace. "About tomorrow night," she began. "If I can change my plans, where shall I meet you?"

"I'll come for you at your hotel."

Meredith shook her head emphatically. "I'll meet you at the restaurant," she insisted. "Just tell me where."

"Do you like Lutèce? At eight?"

"Eight will be fine."

He watched her walk away, smiling to himself as she rejoined her group. He'd been intrigued by her the first time they met, and was even more so now. She was unlike any woman he'd ever known. She was bright and beautiful and independent, traits he found surprisingly appealing. She touched him as no other woman ever had, and he was not sure why he felt as he did. Alexander vowed to himself right then and there that sooner or later he was going to have her, and no one or nothing was going to stop him.

The overhead Fasten Seat Belt sign clicked off abruptly. Meredith stretched her arms and legs as much as the narrow space between the rows of seats would allow. She opened her briefcase and took out the two magazines she'd bought at Kennedy, the current issues of *Vanity Fair* and *Town and Country*. On the cover of *Vanity Fair* was a teaser, a one-line mention of an interview with Italian film star Francesca Correnti. Francesca Correnti . . . Alexander's former lover. Or was she a former lover? There were rumors that their affair had endured over the past few years on an on-again, off-again basis.

Meredith flipped through the magazine until she found the article. There was a full-page black-and-white photograph of the actress at the beginning of it. She *is* beautiful, Meredith thought as she studied the photo. Voluptuous in a world where everyone else wanted to be pencil-thin. Sultry, like a jungle cat. A beautiful woman by anyone's standards. There was also a smaller photo of Francesca with Alexander, who looked almost as handsome and elegant as he was in the flesh. As attractive as he had been at dinner that night at Lutèce, when she'd spent the entire evening fending off his suggestive comments. She told herself it had been a waste of time, since they'd accomplished nothing as far as her interview was concerned. He probably feels the same way —since he went home alone, she thought wryly.

Meredith stared at the picture for a long time, oddly disturbed by the sight of Alexander with another woman. Why should it bother me? she asked herself. It's not as if there's anything between us, though God knows he tried.

So why did it bother her so much? It had never bothered her when she saw photos in the trades or tabloids of Nick with the actresses who appeared in his films. She'd always told herself she wasn't jealous because she had no reason to be. She trusted Nick; it was as simple as that. He worked with beautiful women all the time. It went with the territory and she understood it perfectly. Still. . . .

She closed the magazine and drew in a deep breath. She

wasn't emotionally or physically involved with Alexander Kirakis, yet the photo of him with Francesca Correnti made her feel extremely jealous. It was a feeling that made her acutely uncomfortable. She hated the way he'd managed to get to her. *I don't care what you do, Alexander,* she thought angrily. *I don't care about you!*

She leaned back and closed her eyes. If she had any doubts about her relationship with Nick before, Alexander had managed to further confuse her with minimal effort. In her mind, she could still see his face clearly, that devastating smile, those hypnotic black eyes. *If he knew, he'd have a good laugh over this,* she thought.

But he'd never find out. Not from her.

Malibu.

"Now, close your eyes," Nick told Meredith as they entered the beach house together. "No peeking."

She gave him a quizzical look. "What is this all about, Nick?" she asked irritably. "Why all the secrecy?"

He smiled patiently. "Humor me, okay? It's a surprise."

Meredith forced a smile. It had been enough of a surprise that he'd come to meet her at the airport, and even more of a surprise to her that she hadn't been all that happy to see him. "Oh, all right," she sighed. Closing her eyes tightly, she allowed him to lead her down the three steps into the sunken living room.

"Watch your step," Nick cautioned as he led her around the furniture to the other side of the room. "Okay, you can look now."

She did as he instructed. In front of her, positioned near the windows overlooking the ocean, was a large easel covered with a green velvet throw. Nick lifted it slowly to reveal the painting underneath, the portrait of Elizabeth Weldon-Ryan and her child. Meredith couldn't believe it. Even though Nick had inherited the Ryan estate, she knew that he wanted to keep everything intact, just as Tom had left it. "Why—" she began.

"I know how much you love it," he said simply. "And I wanted to show you how much I love you. This seemed like a good way to do that, and to say I'm sorry for the things I said before you left.''

Meredith embraced him gently. She was happy to have the painting, but she still felt troubled and unable to understand why. Why, she asked herself, wasn't she happy to be home, back with the man she loved? Why did she wish she was still in New York, fighting off Alexander's advances?

SEVEN

〰〰〰〰〰〰〰〰〰

New York City, April 1980.

"As many of you present are aware, this is not by any means the first time we have been faced with a major decision of this nature, of such great importance to the future of the corporation as a whole." Alexander stood at the head of the long conference table in the board room, addressing a group of executives from the upper echelons of the Kirakis Corporation. "Many of you were with us when I first took over as head of the North American operations in 1973 and will surely recall that, at that time, world inflation created a greatly increased demand for oil. As a direct result of this increase in demand, our Athena Maritime tankers were also in demand. At that time, a single voyage of one of our British supertankers—which as a rule commanded a price of approximately two and a half million dollars for a trip from the Persian Gulf down around the Cape—rose to an all-time high of eight million." He turned to George Prescott, who was seated to his right. "What was our net profit that year, George?"

"Twelve billion," George answered.

Alexander nodded. "Twelve billion," he repeated slowly, his dark eyes scanning the group, gauging their reactions. "I believe that was nearly double the profit of the previous year, was it not?''

George nodded.

Alexander smiled. ''Many of the other major shipping companies, having made a similar killing in the marketplace, invested the influx of capital in the expansions of their fleets,'' he recalled. ''Though our advisers—supposedly experts in their fields—recommended that we follow suit, we elected instead to put our profits into the oil itself. My 'father had a theory that this was going to be a fluke, that it could not and would not last—a theory, I remind you, that proved to be correct. The Arab oil embargo that same year brought about one of the worst economic depressions to hit the world at large since the 1930s. Those same shipping companies that had invested so heavily in expanding their fleets found themselves suffering devastating losses. For many, the reverses were brutal. Fortunately for us, our own losses were minimal, but only because my father had the foresight to invest in other markets.'' He turned away from the group momentarily, pausing to stare thoughtfully at the sweeping panorama of downtown Manhattan. ''What I propose now is a move of a similar nature, but on a much larger scale. I believe that the future of Kirakis lies in expansion, in diversity. Real estate, electronics, pharmaceuticals, communications—diversity is the key word, gentlemen. It's the key, not only to survival, but to making Kirakis the world's largest international conglomerate. I feel that—'' He stopped short as his secretary entered the room and addressed him by name. He turned to face her angrily. ''I told you I was not to be disturbed for any reason, did I not?''

She nodded. ''Yes, sir—but this cablegram just came for you. I think you'd better read it—'' she began timidly.

''Can it not wait another hour?'' he asked irritably.

She shook her head. ''It's an emergency.''

He paused for a moment, glaring at her, then motioned her to come forward. ''This had better be important,'' he snapped as he took the cable from her.

''It is,'' she said in a low voice.

As he read it, his expression changed from anger to alarm. ''When did this arrive?'' he asked in a hushed tone.

"Five minutes ago."

He took a deep breath. "Have the car brought around," he told her. "Get Woodhill on the phone. Tell him to meet me at Kennedy right away. Tell him to do whatever must be done to arrange for clearance so we will be able to take off as soon as I arrive." As she started to walk away, he stopped her again. "I will need a helicopter on standby in Athens —and arrange for courtesy of the port at Hellenikon Airport. I won't have time to waste in customs there."

"Yes, sir."

He turned to the group of executives. "My apologies," he said quietly. "You will have to excuse me. I must leave for Greece immediately." He left them staring after him as he dashed out of the conference room.

George caught up with him in his office, where he was getting into his overcoat. "Have you taken leave of your senses, Alexander?" he wanted to know. "The chairman of Donovan Associates is due here this afternoon to meet with you personally—or have you forgotten?"

"I have forgotten nothing," Alexander said sharply. "You will simply have to take care of the matter in my absence."

"I can't!" George ran his fingers through his thick blond hair. "We've been working on this deal for the past six months. Why can't you postpone this trip for one day? Twenty-four hours can't make that much difference—"

Alexander's eyes met his. "Mother is dying," he said quietly. He turned and rushed out of the office without looking back.

As the Learjet taxied down the runway and began its ascent, Alexander leaned back in his seat and closed his eyes tightly. He still found it difficult to believe that this could really be happening. His mother was dying. His father's cable said she was not expected to survive the night. It simply did not seem possible. When she came to New York for Christmas, she had looked wonderful, better than she had in months. She'd appeared to be a bit tired, but that was to be expected; she was seventy-one years old and had a history of heart trouble. She had fared surprisingly well, given her condition, outliving all her doctors' predictions. Perhaps that was the reason he and his father had allowed themselves to be lulled into a false sense of security.

She had asked for him. How many times in the past had she pleaded with him to come home, to spend more time with his family? he asked himself. How many times had he promised her he would come home, then changed his plans at the last minute? How many times had business obligations prevented him from returning home? And how many times had he put off making that trip because he'd been in the throes of passion with his latest conquest? He'd let her down so many times in the past; he could not let her down again, not this time. If he did not get there before she died, he was not sure he could live with himself.

At that moment, his pilot emerged from the cockpit, having turned the controls over to the copilot. Alexander looked up. "What time will we be landing in Athens?" he asked.

Woodhill came forward. "Our ETA is one-fifteen in the morning, Athens time," he said as he took a seat across from Alexander. "We've been extremely fortunate thus far. I had no problem at all in getting immediate clearance for takeoff at Kennedy, which frankly surprised me. The weather conditions between New York and Athens are excellent, and we don't expect any surprises before our scheduled arrival."

"I see," Alexander said distractedly.

"It should be smooth sailing all the way," Woodhill offered.

"And what about after we land?" Alexander wanted to know. "Have all the arrangements been made?"

"Everything's been taken care of," the pilot assured him. "Someone from headquarters will meet you at the airport. You'll be able to bypass all the red tape in customs with no problem. They've already got a chopper on standby to take you out to the island."

Alexander nodded. "Then there should be no delay."

"None that I can see." Woodhill got to his feet. "Is there anything else you want me to take care of?"

Alexander did not respond. He was staring through the window at the Atlantic Ocean below. To the pilot, it seemed as though his employer's mind were a thousand miles away.

"Will there be anything else, sir?" he asked again.

Alexander's head jerked around abruptly. "What? Oh—no. That will be all," he said irritably.

Woodhill nodded. "Yes, sir." He headed back toward the cockpit.

"Woodhill?"

The pilot turned. "Yes, sir?"

"I believe I forgot to say thank you," he said quietly. "I do appreciate all you've done."

Woodhill smiled. "Just doing my job, sir."

Alexander didn't respond. He wasn't even aware that Woodhill had returned to the cockpit. His thoughts were in another place, another time.

Through the window of the jet, Alexander could see the ruins of the Parthenon, illuminated by floodlights atop the Acropolis. As the jet began its descent to Hellenikon Airport, he marveled at the sight, so spectacular when viewed from the air. The plane made its approach, and once again he wondered if he would make it in time, or if he could be too late already.

When the jet landed, an airport official was waiting to escort Alexander through customs. "There are reporters—a very large number of them—waiting for you beyond the gates, Mr. Kirakis," he explained breathlessly as they hurried across the airstrip. "I will have to take you in through another entrance."

"And how did they find out about this?" Alexander asked crossly.

"I have no idea, sir," the man said quickly, almost apologetically. "Only a very small number of our personnel were made aware of your scheduled arrival time, and they were informed only because it was necessary. I was absolutely certain this could be avoided."

"It could have." There was contempt in Alexander's voice. "Apparently, someone among your chosen few cannot be trusted to maintain his silence."

As they entered the main terminal and headed down the busy concourse flanked by three uniformed security guards, the short, balding man found it difficult to keep up with Alexander's long, quick stride. He said a silent prayer that nothing else went wrong. He knew how Alexander Kirakis hated to be kept waiting—for any reason. If there were any further delays, it would make him look bad. More than anything at the moment, he wanted to get Kirakis through customs and into that waiting helicopter as quickly as possible.

Alexander was already annoyed, and he did not bother to hide his displeasure. He stood silently, impatiently, as his passport was stamped by a solicitous customs official and returned to him. Once through customs, he was met by Frederick Kazomides, a senior vice-president of the Kirakis Corporation's European division, who escorted him to the helicopter that waited on another part of the airfield. "I am sorry to hear about Madame Kirakis," Kazomides told Alexander as they hurried down the concourse. "It is most difficult to find the right words to convey—"

Alexander raised a hand to silence him. "It's all right. I understand," he said quietly. "Tell me—do you know what her condition is now?"

Kazomides shrugged helplessly. "I could not say," he admitted. "It has been several hours since I last spoke with your father. He said then that she was very bad, that it was only a matter of time." He saw the tormented look on Alexander's face. "Again, I am sorry."

Alexander nodded but said nothing. Words seemed so inadequate now.

Kazomides opened the heavy glass double doors, then stepped aside. As Alexander stepped out into the cool night air, the helicopter pilot spotted him immediately and started his engines, signaling that he was ready to take off as soon as his passenger was aboard. Alexander turned to Kazomides. "Thank you, Frederick," he said softly.

Kazomides nodded. "I hope you make it in time."

Alexander broke into a run as he crossed the airstrip, covering his face with one arm to block out the blinding glare of the floodlights and the intensity of the wind created by the whirling rotors of the helicopter. He climbed into the machine and looked back toward the exit only once at Kazomides before the chopper lifted off into the night, making a sharp turn southward as it headed for its destination.

To Alexander, the flight from Athens to the Kirakis' private island, a relatively short journey by air, seemed to take forever. He was silent and remote during the entire trip, and could not remember the last time he'd been home. Home. He'd been living in New York for almost nine years, and before that had taken up residence in Boston during the six years he had attended Harvard. He still thought of the island as home. His fondest memories were of his childhood there. Those years, Alexander reflected now, had been the most peaceful years of his life.

The island had been in his mother's family since the Balkan wars. It had been part of her dowry when she married his father. His father had taken that raw land, untouched for many, many years, and transformed it into a paradise. There were stables for the horses Alexander adored, an artificial freshwater lake, a game reserve, a harbor for their yacht, the *Dionysus,* and an airstrip where small planes and other aircraft could land. Outside the villa was a garden filled with flowers and greenery of every kind and adorned with priceless ancient statuary and a fountain especially designed for it by a celebrated Roman sculptor. The magnificent forty-room villa, staffed by twenty-five servants, had been built atop the highest hill on the island. Outside, it looked like a sprawling Spanish hacienda, but the interior looked as though it belonged at Versailles. Evidence of his mother's lifelong passion for anything French was everywhere, from the furnishings, mostly French antiques, to the Impressionist paintings, to the fabrics of the wallcoverings, upholstery, and draperies, all in delicate shades of blue, green, and mauve. The linens and tableware had come from the finest stores in Paris. The beautiful Savonnerie oval rug in the entrance hall and the enormous chandelier of rock crystal and gilded bronze in the dining room had come from some Loire château. Alexander smiled to himself. His father had said more than once that, though his mother had been born in Athens, she was a Frenchwoman at heart.

There were also twelve guest cottages on the island, but to this day Alexander did not understand why his father had them built. For as long as he could recall, no visitors had ever been permitted on the island. Security had always been extremely tight. His father had made no secret of his deep resentment of any intrusion on his most cherished privacy and had gone to extraordinary lengths to make certain that

unwanted intruders would be kept away. His efforts thus far
had been astonishingly successful. The island was the one
place on earth where Alexander could always find privacy,
the one place the paparazzi could not follow him.

Alexander had always suspected that his father's obsession
with privacy stemmed from his outrage at the media onslaught that had taken place at the time of Damian's death.
Alexander's brother Damian had died tragically at the age of
five, only five months before Alexander's own birth in 1948.
Damian had been cursed with the same cardiopulmonary
defects that had made their mother a semiinvalid for most of
her life, but Damian's condition had been worsened by
complications encountered during his delivery. Though his
parents seldom spoke of the tragedy, Alexander knew they
had never really stopped mourning the child they lost so
many years ago. He had heard the whole sad story while still
quite young, mostly from his governess, Helena, who had
come to the island after Damian's death. Helena, one of the
most resourceful women Alexander had ever known, had
managed to learn a great deal of the history of the Kirakis
family from servants who had been part of the household for
many years before her own arrival. It was Helena who had
told Alexander most of what he knew of Damian's short life
and tragic death. Alexander knew that his parents had been
told, almost from the beginning, that Damian's chances of
survival beyond the age of three were slim. He knew, too,
that Melina Kirakis had been warned repeatedly against
attempting motherhood even once, but she had, in fact,
conceived five times. Three of those pregnancies had ended
too soon for the child to survive, but she did bear two sons,
Damian in 1943, and Alexander five years later. Alexander
always suspected that his mother's fierce devotion to him had
been strengthened by the knowledge that he was going to be
the only child she was ever going to have. Alexander never
questioned his mother about Damian, realizing how painful
the memories still were for her, but he always listened with
interest when she was in one of those rare moods to talk
about the brother he'd never known.

Damian's death had been hard on Melina, but as Alexander later discovered, it had been even harder on his father.
Constantine Kirakis, who like most men longed for a son to

carry on his name and his empire, had been devastated by the loss of his firstborn son. For a time, in the months before Alexander's birth, it was said that Constantine Kirakis's world, even his life, had ceased to hold any real meaning for him. His state of mind had been deeply affected then by the insensitive reporters who, sensing a story in the man's personal loss, converged on the estate at Varkiza on the Greek mainland. Fearing the stress of repeated intrusions would be too much for his wife, then four months pregnant, Kirakis had taken her to the island and taken extra security measures to make it impossible for the press to follow them there. He'd ordered round-the-clock patrols of the island by armed guards and instructed them to do whatever had to be done to keep the reporters off the island. He purchased several specially trained guard dogs and had the most advanced alarm systems available at that time installed in the villa. Concerned for his wife and their unborn child, he'd decided they would await the birth there on the island. They had both come to love the paradise they found there so much, they never returned to live at Varkiza. Damian was buried in the garden.

And soon, Alexander thought sadly, his mother would also be laid to rest there.

While Alexander raced against time to reach the island, Constantine Kirakis kept a silent vigil at his wife's bedside, holding her hand as he watched her sleep. Time was running out. How, he wondered, would he ever be able to go on without her? In the dim light, it looked as though she were not breathing. Kirakis reached out and rested his hand just below her bosom, waiting for the reassuring rise and fall of her body that would tell him she was still with him.

Melina opened her eyes slowly and smiled when she saw him. "Costa," she said in a weak voice. "It is not necessary for you to stay here every moment. You must get some rest—you look so very tired."

He shook his head, his eyes bright with tears. "Do not worry about me, *matia mou*. Concentrate on yourself, on getting better," he told her.

Her smile was knowing. "We both know it is too late for that now," she said softly. "My time on earth grows short. You must accept it, as I have."

"No . . ."

"Yes, Costa. It is all right. I have no fear of death now. Life has been good, very good, but . . ." Her voice trailed off.

"No, Melina. You must not give up," he said firmly.

"There is no point in fighting the inevitable," she told him.

He shook his head, not trusting his voice.

"Alexander . . . is he here yet?" she asked.

"He is on his way," Kirakis said, fighting back tears. "I expect he will be arriving soon."

"Good." She paused for a moment. "I have been trying very hard to stay awake, to wait for him."

"Do not fight sleep, *matia mou*. You will need to rest to keep up your strength," he said gently, smoothing her heavy blond hair back, away from her face.

"I must see Alexander," she insisted.

"Of course you will see him," Kirakis promised. "He will be here when you wake—"

"*If* I wake," she corrected him. "No . . . I must stay awake until he arrives."

"If it will give you peace of mind, I will wake you myself as soon as he is here."

"Costa, you must promise me something now," she began, her voice faltering. "You must make peace with Alexander."

"You know I want that as much as you do."

"Yes . . . but I am not sure either of you has been making a genuine effort," she said. "Both of you are very stubborn men. You must learn to put your foolish pride aside if you ever hope to rekindle your relationship with our son." She closed her eyes for a moment, and her breathing became more labored. "My Costa . . . only you can enable me to leave this world in peace."

"How?" he asked. "You know I will do anything—"

"Right the wrongs that have been done," she said in a faint voice. There was an urgency in her eyes that was unmistakable. "Put an end to the lies, the secrets. Make peace at last—with Alexander and with yourself."

Kirakis hesitated for a moment. He turned to Pericles Karamanlis, who had just entered the room. Kirakis shook his head, then looked at Melina again. "Yes, *matia mou*," he said softly. "You are right. It is time to put the past behind us . . . once and for all."

As soon as the helicopter touched down on the lawn in front of the villa, Alexander pushed open the doors and leaped to the ground, not bothering to wait until the pilot had shut down his engines. He raced across the lawn to the main entrance. Helena, who was now in charge of the household staff, was waiting for him in the entrance hall. "Thank God you are here, Alexandros," she whispered as she embraced him gently. "She has been asking for you."

"I came as quickly as I could." His eyes darted toward the top of the staircase, where Pericles Karamanlis had just emerged from his mother's room. "Is she—"

"She is still alive—barely," Helena said sadly, wiping a tear from her eye. "She is very, very weak. Her life hangs by only a slim thread. She insists she has been waiting for you."

Alexander nodded. "I want to see her—now," he said as the doctor came down the stairs.

Karamanlis shook his head. "Not now," he said flatly. "She is asleep—and will be for several hours to come."

Alexander glared at him. "Do you have any idea how far I have come to see her, to be with her before—" He stopped short, unable to finish. The words stuck in his throat.

"I am well aware of how far you have traveled," the doctor said patiently, "but she is asleep now, as I have already explained. She will not know you are there."

"I still want to see her—if only for a few minutes," Alexander said stubbornly.

The doctor hesitated for a moment. "Very well," he said finally. "But only for a few moments—and do not try to wake her. She is weak, very weak. All I can do for her now is make her as comfortable as possible—and I fully intend to do that much."

Alexander let out a deep breath. "I understand," he said quietly. "I won't stay long, but I must see her."

Helena caught his arm as he started up the staircase. "Your father has been waiting for you in the library, Alexandros."

Alexander nodded. "Tell him I'll join him there after I have seen Mother," he told her.

"I will do that." She paused for a moment. "I am glad you have come home. I wish only that the circumstances that have brought you back to us could have been different."

He looked at her for a moment. "So do I, Helena."

He turned away from her and ascended the stairs slowly, deliberately, realizing now that no matter how much time he'd had to prepare himself for this, he was never really going to be ready for his mother's death. Never.

As he entered his mother's bedroom suite, a white-uniformed nurse was checking her vital signs. She looked up at Alexander disapprovingly. "You should not be in here," she said. "She has been sedated. Dr. Karamanlis would not approve—"

"Dr. Karamanlis knows I am here," Alexander assured her. "I have come a very long way to be with my mother and I would like to spend a few moments alone with her now."

"I do not think—"

Pericles Karamanlis appeared in the doorway. "It will be all right, Penelope," he told her. "Madame's son will not be staying long—will you, Alexander?"

Alexander shot him a murderous look.

After Karamanlis and the nurse left the room, Alexander seated himself in one of the Louis XV chairs near his mother's bed. She was asleep. She looked so peaceful. At first glance, if one did not know, it would be hard to believe she could be so close to death. But when he looked at her more closely, he saw that her face was pale, almost chalky white. She appeared to have lost a great deal of weight in a very short time. Her face was sunken, especially around the eyes and the hollows of her cheeks. Her normally prominent cheekbones protruded so that her face looked cadaverous. Alexander, who could not recall ever having cried openly, even as a child, now fought back tears. He reached out and took her hand. It was cold. The chill of death has already set in, he thought.

Melina opened her eyes, smiling up at him. "Alexander," she whispered his name. "I was so afraid you would not get here in time."

"I came as quickly as I could, *manna mou,*" he said softly.

"I am so very glad you are here," she said. "I could not bear the thought of leaving this world without seeing you one last time, without saying good-bye."

Alexander blinked back tears. "Please, Mother, you mustn't talk like that—" he began in a trembling voice.

"I do not have much time left on this earth, my son," she told him. "You must accept this, as I already have. It is - God's will."

His handsome face was dark with rage. "If there is truly a God, then why does He do this?" he demanded angrily. "How can He allow this to happen?"

"All things happen for a reason, Alexander," she said in a weak voice. "It is not for us to question God's will."

"No . . . I cannot accept that," he said tensely, shaking his head. "I'm sorry, Mother, but I'm unable to share your faith. Not now . . . especially not now."

"You must believe, Alexander. You must always have faith," she insisted. "It will make you strong. It will help you to survive, to keep going—no matter how difficult your life may become at times. Everything happens for a reason —even though we may not be able to see that reason or understand it at the time."

Alexander looked at her, so calm, so unshakable in her faith, and he was filled with a bitterness he could barely conceal from her. Faith. He could hardly have faith in a God who would take his beloved mother from him. He could not imagine placing his life, his destiny, in the hands of a Supreme Being whose existence he'd always doubted. How could his mother—or anyone else—expect him to believe, especially now? he asked himself. He nodded hesitantly. "I will try," he promised. Anything to make her happy. "I can guarantee nothing, but for you, I will try."

Melina smiled up at him. "Have I told you how very proud I am of you?"

He tried to smile back at her. "More than once, Mother," he said in a low voice.

"You have always been so strong," she said, her voice growing weaker. "I am counting on you now to look after

your father. You will have to help him through this. He will
not be able to cope."

Alexander forced a slight smile. "Father is much stronger
than you seem to think," he said lightly.

"Perhaps, but after so many years, he is going to find it
difficult to be alone again," Melina said with concern in her
voice. "He is going to need you—more than ever."

Alexander shook his head. "No, I think I'm probably the
last person Father will ever turn to."

Melina looked at him for a moment, not sure what he
meant at first. "Ah, yes, you are making reference to his
threat to disinherit you."

"You knew about that?" he asked, surprised.

She managed a weak smile. "Your father has never kept
anything from me," she said, "though he has tried on
occasion."

"I knew that you were aware of what had happened—"

"I know that the young lady took her own life because she
felt you had rejected her," Melina told him. "Alexander, I
have not always approved of the way you have handled your
private affairs in the past—but I have always made it a rule
never to interfere."

"You never had to," Alexander said. "Father was capable
of enough interference for both of you."

"Your papa feels he has acted in your best interests—and
the corporation's," Melina tried to explain. "He wants only
for you to take a more responsible attitude in the future—in
your personal affairs as well as in business matters. Your
father has always had such high hopes for you. As his only
heir, you have the responsibility of living up to tradition."

"Tradition," Alexander said slowly. "As I recall, tradition has always been extremely important to you as well."

"Your happiness is important to me," she insisted. "I
simply do not think the life-style you have chosen for
yourself really makes you happy."

"I think you know me too well," he said.

"Believe what I tell you now, Alexander, because I know
your father as well as he knows himself—perhaps better,"
she said then. "He was angry with you, yes—he was
furious. If the news of your involvement with the young

Swiss woman had leaked to the media, the result could have been much adverse publicity, both for the corporation and for you personally. He felt he had to do something to make you realize it could not be allowed to happen again, but your father would never really disinherit you. He could never remain angry with you for long. It is just his way. He explodes like a volcano. He unleashes his anger, but he gets over it quickly. He has always been that way. You will see."

"I am not so sure," he said, shaking his head. "You weren't there, Mother. You didn't see him. I have never seen him like that before."

"And you were not here when he received word from his people in Geneva," she said. "He became physically violent. Poor Helena thought a tempest had hit the library. He was quite destructive. But as I have already told you, he blows off steam and then it is over."

"I hope you're right," Alexander said quietly. "I'm not happy that things are so strained between Father and myself."

"Alexander"—she reached out with her free hand and touched his cheek gently—"I want you to always remember one thing: no matter how it may seem to you at times, and there may come a time in the future when you will have doubts, I have always loved you more than my own life. I would never have done anything—intentionally—to hurt you in any way."

"I know that," he assured her.

"You do *now*, my son—but if a day should come when you are not so sure of my love for you, of your father's love for you, remember what I am telling you now. Either of us would have gladly died for you."

"I know that, Mother," he insisted. She was visibly upset.

"You know, you are the miracle I always prayed for, Alexi," she went on. "You are the perfect, healthy child the doctors always told me I would never have. You made my life complete at a time when I had almost given up."

Karamanlis came to the door again. "Alexander, I think you should go now," he said firmly. "Your mother should be resting."

Alexander nodded, then turned back to Melina. "I must

go now, *manna mou*," he told her. "I will come back later."

She nodded. "Do not wait too long," she said in a voice that grew steadily weaker.

He bent down, kissed her cheek lightly, then left the room.

Constantine Kirakis nervously paced the floor in the library. In the past hour he had smoked a half dozen of his specially blended Egyptian cigarettes. His beloved Melina—his wife, his lover for so many years, his best friend—was dying, and there was nothing he could do to prevent it. Never before in his life had Kirakis ever felt so totally powerless. It was an alien feeling for this man who had become so accustomed to always being in command, to having every situation under control at all times. It was bitterly frustrating to be forced to just stand by and watch her slipping away from him, knowing that her death was inevitable.

"Father?"

Startled, Kirakis swung around to face Alexander, who stood in the doorway looking as though he had been subjected to a physical beating. Kirakis gestured to his son to come into the room. Alexander closed the door, crossed the room in silence, and sank into an armchair near his father's desk. He shook his head sadly but made no comment.

"You have already seen your mother?" Kirakis asked, lighting another cigarette.

Alexander nodded. "I still can't believe this is really happening," he said. "The last time I saw her—God, it was only a few months ago, at Christmas—she seemed so well then. She looked wonderful! How can this be possible?"

Kirakis shook his head. "I too am finding it difficult to believe," he admitted. "In the past few months, since we returned from New York, she had been doing splendidly. Better than I have seen her in quite some time." He perched on one corner of his massive desk. "But then, a few days ago . . ." He shrugged. "I am still not sure what happened —or why."

Alexander looked up at him. "A few days ago?" he asked. "This happened a few days ago? Why did you wait so long to contact me?"

"No one thought it was anything to be alarmed about—at first," he answered, stabbing out his cigarette. "She was feeling a bit under the weather, that was all. I have seen her when she's felt worse, so I was not so concerned. She complained of being tired—more so than is usual—but aside from that, she seemed perfectly fine. I actually had no idea how serious the problem was until this morning, when I cabled you. That was also when I sent for Pericles."

"Karamanlis knows what he is doing?" Alexander demanded. "He hasn't simply given up on her, has he?" He looked into his father's eyes questioningly.

Kirakis shook his head. "No, Alexander, that is not possible," he said with certainty. "Pericles would never just give up on her, as you put it. He has done all that is humanly possible to keep her with us."

"Mother seems to think it's all in the hands of God now," Alexander said then, remembering his conversation with her.

Kirakis's smile was sad. "Ah, yes," he said, drawing in his breath. "Your mother's faith has always been strong. Unshakable. I always found it difficult to share her faith myself."

Alexander nodded. "It's just as difficult for me, especially now," he agreed wearily. "But at this moment I would say or do anything to keep her happy. I promised her I would at least try. It seemed so important to her."

Kirakis nodded. "I feel exactly the same way," he said. He found himself thinking of the promise he'd made to Melina just before Alexander's arrival. The promise he was not at all sure he would be able to keep, even as he had spoken the words to her. "There is nothing I would not do to make her last hours peaceful ones."

Alexander was silent for a little while. "I thought I was prepared for this," he said finally. "After living with Mother's illness all my life, I thought I'd be ready for the day when—" He shook his head, unable to go on.

"So did I," Kirakis admitted solemnly.

Alexander leaned back in his chair and closed his eyes tightly. He was exhausted. Only now did he feel the effects of jet lag, compounded by the emotional stress he was suffering. He felt as though he were about to collapse.

Kirakis studied him for a moment, for the first time realizing the impact the time difference and the distance he'd traveled must be having on him, both physically and mentally. "You have come a long way, Alexander," he said quietly. "Perhaps you should try to get some sleep."

Alexander shook his head emphatically. "I am exhausted, but I couldn't sleep," he insisted. "Not now."

"I know how you feel," Kirakis said with an understanding in his voice Alexander had not heard in a good many years. "But we cannot do anything for your mother now. We can only wait—and hope. She is asleep—and I expect she will be until morning."

"Or she may not wake at all," Alexander said darkly. "No, Father, I will force myself to stay awake. I must. I must be here for her if she should ask for me."

"You *are* here," Kirakis said firmly. "Do you not think I would wake you if—if anything should happen?"

Alexander looked up at him. "And what about you, Father? When will you find the time to rest?"

"Soon." Kirakis moved around the desk, pausing to glance through the French windows at the garden beyond. "I see the helicopter is still here," he observed.

"I asked the pilot to stay on," Alexander explained. "I left New York without even a change of clothes. I will be sending him into Athens to get some things for me."

Kirakis nodded. "Helena told me you brought nothing with you."

"There was no time to pack. I left as soon as I received your cable." Alexander paused, managing a slight smile. "I see Helena is still the unquestioned main source of all information around here."

His father nodded. "Old habits are difficult to break, are they not?" he asked. He paused. "I am sure nothing has been removed from your closets, but if there is anything else you need . . ." He was rambling on about trivial matters, not really thinking, not really caring, but afraid to stop, afraid the silence would give him time to think, and the tears a chance to surface again.

"I was thinking, on the plane en route to Athens, and then again in the chopper," Alexander began. "I kept thinking about all the good times spent here, all the happy memories.

The most peaceful moments of my life have been spent here.''

Kirakis smiled in remembrance. ''I too have been recalling happier times,'' he admitted. ''When you were a child, keeping you in line was no easy task. You had two adoring women running interference for you. I remember how your mother and Helena always managed to prevent me from imposing strict discipline upon you. I was never quite sure which of them was the more guilty when it came to spoiling you.''

''They did know how to indulge a child, didn't they?'' Alexander agreed, smiling as he remembered the many times his mother and his governess had managed to conceal his mischief from his father, his unquestioned disciplinarian.

Kirakis laughed for the first time since Alexander's arrival. ''I was thinking about the day you broke that antique vase I'd bought for your mother in Rome,'' he said. ''I knew it was an accident and had no intention of inflicting punishment, but your mother was taking no chances. She insisted she had broken it herself. She would have done anything to keep you from being punished in any way.''

''I think you're probably right.'' Alexander studied his father's face for a moment, realizing this was the first time in many years that he and his father had spent time together without ending up at each other's throats, the first time since he'd left the island to go to the States that they'd spent time just reminiscing as they were doing now. Until this moment, Alexander had not realized just how much he'd missed it. ''Mother could never have been the disciplinarian,'' he said, recalling how patient and indulgent she had always been with him.

Kirakis shook his head. ''No, she could not.'' He started to cry, and his tears came freely now. He felt no shame in crying in his son's presence. ''I do not know what I am going to do when she is gone,'' he told Alexander. ''I feel as though my whole life, my reason for living, is being torn away from me. After fifty years of marriage, I do not know what I will do without her.''

Alexander wanted to reach out to his father now. He wanted to tell him that it was going to be all right, that he would be there for him, that they would be there for each other. He wanted to bridge the gap between them at last, but he was held back, as always, by that invisible wall that had separated them for so many years, the wall that had been strengthened by the foolish actions of a troubled young woman in a hotel room in Geneva. Alexander wondered if things could ever be put right between himself and his father. They had once been close. They'd shared the same goals, the same intense ambitions. They had been bound together by their shared dreams to make the Kirakis Corporation the world's largest international conglomerate. His mother insisted that his father would never disinherit him. Alexander was not so sure.

He took a deep breath, then reached out and touched his father's arm gently. "We must both be strong now, Father," he said in a low voice. "We must try—for Mother's sake."

Kirakis looked up, staring at his son's face. He nodded slowly. He wanted to reach out to Alexander as much as Alexander wanted to reach out to him, but so much had happened in the past few months, so much had gone wrong between them. Even so, even with all that had kept them apart, Kirakis realized at this moment that he had only to look at his son, to see the pain in those black eyes, to know that he was not going through this hell alone.

Melina Kirakis passed away quietly in her sleep just before dawn the next morning. Constantine was with her at the time of her death, still holding her hand, still talking to her as though she could hear him and knew what he was saying to her. Though Kirakis openly admitted that he had never shared his wife's deep and unquestioned faith, he realized now that ever since he'd entered her room four hours earlier, he had silently been praying for a miracle. Praying that, somehow, Melina's life would be spared once again. If there *is* a God, he thought as he watched her slipping away from him, little by little, He would not be likely to listen to the likes of me. Even as he prayed, something in the back of Kirakis's mind told him he was wasting his time. It was too late.

"This is God's mercy, Constantine," Karamanlis told him as he drew the sheet over Melina's pale, lifeless face. "In the past few weeks, her heart has been growing steadily weaker. It could not keep going. It was inevitable that it would stop. The damage was too great."

Kirakis nodded. "As long as I have lived with this . . . so many years . . . I find that I am not ready for it," he said.

Karamanlis shook his head. "I think we are never truly prepared for death, even when we have known for some time that it is coming," he said. "Melina herself was probably more resigned to it than any of us were."

Kirakis looked at him. "You really believe that?"

"Yes, I do," Karamanlis answered without hesitation. "I think you were able to do more for her in that respect than I was."

Kirakis looked puzzled. "How?"

"I was able to ease her pain, to make her comfortable physically. But you, my friend, you gave her something she has wanted for a very long time," Karamanlis said. "Just before Melina lost consciousness, while you were with Alexander, we had a talk. She told me she could leave this world without fear because you had finally promised to right a wrong ignored for too long."

Kirakis stiffened. "Did she tell you what she was talking about?" he asked carefully.

"No, but I think I have a good idea." Karamanlis put his instruments into his black leather case. "It is no secret that she has been concerned for some time about you—and about Alexander."

Kirakis nodded. "Yes," he said slowly. "Yes, she was."

"I am glad you made that promise to her, Constantine," Karamanlis told him. "It meant a great deal to her."

Kirakis stopped in front of the bay windows, staring out at the Aegean stretched out before him. "I would have promised her anything to give her peace of mind," he said finally. "But will I be able to live up to that promise?"

"Nothing else could have given her so much contentment, but I don't have to tell you that," he said.

Kirakis turned to face him again. "How did this happen?" he asked. "How could it have happened so suddenly? She seemed to be doing so well. Even Alexander commented on how marvelous she looked—"

"It is very hard to say," Karamanlis replied. "I suppose there are some who might say that Melina knew, somehow, that there was not much time left and summoned up all her strength to make those last months the best possible for all three of you—like making that trip to New York so you could all be together at Christmas after I'd expressly forbidden her to make any long trips."

"You think the trip was too much for her?" Kirakis asked.

"It is possible, yes."

"I would prefer that you not mention this to Alexander," Kirakis said firmly. "He blames himself now for placing too much stress on Melina emotionally."

Karamanlis nodded. "Have I ever told him anything you did not wish him to know?"

Kirakis shook his head. "No, you have not, and I am deeply grateful for that," he said quietly.

"I know Melina would not have wanted him to feel that he was in any way responsible for this," Karamanlis said, knowing why Kirakis was concerned. He paused for a moment. "Alexander is a grown man now, Constantine. When are you going to finally accept him as such?"

Kirakis sighed deeply. "Sometimes I think perhaps it happened too soon—that my son became a man too soon." He was staring out at the Aegean again. "Melina tried to keep too much to herself," he said at last, changing the subject again. "Why did she never tell me how badly she felt?"

"She did not wish to alarm you, and she did not want Alexander to know what a toll that trip to New York had actually taken on her," Karamanlis answered. "She told me how concerned he was when she showed up there unexpectedly. He was worried that she had traveled too far in her condition. She was afraid that he would blame himself because he had not made time to come home as she had asked him to do on so many occasions. She decided it would be best not to tell anyone."

"Melina understood Alexander's business obligations," he said. "God knows she has lived with businessmen all her life—her father, myself, and Alexander. She just couldn't bear to be parted from him over the holidays." He slammed his fist against the wall, unable to contain his bitterness and frustration any longer. "Do you have any idea how it feels, Pericles, to have to stand by and watch someone you have loved and lived with most of your life just slip away from you? Do you know how helpless I felt?"

"It is a feeling I have known many times in my profession," Karamanlis said softly.

Kirakis shook his head sadly. "I have to go tell Alexander," he said. "I cannot allow him to just walk in here, unprepared, and see . . ." He was unable to finish.

"You will not find him in his room," Karamanlis said as he started for the door. "I saw him down in the library about an hour ago. He fell asleep in one of the armchairs."

Kirakis nodded. "He was so determined to stay awake, to be here for Melina if she called for him," he said, recalling his conversation with Alexander earlier. "But he was exhausted. I suppose he was unable to hold out any longer." He gave an exaggerated gesture of helplessness.

As Kirakis left the room, Karamanlis turned his attentions to completing the death certificate, something he had not wanted to do in Kirakis's presence. He was filled with a growing concern, wondering which of them would take Melina's death hardest, Kirakis or Alexander.

Alexander woke with a start. At first, he was not sure where he was. He sat up, realizing that he was home, that he'd fallen asleep in the library. He'd been having a nightmare, a terrifying dream, but he could not recall much about it. Then, suddenly, it came to him. It had not been a dream at all. He was home, on the island. He had come home because his mother was dying. He pulled himself upright and switched on a lamp. His neck and shoulders were stiff, and he wondered how long he'd been asleep. Where was his father? Surely nothing had happened or he would have come for him.

At that moment Kirakis entered the room. Alexander got to his feet quickly and turned to face him. "Mother—" he began.

Kirakis shook his head. "It is all over, Alexander," he said gravely.

Alexander drew in his breath, shaking his head as though his mind were unable to accept the reality. "I . . . was she . . . was she in a great deal of pain at the end?" he asked finally, his eyes cast downward, unable to face his father.

"Karamanlis says not," Kirakis answered quietly. "He tells me the end was very peaceful for her."

Alexander nodded slowly. "That's good," he said. "I was afraid she might have to suffer before she—" He turned away, gazing blankly through the windows. "I'm glad he was able to make her comfortable. At least modern medicine is capable of that much, if they cannot . . ." His voice trailed off.

Kirakis studied his son with concern. He had expected Alexander to be upset. He had expected tears. He had even expected uncontrollable rage. He had not expected this. Alexander seemed disoriented. Kirakis reached out and touched his son's shoulder. "It is all right, Alexander," he said in a low voice. "There is nothing wrong with crying at a time like this."

Alexander shook his head emphatically. "No," he said in a strained voice. "What good are tears? Will they make the pain go away? Will they bring Mother back to us?" There was bitterness in his voice as he gripped the edge of the desk.

Kirakis shook his head, looking down at the floor. "No . . . nothing can bring her back now," he said slowly, "but it is not good to keep your feelings bottled up inside you this way, Alexander. You must let it out, come to grips with it."

"It won't help," Alexander said stiffly. He took a gray suede jacket from the back of a nearby chair and put it on. "If you'll excuse me, Father, I feel the need to be alone for a while. I think I'll take a long walk in the reserve."

Kirakis did not try to stop him as he headed out the door, almost knocking Helena down in the wake of his hasty departure. She stared after him for a moment, not sure whether to speak or not, then turned back to Kirakis. There was concern and grief on her heavily lined face. "Alexander —is he all right?" she asked hesitantly.

"He will be," Kirakis said quietly.

"It is not a good idea for him to be alone right now," she said, worried. "He is not himself."

"On the contrary, Helena. This is Alexander's way—the

only way in which he will feel comfortable in dealing with his loss. Alexander has never been one to show his deepest emotions openly. He will give in to it only when he knows he will not be observed.'' He paused. ''Alexander is a man now, a fact that even I must be reminded of at times. If this is what he needs, I will not interfere. I understand my son much better than he seems to think I do. Besides, I feel the need to be alone myself right now.''

''Saddle Casablanca for me, Nicos,'' Alexander snapped irritably as he entered the stables.

The young groom nodded. ''Yes, sir, Mr. Kirakis,'' he said pleasantly. ''It will only take a moment.'' He turned on his heel and headed down the long row of stalls to fetch Alexander's favorite mount.

Alexander paced back and forth in the aisle impatiently, lightly slapping his riding crop against the palm of his left hand in frustration. He felt as though there were a time bomb inside him, waiting to detonate at any moment. He told himself everything would be all right if only the tears would come. Why wasn't he able to express his grief? He'd just lost his mother. Why couldn't he cry? Why were feelings of rage and betrayal now overpowering his feelings of loss and sadness? Instead of mourning, instead of feeling a deep sense of grief, Alexander felt only anger, as if his mother had deliberately abandoned him. Why? he asked himself. Why did his mother's death leave him feeling so angry and betrayed? Why was there no relief from his pain?

''Nicos!'' he roared, his impatience growing by the second. *''Nicos!''*

The groom appeared from a stall at the far end of the stable, leading a spirited black Arabian mare. ''It will take just a moment to saddle her—'' he began.

''Don't bother!'' Alexander barked. ''I'll take her as she is!'' He leaped onto the horse's back, gathered up the reins, and dug his heels into her flanks, urging her into a headlong gallop. Then he rode away as though he were being pursued by the devil himself.

EIGHT

Melina Kirakis was buried on a beautiful spring morning in late April in the garden outside the villa, among the flowers and statuary she had always loved so much. Though Alexander had planned to leave for New York immediately after the funeral service, his father had managed to persuade him to stay on for a few days, insisting that he was not up to the pressures and demands of the workload that would be awaiting him upon his return to the States, either physically or mentally. Kirakis knew that his son wanted only to get as far away from the island as possible, but he was convinced it was the worst thing he could do.

Now, three days later, Constantine Kirakis sat at his desk in the library, staring up at the oil painting of Melina hanging over the fireplace. Melina, his beloved Melina—just as she had looked on their wedding day in 1926. She had been so breathtakingly beautiful then, only eighteen years old and the most incredibly lovely young woman he had ever known. She had been such a beautiful bride in her high-necked, Victorian wedding gown—a Paris original, since her father would have it no other way—white silk with a ten-foot train, covered with yards of the most delicate antique lace and tiny seed pearls. Her thick blond hair had been pulled up in a loose topknot, adorned by the traditional coronet of white flowers they had both worn during the Greek Orthodox ceremony. Kirakis could still hear the words she had spoken on that joyous day as he whirled her across the dance floor at the reception: "Costa, you are going to be the only love of my life." *The only love of my life*. Kirakis smiled in remembrance. In over fifty years of marriage, he knew with certainty that she had never been unfaithful. Melina would have died before she would have allowed another man to touch her.

Kirakis had not thought it possible then that he could ever have loved her more than he had on their wedding day, but he had been wrong, so very wrong. As the years had passed, as they shared both triumph and tragedy, the bond between them grew stronger with the passing of time. They had weathered many storms together, but they'd also rejoiced. In the end, the good had outweighed the bad because they had endured it all together. Melina, he reflected now, had matured. She had made the transition from a willful, spoiled, impetuous but fiercely loyal girl to the poised, elegant woman whose graciousness and regal bearing made her specialness apparent even to those who did not have the good fortune to know her well.

We both changed a great deal, did we not, *matia mou?* he thought as he looked up at the portrait. You, from a headstrong, idealistic girl with dreams of princes and knights in shining armor to a fine, elegant woman of the world—and me, from a tempestuous, hotheaded kid from the slums of Piraeus to a respected, powerful man. God, what am I going to do now that you are gone? How will I ever be able to go on without you, my love?

Helena came into the library carrying a heavy silver serving tray laden with food. "I know you have been busy all morning, sir," she said as she placed the tray on one corner of the desk. "I thought you would probably prefer to take your lunch here."

"I would, Helena, thank you," he responded, returning to the present abruptly. "I am afraid it has not been easy to concentrate on business matters today."

"I am not surprised," she said as she poured him a cup of

coffee. "If you do not mind my saying so, sir, I think perhaps you chose to return to your business affairs a bit too soon after Madame's funeral. You need more time to yourself, I think."

Kirakis's smile was sad. "I appreciate your concern, Helena, but this is exactly what I need now. It keeps my mind occupied." He paused for a moment. "Will Alexander be taking lunch in the dining room? If he is, I think I should join him."

"Alexander is not having anything," Helena said quietly, busying herself with the tray. "Missing meals has become a habit with him, I am afraid."

"He told you he did not want anything?" Kirakis asked, concerned.

"In no uncertain terms, sir," Helena replied. "I am worried about him. He barely eats enough to keep himself going. He does not sleep well. I have heard him roaming the halls at all hours."

Kirakis frowned, shaking his head. "I, too, am worried about him," he admitted. "Do you know where he is now?"

"He went for a walk—again," Helena told him. "He has received several transatlantic calls from New York in the past few days. He will not speak to anyone. He does not return any of his calls, and I think some of them have been quite important."

"I will have a talk with him," Kirakis declared. "You will let me know when he returns?"

Helena nodded. "Of course I will, sir."

"Thank you."

Helena left the room quietly. Kirakis sipped his coffee thoughtfully, staring absently through the French doors at the men working out in the garden. He was very worried about Alexander. His son had not been himself since the morning Melina died. Kirakis had expected him to grieve, but Alexander had shown no emotion whatsoever since that morning. No tears, no rage, nothing. It was as if something deep within his soul had died with Melina. Though Alexander's attachment to his mother had always been strong, Kirakis had not been prepared for the ordeal his son would experience at her loss. He suspected that something inside Alexander was afraid of losing control. He thought about the morning Melina was buried. Alexander had been silent and remote during the long graveside service, staring off into the distance at something only he could see. When the few close friends who had been permitted to attend the service tried to offer their condolences, Alexander had turned away from them, refusing to respond. He'd gone off by himself afterward, and Kirakis had not seen him again until late that night. Alexander had offered no explanation for his rude behavior or his unceremonious departure, nor had he bothered to tell his father where he had gone.

As the next few days passed, Alexander showed no signs of reconciling himself to his loss, as Kirakis had been certain he would. If anything, he had become even more withdrawn. This has gone on long enough, Kirakis thought as he finished his coffee. It is time for my son and I to have a long talk.

Late in the afternoon, Helena poked her head in the door of the library. "Sir, you asked me to let you know when Alexander returned—" she began.

"Yes. Where is he?"

"He went upstairs a few minutes ago. I think you will probably find him in his bedroom," Helena said. "He walked past me as if he did not even see me."

"Thank you, Helena."

"Yes, sir." She closed the door.

Kirakis stood up and paused for a moment in front of Melina's portrait. "Perhaps you have been right all along, *matia mou*," he said sadly. "It is time to put the past behind us—once and for all. Alexander and I, we must now look to the future."

Alexander was packing a large carry-on bag when Kirakis entered the bedroom. "Do you not normally allow one of the servants to do that?" Kirakis asked casually. "It is, after all, one of the many things they are paid to do."

Alexander did not look up. "I'm perfectly capable of doing it myself," he said quietly. "I would prefer not to have anyone underfoot right now."

"I see," Kirakis started slowly. "You plan to leave soon?"

"Tonight," Alexander replied. "I've been away from my

office much too long now. I do have responsibilities awaiting me in New York, responsibilities that will not wait just because—'' He stopped short.

''Just because your mother has died?'' Kirakis finished. ''Do you not have men on your staff who are able to handle corporate affairs in your absence?''

''Yes, of course, but—'' Alexander began, drawing in his breath.

''Then what is the rush?'' Kirakis sat down on the bed. ''I think it would be best if you were to stay here a while longer.''

Alexander looked at him. ''Is that a direct order from the chairman of the board?'' he asked.

Kirakis shook his head. ''No, Alexander. It is a request from your father.'' There was a deep, overwhelming sadness in his voice as he spoke. Alexander started to say something, but Kirakis held up a hand to silence him. ''I know what you are thinking. You are an adult and I have no right to make decisions for you. I am not pulling rank on you, as they say in the States. But no matter how many years pass, our relationship is what it is, Alexander. When you are eighty, I will *still* be your father. My feelings toward you will never really change. You and I have been through a great deal in the past few years, and I am aware that you resent my interference in your personal affairs. I think perhaps now is the time to try to put all of that unpleasantness behind us and take the time to get to know one another again. I would like us to be close again, my son.''

Alexander paused for a moment. ''What's the use?'' he asked finally, hopelessness in his voice. ''Caring is too painful. You make that emotional investment in another human being, and they leave you or they die. Or they betray you. Women leave their children. Husbands betray their wives. What good is it? Better to be detached, to never allow oneself to care too much about anyone.''

''Your mother hasn't abandoned you, Alexander,'' Kirakis said carefully, alarmed at the way his son was talking. ''Your mother died. There is a difference. It would be a rather hollow existence, don't you think?'' Kirakis continued. ''Never caring, never allowing anyone to get close enough to care for you?''

"It would certainly make life less complicated," Alexander said coldly, turning away from him again.

"It would also take the joy out of that life," Kirakis told him. "I started out with nothing. I built the Athena Shipping Company from the ground up, and it was not an easy task. But to this day, I am convinced that my ambitions alone would never have been enough to sustain me during those trying times. My drives were born out of fear of poverty —and out of love. The person who mattered most in the world to me while I was growing up in Piraeus—my mother—died a long, lingering death because we were too poor, and it left its mark on me. I named Athena for her. And then there was your mother. Without her, without her love and support, I doubt I could have kept fighting as long as I had to in order to ensure Athena's survival in those early years. I, too, grieve her death. I am not at all sure I can go on without her now. But I would not trade the years we had together for anything. Melina made me strong, helped me to become the man I always wanted to be. Somehow, I always saw myself through her eyes. I measured my own worth through her love, her belief in me. We endured a good many tragedies in our years together, but on balance it was a good marriage. A strong one. We were very happy, your mother and I."

"Even when Damian died?" Alexander asked sharply.

Kirakis looked up at him. Leave it to Alexander to make a direct hit every time, he thought. "That was the most difficult period of our lives," he said. "I could not have survived it without her. Our love made us stronger than we would have been alone."

"I never thought of you as an idealist," Alexander said quietly as he continued to pack.

"Nor have I ever thought of myself as such," Kirakis said, eyeing his son carefully. He could almost feel Alexander's inner tension building. "One does not have to be an idealist to care, you know."

Alexander did not respond but went back to his packing.

Kirakis decided this approach was going nowhere. "Your mother was an exceptional woman," he said. "She wanted children very much. She knew, too, how much I wanted a son. I was afraid for her. I did not want her to put her own life at risk as she did, but Melina was a woman with a mind of her own. Once she decided to do something, God help anyone who got in her way.''

"Father, there's really no point—" Alexander began with a weary sigh.

"Let me finish," Kirakis said firmly. "After so many failed attempts, after losing Damian, she had almost given up on having a child, a healthy child. Then you came along. You, Alexander, were the light of her life. She loved you more than I would have ever thought any woman could love her child. She worshipped you.''

"If you don't mind, I'd rather not talk about this—about Mother—right now," Alexander said stiffly.

"I *do* mind. I think this is necessary, Alexander. I think it is something we both need right now," Kirakis insisted. "Your mother always worried about you. She never cared for the idea of your being alone, but she knew she could not hold on to you forever. She accepted that because she wanted you to be happy. She would not want to see you like this—"

"Dammit, I know what she wouldn't want!" Alexander exploded suddenly, snatching a silver-framed photograph from the nightstand and hurling it at the wall in his rage. "I can't help how I feel, Father! I can't control my emotions! I just wish the pain would go away!" He sobbed openly now, and Kirakis got to his feet and held him close, something he had not done since Alexander was a child, crying with him until their sobs came in dry, choking gasps.

At last, Kirakis thought. At last we will both begin to find peace.

Malibu.

Nick Holliday, in his tuxedo, stood in front of the mirror, muttering profanities under his breath as he fumbled with his bow tie. "I think whoever designed these goddamned monkey suits must have been a member of the Inquisition," he grumbled irritably. "They've got to be a throwback to some fifteenth-century torture method."

Meredith laughed. "You complain like this every time you have to wear a tux," she reminded him. She stopped what she was doing and crossed the room to adjust the errant tie. "Personally, I think you look dashing."

He frowned. "I look like the headwaiter at Chasen's."

"Nonsense." She kissed him lightly. "I think you're going to look very impressive when you step up on that stage to accept your Oscar."

"*If* I go up to accept," he corrected her.

She looked at him and smiled. "I don't believe it," she said in a teasing voice. "You're really nervous."

"Don't be ridiculous," he growled. "It's just this damned tux—"

"Come on, Holliday—admit it," she said. "You *are* nervous about the awards."

He hesitated for a moment, then nodded. "Yeah, you're right," he said. "I'm nervous. This is the first time I've been nominated. To win the first time out, on the first nomination—" he shrugged—"you can't even get odds on that in Vegas."

She placed her hands on his shoulders. "Relax. If the members of the Academy have any brains at all, they'll recognize a true creative genius when they see one."

"That's what I'm afraid of."

"What happened to all that self-confidence and optimism?" she asked. "Where's the Nick Holliday I fell in love with?"

"Out to lunch," he replied glumly.

"I don't believe that for a minute," she said. "Weren't you the one who told me winning an Oscar doesn't really mean anything because the awards usually have more to do with Hollywood politics than with talent or achievement? Weren't you the one who said you didn't really care if you won or not because box office receipts were all that really mattered?"

"I lied."

"Listen," she said softly, "even if you don't win, just remember—it's quite an accomplishment just to be nominated. How many big-name directors—*and* big box-office stars—go through their entire careers and never get a nomination?"

"You're just trying to make me feel good," he said, his eyes narrowing suspiciously.

"But I'm *not* lying," she insisted. "And if by some error

on the Academy's part you *don't* win, there's always next year.''

He grinned. ''There will *always* be next year.''

She kissed him again. ''It's true, you know—the box office receipts are what counts, and we both know you're a smash there.''

''You're absolutely right,'' he said. ''What have I got to worry about?'' He embraced her tightly. ''How would I ever get along without you?''

She smiled. ''Let's hope we never have to find out.''

He drew back and studied her for a moment. ''Have I told you how good it is to have you home again?''

''Only twenty or thirty times, but you can tell me again if you like,'' she said playfully. If only it could always be like this, she thought. If only they could be as happy as they had been in the beginning.

Her encounter with Alexander Kirakis still bothered her. She was never quite sure which had unnerved her most—the way Alexander had come on to her, or her response to his overt attentions. But she tried to tell herself it didn't matter now. She was home, she and Nick were working out their problems, and she had finally put Tom Ryan and the documentary behind her. She had accepted the reality that her questions might never be answered, that the story was dead. It had died with Tom Ryan. It was hard to forget when she was reminded of it every time she looked at the portrait of Elizabeth and David, but she knew without Tom there could never be a story.

''Know what?'' Nick was saying as he held her close. ''I think even if I don't win tonight, I can live with anything —as long as I've got you by my side.''

''Just try to get rid of me,'' she teased.

''Not on your life!'' He looked down. She was still in her slip. ''I think I'd better go downstairs to wait for you. It would be very easy right now to forget all about the awards presentation.''

''I won't be long,'' she promised.

After he left the room, Meredith went to her closet, took out her gown, and stared at it speculatively. She'd spent an entire afternoon on Rodeo Drive looking for the perfect gown to wear to the Academy Awards ceremonies, and she was convinced she'd found it. It was spectacular, a real showstopper. Made of royal blue silk satin, it was the latest creation from the year's hottest new designer. It clung to her body from her bosom to her hips, widening only slightly from her hips to the floor. It had a wide ruffle that extended over her breasts and up over her left shoulder, and a provocative slit starting at mid-thigh that revealed quite a bit of leg when she walked. She put it on, then slipped into her silver high-heeled pumps and stood in front of the full-length mirror. She was satisfied, knowing that she'd never looked better. The gown was flattering. It had been ridiculously expensive, but it was worth it. The eyes of the world would be on them tonight. They would be seen on television in homes all over the world. The cameras would be on Nick as he achieved the greatest triumph of his career to date. She was sure he was going to win. She could feel it in her bones. She would be at his side, sharing it all with him, and she wanted to look her best.

She reached for the diamond necklace and earrings on her dressing table, Nick's Christmas gift to her. They were magnificent, the most incredible blue-white diamonds she'd ever seen, but he had insisted they paled in comparison to the light in her eyes. She smiled to herself as she studied them for a moment. Well, my dear, you've come a long way from your dreary, middle-class beginnings, she told herself. But you still have a long way to go.

She paused, gazing at her reflection in the mirror once again. I do love Nick, she thought. No relationship is perfect. Every couple has their problems. So why do I have to keep reminding myself . . . ?

Suddenly Alexander's face was staring back at her from the mirror, looking as he'd appeared the last time she'd seen him, that night at Lutèce. This is crazy, she scolded herself. It's not Alexander Kirakis I want. God knows he's the last thing in the world I need! She tried to tell herself it wasn't Alexander she wanted, but the life-style he represented. That was what she longed for. And yet. . . .

She combed her hair carefully, allowing it to fall loosely around her shoulders, added the finishing touches to her makeup, collected her silver evening bag, then went down-stairs to join Nick.

Television crews were stationed outside the Dorothy Chandler Pavilion, catching on camera the multitude of famous faces as they arrived at the fifty-second Academy Awards presentation. Reporters and photographers lined the entrance, aggressive in their pursuit of the nominees. As Meredith and Nick emerged from their limousine, they were temporarily blinded by the never-ending series of popping flashbulbs. One overzealous reporter shoved a hand mike in Nick's face and asked, "What do you think your chances are of winning the Best Director award?"

Nick grinned. "About as good as those of the other nominees, I'd say," he responded easily.

"Do you think *Reflections* will be named Best Picture?" the reporter pursued.

"I've got my fingers crossed," Nick answered, concealing his nervousness from the cameras.

Meredith leaned against him as they made their way inside. "And I always thought the tough part was being on the *other* end of the mike," she quipped in a barely audible voice. "After this, I'm going to have a little more sympathy for my victims." She paused. "But I may not necessarily show them any more mercy."

Nick laughed. "Listen, babe, some of these Hollywood hotshots may *act* like they're annoyed with all the reporters and photographers getting underfoot," he said, "but believe me, they'd be even more upset if the press didn't show up at all."

They were seated with the other nominees in an area next to the stage. Down on the floor television crews appropriately attired in formal dinner jackets and armed with hand mikes and minicams took up their positions as a network anchorwoman and her director gave them last-minute instructions before retreating to the control booth. Down on the floor, the minicams scanned the crowd. Meredith knew from experience what they were attempting to accomplish. They wanted to catch some of those famous faces unawares, to give the public at large a glimpse of the very human emotions behind those celebrated faces: anxiety, hope, and—in some cases—disappointment. Though Meredith knew she would garner more attention right where she was, she felt slightly disappointed, wishing she could have been in that control booth, covering the awards herself.

A cinematographer who had passed away two weeks after the nominations were announced was awarded an Oscar posthumously. As his widow and daughter stepped up to accept it, Meredith thought of Tom Ryan at the 1954 Academy Awards. What must it have been like for him, having to step forward and accept his wife's Oscar so soon after her death? It had been less than a year. What must he have been thinking as he took the gold statue in his hands, the award Elizabeth had wanted so desperately to win, having lost both his wife and his son because of that picture? Meredith thought of the glittering gold statue on the mantel at the Ryan house, next to the painting of Elizabeth and David. Suddenly she knew why Tom Ryan had chosen to leave the house to Nick. He did think of Nick as the closest thing he had to a son since David's death, but it was more than that. Ryan had known Nick well enough to know that Nick would respect his wishes to the end. The house would be maintained as Ryan had always insisted it be kept. It would always be 1953 at the Ryan estate. Nothing would ever change.

The theme from *Reflections,* a song called "In the Eyes of a Stranger," was one of the Best Song nominees. The vocalist who had performed it on the film's soundtrack came onstage to perform it now against a haunting dark backdrop punctuated by an enormous pair of mysterious eyes, peering through a sheer screen, the same eyes that appeared on the posters and advertisements for the picture. Nick leaned over to Meredith and said in a low voice, "This one's going to be the winner. The only thing you can turn on nowadays and *not* hear 'In the Eyes of a Stranger' is a faucet!"

Meredith smiled, realizing how hard he was trying to hide his nervousness. She reached out and took his hand, squeezing it gently. He turned to look at her and smiled. "If only I could be as sure about all the nominations the picture received," he added.

The presentation ceremonies were nearing the end when

the nominees for Best Director were finally announced. Meredith could feel Nick's tension as the names of the five nominees and the films for which they had been nominated were read. She reached out and touched his arm reassuringly as the envelope was opened. "The winner is Nick Holliday for *Reflections*!" Nick got to his feet and Meredith watched proudly as he made his way to the stage amid thunderous applause. He'd told her he hadn't even bothered to prepare an acceptance speech. She wondered what he planned to say.

He stepped up to the podium and accepted the award, then leaned forward into the microphone. "I'm not really prepared for this," he admitted to the audience, "but I do want to say thanks to the people who helped to make *Reflections* —our great cast and crew, each of whom contributed to the final product. I also owe a debt of gratitude to the late Tom Ryan, who got me in the gate at Centurion. But most of all, I want to thank Meredith for putting up with me—love you, babe!" Looking up in her direction, he raised the Oscar high into the air.

When he returned to his seat, Oscar in hand, he was beaming proudly. "See?" Meredith whispered. "All that anxiety for nothing." He turned to look at her. Their eyes held for a moment, then he leaned over and kissed her. Neither of them was aware that one of the television cameras happened to find them in the audience, capturing that intimate moment between them.

Athens.

The Kirakis Corporation's world headquarters occupied a modern, twenty-story office complex in the exclusive Kolonaki section of Athens, within walking distance of the Bank of Greece. It had been a long time since Alexander had visited his father's offices. The last time had been the day he'd refused his father's offer of a high-level position within the global operation. He'd just received his M.B.A. from Harvard and was intent upon remaining in the United States. New York, he'd discovered, was the most exciting, electric city in the world—*his* kind of city. In spite of his father's objections, he had been determined to make his home there. Unfortunately, his father had never quite understood his need to be in control of his own world. Had he decided to remain in Greece, he would not have achieved the autonomy, the unquestioned power he now had in New York. Here, he would have been ''the boss's son.''

Now, as he stood outside the corporation's headquarters building on Leoforos Venizelou, across from Klafthomonos Square, Alexander decided the time had come to go home to New York. He'd been grateful for the past few weeks, grateful to have had the chance to renew his bond with his father, but suddenly he was eager to reenter the business world, the supercharged world of high-stakes negotiations and deals.

As he entered the building and crossed the lobby to the bank of elevators, the uniformed security guard recognized him immediately and rang for the express elevator that would take him to his father's offices on the twentieth floor. The guard held the door for him, nodding politely as he stepped inside. Alexander smiled but did not speak. As the door closed and the car began its ascent, he thought about the hours his father had been putting in the past week.

When he emerged from the elevator, his father's secretary, Elena Roumelis, spotted him immediately and jumped to her feet to greet him. ''*Kaliméra*, Mr. Kirakis,'' she said as he approached.

''*Kaliméra*, Elena,'' he responded. ''Is my father in his office?''

''Yes, he is—but I believe he is on the telephone right now,'' she said hesitantly. ''Is he expecting you?''

''No, he isn't,'' Alexander said, shaking his head. ''I thought perhaps I might be able to convince him to leave long enough to join me for lunch.''

''I doubt it—not today,'' Elena said quickly. ''This has been a most difficult morning. He received word that there was an explosion in one of the diamond mines in the Namib Desert just before dawn this morning. Several men were killed. He's in touch with the Cape Town offices now.''

''I see,'' Alexander said slowly. ''I don't think, under the circumstances, he would object if I went in anyway . . .''

''Oh, no—of course not,'' Elena agreed readily. ''Could I get you something? Coffee, perhaps—''

"Thank you, no," Alexander said with a smile. He turned and entered his father's office. Constantine Kirakis was at his desk, the telephone receiver cradled on his shoulder as he scribbled notes on a yellow legal pad. He looked up as Alexander entered the room, motioned to him to be seated, then turned his attentions back to the phone. Alexander took a seat and looked around. It had been a long time since he'd been in this office, the real seat of power within the corporation. He remembered when his mother had taken on the task of redecorating it. She'd personally selected the fabrics, the colors, and the furnishings with her husband's tastes and preferences in mind, from the antique desk that dominated the room to the chamois leather couch and matching chairs, from the inlaid lacquer cabinet to the Renaissance paintings on the walls. She'd supervised the design of Kirakis's private dressing room, which she considered a necessary convenience since they were living on the island at the time and he had had to travel so far to his offices on the mainland. She had insisted upon the cedar closets and lined drawers for his clothing and other personal items. She'd personally chosen the tiles used in his shower stall and ordered warming racks for his towels. Mother really *did* keep our lives organized, Alexander thought now.

Kirakis ended his call and put the receiver back on its cradle, then turned to Alexander. "All hell has broken loose in the Namib mines," he said wearily. "Fifty men are known to be dead and several others are still missing. I am going to have to fly down there."

"Would you like me to go in your place?" Alexander offered, knowing his father was not looking forward to this trip.

Kirakis shook his head. "I do appreciate the offer, but no, I will have to do this myself. But if you would like to go with me . . ." He paused, studying his son for a moment. "What brings you to Athens today? I thought you wanted to spend time alone."

"I've decided it's time for me to get back to New York, to my own responsibilities," Alexander told him. "I plan to leave within the next few days, so I won't be here when you return from Africa." He paused. "I came to see if you'd like to join me for lunch at Gerofinikas.'' The restaurant was nearby and had long been one of his father's favorites. "I see now that it's not likely.''

Kirakis frowned. "No, I am afraid not,'' he said wearily. "But perhaps tonight we could have a late supper at the Helleniki Leschi Club—have a few drinks, perhaps indulge in a bit of gambling. It has been a long time since we have done such things together. Unless, of course, you have other plans—''

"No, no other plans,'' Alexander said. "Would you like me to meet you here?''

"Yes. Seven-thirty,'' Kirakis told him. "I should be through by then.''

Alexander got to his feet as his father took yet another call from the offices in Cape Town. He let himself out of the office and left the building.

Alexander loved to walk. It helped him to relax. For as long as he could remember, he'd always hated crowds, hated closed-in places, though he'd never quite understood why. In New York, he often dismissed his driver and walked to his destination. There were times, when he felt particularly closed in, that he would take long walks on the streets of Manhattan late at night or in the early hours of dawn. In Paris, he liked to walk along the banks of the Seine at dusk. On the island, he walked at night in the game reserve or on the white beaches. He walked in any kind of weather, no matter where in the world he happened to be, especially when he felt the need to unwind. Now, as he walked down a busy street in Athens, he felt exhilarated, as though a great weight were being lifted from his shoulders. His mother's last wish that he and his father reconcile their differences had brought about a truce, and Alexander felt as though he had been set free.

He ended up at the Taverna Ta Nissia at the Hilton, meant to resemble the island tavernas, but Alexander thought with mild amusement that it would have to be a very fashionable island to feature such a swank taverna. The forty-foot-high ceiling was redwood, the floors marble, and the decor featured plenty of copperware. The persimmon table linens and turquoise china were impressive, and the menus came in hand-woven binders. He sat alone in one corner of the room, looking over the menu, but his mind was not really on food. So much had happened since he had arrived in Greece a few weeks earlier. So much had changed. He had lost a mother and regained a father. He no longer felt threatened by the ultimatum his father had delivered in New York. Marianne's ghost no longer haunted him.

"Alexander? Alexander Kirakis?"

Hearing his name, Alexander looked up. Frederick Cocyannis, a longtime friend and business associate of his father's, had just entered the restaurant. It had been many years since Alexander had seen Cocyannis, and he did not recognize the man at first glance. Cocyannis was older now, probably in his early fifties. His hair and mustache had gone completely white. In his youth, he had been a handsome man, Alexander remembered, and even now he was attractive in a distinguished, subdued way.

Alexander got to his feet and smiled. "Frederick—it's good to see you," he said as they shook hands. "It's been a long time."

"Too long." Cocyannis paused. "I was sorry to hear about your mother, Alexander. Irene and I were in Biarritz at the time—"

Alexander raised a hand to silence him. "It's all right, Frederick," he said. "There was nothing anyone could do."

Cocyannis nodded. "I have wanted to see your father, but"—he shrugged—"it is hard to know what to say at a time like this."

"Yes, it is," Alexander agreed. "Father's holding up well, under the circumstances. And how is Irene?"

"Well, very well indeed. In London at the moment. She is visiting Thione." Thione was Cocyannis's daughter. She and Alexander were close to the same age, and Cocyannis had never stopped hoping that his daughter would one day become Alexander's wife. Alexander was trying to think of a subtle way to change the subject, when a woman entered the restaurant and waved to them to join them. Cocyannis motioned to her to join them, and Alexander was both relieved and curious. Could the rumors be true? he wondered. Was Cocyannis having an affair? It certainly looked that way. This woman could not possibly be a business contact. As she approached, Alexander decided she was probably in her late thirties. She was tall and full-figured, dressed in a black Valentino dress that showed off her splendid figure. She was one of the most beautiful women Alexander had ever seen, with strong, perfect features and a thick mane of dark hair worn loosely about her shoulders. He knew that she was probably a call girl, a woman who made her living off satisfying the more unorthodox sexual desires of her wealthy clients. He knew that one of those clients was Frederick Cocyannis, something he would never have believed if he had not seen it with his own eyes, seen the knowing glances they exchanged. He also knew his father would be furious if he found out what he had in mind for this woman. None of that mattered to Alexander now as he stood looking at her, trying not to be too obvious. All that mattered was that he wanted her, and before the day was over, he intended to have her.

He looked at Cocyannis, who said nothing but smiled nervously, embarrassed at having been discovered. "Alexander, this is Anna Constantelos," he said finally. "Anna, Alexander Kirakis."

"I am very pleased to meet you," the woman said in a low, soft voice that could have been likened to the purring of a cat.

Alexander smiled appreciatively. "I assure you, the pleasure is all mine," he responded. Or it soon will be, he thought.

He tried to think of a way to speak with her alone, to tell her what was on his mind, when Cocyannis inadvertently provided him with the opportunity. "Anna, I must telephone my office," he said, checking his watch. "I am expecting a very important call from one of my people in London. If you will wait for me at our table, I will not be long."

"Of course, Frederick," she said pleasantly. "I am sure Alexander will not mind keeping me company until you return."

Cocyannis's eyes moved nervously from Anna to Alexander. "I will be right back," he promised.

"Take your time," Anna told him. "I will not leave."

After Cocyannis disappeared through the exit, Alexander

turned to Anna. "You're very sure of yourself, are you not?"

"No," she said simply. "I am sure of you."

He raised an eyebrow. "Oh? And why is that?"

She laughed. "You have been staring at me ever since I arrived. You try not to be obvious about it, but I know. Tell me, do you like what you see?"

"If I say yes, what will it cost me?"

She looked at him with mock disapproval in her eyes. "Did your mother never tell you it is impolite to ask a price in advance?"

"Perhaps—but my father has always told me of the importance of knowing in advance what I am buying and what it will cost."

"I should have guessed," she said with a throaty laugh.

"I want to see you."

"Where and when?"

"Your place, this afternoon, after you leave Frederick."

"Impossible. I have another appointment."

"Get rid of him. I'll be there at three."

She hesitated for a moment, then took the card he offered her and wrote her address on it. "Do not come before three," she warned. "Getting my—friend to leave will not be easy. I will need time."

Alexander smiled. "I'm sure you'll be able to handle it." He saw Cocyannis coming back into the restaurant. "Tell him I had to leave."

He walked out without a backward glance.

Anna Constantelos lived in a new high-rise apartment building on Patriachou Yoakim, within walking distance of Kolonaki Square. Alexander glanced at his watch as he entered the lobby. Two fifty-six. He wondered if she had gotten rid of her client yet as he rang for the elevator. He went up to the tenth floor and found her apartment. He rang the doorbell, and when she did not answer immediately, he rang again, impatiently. She finally opened the door and motioned him in, dressed in a red silk robe that left no doubt in Alexander's mind that she wore nothing underneath. "You are punctual," she observed. "Almost too punctual."

He looked at her.

"My friend," she explained as she walked barefoot across the room to the bar. "I am afraid he did not want to leave. You see, his wife is out of town for the next two weeks and he expected to spend most of his free time with me."

"His disappointment is of no concern to me," Alexander said indifferently.

"No. Of course not," Anna said with a smile. "He is very rich—head of one of the largest brokerage firms in all of Athens—but of course his wealth is nothing compared to your own."

"I take it you favor rich men."

"Of course," she said. "All of my lovers are rich. Only a very wealthy man could afford me."

"I see." He studied her speculatively. "So you're an expensive pleasure. Are you worth it?"

"My lovers all seem to think so," she said arrogantly. She held up a glass. "What will you have?"

"You," he answered without hesitation.

She poured herself an ouzo. "You are far too impatient," she told him. "You are sure you will not have a drink with me?"

He shook his head. "I did not come here to drink."

"Oh, I am quite sure of that," she said as she came forward, loosening his tie. "But you forget one thing. We have not yet settled upon a price."

"How much?" he asked tonelessly.

"That will depend upon what you expect of me," she replied, sipping her drink.

"I see." He took several large bills from his pocket and tossed them at her feet. "I think this will satisfy you."

She dropped to her knees on the carpet and collected the bills, counting them slowly. "This is a great deal of money," she said, looking up at him.

"I want to spend the night," he told her. "I'll have to leave for a while, but I'll return later."

She nodded slowly. "This is a great deal of money." She stood up and smoothed the front of her robe. "You're not interested in perversions, are you?"

"What if I am?"

Anna shrugged. "You get what you pay for, I suppose," she said. "But I am curious. Why would someone as attractive as yourself have to pay for it? It seems to me that you could have almost any woman you wished."

"I don't have to pay for it, as you so aptly put it," he said. "However, I am willing to make an exception in this case. I want you—and I'm accustomed to getting what I want."

"At least you are honest," she commented. "It will be a pleasant change, at any rate. My lovers are not often young and handsome."

He untied the sash on her robe and pulled it open. "Perhaps, then, I should make you pay me," he suggested as he reached for her.

She gave a throaty laugh. "No man is *that* attractive to me," she told him as his hands roamed over her flesh. His mouth came down on hers, hard and demanding as he squeezed her breasts. Her robe slipped off her shoulders and fell to the floor. She reached up and pulled his tie from around his neck. "Let's go into the bedroom," she whispered as she unbuckled his belt.

"Finish undressing me, Anna," he rasped as he pressed himself against her.

"In the bedroom."

"Here. Right now."

Obediently, Anna reached up and pushed his jacket off his shoulders and started unbuttoning his shirt. She ran her fingertips lightly across his chest and nuzzled his nipples, encircling each of them with her tongue. She unzipped his pants and found his organ already swollen hard. She began to stroke it as his excitement grew. "Let's go into the bedroom now," she whispered.

He held her face in his hands and kissed her roughly. Then he cupped her breasts in his hands and squeezed them hard. She pulled away from him abruptly and started for the bedroom. "*Now*, Alexander," she said hoarsely. "Take me now."

He shed the rest of his clothing hurriedly and followed her. The heavy drapes in her bedroom were drawn, and the room was in total darkness. He pushed her down on the bed and mounted her, entering her with such urgency that she cried out in pain. "Hey, lover, you like to play rough, don't you," she moaned as he thrust deep inside her. She began to writhe beneath him as he pounded himself into her with a force even he did not understand. He took her quickly, reaching an explosive climax, then rolled off her and lay motionless at her side, staring up at the ceiling. Anna turned over and stared at his face. She had the feeling that his desire for her was more complicated than the fulfillment of his physical needs. He was like a man possessed.

What, she wondered, did he really want from her?

At eight-thirty, Constantine Kirakis was still in his office, still waiting for Alexander. He was furious. Alexander knew how he hated to be kept waiting. He was supposed to be here an hour ago. Where the hell was he—or, more accurately, with whom? When Alexander, normally punctual to a fault, was late for an appointment or a social engagement, there was always a woman behind it. His son was like a sexual magnet, attracting women of all ages and types without making any real effort. Kirakis hoped Alexander would be wise enough to avoid the kind of scandal he had narrowly escaped with Marianne Hauptmann in Switzerland. Perhaps, Kirakis reflected now, it was fortunate that Alexander had never fallen in love. Alexander's passions were strong, often stronger than his common sense. He could easily lose his head over a woman if he ever did fall in love.

Kirakis stood at the windows, staring blankly at the Acropolis in the distance. As much as he would like to question Alexander about his whereabouts when he finally did deign to show up, he knew he could not. In the weeks since Melina's death, they had both made a monumental effort to bridge the gap that had divided them for so many years. Kirakis had promised not to interfere in Alexander's personal affairs, and for his part, Alexander had sworn he would avoid involvements that could result in a scandal such as Marianne's suicide. Kirakis knew that questioning Alexander now could mean a breach of that trust.

At that moment, the door opened and Alexander entered, carrying a large garment bag over one shoulder. "I'm sorry to have kept you waiting, Father," he apologized. "After I

left you this afternoon, I realized I would need suitable attire
for the Helleniki Leschi Club. Since I brought nothing with
me, it was necessary to visit some of the shops.'' He paused.
''I will need to take a quick shower, but I won't be long.''

Kirakis nodded. ''Go ahead,'' he said, his irritation at his
son quickly evaporating. ''I think, since it is so late, we
should plan to remain in Athens tonight.''

Alexander smiled. ''Exactly what I had in mind, Father,''
he said as he disappeared into the dressing room.

Constantine Kirakis left for Cape Town the next day.
Though Alexander accompanied him to the airport, he
decided against telling his father of his own last-minute
decision to postpone his return to New York. Kirakis would
have asked questions, questions Alexander was not yet ready
to answer. He could not have told his father that Anna
Constantelos was the reason he'd changed his mind about
leaving. He saw no reason to jeopardize their newly established closeness over a woman he'd just met, a woman with
whom he probably would not share anything more than a
passionate encounter that would end when he left Greece. At
this point, he was sure of only one thing: after having spent
the night with her, he was no longer eager to leave. Anna had
satisfied a need, filled a void in his life he had been able to
acknowledge only to himself.

Since his mother's death, Alexander had been consumed
by a deep, overwhelming loneliness. He had felt the need to
reach out to someone—anyone—for comfort. For him, sex
had been an emotional release valve, the only form of close
communication he'd ever been capable of achieving. Anna
Constantelos had entered his life at exactly the right moment
to take care of that need.

Alexander remained in Athens for another week, and most
of that time was spent in bed with Anna. Sex between them
was exciting and uninhibited and she allowed him to do as he
wished with her. It did not matter to Alexander that there
was no emotional involvement between them, that he had
paid her to have sex with him. He did not care about what
she was or what she might want from him. He cared only
about the pleasure she gave him in bed, the escape, however

temporary, from his loneliness. She had eased the pain of his loss, and he could never put a price on that.

As he lay in the darkness thinking about it, he realized he was not ready to give her up. Not yet. He was not willing to return to New York without her. He had no idea how long it would be before he no longer felt a need for her, but that did not matter. *Now* was all that mattered. He wanted to hold onto her for as long as it lasted.

By sunrise, he had come up with a solution.

The bright morning sunlight streaming through the bedroom windows cut a brilliant path across the shaggy blue carpet, which was strewn with Alexander's hastily discarded clothes. Anna's silk robe was in a heap next to the white-canopied bed. Alexander lay on his back, arms folded behind his head, staring ahead without really seeing anything. Beside him, Anna slept peacefully, the ice-blue satin sheets pulled up only as far as her waist, her dark hair spread out on the pillow like a great fan. Alexander turned over to look at her, lying on her back, her large breasts upthrust and firm, rising and falling gently. He reached out and touched one of her nipples, and almost instantly it hardened. He bent his head and took it into his mouth. As he began to suck at it, Anna opened her eyes and looked down at him. "Do you never get tired?" she asked.

He released her abruptly and looked up. "Ah, so you *are* awake," he said with a knowing smile.

"And who could sleep with you doing that?" she asked, promptly drawing the sheet up over her breasts.

His hand moved under the sheet, caressing her. "Tell me, Anna, do you plan to remain in Greece always?" he asked. "Or would you consider leaving if the opportunity presented itself?"

She propped herself up on one elbow and stroked his chest with her fingertips. "I have never been one to pass up an opportunity to better my circumstances. Are you making me an offer?"

"I'm thinking of taking you back to New York with me," he said as he pulled her to him. "Are you interested?"

"I might be," she said coyly. "Suppose you tell me

exactly what I would gain by going with you. After all, if I leave here, I will be giving up a great deal—this apartment, my many generous lovers—''

"You would become my mistress," he said as his hands began to explore her nakedness again. "You would have the use of a luxury apartment in Manhattan, a generous allowance, and gifts now and then."

"What kind of gifts?" she asked.

"Furs, jewels."

"And I would be living with you?"

He shook his head. "No. We would maintain separate residences. I'd come to you every day—sometimes in the afternoon, sometimes at night. We'd do the New York nightlife. You would have to be available to me whenever I want you, but when I'm out of town your time would be your own."

"And what about other men?" she asked. "I am accustomed to variety."

He shook his head. "Out of the question. There will be only me, but I'll be all you will be able to handle," he assured her.

She smiled. "It sounds good, almost too good to refuse," she admitted.

"Then I suggest you accept." Alexander pulled back the sheets, then rolled her over on her back and got on top of her, thinking that she had been exactly what he needed to take his mind off his grief over his mother. Though Anna had not yet given him her answer, he did not have the slightest doubt what it would be.

New York City, September 1980.

In his office at the Olympic Tower, Alexander was seated at his desk, reviewing reports he'd received that morning from his people in Singapore on the corporation's oil drilling operations there. The figures were good—no, they were excellent. The offshore tracts were now producing 875,000 barrels of crude daily. Translated into dollars and cents—he leaned forward and punched some buttons on the large calculator on his desk—the figures were impressive,

even by his standards. He smiled to himself. His father
would be pleased.

"Mr. Kirakis?"

His secretary's words cut through his thoughts. His head
jerked up abruptly. She stood in the doorway, a pen and
yellow legal pad in one hand. "Yes?" he asked.

"Your reservations at the Beverly Wilshire for the polo
match next week have been confirmed, and your horses
arrived in L.A. this morning," she told him. "Is there
anything else?"

He shook his head. "No, Stacey, thank you."

She left the office, closing the door behind her. Alexander
leaned back in his chair, tapping the eraser end of his pencil
on the desk in a steady rhythm without realizing it. Los
Angeles. Maybe he should give Meredith Courtney a call.
After all, they hadn't settled anything on that interview of
hers when she was in New York. He smiled to himself. It was
odd, the way she stuck in his mind. Even now, with a woman
as skilled as Anna to take care of his needs in bed, he hadn't
been able to get Meredith off his mind. Why?

On an impulse, he buzzed Stacey and told her to contact
Meredith at KXLA in Los Angeles. Ten minutes later, she
buzzed him on the intercom. "Miss Courtney on line two,
sir."

"Thank you, Stacey." He picked up the phone, punching
the lighted button on the console. "Meredith—how are
you?" he greeted her cheerfully.

"Busy," she responded. He could hear a rustling sound
on the other end. Papers. "Is this call social or professional?"

"Social."

"In that case, you'll have to make it brief," she told him.
"I'm really busy."

"Actually, it's both," he admitted, determined to hold
her attention. "I thought if you still want that interview, we
might be able to arrange a meeting. I'll be playing in a polo
match at the L.A. Equestrian Center next weekend—"

"Sorry, I don't cover sports," she said briskly.

"Do you want the damned interview or not?" he asked,
annoyed. "I don't get to the Coast very often these days."

There was a long pause on the other end. "Give me the specifics," she said finally. "I'll see you there."

"I don't know what you're so angry about." Meredith was curled up on the couch, a sheaf of papers lying on her lap. "It's just an interview. I've done hundreds of them."

"Not with Alexander Kirakis." Nick stood at the windows, staring absently out at the ocean.

"No one has done hundreds of interviews with Alexander Kirakis," she pointed out. "He almost never gives any —avoids the press as though we all have the Black Plague."

Nick turned to look at her, his face tight with anger. "Apparently, he doesn't think you're contaminated."

Meredith was annoyed with him for behaving like a jealous husband—and with herself for putting up with his tirade. "You're making a big deal out of nothing," she said angrily. Throwing her papers down on the couch, she got up and headed for the stairs. She had no intention of arguing with him. "I met Alexander Kirakis last summer when his father held a press conference here at the Beverly Wilshire, and—"

"And again in New York," Nick finished crossly.

She stopped in her tracks and turned to face him. "You knew about that?" she asked.

"I knew about it before you got back to L.A.," he said tightly. "Two of the studio people were at the Rainbow Room the night Kirakis was pawing you on the dance floor. When they got back here, they couldn't wait to tell me about it."

"Just hold it a damned minute!" Meredith snapped, infuriated by what he was insinuating. "He wasn't pawing me, as you put it. We were dancing—"

"And his hands were all over you," Nick finished, pouring himself a drink.

Meredith hesitated for a moment. "Why didn't you mention this before?"

"I was hoping you'd come home and tell me about it. I figured you'd tell me there was nothing to it and we'd have a good laugh over it, and that would be it."

"Well, there wasn't anything to it!" Meredith stormed up

the stairs and into the bedroom, slamming the door behind her.

The seconds ticked away on the huge scoreboard of the Los Angeles Equestrian Center. The spectators were on their feet, cheering a blistering charge toward the goal. Alexander Kirakis, riding a large chestnut gelding, led that charge, a lean, tanned figure in blue and white, the colors of the Kirakis team. Swinging his mallet forcefully, he struck the ball viciously as a player from the opposing team failed in an attempt to block him. The ball skimmed the ground, landing several yards ahead. Another long, cracking hit sent it to the goal. The spectators gave a round of thundering applause as the numbers on the scoreboard changed.

Meredith leaned against the railing, entranced by what was taking place in the arena even though she knew virtually nothing about the game. One did not have to be an expert, she decided, to be caught up in the electric excitement of what was happening. Nor did one have to be an authority to sense the power, the absolute control with which Alexander Kirakis dominated the play, the instinct and intelligence that enabled him to act with split-second grace at the cutting edge of danger. Elegance in action, she thought, intrigued.

"He could ride in on a jackass and turn out eight or nine goals," her cameraman commented, almost as if he'd read her mind. "The expert strategist, team player, and athlete —not to mention the fact that he happens to own some of the best ponies in the game today."

"Who?" Meredith asked, her eyes still on the field.

"Alexander Kirakis," Brian answered, making an adjustment on his equipment. "He has a ten-goal handicap and is considered one of the best players in modern polo. It's damned unusual when you consider that his game has to take a back seat to business."

"Why unusual?" Meredith asked, turning to look at him for the first time.

"Well, the world's top-ranked players—Gonzalo Pieres, Antonio Herrera, Howard Hipwood—they're all guys who devote themselves totally to the game. They eat, sleep, and breathe polo. Kirakis is at best a part-time athlete," Brian

explained. "But he's such a perfectly conditioned athlete
that he's been able to maintain his ten-goal status in spite of
his inability to play regularly."

Meredith smiled. "Where did you learn so much about
the game?" she asked.

"I played intercollegiate at Yale," he told her. "Used to
be pretty good, too—if I do say so myself."

A burst of wild applause signaled that the match was over.
Meredith instructed Brian to move in for a closeup shot as
Alexander Kirakis accepted the trophy. "Come on," she
told him as she turned on her heels and headed for the exit.
"I want to get comments from some of the players."

"Okay, boss lady." He followed cheerfully.

Positioning herself at that spot near the arena exit each
player would have to pass as he left the field, Meredith found
the men to be exhausted and eager to leave, but surprisingly
willing to discuss the match with her for the cameras.
Alexander Kirakis, the last to leave the field, turned his pony
over to one of his grooms as he reached the exit. Spotting
Meredith, he smiled appreciatively as he pulled off his
helmet. "Meredith Courtney," he said in that low, seduc-
tive voice as he walked toward her with the athletic ease and
sexual negligence of a born predator. "It's good to see you
again."

"Congratulations on your victory," she said, taking a
step forward, brushing his last comment aside as if it had no
particular meaning. "From where I sat, it certainly didn't
look like an easy one."

His smile was disarming. "None of them are ever easy,"
he assured her. "But it was the kind of game I enjoy
most—a genuine challenge. There's nothing quite as exciting as truly aggressive play between topflight competitors."

Mentally, Meredith recalled some of the comments some
of the other players had made about his style and game:
mercurial . . . calculating . . . lightning-fast . . . a single-
minded perfectionist. But she had the feeling that his
comments about enjoying a challenge, about finding aggressive play exciting, actually had nothing to do with polo. The
way he was looking at her, not bothering to conceal his
attraction to her, made her think of their last meeting in New

York. "I'd like to get a few comments from you—on camera," she said, her clear, crystalline voice not betraying the uneasiness she felt under his powerful gaze.

Alexander looked at the cameraman as though he were an inconvenience that had to be tolerated. Then he looked at Meredith again and nodded. She asked his views on the outcome of the match and his opinion of some of the other players, and he spoke easily, ignoring the camera that was on him all the while. When the camera stopped rolling, Brian gathered up his cables and wires. "I'll catch you back at the van," he told Meredith.

She nodded. "I'll be along in just a minute."

She started to walk away, but Alexander caught her arm. "I think we have some unfinished business, don't we?" he asked, smiling at the look of surprise on her face.

"The interview," she concluded, withdrawing her hand.

"Among other things."

"There is nothing else as far as I'm concerned," she said pointedly.

"Have dinner with me tonight."

She looked at him. "You never give up, do you?"

"Never," he replied promptly. "Give me the bottom line, Meredith. What's it going to be?"

She shook her head. "I can't."

He grinned. "So, the director is jealous," he concluded. "Does he always object to your meeting socially with prospective interviewees?" There was a twinge of amusement in his voice.

"No, of course not—when it's strictly business," she said. "But you and I both know you won't let it go at that."

He leaned nonchalantly against the wall, arms folded across his chest, studying her for a moment. "I'm many things to many people," he said, still smiling. "And not all of them are complimentary. But I'm honest about what I want. I make no secret of it."

Meredith glanced around, hoping no one who knew her or Nick had overheard their conversation. "You also don't take no for an answer," she said, her voice barely audible.

His black eyes glittered wickedly. "If you won't have dinner with me, then perhaps we could have a drink together

later and discuss the interview. I'm staying at the Beverly
Wilshire.''

"I told you before that I couldn't. Not tonight."

"Do you want to do this interview, Meredith?" he
pressed.

"I want the interview," she insisted. "But that's *all* I
want. If you're willing to accept that and still talk business
with me, I'll meet you tomorrow for lunch at La Bella
Fontana."

He shook his head. "I'm afraid that won't be possible,"
he said. "I'm leaving for New York in the morning. You
know, it's most unfortunate that we can't come to some sort
of agreement. Though you want only an interview, you see, I
want you."

She stared at him for a moment, surprised that even he
could be so blunt. "I'm sorry," she said evenly. Without
another word, she turned and walked away without looking
back.

As he watched her leave, Alexander was once again
confounded by the effect the woman had on him. He'd had
some of the most beautiful women in the world, women who
were not only willing, but eager to share his bed. He had
Anna waiting for him in New York—Anna, with her
superbly skilled hands and mouth and her intoxicating body;
Anna, whose erotic expertise satisfied even his most unorthodox desires. Yet all he could think about was Meredith
Courtney, slim, golden Meredith with her blue eyes and
sassy spirit, who seemed totally uninterested in him. Meredith, who wasn't even his type, wasn't dark and voluptuous
like his other women. Meredith, who fascinated him more
than anyone he'd ever known. What was it about her that
made her special, made him want her more each time he saw
her? Was it her firm refusal to surrender herself to him, or
was it something more, something about the woman herself
that attracted him as he'd never been attracted to anyone
before? He was tempted to postpone his return to New York,
to stay on in California and have lunch with her. It would be
a start, he thought. It would be worth giving her that damned
interview if it meant she would finally be his, even for one
night. But Alexander knew it was out of the question. His

father was flying in from Athens that night, and there was the board of directors meeting tomorrow afternoon. The last thing he needed now was to antagonize the old pirate, to miss a board meeting because he was trying to seduce a woman who'd consistently refused him. No, Meredith would have to wait. For now.

Next time, he thought as he disappeared into the crowd. Definitely next time.

NINE

༺༻༺༻༺༻༺༻༺༻

New York City, January 1981.

From the bedroom windows of her apartment on Central Park South, Anna watched the falling snow with disgust. It had snowed all night. Central Park was covered in a blanket of white, not yet violated by the pedestrian traffic that would soon invade its perimeters. To most people, she thought, it would be a beautiful sight. But to Anna Constantelos, who was neither sentimental nor romantic, it meant only that it was going to be another cold, miserable day for shopping. While finding a taxi on Fifth Avenue was normally difficult, on a day like this it would be virtually impossible. Damn Alexander, she thought bitterly. He could have given her the use of his limo—at least when he was going to be out of town. Though she'd complained about the situation on several occasions, he'd made it clear that it was out of the question. His driver, he pointed out, was on call around the clock, and he expected his car to be available on very short notice. Alexander had reminded her that she was already receiving a great deal from him: he'd given her the use of the apartment, which had been kept vacant in the past for the use of visiting corporation executives and business associates; he'd provided her with a generous allowance that enabled her to indulge her passion for beautiful clothes and other luxuries; he bought her jewelry and furs and took her to all the best places. In return, he expected her to take care of his sexual needs. Anna had learned early on that Alexander was most generous when she kept him satisfied in bed, but she was absolutely convinced that she had earned everything he gave her. In bed, Alexander was rough and demanding, and his sexual appetites were insatiable. When he took her, she still had the feeling that his passions were the result of rage, not desire. There was no real intimacy between them. Not that Anna wanted any—she was only in it for the money —but there were times when even she was unnerved by Alexander's behavior. He no longer bothered with prolonged foreplay. He simply satisfied himself and left her alone afterward. His lovemaking was quick and brutal, his body pounding into her with a force that made her feel she'd been subjected to a fierce beating. And the look in his eyes . . . he was like a man possessed. Never in the eight months she'd been his mistress had she ever questioned him about it. Anna knew her place with Alexander. As long as she kept him sexually satisfied, he would give her almost anything she asked for, and that was all that mattered.

Her main concern was to accumulate as much as possible as quickly as she could, squirreling away as much money as she could manage, insurance against the day when Alexander became bored with their arrangement and found someone else. Anna knew from past experience that this was inevitable. Sooner or later, the married ones always went home to their wives, and those who were unattached grew disenchanted and turned to marriage or another mistress. This did not bother Anna, for by the time it happened, she'd invariably managed to accumulate enough money and jewelry to live quite splendidly until the next man came along.

You have come a long way, she mused. A long way indeed from the illegitimate daughter of a shopgirl from the Plaka. A long way from the bastard child of a Nazi pig whose identity you will never know. . . .

"You have managed a takeover of Donovan Associates?" Even the sometimes poor quality of the transatlantic telephone connections had no drastic effect on the resonance of Constantine Kirakis's voice. "Excellent! I have no idea how you managed this, Alexander, but I am pleased. Extremely pleased.''

"I knew you would be, Father, which is why I wanted to be the one to tell you about it." Alexander was aware that ten years earlier Kirakis's own attempts to take over the same company had failed.

"I am glad you called, Alexander," Kirakis said. There was an ominous pause on the other end of the line. "There is something else I think we should discuss.''

"Business?"

"Personal.''

Alexander knew what was coming. His father had learned of his arrangement with Anna. "Father, I know what you're going—''

"Let me finish, Alexander," Kirakis cut in. "I know I have promised not to interfere in your personal affairs. I do not intend to tell you how to live your life or with whom to sleep. But I wonder if this is a wise move, this present relationship of yours.''

"You're talking about Anna Constantelos," Alexander said.

"You know, of course, what kind of woman she is.''

"I know all there is to know about Anna Constantelos," Alexander assured him.

"And you do not foresee problems with her?''

"Father, you disapproved of my brief affair with Marianne Hauptmann because you felt I had taken advantage of a vulnerable young woman," Alexander reminded him. "Anna is neither innocent nor vulnerable. She was a high-priced call girl when I met her in Athens. She has no illusions. She realizes that when I no longer have a need for her . . . her services, the arrangement will come to an end.''

"You must be careful, Alexander," Kirakis warned. "I think she would like to trade what every woman carries between her legs for the power that is your birthright.''

Alexander laughed. "Anna knows better than to try to use sex for bargaining purposes," he said. "Right from the beginning, I've made it quite clear that I make the rules. She knows what she will gain from our arrangement and what's out of the question.''

"And you think she can be trusted to live up to this arrangement?" Kirakis asked.

Alexander laughed aloud at the thought. "I would trust Anna no further than I can see her, Father," he responded without hesitation. "But she's a pragmatist. She knows I want only one thing from her. I make no promises I don't intend to keep. Anna's been through this before with other men. She's not going to kill herself when it's over."

"And if she chooses to create a scandal?"

"Anna is not going to cause a scandal," Alexander said confidently. "She prefers to keep a low profile for obvious reasons. Her past would not bear close scrutiny."

Kirakis paused. "Tell me, Alexander, do you think you will ever find the right woman and settle down?"

Alexander hesitated for a moment. "I found her over a year ago," he said slowly.

"You—" Kirakis stopped short. "She is married? Is that what you are saying?"

"No," Alexander answered quietly. "She's involved with someone. A serious relationship."

"You are sure of that?"

Alexander took a deep breath. "Father, I'd rather not discuss it," he said in a low, controlled voice. "I only called to tell you about the Donovan deal—"

"Ah, very well," Kirakis sighed. "I cannot help my concern for you, my son. You are all I have left now, and I want only for you to be happy."

"I know that, Father," Alexander said wearily. "I have to go now—I have another call." He didn't, but he wanted to end their conversation as quickly as possible.

"I will talk to you later in the week?"

"Definitely."

Alexander replaced the receiver slowly. His statement had surprised him even more than it had surprised his father. Until now, he hadn't given much thought to the nature of his attraction to Meredith. He desired her sexually, of course, just as he'd desired other women. But no, that wasn't exactly the case. It had been different, right from the beginning. As much as he wanted Meredith, he didn't feel a need to dominate her sexually. There was none of the unexplained rage he'd felt with Anna or Francesca—or, to a degree, with Marianne. None of the feelings that made him eventually lose interest in his other women, just as he was growing tired of Anna. There was a need, yes, but it was something he couldn't quite put his finger on.

He drummed his fingers on the edge of the desk in frustration. Why couldn't he get her off his mind? What was it that set her apart from the others? And why, when he was having sex with Anna, was it Meredith he was thinking of? What did he really feel for her?

Alexander stared thoughtfully at the photographs spread out on the desk in front of him, photographs of Anna with other men, either entering or leaving the apartment. These photos, he thought ruefully, confirmed his suspicions that Anna had not been living up to her end of their agreement. She had not been a faithful mistress. He looked up at the man seated across from him. "You know the identities of these men?" he asked.

The private investigator nodded. "I thought you might ask. I have a complete report for you right here," he said, producing a manila folder from his attaché case. "You'll see that I've included not only their names, but their occupations and background info as well. I've also noted the dates each of them was with her and for how long each time."

Alexander took the report and scanned it quickly, then turned to the investigator again. "I'm impressed," he said. "You do not misrepresent yourself. You've been meticulously thorough." He took an envelope from the drawer and passed it across the desk.

The man took it and opened it carefully. Inside were several large bills. "Cash?" he asked, surprised.

"I prefer to handle it this way, Mr. Hayes," Alexander said, not bothering to offer an explanation. He handed the investigator a typewritten document. "Sign this—to acknowledge receipt of the money."

Hayes nodded, then scribbled his name on the dotted line. "You want me to stay with it, Mr. Kirakis?" he asked, returning the signed paper.

Alexander shook his head. "That will not be necessary.

You've already provided me with all the information I will need—or want. But I'm sure if you prove to be as discreet as you are thorough, I'll be calling on you again in the future.''

"I assure you, Mr. Kirakis, I never discuss my clients," Hayes said as he got to his feet. "Not with anyone."

Alexander stood up and extended his hand. "Perhaps, then, we shall meet again," he said as they shook hands.

After Hayes had gone, Alexander turned his attention back to the report. This time he read it carefully, considering the contents. He was not at all surprised to find that the men Anna had been seeing were all connected in one way or another to the entertainment industry. So, he thought with mild amusement, she'd been serious about pursuing a show business career. How like Anna to try to capitalize on her natural assets to attain her goals. But, then, why shouldn't she? Had they not served her well in the past?

Oddly enough, Alexander was not angered, as he had expected to be, to learn that his mistress had been spending time with other men whenever he was out of town. Lately he'd found himself becoming increasingly dissatisfied with their relationship. At first, Anna had been able to satisfy his needs, and satisfy them quite well. Now, however, those needs had changed. *He* had changed. A strictly physical relationship with a woman was no longer enough. He'd begun to feel the need to care, to feel something more than sexual desire when he took a woman in his arms. He realized now it would not bother him if Anna were gone.

He thought about it for a moment, then leaned forward and flipped the switch on the intercom on his desk. His secretary came on immediately. "Yes, Mr. Kirakis?"

"Stacey, I'll be leaving shortly," he told her. "I plan to be out of the office for the rest of the afternoon."

"Would you like me to have your car brought around?" she wanted to know.

"No, thank you. I plan to walk."

"Yes, sir."

He put the photographs and the investigator's report in a large brown envelope, then went to the closet for his overcoat. He would not bother to call first. If for some reason Anna was not there when he arrived, he would wait for her. And if by some chance she was there and was not alone, he would still confront her.

It was time to put an end to this farce.

"You had a detective following me?" Anna looked at the photographs scattered across the bed, then turned back to Alexander, her eyes narrowed in anger. "Why?"

"That should be obvious, even to you, my dear Anna," he said coldly, his black eyes blazing with anger. "We had an arrangement, and you have not lived up to the terms of that arrangement."

"I have taken care of your desires, have I not? I have been available to you whenever you wanted me, have I not?" she demanded hotly, her features distorted with rage.

"I made myself quite clear when I brought you here, Anna," he reminded her. "I told you as long as I supported you, as long as I paid the bills, you were to see no one but me. I made it quite clear that I would not tolerate any indiscretions on your part. Didn't you take me seriously?"

She stared at him for a moment, her eyes dark with fury. "It makes no sense to me," she said finally. "It is obvious that I am nothing to you beyond a means to satisfy your physical demands. Why would you care if I see other men or not? Why would it make any difference as long as it never interfered with your plans?"

"It matters because I have been paying for exclusivity and I expect to get what I pay for," he said angrily. "These men are all connected with the theater and show business. I take it this is your way of breaking into that business yourself?"

"What if it is?" she demanded. "Do you intend to stand there and tell me you have not indulged in a bit of extracurricular activity while you are away on all of those business trips? Do you not think I have heard of the way you carried on over that newscaster at the polo match in California—"

He grabbed the front of her purple silk blouse and pulled her close. "I don't think you understand, Anna," he said in a menacing tone. "I don't care what you choose to believe. I don't think you really care what I do when I'm away, and it wouldn't make any difference if you did. It is I who am paying you, I who make the rules in this mockery of a relationship!''

"Let go of me!'' she hissed, her beautiful face a mask of fury.

"With pleasure!'' He released her abruptly and she stumbled backward, stunned. "You should be pleased to know that the investigator will no longer be following you. I no longer care whom you see or what you do with your time. I came here today only to tell you that I'm dissolving our so-called arrangement as of now.'' He collected the photos and papers and put them back in the envelope.

"You are not serious,'' she said incredulously.

"I have never been more serious in my life,'' he assured her. "I want you out of this apartment—and out of New York, if possible—immediately. You may take your clothing and other personal belongings. Nothing else. Just make sure you're out of here by tonight.''

"Tonight?'' She stared at him wide-eyed. "Impossible!''

"You'd damned well better make it possible, Anna, because if you're here when I return, I'll evict you myself,'' he warned.

"It is not enough time! I—'' She waved her arms in frustration.

"You should have thought of that when you took on your other clients,'' he snapped. "Just make certain you're out by seven this evening, or I will remove you bodily.'' He turned and headed for the door.

Anna ran after him. "You bastard!'' she screeched. "You cannot do this to me!''

He stopped in his tracks and turned to face her again. "You're wrong about that, Anna. I not only can, I will.''

"But on such short notice—where will I go?''

"That's your problem.'' He left the apartment, slamming the door with such force that one of the paintings fell from the wall.

"You are going to be very, very sorry you have done this to me, Alexander!'' Anna screamed after him as she picked up a crystal wine goblet and hurled it at the door. It smashed against the frame, falling to the carpet in a shower of tiny fragments as she shouted profanities in her native Greek.

As Alexander emerged from the elevator downstairs and

crossed the lobby to the glass doors facing Central Park South, his rage began to cool considerably. Anna had always brought out the worst in him, he realized as he headed east toward Fifth Avenue. Even now, he felt out of control. He'd wanted to lash out at her, to physically attack her for betraying him. Yet he was not sure why. Why did he feel betrayed? Why did it matter, one way or the other? He drew in a sharp breath. It had been a mistake from the beginning. At least he'd come to his senses and put an end to it. He'd taken the first step.

He walked down Fifth Avenue, oblivious of the crowds of shoppers in their bulky winter coats, armed with packages and large shopping bags, oblivious of the blasting winter wind that whipped through his hair and made his cheeks burn and flush with color. He'd left Anna in such a fury that he had not bothered to buckle the wide belt of his overcoat, and now it flapped about him furiously in the wind. Alexander didn't notice. Now that he'd ended his relationship with Anna, what he felt came as a complete surprise.

He felt as though he'd been set free.

TEN

~~~~~~~~~~~~

Los Angeles, May 1981.

Meredith climbed out of the KXLA mobile production van and dashed across the parking lot to the station entrance. She was exhausted. She'd spent a harrowing morning covering a bank robbery in Marina Del Rey, a tense three-hour drama during which a half-dozen bank employees and an equal number of customers were held at gunpoint by four men who'd threatened to kill their hostages if police did not comply with their demands.

In the KXLA News Center, the nerve-racking race to meet the five o'clock deadline had already begun. Meredith made her way through the chaotic jumble of the newsroom—a sea of desks covered with papers, dirty ashtrays, crumpled cigarette packs, and half-empty coffee cups—to the assignment desk. Ted Hammond, the director of news services, a portly man in his mid-fifties, sat behind the desk, surveying his domain. He smiled when he saw Meredith. "Back so soon?" he asked in a joking voice. "What happened? SWAT team show up too soon and ruin your day?"

"Very funny." She leaned on the desk as she spoke. "Just between you and me, I'm glad it's over. Besides, I have plenty of tape."

"Great! It's good to hear something's going right today." He leaned to one side as another newscaster came forward to check the board, an ever-changing menu of the items being tapped for the evening broadcast. "This has been one hell of a lousy day."

"What's the matter, Ted? Is this place getting to you—" She stopped short as she looked up and caught sight of something different on one of the large-scale maps on the wall behind the assignment desk. At the map's center was the KXLA building, and just above it, someone had tacked a small photo, probably clipped from a newspaper, of a B-51 bomber discharging its deadly cargo. Meredith laughed at the implication. "Who did *that*?" she wanted to know.

"I did," he answered with a sheepish grin. "I told you, it's been a rotten morning."

"Come on, Ted," she chided him. "We both know you wouldn't know what to do with yourself if we ever had a quiet day around here."

"Maybe," he conceded, "but I'd sure as hell like to give it a try."

"Meredith!"

They both turned. Chuck Willard stood outside his office, waving to her. "I need to see you—pronto!"

Meredith turned back to Hammond as Willard went back into the office. "I wonder what that's all about?"

Hammond grinned. "Maybe it's supposed to be a surprise."

Meredith made a wry face. "Pearl Harbor was supposed to be a surprise, Ted, and we all know how that turned out." She crossed the busy floor to Willard's office. "What's up, Chuck?" she asked as she entered.

"Close the door." He seated himself behind the desk.

She did as he instructed, then took a seat across from him. He took a network memo from the drawer. "It seems the network brass were quite impressed with the job you did in New York last spring," he said, leaning back in his chair.

"Not well enough to offer me Carla Granelli's job when she didn't renew her contract in January," Meredith pointed out. It had been her biggest professional disappointment to date.

"But they were impressed enough to make another offer," Willard said. "You're familiar with *World Focus,* aren't you?"

"Of course." It was the network's top-rated morning news and features show. There had been rumors flying for the past six months that the program's female cohost, Tiffany Gordon, would not be renewing her contract in July, but neither Tiffany nor the network had ever confirmed those rumors.

"Tiffany Gordon's not renewing," Willard said, as if reading her mind. "The producer, Harv Petersen, wants you to replace her. Interested?"

"What a question!" Meredith laughed. "I'm not only interested, I'll give you my resignation now if you like."

"You'd have to be in New York in time to start the first week in July," he told her. "Any problem with that?"

She shook her head. "I'd like to leave L.A. by June fifteenth," she said thoughtfully. "I'll need time to find an apartment and get settled. Is there any chance you could replace me here by then?"

"No," he said. "No problem on this end."

She smiled. "Then it's settled."

"I'll call New York and let them know you're accepting," Willard said then.

She raised a hand to stop him. "I'd like to call them myself, if you have no objection."

He shook his head. "Fine with me." He grinned. "You know, I figured you'd take it, but somehow I didn't think it was going to be so easy."

Meredith got up and opened the door. "Neither did I," she admitted. "But I suppose there was never really any doubt in my mind that I'd accept if an offer were made."

It *had* been easy, she thought as she negotiated the sharp turns on Route 1 en route to Malibu that night. Much easier than she'd expected. She had not had to think it over because there was nothing to think about. The network's offer was a wonderful opportunity for her. She'd worked hard for it and firmly believed it was well deserved. She had no reservations about accepting it. None whatsoever.

When she accepted, the one thing she had not taken into

consideration was how Nick might feel about it. His feelings had not even entered her mind when she'd told Chuck Willard she wanted *World Focus*. There once was a time when she might not have made a decision so important without at least discussing it with him first. But since she had returned from New York last year, nothing had been the same between them. She had tried, perhaps not as hard as she should have, she realized, but she'd tried to rekindle the flame between them. Nick had tried, too, but he'd never quite managed to convince her that he didn't resent her career, that he wouldn't have been happier if she'd given it up to be with him wherever his moviemaking took him. In that moment, as if struck by lightning, Meredith realized that things could never be the same for them again. Her fading passion, she told herself now, had begun during the past year, fueled by resentment on both sides. She was angry with him for trying to dominate her, for trying to hold her back professionally, and he resented her for not putting his needs above her own. He was so accustomed to his self-sacrificing mother who'd always put him first that he couldn't understand why she didn't do the same. Her stint in New York had been the turning point, the moment of truth for both of them.

"You've already accepted?" Nick stared at Meredith, dumbfounded. "How could you just give them an answer, just like that, without even discussing it with me?"

She met his gaze defiantly. "There was nothing to discuss!" she shot back at him. "If you were going to do a picture and it meant you'd have to be away on location several months to do it, would you discuss it with me first, or would you give the studio your answer before leaving the production meeting?"

"That's different," he countered. "You know that."

"I don't know anything of the kind!" she snapped. "That's the problem, Nick—I feel like I don't even know *you* anymore!"

"That door swings both ways, you know!" he exploded. "Didn't I tell you last year that if you went to New York for the network that everything would change for us? Didn't I tell you it was just a matter of time before they offered you something permanent? God, you haven't been the same since you got back! I've bent over backward to patch things up between us—''

"Sure you have!" Meredith raged. "You've done it all, haven't you? And I'm the villainess for not seeing the light and letting you control my life! I'm not your mother, Nick! I can't just put my life on hold to make you happy!"

"You've all but shut me out of your life," he responded. "Do you think I can't tell? Jesus, even when I make love to you, I get the feeling you're not really there—like your mind's on someone or something else!"

Meredith faced him squarely. "Did it ever occur to you that my lack of enthusiasm might be due to your attitude?" she asked defensively.

"No," he said coldly. "Did it ever occur to you?"

"I used to think we had something special," she said, biting off each word as if they left a dreadful taste in her mouth. "We had so much in common—we were so much alike. You knew what it was like to have to struggle. I really thought it had a chance of working!" Tears welled up in her eyes. "I wanted it to work!"

"Not enough, apparently!" Nick grabbed his coat and stalked across the room to the front door.

Meredith started after him. "Is that your solution to everything, Nick?" she demanded. "To run away from the problem?"

He didn't respond.

"Where are you going?"

He whirled around to face her. "Do you really give a damn?"

"Yes, of course I do!"

"Out—and don't bother to wait up for me. Not that you'd care enough to!" He stormed out the door, slamming it so hard the entire wall shook.

Meredith hugged herself tightly, tears streaming down her cheeks. Where did it all go wrong? she asked herself.

At three in the morning, Nick still had not returned. Meredith, bundled in a long, pine-green velour robe, was curled up on the couch in the darkness, hugging a large throw pillow. He was due to leave for Sri Lanka in a matter of hours. More location shooting. Surely he'd come home to pack first. But would she be here when he did?

Nick was right, though she hadn't been able to admit it at first. She *had* changed. She hadn't been the same since New York. She'd tasted a life-style there she'd yearned for all her life, and now she craved it. Her life with Nick had always been glamorous and exciting—she'd enjoyed the parties and premieres—but in New York it had been different. In Manhattan she had been in the spotlight, and she'd thoroughly enjoyed the attention. The recognition had been hers, not Nick's, and it had confirmed what she'd always felt deep inside: she was not a woman who could live in any man's shadow, no matter how much she loved him.

I do love you, Nick, she thought. No matter what had happened between them, no matter what had gone wrong, she would never forget how wonderful it had been in the beginning.

Until he tried to take away her dreams.

Meredith wasn't sure when she'd drifted off to sleep. She woke with a start, not knowing at first where she was. She looked down at the pillow in her arms and remembered. The house was dark and silent. Maybe he wouldn't come home at all this time, she thought dismally. She looked at the clock hanging over the fireplace. Five-thirty. She decided she might as well go to bed and get at least a couple more hours' sleep before she had to be at the station.

As she started up the stairs, she heard a sound coming from the master bedroom. She stopped to listen, her heart pounding. There it was again! Of course—Nick *had* come home. Was he still so angry he hadn't wanted to wake her? She went up the stairs and opened the door. The first thing she noticed were the suitcases. Nick was bent over the bureau, removing a stack of T-shirts. One suitcase was still lying open on the bed, only half packed.

"Were you just going to pack and go? Not even a good-bye?" she asked.

He didn't look at her. "I think we said all we have to say to each other last night," he replied coldly.

"So you won't even discuss it with me?"

"What's there to discuss?" He didn't bother to hide his

irritation. "I think you already have your mind made up. You had a decision to make and you made it, and you didn't see fit to talk it over with me first, so why talk now?"

"It's my career and my decision," she said firmly. "We could work it out if you'd just be reasonable."

"So now I'm unreasonable!" he said sharply, throwing the shirts into the open suitcase. He turned to face her for the first time. "Tell me, Meredith, what's there to work out? What's left, anyway?"

"We could still be together—"

"On weekends, I suppose?" There was open contempt in his voice. "The way I see it, we won't have any time together to speak of. You'll be in New York all week, and most weekends I'm filming, so what's the use?"

"You could come to New York. One of the women at IBS told me about an apartment I can sublet from someone she knows. It's ready for occupancy right now," Meredith told him. "And I could visit you on location—"

"We might as well stop trying to convince ourselves this has a ghost of a chance of working," he said tightly. "I love you, Meredith, but I don't want a part-time romance. I've had it with this business of loving someone and then they just walk out one day and don't come back!"

She stared at him as if he'd slapped her. She knew he was referring to his father's death, and knowing how he felt, she realized at that moment that if she stayed with him, it would probably always be this way. It would always be a wedge between them. She turned as he picked up his bags and started for the door. "You're leaving now?"

"No time like the present."

She drew herself up straight. "I won't be here when you get back."

He stopped in his tracks but did not face her. "Suit yourself," he said tonelessly.

Meredith didn't respond. She went to the top of the stairs and watched him go. Only when she heard the front door slam did she start to cry.

"Keep in touch." Kay stood in the doorway of Meredith's small office, looking on as Meredith packed her personal items into a cardboard box on her desk. "Drop in and see us whenever you're in the neighborhood, okay?"

"I will," Meredith promised. "And you'll come and see me whenever you get to New York?"

"Yeah, sure." Kay made a face, but it was clear she was trying not to cry. "As if I'm ever going to get to New York."

Meredith managed a slight smile. She was going to miss her old friend and confidante. "There's always your vacation," she pointed out.

"Yeah," Kay agreed, though unconvinced. "Maybe."

Meredith picked up the framed photograph of Nick she'd kept on her desk and stared at it. "I really should get rid of this," she said, finally putting it into the box.

"It's going to hurt—for a while, anyway," Kay said. "But take the word of someone who's been there: time really is a great healer."

"I never thought it would end like this," Meredith said softly, more to herself than to Kay.

"None of us ever do," Kay told her. "We all think our men will be with us forever—and that ex-husband of mine probably will, unless someone drives a stake through his miserable heart." She forced a smile. "But you—any woman who looks like you will find another man in no time at all."

Meredith shook her head. "No," she said thoughtfully. "Not for a very long time, anyway."

As she carried the last of her suitcases down the stairs and put them next to the bags already waiting at the door, Meredith paused and looked around the living room, wondering if she'd forgotten anything. The air freight company had picked up the things she was having shipped that morning. She'd sold her car and was leaving the one she'd rented at the airport. Her bank accounts had been closed and her address change filed. It's all been taken care of, she thought dismally. It's like dissolving a business partnership. All reduced to a question of what belongs to whom.

Crossing the room, she looked up at the painting of Elizabeth and David. She'd loved that painting from the moment she saw it at the Ryan estate. She wanted to take it with her but wasn't sure she should. Why shouldn't I? she asked herself. Nick did give it to me, so it is rightfully mine! Hesitating for only a moment, she reached up and took the painting off its hooks, then carried it over to the door. He wouldn't dare ask me to return it, she thought as she leaned it against the wall.

She rummaged through her shoulder bag until she found her keys. She carefully removed the house keys from the large gold ring and left them on the desk with an envelope addressed to Nick. My last good-bye, she thought.

In spite of the problems, in spite of the bitterness that had torn them apart, leaving this house—and Nick—was painful. She felt as though she were closing the door on one chapter of her life and opening the door on another, and she wasn't at all sure what it was going to hold for her. Now, as she looked around the room one last time, she wondered how breaking up with someone she felt she could no longer share her life with could hurt so much.

It's true, she thought. One lifetime has ended . . . and another is about to begin.

ELEVEN

𝔯𝔲𝔯𝔲𝔯𝔲𝔯𝔲𝔯𝔲

Athens, December 1981.

"How long do I have, Pericles?" Constantine Kirakis asked as he buttoned his shirt. "And do not try to spare me. It is imperative that I know the truth, especially now. There is much to be done, and if I have but a short time left—"

"Six months," Karamanlis answered gravely. "Six months at the most. Possibly less. Probably less."

"With all of my faculties?" Kirakis wanted to know. He eyed the doctor warily. "This is very important. You must be completely honest with me."

Karamanlis shook his head. "I cannot predict. Probably. There are no guarantees where cancer is concerned," he said truthfully. "You see, Constantine, when cancer cells begin to spread, they generally do so through the lymphatic system. They have the tendency to attack the vital organs first—heart, lungs, kidneys, brain—"

Kirakis frowned. "Then you are saying I may *not* be in control at the end?"

"I cannot make any guarantees," Karamanlis answered. "You may need chemotherapy or cobalt treatments."

Kirakis looked at him for a moment. "These treatments —they will buy me time?" he asked.

"A month or two, perhaps a bit more," the doctor said quietly. "The cancer is quite advanced. Had it been detected sooner—"

"There is no point in elaborating on what might have been," Kirakis said darkly. "It is clear to me that nothing can be done to stop what is happening or even slow it down. I must concentrate now on preparing Alexander to assume full control of the corporation."

"You *are* planning to tell Alexander of your condition . . ."

"I am not," Kirakis answered without hesitation. "And under no circumstances are *you* to tell him either. I will not have my son spending the final days of my life watching me as though he expects me to drop dead at any moment. I do not want him to feel that he must be with me every moment until the end. There will be other, more important things for Alexander to be doing with his time now."

"Do you not feel he has the right to know?" Karamanlis pursued.

Kirakis turned on him in anger. "The right to tell him—or not tell him—is mine, Pericles," he said irritably. "I wish to spare my son for as long as possible. Is that so wrong?"

"No," Karamanlis said. "But I think he will resent having been kept in the dark about such an important matter. He feels you keep too much from him now. If you were to tell him—"

"No," Kirakis said with finality.

As the Learjet began its approach to Kennedy Airport, Kirakis leaned back in his seat and closed his eyes. He massaged them with his fingertips, exhausted after his long flight. He had not felt up to traveling, but he had to have a talk with Alexander, and what he had to say had to be said face-to-face. He owed that to his son. He had to prepare Alexander for the task that lay ahead of him, and after weeks of deliberating, Kirakis had come to the conclusion that there was only one way to do it properly.

As soon as the jet landed, Kirakis was met by a harried airport official who explained that Alexander had arranged for him to have courtesy of the port. Kirakis idly wondered why his son had gone to the trouble. He had made so many trips to New York, especially in the past few years, and there had never been any need for it. Why now? he asked himself as they crossed the airfield. Then he saw them—a mob of reporters and photographers gathered on the other side of the high fence surrounding the field where the private aircraft usually landed. When they spotted him, they began to call out his name and flashbulbs popped.

"Mr. Kirakis, is it true . . ."

"Rumor has it you're planning to retire . . ."

"Will your son become the new chairman . . ."

"Does this have anything to do with your . . ."

"One more picture, please . . ."

Kirakis waved them off. "No comment," he responded curtly. How did this happen? he wondered. How had the rumors of his retirement reached the United States so quickly? He knew there were those within his offices in Athens who had become suspicious when he set the wheels in motion to transfer more and more power to Alexander, but he'd been sure he would have time to discuss his decision with his son before the press got hold of it. He wondered if Alexander had heard the rumors.

"I'm sorry about this, Mr. Kirakis," his escort said apologetically. "I have no idea how your arrival time leaked to the media."

Kirakis shook his head. "Who knows how they get their information? Reporters!" He snorted disapprovingly. "How much simpler my life would be without them!"

He was whisked through customs without delay and taken to another part of the airport where Alexander's limo waited near one of the exits. The driver opened the door for him as a porter piled his luggage into the trunk. As Kirakis ducked his head to climb into the car, he saw Alexander seated alone in the back. "Hello, Father," he said with a smile. "It's good to see you."

"Alexander—I did not expect you to come all the way to the airport to meet me," he said, not hiding his surprise. "You do not normally come when I am—" He wondered if Alexander knew why he was here. Could he have spoken to Karamanlis?

"I knew the press would be waiting for you. They're

rather like a school of piranha, aren't they?'' Alexander
commented with a wry smile. ''What have you done to gain
so much attention?''

''I? I have done nothing,'' Kirakis insisted. ''The international grapevine has done it all for me.''

''Rumors again,'' Alexander concluded.

His father nodded, lighting a cigarette.

''What brings you to New York, Father?'' Alexander
asked.

Kirakis looked at him. ''Must I always have a reason to
visit my only son?''

''No,'' Alexander replied, ''but since you normally do, I
thought I'd ask.''

He hesitated for a moment, then nodded. ''You are
right,'' he said. ''I do have a reason for this visit, a very
important one. I am about to make an announcement to the
press, but I thought I should tell you—in person—first.''

Alexander's expression changed from mild amusement to
concern. ''It sounds ominous,'' he said as he looked at his
father questioningly.

''Ominous? Perhaps.'' Kirakis looked at him. ''I am
about to officially announce my retirement—and that you
will succeed me within the corporation.'' He waited for
Alexander's reaction.

Alexander stared at him in disbelief. ''You're joking, of
course—'' But then he realized that his father did not make
jokes. Not about anything as important as this. ''When did
you decide this?'' he asked carefully.

''It is something I have been thinking about ever since
your mother died,'' Kirakis lied. Nothing could have been
farther from the truth. His work had become the most
important thing in his life since his wife's death—next to his
son, of course. It had kept him going. ''I reached a decision
only a few days ago. I have prepared a formal announcement
for the stockholders, as well as a press release.''

''Are you sure this is what you want to do?'' Alexander
asked dubiously.

Kirakis nodded. ''It is. But I thought you would be
pleased. Becoming chairman of the board is something I
know you have always wanted.''

''It is,'' Alexander admitted, ''but I cannot help thinking

that perhaps there is more to this decision of yours than meets the eye, something you are not telling me.'' He turned to look at his father again, searching the older man's face for answers to his unspoken questions.

''You imagine things,'' Kirakis growled.

Alexander studied him for a moment. Something about his father seemed different. He couldn't put his finger on it, but he sensed the change. There had never been any doubt in Alexander's mind that his father would continue to run the corporation from his fiefdom in Athens until the day he died or became too senile or feeble to go on. The thought of his father retiring was like trying to imagine the abdication of a king who'd ruled for an eternity. What could have happened to make his father decide to retire while he was still active and apparently in good health?

The retirement of Constantine Kirakis created shock waves throughout the entire world of international business. It made headlines in the *Wall Street Journal, Fortune, Forbes,* and other business periodicals. One publication announced it with banner headlines: ''Shakeup at Kirakis?'' But once the furor died down, it was Alexander who emerged as a new kind of media celebrity. His photos appeared in the same periodicals that had announced his father's retirement, proclaiming him the new chairman of the board of the Kirakis Corporation. The heir apparent of Constantine Kirakis, already a familiar face in the gossip pages, had emerged with a new image. One reporter made reference to the Kirakis Corporation as ''Alexander's empire,'' and the handle stuck. Before long, everyone from the financial reporters to the gossip columnists to the man on the street was making reference to ''Alexander's empire.''

Constantine Kirakis, in spite of the circumstances surrounding his sudden retirement, found himself taking greater pride in his son's headline-making ventures than he ever had in his own achievements. It was a relief to him to have positive publicity surrounding his son for a change. Alexander had moved in, taking control of the corporation as though he'd been born to it, which indeed he had.

Alexander's first major action as the new chairman was a formal announcement to the corporation's board of directors

—and to the press—that the corporation would be relocating its world headquarters to New York City, predicting that this would trigger a phenomenal growth within the corporation that would surpass anything preceding it. Kirakis had not been surprised by Alexander's move. He'd known it would be only a matter of time before the headquarters were relocated. Kirakis hoped, for Alexander's sake as well as the corporation's, that his instincts were correct.

In the next three months, Alexander was busier than he had ever been. He put in long hours, often from six in the morning until two or three the next morning. He read contracts and other legal documents. He reviewed reports concerning potential business deals. He always discussed them with his father at length, and even Kirakis himself was amazed at the depth of Alexander's knowledge and understanding of the intricacies of international business. He is ready, Kirakis thought with pride as he sat in on Alexander's first meeting with the board of directors. He is more than ready.

During those three months, Alexander and his father managed to spend a great deal of time together in spite of Alexander's hectic schedule, often in Alexander's study, late at night. After he read contracts and reports until he was bleary-eyed, he leaned back in his high-backed chair and listened as his father reminisced about his childhood in Piraeus and his early struggles to start—and later save—the often floundering Athena Maritime, the flagship company of the Kirakis empire. Alexander had heard all of the stories before, but he enjoyed hearing them again. It brought back memories of another time, of his own childhood in Greece, a time when he and his father were close, before the conflicts that had driven them apart. In the two years since Melina's death, they had both made a concerted effort to renew that closeness, but now something was definitely different. Alexander could feel it, but he was unable to identify it. It was as if his father had arrived in New York with a mission in mind. After his retirement had been announced, he'd made no mention of returning to Greece. Alexander could not remember a time when he'd stayed away so long, and he could not help wondering what could possibly be on his father's mind.

In late March, Alexander leased offices in the World Trade Center that would become the Kirakis Corporation's new world headquarters. *People* magazine did a cover story that included photographs of him supervising the remodeling of those new suites, walking on the streets of Manhattan, and launching one of Athena Maritime's supertankers in Great Britain. The cover line, emblazoned across the bottom of a flattering photograph of Alexander, read: "Alexander's Empire: A Contemporary Conqueror Aims High." Alexander hated the article and had resented the intrusion upon his privacy, but his father was pleased with its positive tone. It was going to be good for Alexander's public image, he maintained, adding that he definitely felt his son's image needed a radical change. Though the collective attitude of the media and the international business community had changed toward him considerably since he became the new chairman of Kirakis, his father felt he still had a long way to go before he would completely overcome his playboy image. "Use the media to your advantage, Alexander," Kirakis advised. "You need them now. Cooperate with them. Change the way the world sees you." Alexander had finally realized that his father had been right all along. The playboy image *had* created problems for him, both professionally and personally.

It was time for a change.

Constantine Kirakis stood near the floor-to-ceiling windows in Alexander's study, staring thoughtfully at the gray, gloomy March sky. He was recalling how, as a youth, he had stood on the docks in Piraeus, watching the changing weather conditions, hoping to predict a tempest before it actually hit the mainland. When one worked on the ships, he remembered now, it was important to know in advance of turbulent weather conditions. He rubbed his eyes, feeling the strain. He realized that he was spending a great deal of time living in the past. Was it because his time on earth grew short? He often found himself thinking about people and events he hadn't thought of in years: men he'd worked with on the docks during his stevedore days; the run-down shacks he'd lived in, stealing from local merchants as a child because he was hungry; the middle-aged hooker with whom he'd had his first sexual experience at the age of fourteen. It is true, he thought now. One's life does pass before one's eyes before the moment of death.

Everyone, including Alexander, thought he had come to New York to announce his retirement and help his son during the transition of power. But his main purpose in coming here had been to spend as much time as possible with Alexander in the little time he had left. They'd been apart for so many years that he felt the need, now more than ever, to make it up to his son. How could he ever make Alexander understand why he had been so against his decision to remain in the U.S., to live in New York and take charge of the corporation's North American offices? How could he ever tell his son he'd been afraid that the longer Alexander stayed here, the greater the risk that he might find out what kind of man his father really was? How could he ever tell Alexander about the real man behind the legend? How could he allow him to find out just how far his father had been willing to go to ensure the future of the Kirakis empire? Alexander was a tough, hard-nosed businessman: he knew it was sometimes necessary to step on a few toes, pull a few punches, just to attain an objective. But even Alexander, ambitious as he was, would not understand what he'd done. How could he? How could his son ever forgive the sins of a lifetime? How could he be expected to forget the pain and anguish he'd had to suffer for so many years—no matter what the reason?

Kirakis thought of Melina, of the promise he'd made to her just before her death. A promise that, in the years that had passed since, he had not been able to fulfill. It was the first time he had not kept a promise to her. He could still hear her words echoing through his mind: You must make peace with Alexander. Put an end to the lies, the secrets. Make peace at last—with Alexander and with yourself. He knew, even then, that she had been right, but did he have the courage to do what he knew had to be done? Forgive me, *matia mou*, he thought, if for the first time in all our years together I have made a promise I am unable to keep.

He was gripped by an intense pain in his upper right abdomen, yet another sign that his time was running out. Two weeks ago, after a long transatlantic telephone conversation with Pericles Karamanlis, he had consulted Dr. Eric

Langley, a leading oncologist on the staff of Memorial Hospital. Langley had ordered several tests on an outpatient basis: a liver scan, a bone scan, endless blood tests, and X-rays. The news had been bad. What Karamanlis believed to be a primary lung cancer had spread to his liver and spine. Langley had discontinued the chemotherapy begun by Karamanlis in Greece and prescribed painkillers, explaining that to continue therapy now would be pointless. It was too late, he told Kirakis bluntly, to do anything about the deadly cells spreading now like a forest fire out of control throughout his body. A primary lung cancer would not respond to chemotherapy, no matter what. Langley advised Kirakis to check into the hospital, but Kirakis had flatly refused. Not yet. He had to tell Alexander first.

Kirakis began to cough, that same violent, uncontrollable cough that had plagued him for months now. Alexander had expressed concern about it when he first came to New York, but he'd insisted it was nothing serious, just the result of heavy smoking for too many years. It wasn't far from the truth. He'd started smoking at the age of nine, and Karamanlis was convinced it had definitely contributed to the cancer now spreading through his system. He continued to cough, unable to stop. He was finding it difficult to breathe. There was blood on his handkerchief. He lowered himself into a chair near Alexander's desk, gasping for air. When the coughing finally subsided, he rang for Alexander's valet, who came immediately. "Martin, I need you to summon an ambulance for me," he said in a raspy voice. "I will be going to Memorial Hospital." He took a card from his pocket and gave it to the valet. "Call this man, Dr. Langley, and tell him to meet me there."

"Sir, if you—" Martin began, confused.

"Please, Martin, there is no time!" Kirakis gasped, now fighting to breathe. "You must get the ambulance—quickly. And phone my son—tell him where I have gone." He gestured toward the phone on the desk.

"Yes, sir." Martin picked up the phone and dialed hurriedly.

Time is running out, Kirakis thought. More quickly than I had anticipated.

Alexander arrived at Memorial Hospital shortly after his

father was admitted. He was intercepted outside Kirakis's room by Dr. Langley, who ushered him into a nearby lounge and closed the door to indicate he did not wish to be disturbed. "I think we should talk before you see your father," the doctor said. "He tells me you have not been aware of his condition up until now."

"That's in the nature of an understatement," Alexander responded tightly. "What, exactly, is his condition?"

"For the hospital records, he's listed as having malignancies of the lung and spine, hepatic carcinoma and insufficiency, pulmonary edema, and pneumonia," Langley answered. "In layman's terms, cancers of the lung, spine, liver, and possibly other sites. Fluid has accumulated around his heart, and a sampling of that fluid indicates the presence of malignant cells. His liver has failed—there are signs of jaundice. The pneumonia resulted from the weakness in the pulmonary system. I've ordered antibiotics and steam aerosol."

"How long has he been . . . like this?" Alexander asked carefully, staring down at the floor.

"I'd say it's something that's been spreading throughout his body for some time now—a year, perhaps even longer."

Alexander looked up in surprise. "He's known about it for over a year?"

"No," the doctor said quickly. "I said the condition had probably existed for at least a year. He's actually known about it for three, maybe four months. It was discovered by his doctor in Greece, who referred him to me when he decided to remain in New York."

"Karamanlis," Alexander said slowly, anger in his voice.

"Yes." Langley paused. "By the time your father sought medical help and the cancer was detected, it had already spread from his lungs to other organs. There was nothing anyone could do. It was already too late."

Alexander nodded, clasping his hands together. "How long—" He couldn't finish.

"Not very long," Langley said honestly. "He's very weak. He'll have to remain in the hospital, of course, where we can take care of him properly. We'll have to watch him closely, in case fluid builds up around his heart again. He'll have to stay on the respirator, since right now he can't breathe on his own. I suspect he'll be here until he—'' He shrugged.

"I understand," Alexander assured him. "However, I don't think my father will want to remain here. He'll want to go home—to Greece—to die."

Langley shook his head. "It's out of the question," he said without hesitation. "Even by air, he couldn't survive such a long journey. I couldn't, in all good conscience, approve of such a trip—or even release him from the hospital."

Alexander was thoughtful for a moment. "I'll try to dissuade him," he said finally, "but I can promise nothing. My father can be a very stubborn man."

"I know," Langley said with a tired smile.

"I'd like to see him now," Alexander said, getting to his feet.

Langley nodded. "He's been asking for you," he said as he stood up. "But don't stay too long. He's been sedated."

Alexander looked down at the floor, trying to compose himself. The doctor left him at the door. Alexander entered the room and walked over to the bed. His father's eyes were closed. There were tubes in his nose and i.v. needles in his arms. The steady beeping sound of the cardiac monitor was reassuring. Alexander leaned forward and touched his chest lightly. His breathing was labored. "Father," Alexander said in a low voice.

Kirakis opened his eyes slowly. "Alexander," he said hoarsely. "I am glad you are here . . ."

"Why did you not tell me, Father? Why do you always keep things from me?"

"I wanted to spare you," he said, his voice faltering. "I did not want you to waste your energies worrying about me. There was nothing you could have done, and there is so much you must do now, so much that it is so very important to your future . . ."

"This is why you suddenly decided to retire, yes?" Alexander asked, searching his father's face for answers.

"I knew there was not much time left." Kirakis's voice was barely audible now. "I wanted more than anything to spend that time with you, to make up for the time we have lost in the past few years, to help you prepare for your new role as board chairman . . .'' He began to cough, gasping for air.

"Father," Alexander said in a trembling voice. "I've waited far too long to say this, I know . . . but I love you."

For the next two weeks, Alexander spent hours at a time at his father's bedside, sometimes just sitting with him, sometimes talking with him. Kirakis went through alternating periods of unresponsiveness, drug-induced twilight, and mental alertness. There were times when he was able to sit up and even carry on a conversation with his son. He was pale and drawn and had lost far too much weight for his large frame, but Alexander still found it difficult to believe he could really be dying. His father had always seemed somehow immortal to him. Even after his mother's death, when Alexander realized just how human his parents really were, he could not imagine his father—that living legend, that giant among men—meeting the same fate.

One night, when he was more alert than usual, Kirakis had insisted he and Alexander have a talk. "You know, Alexi, I think I would not be so concerned about dying if I knew you were not going to be alone," he told his son. His eyes met Alexander's, his gaze questioning.

Alexander shook his head. "I haven't been as fortunate as you and Mother," he said quietly.

"A good marriage and children, Alexander—they are every bit as important as power. More so," Kirakis told him. "Even I have never doubted that." There was an urgency in his voice Alexander did not understand.

"I don't doubt it, Father," said Alexander. "I do doubt, however, that I'm cut out to be a proper husband."

"Perhaps you have not given yourself a chance," Kirakis suggested. "I could leave this world without regret if I knew that you had someone you really cared for. Your mother . . . she always worried about you." He took his son's hand and squeezed it tightly.

"She worried about both of us, Father," Alexander said, his eyes moist with tears.

Kirakis nodded. "Before she died, she made me promise that things would change between us."

"They have, have they not?"

Kirakis coughed. "She wanted to go to her grave with a clear conscience, as I hope to myself," he gasped. "She begged me to put an end to all the lies, the secrets—" He was coughing violently now, struggling to get air. "She wanted me to tell you—" He began to choke, unable to go on.

"Don't try to talk, Father," Alexander said as he rang for the nurse. "Lie back. Try to relax."

The nurse came immediately. She administered a sedative and reinstated the respirator, which had been shut off when Kirakis had no need of it. She ordered Alexander out of the room and began checking Kirakis's vital signs. From the corridor, Alexander watched as another nurse and a doctor rushed into the room, surrounding the bed. They spoke in hushed tones, and Alexander was unable to hear what they were saying. He moved closer to the door, but it did no good. An icy fear grew inside him.

Dr. Langley arrived a short time later and was in the room for almost fifteen minutes, then came out into the corridor to talk with Alexander. "The cancer is obstructing the bronchial tubes, blocking off his breathing." He paused. "He also has fluid around his heart and lungs again."

"He doesn't have much time left, does he?" Alexander said softly.

Langley shook his head. "I'm afraid not."

Alexander went back into the room as soon as they would let him. He sat at his father's side, hoping against hope for an eleventh-hour miracle, but in his heart he knew that this was the end. He thought about the conversation they'd been having before. His father had wanted to tell him something. What was it? He thought back, recalling the talk he'd had with his mother before she died. She'd also been trying to tell him something, but her words had made no more sense to him than his father's did now. His father talked about the past, about putting an end to the lies and secrets. What secrets? What lies? Alexander asked himself.

Shortly after midnight, Constantine Kirakis drifted into a coma. Alexander remained at his side all night and most of the next day. In that time, his father never regained consciousness, even for a moment. As Alexander kept his silent vigil, he thought about all his father had been through in the past few months, living with his illness and his impending death, trying to carry that burden alone, trying to prepare Alexander for his new role as board chairman. Alexander was grateful for the reconciliation that had occurred between them. He'd realized just how much his father did care about him.

At four in the afternoon, Dr. Langley looked in on Kirakis for the third time that day. He was about to leave the hospital and advised Alexander to do the same. "You need to get away from here for a while," he urged. "It's going to happen, but I doubt it'll happen tonight. Go home. Go out to dinner. Anything. Just don't stay here."

Reluctantly, Alexander left. He called for his car and returned to his apartment. Once there, he retreated to the quiet solitude of his study. His valet brought him a tray, but he found he was unable to even look at food. There was a backlog of paper work piled up on his desk, but he knew he would not be able to concentrate. He sat on one corner of the desk, staring out at the sky until the gray, overcast gloom turned to darkness. He could not remember ever feeling so painfully alone. He wished there were someone he could turn to now who could ease his pain. He'd always believed he was destined to be a loner all his life, but now he realized how much he would hate spending the rest of his life alone. He needed to care, to have someone care about him. He looked up at the portrait on the wall—the portrait commemorating his parents' fiftieth wedding anniversary—and he was filled with sadness.

He had no idea how long he had been sitting in the darkness when the phone rang. He ignored it at first, expecting his valet or housekeeper to answer it. When it continued to ring, he snatched it up irritably. "Hello?"

A woman's voice on the other end asked, "May I speak to Mr. Kirakis, please?"

"Speaking," he said, annoyed.

"Mr. Kirakis, this is Mrs. Hanover at Memorial Hospital." She hesitated for a moment. "Your father passed away at eleven fifty-six this evening."

Alexander switched on the desk lamp and looked at his watch. It was 12:03.

"Mr. Kirakis?" she asked.

"I'll be right there," he said quietly.

He replaced the receiver slowly and looked up at the portrait again. His father was dead. When his mother died, she had been worried about who would take care of him after she was gone.

Now she could do it herself.

TWELVE

᠍᠍ᘓᘓᘓᘓᘓᘓᘓᘓᘓᘓ

Alexander had hoped to keep the news of his father's death out of the media until he'd made all the necessary arrangements to return the body to Greece for burial. He wanted to be left alone, to be able to go through the rituals of death in peace. Though he knew there were at least a dozen people on his staff who could be trusted to take care of these things for him, he felt he had to do it all himself. He owed it to his father.

Unfortunately, word leaked to the press immediately. Reporters mobbed him outside Memorial Hospital. They stalked him for the next three days as he went through the painful process of selecting the coffin and taking care of arrangements to have his father's body taken to the airport. They waited for him outside the Olympic Tower. They followed him to Kennedy Airport on a bleak, cold Friday morning as he prepared to leave for Athens. They photographed the coffin as it was loaded onto the corporate jet while Alexander scowled at them, unable to conceal his rage. He refused to comment when approached. If he had resented the press before, he loathed them now. Did they not have the common decency to leave him alone with his grief? he thought angrily as he boarded the jet. Did they have to turn his father's final return to Greece into a media side-show? Was nothing—not even death—sacred to them?

As the jet taxied down the runway and began to climb into the overcast sky, Alexander put his seat into a reclining position and closed his eyes. He was exhausted. For the past four days he had willed himself to keep going, to work as quickly as possible to put everything in order at his office and make arrangements to take his father home to the island. He knew he would not be able to continue that pace much longer. He was near collapse. Now that they were finally on their way, he found himself surrendering to the needs of his body and his mind. As he drifted off, he wondered if there would be a scene at the airport in Athens. He was not sure he could face the press again without losing control.

Constantine Kirakis was buried on the island, next to Melina and Damian. Alexander elected not to attend the memorial service held at the Greek Orthodox church in Athens, a final tribute arranged by his father's friends and business associ-ates, nor did he permit any of them to come to the island for the burial. He made it clear to all concerned that the island was *his* domain now, and he wanted to be left alone there. He received no visitors and accepted no phone calls in the week following the funeral. Even the household staff saw little of him. He was up before dawn every morning and seldom ate breakfast. He left the villa without telling anyone where he was going or when he expected to return. He spent hours walking on the beach or in the game reserve. Other times he went horseback riding or drove around the island in one of his father's Jeeps. He was restless and had difficulty sleeping. Helena expressed concern for his health, but Alexander insisted he was all right. "I've a great deal on my mind, that's all," he told her.

It was the truth. He hadn't wanted to stay on in Greece after his father's burial, but he knew it was necessary. There was much to be done. The following week his father's will would be read at the offices of his attorneys in Athens. After that, there would be documents to sign, decisions to be made. It would not have been practical to go back to New York immediately after the burial, only to have to return to Greece in less than two weeks.

One day he returned from an afternoon of riding to find Pericles Karamanlis waiting for him in the library. "What are you doing here?" Alexander asked coldly, tossing his riding crop down on the desk and pulling off his gloves. "I thought I made it clear I did not wish to see anyone right now."

"I have been concerned about you," the doctor said quietly. "I wanted to see for myself that you are all right."

"How touching. Now that you can see that I'm quite all right, you may go." There was undisguised contempt in Alexander's voice. "Tell me, Doctor, are you so conscientious where all of your patients are concerned?"

Karamanlis looked at him. "I have never thought of you as just a patient, Alexander," he replied. "I think you know that. Your parents were my very close friends for many years."

Alexander turned on him in anger, unable to hold it back any longer. "Why didn't you tell me my father was dying, Doctor?" he demanded.

Karamanlis drew in his breath. "Because he forbade me to tell anyone," he answered. "Especially you."

"You should have come to me, no matter what he said," Alexander insisted. "You should have told me what he was going through!" The rage in his face, in his voice was unmistakable.

"You know better than that, Alexander," Karamanlis said sternly. "It would have been a blatant violation of the doctor-patient relationship."

"Don't give me that sanctimonious bullshit about medical ethics!" Alexander snapped. "I have no interest in the sacred vows—"

"Perhaps not, but as a physician I was bound by those ethics," Karamanlis told him. "Your father made it clear he did not want you to know—did not want *anyone* to know."

"I had the right," Alexander said stubbornly. "I'm his son—the only family he had left!"

"I urged him to tell you," the doctor said, trying to defend himself. "I told him it was wrong to keep it from you, that he had already kept too much from you—" He stopped short.

Alexander's black eyes narrowed suspiciously. "Before he died—when I was with him at the hospital in New York —Father said something to that effect. He said the time had come to put an end to the secrets and the lies. *You* know what he meant by that, don't you?" He took a step forward.

Karamanlis was visibly nervous. "No, only that he always felt he could spare you unnecessary concern by keeping certain things from you, things like his illness," he said in a faltering voice. "He was the same way about your mother —always trying to protect her, or so he thought. Melina knew him well . . . she was not often fooled . . ."

"I think you're lying," Alexander said in a menacing tone. "I think you know more than you're telling me."

"Absurd!" There was anger in the doctor's voice now, but an unmistakable uneasiness in his manner as well. "You knew him as well as anyone could know Constantine Kirakis. You, of all people, should know that he never confided in anyone."

Alexander turned away from him abruptly. "This is all quite pointless," he said finally. "I don't believe you. You will not tell me what I wish to know. You have wasted your time—and mine—by coming here. I would like you to leave now."

"I—" Karamanlis stopped short, realizing it was no use. He turned to go, then paused at the door. He opened his mouth to say something, then changed his mind, turned, and left the room.

Alexander slammed his fist against the wall in frustration. Perhaps he'd mishandled the situation. The doctor wasn't talking, but Alexander was sure he knew something.

What could Karamanlis be hiding? he wondered.

In May, Alexander returned to New York. For the next eighteen months he threw himself totally into his work, into the growth and expansion of the Kirakis Corporation. He became personally involved in every aspect of that expansion. He went to great lengths to learn everything he could about the businesses he was interested in acquiring. He traveled extensively, spending weeks in an automobile plant in Germany, observing and questioning both the executives and the men who worked in the assembly plant . . . visiting an advertising agency in London to learn how ad campaigns were developed and executive decisions made . . . checking out the corporate offices of a major airline in Paris to find out all he could about that business and to learn about flaws in airport security. In Montreal, it was a computer company. In Rome, a pharmaceuticals manufacturer. In Japan, a television network. "I find myself getting an education I never had at Harvard," he confided to George Prescott.

Whenever he needed advice, he called in the experts. If he was asked a question for which he did not have an answer, he was not afraid to pick up the phone and locate someone who did. It was not unusual for Alexander to drop in unannounced on the platoon of corporate lawyers who handled the legal end of the corporation's business affairs. Nor was it a surprise to the president of a major Manhattan bank when he received a call from Alexander in the early hours of the morning to discuss a possible merger or ask a question about finances or taxes. If it was technical information he sought, he would look for an acknowledged expert in that field. He was thorough, asking questions about even the most minute details and remembering their answers.

George once accused him of trying to become an expert at everything. "It isn't necessary, Alexander," he insisted. "You can always hire the experts when you need them!"

Alexander only laughed. "Such a trusting soul you are, my friend," he said. "Do you think for a moment that I'd turn important matters over to others, ignorant of what might be going on within my own corporation? Only a fool would do such a thing when so much is at stake! I'll hire the experts, yes, but I'll also gain enough fundamental knowledge of my own to know what they're doing."

George studied him for a moment. "What is it you really want, Alexander?" he asked.

"Everything. I want to own the world," he answered simply.

George laughed at the enormity of Alexander's statement. "If anyone knew how to do that—" he began.

Alexander smiled. "Be patient, my friend. I'll show you how."

* * *

"A little more to the left," Meredith instructed the uniformed maintenance man who was perched on a low stepladder as he struggled to hang Elizabeth's portrait. Meredith gestured slightly with one hand. "There—that's it! Perfect!"

"Thank God!" the man declared as he came down the ladder. "Anything else you need me for, Miss Courtney?"

She shook her head. "No, that's all. Thank you."

"Anytime." He folded up the ladder, then paused to look up at the painting. "She was a knockout, wasn't she?"

Meredith nodded. "Very beautiful."

"I saw her last picture," he commented as he carried the ladder to the door. "She was at her best. Too bad she died."

"Yes, it was," Meredith agreed as she held the door for him. "Thank you again for all your help."

"Glad to be of service," he said with a wave of his free hand.

Closing the door behind him, she turned and looked around. My sanctuary, she thought with satisfaction. A real home—at last!

Her first apartment, which she'd sublet sight unseen from an IBS newscaster who'd been sent to Washington at the time Meredith herself was coming to New York, had been located on the Lower East Side and was much too small for her needs. It was a studio in a good building, but it had a kitchenette the size of a postage stamp—that was how she described it to colleagues—and a bathroom with barely enough space in which to turn around. She'd promised herself almost immediately after unpacking that she would move as soon as she found what she was looking for. A month ago, Casey Rinaldi, a colleague at IBS, told her of a vacancy in her building at Seventy-first and West End Avenue. Casey had put Meredith in touch with the building manager, and Meredith had signed the lease the same day she looked at the apartment.

It had taken weeks of spare-time work to make it look just the way she wanted it to, but now it was finished, and she was pleased with the results. The apartment was airy, modern, and distinctly feminine. The living room was decorated in shades of pale blue and white, and the couch and chairs were overstuffed and comfortable. Her bedroom was done in rose and mauve, and she'd turned the spare bedroom into a study, furnishing it with two bookcases and a roll-top desk she'd found at an antique shop.

Now it feels like home, she thought as she looked up at the painting of Elizabeth and David. Unconsciously, she pushed her hands down into the pockets of her gray wool slacks. Ever since she'd left California, she'd longed for another place she could call home, and at last she'd found it. But will it ever erase the emptiness I feel inside? she asked herself.

Even now, the pain of splitting with Nick was still with her. The bitterness she'd felt the last time she saw him was as strong as it had been that morning at Malibu. She promised herself now that it would never happen again. No other man was ever going to hurt her as Nick had, because no one would get the chance. She wouldn't let anyone get that close.

She had her work, and that would have to be enough.

On a cold gray afternoon in mid-December, Meredith stood at the window of her office on the ninth floor of the IBS Broadcast Center, staring down at the traffic on West Fifty-second Street below. Across the street, a man in a red Santa suit stood on a busy corner, handing out candy canes to the children clustered around him. Meredith smiled to herself. She loved Christmas in New York; the holiday feeling here was so different from that on the West Coast. So much more traditional, with snow, so like the ones back home . . .

She turned back to her desk. On the wall behind her was tangible evidence of her success as the co-anchor of *World Focus:* framed newspaper clippings in which she was mentioned or quoted, magazine covers on which she'd been featured. She looked at each of them now as if seeing them for the first time: *The New York Times . . . Newsweek . . . TV Guide . . . Ms. . . . Working Woman.* She'd become one of the most visible, perhaps *the* most visible newscaster on the IBS network. On her best days, this knowledge gave her a sense of pride; on her worst it gave her comfort. One look at that wall told her she'd finally achieved her goal. She had arrived.

She was deep in thought when her secretary tapped lightly on the open door. She looked up. "What is it, Cindy?"

"We're already getting responses to your invitations to the businessmen for the new interview series," the young woman said as she entered. "The president of Exxon has accepted. Lee Iacocca is willing, but there may be a scheduling problem. Brown of AT&T is unavailable at this time. Alexander Kirakis is willing to consider but will have to speak to you before he gives us a green light."

Meredith nodded. "Now, why am I not surprised?" she asked herself aloud.

"Probably because he's never been available to the media," Cindy answered.

"What? Oh, yes," Meredith said, suddenly realizing her secretary had thought she was talking to her.

"Shall I call them?" Cindy wanted to know.

Meredith shook her head. "I'll call him myself. Thanks anyway," she said, still reviewing the list her secretary had given her.

As Cindy returned to her desk, Meredith recalled her last encounter with Alexander Kirakis. She'd never gotten the interview he promised her. God only knows what I'd have to do to get it now, she thought with a twinge of amusement. Was he really unavailable, or was he simply a man who held a grudge? she wondered. So much had changed since that meeting. Alexander Kirakis was now the chairman of the board of the Kirakis Corporation. She was now cohosting a nationally successful television news show. Only one thing had remained the same: Meredith's determination to get whatever story she was after.

She flipped through the Rolodex on her desk and found his number, then reached for the phone. As she dialed, she thought about the three times she'd encountered Alexander in the past, the way he'd come on to her in Los Angeles, knowing she was living with Nick. What would it be like this time, now that she was free?

A woman's voice answered after the second ring. "Good afternoon, Kirakis Corporation," she said with a faint British accent.

"Alexander Kirakis, please." Meredith settled into her chair.

She was put on hold for several moments. Then another woman came on. "Mr. Kirakis's office."

"I'd like to speak with him, please," Meredith said in a businesslike tone. "This is Meredith Courtney, IBS."

There was a pause. "One moment, please. I'll see if he's available." She was put on hold again. She leaned back in her chair, absently tapping her pencil on the corner of the desk.

At the World Trade Center, Alexander was reviewing the latest reports he'd received from his scouts all over the world, men and women dispatched to other countries in search of potential acquisitions. He was discussing those possibilities with George Prescott, who normally checked out each one personally before Alexander took any action. "How does your schedule look for the next week?" he wanted to know.

George shrugged. "Nothing critical. A couple of meetings, a conference in Seattle on that lumber mill deal—"

"Cancel everything," Alexander interrupted. "I want you to fly to Singapore to represent the corporation in bidding for some oil leases in the Java Sea."

George settled into a chair near the desk, his strong, regular features shadowed by the dim light of the partially hidden sun. He ran one hand through his thick, sandy-blond hair as he paused to think. "You sure you want to get involved in that crapshoot?" he asked. "I've heard—"

"I've read all the geological reports," Alexander cut in as he seated himself. "These tracts show great promise."

"I'm sure they do," George said slowly. "I've seen some of those reports myself. If they're accurate, there's so much oil down there we could practically suck it up with a straw."

"And still you have reservations," Alexander concluded.

George nodded. "You're talking about unpredictable territory," he said. "It's like playing Russian roulette. You go in and buy your tracts, and if your number comes up, there's a revolution in some obscure Indonesian country and your tracts become nationalized. I don't like it. Too risky."

"Of course it is," Alexander agreed. "But there's always that element of risk in any worthwhile endeavor of this kind, isn't there?" He paused thoughtfully. "I've considered the risks, and after weighing them against the potential profit, I've decided it's a gamble worth taking."

"It's your decision," George said with a shrug of resignation. "When do I leave?"

"Is Monday morning too soon?"

"Monday's fine."

Alexander's secretary buzzed him on the intercom. "Mr. Kirakis, Meredith Courtney from IBS is on line one," she told him. "Shall I tell her you're unavailable?"

Alexander smiled. "No. Ask her to hold for just a moment." He turned to George. "We'll finish this discussion later."

George nodded, flashing him a knowing grin. "Later," he agreed, and he got to his feet and left the office.

A moment later, the light on Alexander's telephone console came on. He picked it up and leaned back in his chair. "Hello, Meredith," he said pleasantly. "I've been expecting your call . . ."

THIRTEEN

᠌᠌᠌᠌᠌᠌᠌᠌᠌᠌

"These just came for you, Meredith," Casey announced as she entered the dressing room on the third floor of the Broadcast Center, carrying a large crystal vase containing a dozen red roses. "Shall I leave them here or take them to your office?"

"Take them up to my office," Meredith said without looking. She was giving her secretary some notes for calls that needed to be made and letters to be sent out that day.

"Don't you want to see who they're from?" Casey asked.

"What—" Meredith turned, stopping short when she saw the roses. She did not have to look at the card. She knew who had sent them. She pulled the small card from its envelope and read the message: *Looking forward to tonight. A.* She smiled tightly as she reread the card. He never stopped trying, did he, she mused. When he invited her to dinner on the telephone yesterday, she'd accepted, making it clear that it was to be strictly business, to discuss the interview she wanted, but even as he'd agreed, she had known he'd never let it go at that.

"Somebody likes you," Casey commented with a grin.

"Unfortunately," Meredith said grimly.

"Why unfortunately?"

"It's a long story," Meredith said evasively as she climbed into the makeup chair, tucking a large paper napkin into her collar like a child's bib to protect her dress from drops and particles of makeup. As a hairdresser removed hot rollers from her hair, the makeup woman put the finishing touches on her face. Meredith looked over a sheet of copy paper handed to her by Barrie Matlock, the producer's secretary. "Is this all we've got for the tease?" Meredith wanted to know.

"What would you suggest?"

Meredith thought about it for a moment, then began to scribble some notes on the back of the page. "How does this sound? 'Jessica Sherry talks about her scorching new novel; I'll have the second installment in my three-part series of interviews with political wives; and Tony Corrigan will have a report on the recent wave of terrorism in Europe. This, and more, on *World Focus.*'" She looked up at Barrie questioningly.

Barrie shrugged. "Harv will probably like it," she said agreeably. "Let me get it upstairs, and—"

As she opened the door, Kent Mason, the stage manager, nearly collided with her. "Quick!" he said breathlessly. "For the chroma-key—what's Meredith wearing today?" He looked over at her and threw up his arms in frustration. "Beige! Jesus Christ—we're in chroma-green!" He turned on his heel and ran out again.

"He always acts as though he's on the verge of a stroke," Meredith said, laughing.

Barrie made a wry face. "He's been like that as long as he's been with IBS," she said. "He's always rushing around as though he's headed for eternity and has less than ten minutes to get there."

Meredith looked up at the clock on the wall. She wished the hairdresser would finish. Twenty minutes to airtime. She glanced over at her own secretary, who silently proofread letters Meredith had dictated to prospective guests for the show. This afternoon she had half a dozen calls to make and twice as many to return. There were interviews to think about—what approach to take, what questions to ask. She still wrote a great deal of her own material, as she had while at KXLA. And while you're at it, she thought, you'd better come up with something good enough to impress Alexander Kirakis tonight.

At that moment, Kent Mason poked his head in the door again. "Anytime you're ready, Meredith," he said, pointing frantically at his watch. "Ten minutes and you go live!"

"All right!" Meredith jumped to her feet and pulled the napkin from her collar as the hairdresser tamed a few stray hairs. She headed for the exit with her secretary trailing behind.

Five minutes later she was in the elevator riding up to the ninth floor with her secretary and Kent. She taped the tease with her cohost, Cole Richards, an attractive, amiable man in his late thirties who'd once been a correspondent for Associated Press. For the next ten minutes she shuttled back and forth between her office and the set, while the show's staff filtered in and out, leaving messages and delivering mail. Her secretary followed her back to the set as airtime neared. "Who do you want for the 'Faces in the News' segment—Prince Charles or that fellow who's leading that band of mercenaries in North Africa?" Cindy asked.

"Prince Charles, if we can get him. I'd be interested in talking to the mercenary, but the prince will draw a bigger audience," Meredith answered.

Cindy nodded. "Before his marriage, he was almost as popular with the ladies as Alexander Kirakis," she said cheerfully.

The words stung. Why did it bother her that there had been so many women in his life? Meredith asked herself. Why should it matter to her, one way or the other?

She put it out of her mind as she turned her attention to the morning telecast. As she settled onto the couch next to Cole Richards, facing the cameras with one eye to the Teleprompter, she thought of only one thing: the program.

Meredith sat at the dressing table in her bedroom, applying lip gloss with her fingertip. Pausing to study her reflection in the mirror for a moment, she smiled to herself. You're going to a lot of trouble for a man you're not interested in, my dear, she thought. Just what is it about him that makes you go against your own nature?

She got up and went over to the closet. After considering the possibilities, she chose a simple navy blue silk dress that was elegant but not provocative. She had to be careful not to look provocative when she was with Alexander, not that he needed any encouragement. She slipped the dress on and fumbled with the zipper. She put on her shoes—black high-heeled pumps—then went back to her dressing table. Taking her jewel case from the drawer, she selected a single strand of gray pearls and matching earrings. As she was putting on the earrings, she paused. Something was not quite right. The hair. To match the simple elegance of the dress, she pulled her hair up into a twist at the back of her head and secured it with several large hairpins. That's better, she thought as she checked herself in the mirror one last time.

The sound of the doorbell cut through her thoughts. She looked at her watch. Seven-thirty, on the button. He's certainly punctual, she thought as she got to her feet and went to let him in. She'd wanted to meet him at the restaurant, but he wouldn't hear of it. "My father always told me a gentleman calls for the lady at her door," he'd told her.

As she opened the door, she was once again struck by how devilishly attractive he was. He wore a dark blue suit, white silk shirt, and a light gray and black striped tie. A lock of his dark hair fell carelessly across his forehead, and his smile extended all the way to those incredible black eyes. "Are you always so punctual?" Meredith asked casually as she stepped aside to let him enter the apartment.

"Most of the time." He turned to face her. "I've made reservations for eight."

"In that case, we have a little time. Would you like a drink before we go?" she asked.

"Thank you, I would."

Meredith went over to the small wet bar across the room. "Lillet all right with you?" she asked, opening the ice bucket.

He nodded, looking up at the painting of Elizabeth and her son. The woman in the portrait was beautiful. She looked like a southern belle from the American Civil War era in her low-cut white ruffled dress. The child looked incredibly like her, a tiny replica of the woman, with the same features and dark coloring. There was something about the woman Alexander found strangely familiar, as if he knew her.

"Who is she?" he asked.

Meredith handed him the drink she'd poured for him. "Her name is—was—Elizabeth Weldon-Ryan," she answered. "She was a big star back in the late 1940s."

Alexander turned to look at her. "Star? A movie star?"

Meredith nodded. "She and her son died during the filming of one of her movies," she said, remembering Tom Ryan and all the time she'd spent talking to him, learning about Elizabeth and David.

"Then the child is hers?"

"Yes. His name was David. He was four when he died."

"She looks familiar," Alexander admitted. "I thought I might have known her from somewhere."

Meredith shook her head. "I doubt that," she said, sipping her drink. "She's been dead for thirty years."

"Perhaps I saw one of her films, then," Alexander concluded, finishing his drink. "On the island, we have a private projection room. My mother adored American films."

"That's possible. Or maybe you've seen photographs of her here in the States. She is still talked about."

Alexander looked at his watch, as if suddenly breaking the spell. "It's time we left," he said quietly. "The crosstown traffic is a bit heavier than usual tonight."

Meredith nodded. "I'll only be a moment." She went into the bedroom to get her handbag.

When she returned, he was still staring at the painting.

"Did you like the roses?" Alexander wanted to know.

They were seated at a table near the large square pool in the Pool Room of the Four Seasons. The large, three-story dining room was filled to capacity, while in the marble corridor people waiting for tables stopped to admire the immense Picasso stage curtain. From the high windows in the dining room, Meredith could see the lights of a glass-walled skyscraper across the street. She sipped a glass of

white wine slowly. "They were beautiful," she said carefully. "But we had an agreement, remember? This is to be
strictly business—"

"Of course," he agreed. "I was simply being
—courteous. A beautiful woman deserves beautiful roses."

She studied him for a moment. No excuses, no veiled
suggestions. She managed a slight smile. In spite of the
antagonism he aroused in her, she was beginning to feel the
full force of his remarkable charm.

"I've been following your career," he told her.

She looked at him, unable to hide her surprise. "Oh?"
was all she could manage to say.

"I'm impressed," he said, smiling. "I like your style."

"Thank you." Right from the beginning, Meredith had
known Alexander's interest in her was more personal than
professional. You're wasting your time, she thought defiantly. He was handsome, charming, and the most fascinating
man she'd ever met, but Meredith was only too familiar with
his long-standing reputation as a womanizer. She was not
about to allow herself to fall under his spell. This is a man
who wants only one thing from a woman, she reminded
herself. A man like Alexander Kirakis could destroy you.

In spite of her reservations, however, she found herself
relaxing in his company, enjoying the evening tremendously.
They discussed the interview she wanted to do. He asked
questions about her work and seemed genuinely interested in
her answers. He entertained her with amusing anecdotes
about his travels, about some of the bizarre customs and
culinary practices he'd encountered. He acted as though, for
him, there was no one in that room but her. As flattered as
she was by his attentiveness, it also made Meredith slightly
uncomfortable. She wanted to present herself as a total
professional, but he wasn't making it easy. She looked
across the table at him. He was watching her, smiling at her,
as he had that night at the Rainbow Room. He'd barely
touched the crisp duck with peaches on his plate, not
bothering to even try to conceal his fascination with her. I'm
a curiosity to him, Meredith decided. A woman who doesn't
fall all over him.

As they were leaving the restaurant he suggested they have

a nightcap. "The evening is still young," he pointed out. "I know a place where we can talk privately and relax with the best wine in all of Manhattan."

"And where might that be?" she asked.

His eyes met hers. "The Olympic Tower."

The apartment was in darkness when they entered. "My household staff has retired for the evening," Alexander explained as he took Meredith's coat, almost as if he'd read her mind. As he removed his own overcoat, she walked into the darkened living room ahead of him. It was exactly as she'd imagined it would be: elegant, starkly modern, and overtly masculine. From the black leather couch and chairs to the dove-gray carpeting to the glass and chrome tables to the wall of mirrors that reflected the magnificent view of midtown Manhattan at night, it was exactly what she would have expected of a man like Alexander Kirakis. Sleek, elegant, and powerful. From the windows, Manhattan looked like a magnificent jewel box, its glittering lights sparkling as far as the eye could see. The same view was reflected in the gigantic mirrors on the opposing wall, making it seem as if they were surrounded by diamonds. She felt Alexander's presence in the room as he moved up behind her. "It is beautiful, is it not?" he asked.

"It's breathtaking," she admitted.

"And you take my breath away." In one quick movement, his arms folded tightly around her, pinning her arms to her sides. She felt his lips on her neck as he began kissing her, moving downward toward her shoulder.

"No . . ." she whispered in weak protest.

"Don't fight it," he said in a low, husky voice. "Let it happen, Meredith. The chemistry between us—it's been there from the moment we met. I think you felt it too."

"No," she repeated, trying to be firm. The effect he had on her was unnerving. She tried to pull away, but he was too strong and seemed intent upon holding her. Finally, in a burst of determination, she summoned up all of her strength to break his embrace. She moved away from him quickly, before he could recapture her. "I should have known," she fumed.

"You did know."

She shook her head.

"Yes, you did," he insisted. "I've made no secret of the desire I feel for you. I've been drawn to you from the first time I saw you." He took a step toward her.

She turned on him in anger. "Of all the—" she began.

His mouth came down on hers as he caught her up in his arms again. She struggled for only a moment. She began to relax against him, responding to his kisses without wanting to. He reached up and removed the large pins from her hair, allowing it to fall down around her shoulders. He tangled his fingers in it as he continued to kiss her longingly. Finally, he drew back and smiled at her. "You see? I was right," he said softly.

She shook her head, not trusting her voice.

"Stay with me tonight, Meredith," he whispered. "The two of us, making love . . . it would be magic."

"No." She backed away from him again. "I came here to talk to you about the interview, nothing more."

"You're only lying to yourself," he told her. "You say it has to be strictly business between us, but your body is saying something else. I want to make love to you, and I believe you want it to happen as much as I do. Don't you think I could feel it when I held you in my arms? You didn't fight me."

She shook her head. "You've got it all wrong," she insisted stubbornly.

He smiled patiently. "I don't think so."

"I have to go." She was trembling with anger and confusion.

"Are you no longer interested in getting your interview?" he asked.

She stared at him. "Tell me something," she began carefully. "Do you expect me to go to bed with you to get an interview?"

He frowned. "You insult my integrity," he said quietly. "One has nothing to do with the other—beyond the fact that I used your proposed interview to get you here. You and I, Meredith, will become lovers sooner or later—regardless of the outcome of this interview of yours. It was meant to be."

"I have to go," she said again, picking up her bag.

Alexander followed her, insisting upon helping her into

her coat. "If you are so determined to go, then I will take you home."

"No. I'm going home alone."

"My driver will take you."

"I can get a cab."

"I won't hear of it." His eyes met hers in the darkness. Impulsively, he leaned forward and kissed her again, gently pressing her back against the door. Meredith steeled herself against the sexual tension she'd begun to feel when he held her in his arms, willing herself not to respond to him. When he finally released her, he looked into her eyes again and whispered, "Think about how wonderful it could be for both of us . . ."

She pulled away. "I have no desire to become one of your romantic casualties," she said contemptuously.

He touched her hair. "You? Never," he breathed. "I can't explain it. I felt it that first time in Los Angeles. Are you telling me you didn't?"

"That's exactly what I'm telling you," she answered sharply. She pulled away from him, opened the door, and walked out. Long after she had disappeared into the elevator, Alexander was still staring after her, smiling.

We shall see, he thought. We shall see.

FOURTEEN

In his office at the World Trade Center, Alexander watched with interest as Meredith interviewed a controversial U.S. senator on *World Focus*. He loved her direct, hard-hitting interviewing style. She went for the jugular every time. Alexander felt she was really too good for the relaxed, informal-type interviews that were the show's trademark. She belonged on the network's evening news team. He smiled to himself as he studied her face on the television screen. She photographed like an angel. It was hard to believe, even for him, that anyone so beautiful could also be so tough. But then, no one knew better than Alexander just how tough Meredith could be. Though two weeks had passed since the night she walked out on him at his apartment, not a day passed that he did not think about it. Her rejection of him had only fueled his desire for her. He wanted her more than he'd ever wanted any woman, more so since she'd made it clear that she wanted no part of him.

The credits were rolling across the television screen now, signaling the end of the program. Alexander picked up the remote-control device lying on the desk and switched off the set. Automatically, a heavy mahogany panel descended over the large screen, concealing it from view. He paused for a moment, staring at the telephone on his desk. He wanted to call her, to tell her what he thought of the interview and ask her to join him for dinner, but he already knew what her answer would be. Better to wait until she came to him—and he knew she would eventually. She would have to. They still had unfinished business to take care of. The interview. Alexander smiled to himself, wondering what she would say if she knew this interview was as important to him as it was to her, part of his plan to change his public image. First things first, he thought.

He had to change his image in her eyes first.

Harv Petersen, the executive producer of *World Focus,* was a tall, wiry man in his late fifties with a strong, weathered face and thinning hair the color of gunmetal. A former newspaper correspondent, he had covered the Korean War from the front lines. He had a voice like gravel and the manner of a Marine drill sergeant. He occupied an impressive walnut-paneled corner office on the tenth floor of the Broadcast Center, high over Fifty-second Street.

Meredith entered the office wondering why Petersen wanted to see her and what could possibly be so important that it could not wait. His message read "as soon as possible" in big block letters. "Sit down, Meredith," he said with a pleasantness that was out of character.

Meredith nodded and took a seat. "What's the emergency, Harv?"

He minced no words, getting right to the point. "I hear you have an inside track on getting an exclusive interview with Alexander Kirakis." He lit a cigar and leaned back in his chair. "Rumor has it the two of you are on quite friendly terms—dinner at the Four Seasons, flowers . . ."

Meredith looked surprised. "You knew about that?"

He grinned. "News travels fast around here. After all, it is our business to stay on top of things, even when it concerns someone within our own ranks. Especially then."

"I'm afraid the rumors have been greatly exaggerated," Meredith told him. "Sorry to disappoint everyone."

"You're not seeing him?"

"Hardly," she answered. "I met him on three occasions

over the past few years—briefly—then we had dinner at the Four Seasons to discuss the possibility of doing an interview. That's all."

"That's more than anyone else has gotten from him."

"But it's hardly a commitment to an on-the-air interview."

"But there's a chance?"

"There's always a chance. But Alexander Kirakis is one man I would not stake too much on," she said, amused. "He's too unpredictable."

"This is one time you may have to play that long shot," Petersen said.

She gave him a quizzical look. "What do you mean?"

"Getting this interview could mean a great deal to your career," he told her. "The network has a new prime-time interview show on the drawing board for the fall season. They're calling it *Manhattan Observer*. It's going to be a weekly one-hour program, focusing on politics, business, serious issues. The interviews will be more serious and more investigative than what you've been doing. They want to feature world leaders and other influential persons either living in Manhattan or visiting."

"Alexander Kirakis isn't a politician—"

"No, but no one can deny he's one of the most powerful men in the world," he pointed out. "The Kirakis Corporation is so big it can tip a nation's economy just by starting a business operation there—or declining to, as the case may be."

"Exactly what are you trying to tell me, in your roundabout way?" Meredith asked carefully.

"You're the number one contender for the show's hostess, and you'll have it in the bag if you can get this interview with Kirakis," Petersen said, tapping ash from his cigar into a large ashtray on one corner of the desk. "His dislike of the media is common knowledge. When he wants to be, he can be harder to reach than the Pentagon. Land him and you'll eliminate all your competition for the new show."

"Okay, Harv, your message is received," Meredith said as she got to her feet. "I can't guarantee anything, of course, but he did agree to consider it. I'll talk to him again."

She could feel the rage building inside her as she returned

to her own office. It was unfair that her professional future should hinge on the whims of a man who wanted only one thing from her.

If he ever found out, he would make her life hell.

As Meredith crossed the busy concourse, heading for One World Trade Center, she felt apprehensive about this meeting. She could only hope it didn't show, that her ambivalence would not be too obvious to him. It seemed to her that Alexander had the sensitivity of the most advanced radar system; he could almost sense the moods and attitudes of others. Meredith had no idea what to expect from him at this point. He'd been surprisingly easy to reach, and when she spoke to him, he was cordial but businesslike, and agreed to meet with her at his office.

"May I help you?" the receptionist asked.

"Meredith Courtney, IBS," Meredith said. "I have a ten o'clock appointment with Mr. Kirakis."

The receptionist hesitated for a moment, then reached for one of the telephones and pressed a button. "Ms. Courtney is here to see Mr. Kirakis," she announced. There was a brief pause. "All right. Yes, I will." She replaced the receiver and looked up at Meredith. "Through those doors, follow the corridor down to the end and turn left. He's expecting you."

"Thank you."

Meredith found Alexander's suite with no problem. She was met by his executive secretary, Stacey Harcourt. "Mr. Kirakis had to step out for just a moment, but he told me to show you into his office and tell you he would be with you shortly."

Meredith nodded. She looked at the engraved silver name plate on the wall next to the intricately carved double doors: "Alexander Kirakis—President/Chairman of the Board." There were a few things she could have added herself, but none of them suitable for public display.

The secretary opened the doors and led her into the office. It was quite large, and even more impressive than she had expected it to be. The two outside walls were floor-to-ceiling windows, and the inner walls were mahogany-paneled.

There were built-in bookshelves to the right of his desk, and in the center of the shelves was a large, carved panel half-descended over a built-in television screen and video-cassette unit. His desk was a solid block of black mahogany, his high-backed executive chair covered in gray suede. Behind the desk was a communications complex on a large console table consisting of a battery of phones with direct lines to corporation offices all over the world, two red phones equipped with scramblers, an intricate intercom system, and a computer terminal. A couch and several chairs, all covered in the gray suede of his chair, stood in different parts of the room. At the opposite end was a well-stocked bar in a beautiful antique cabinet. On the wall over it hung an enormous portrait of Constantine Kirakis.

After a while, Meredith began to wonder what was keeping him. She glanced at her watch. Ten-thirty. His secretary had said he would be right back. She'd been waiting over half an hour. She shifted around in her chair and looked expectantly at the door. She was beginning to wonder if he had really been called away from his office or if he was keeping her waiting deliberately. She had a luncheon appointment at noon—another prospective interview—but she knew if she left without seeing him, she might not get another chance. She needed Alexander—more than she could ever allow him to know. She would stay and wait, no matter how long this took.

At eleven-fifteen, the double doors opened and Alexander entered the room, smiling. "Good morning," he said in that familiar deep voice as he seated himself behind the desk. "It's good to see you again, but, quite frankly, I am surprised." He looked at her for a moment, impressive in her dove-gray suit, and smiled appreciatively.

"Why?" Meredith asked coolly. "We do have some unfinished business to take care of." She saw the look on his face and knew what he was thinking. "You did promise me an interview." Her eyes met his defiantly.

"Ah, yes—the interview," he said pleasantly. "I thought you had changed your mind about that."

"Where would you get an idea like that?" she asked, surprised.

"It has been two weeks since I have heard from you. Since you walked out on me," he reminded her. "You were quite angry, as I recall."

"Not without good reason," Meredith said carefully. "But I didn't come here to discuss our personal differences with you. I came to find out if you intend to go through with the interview, and if so, to arrange a meeting to work out the details."

He studied her for a moment. "Whatever else I may be, Meredith, I am a man of my word," he told her. "You'll get your interview—with certain conditions, of course."

She looked at him suspiciously. "What conditions?"

"I must have full approval of all questions you plan to ask, all topics you wish to discuss," he explained. "The interview cannot be done live. It must be videotaped and I must have the opportunity to view and approve it before it is aired." He leaned forward, his arms on the desk, his hands clasped together.

"You expect a great deal."

"Those are my terms," he said simply. "Take them or leave them."

He is going to be impossible, Meredith thought. "And if I agree?"

"Then we'll meet again," he answered. "At that time, I'll expect you to provide me with a list of the subjects you would like to discuss. I'll either approve or disapprove."

"As it happens, I've already prepared such a list," she said. "I drew it up when the possibility of doing this interview first arose."

"Oh? And do you have it with you now?"

She shook her head. "I thought it best to wait until I was sure you would agree to it," she replied.

Alexander nodded. "Perhaps we could discuss it over dinner tonight," he suggested.

"No," Meredith said quickly. "The only way this is going to work is by keeping our relationship strictly professional—no romantic dinners, no nightcaps, just business. Preferably conducted right here in this office. I think it will save us both a great deal of trouble."

He tapped the eraser end of a pencil on the desk, never taking his eyes from her. "I'm afraid we have a problem," he said at last. "You see, my schedule makes it impossible for me to see you here during regular business hours. If you wish to do this interview, it will have to be done at my convenience."

"I see," she said tightly. "More conditions." She looked up at him, her eyes blazing with anger. She hated herself for letting him get to her.

He smiled. "If you're concerned about seeing me socially or being alone with me because of what happened between us at my apartment, let me put your mind at ease," he said patiently. "I have never taken any woman against her will and do not intend to start now."

Meredith looked at him but said nothing. He was teasing her, and it took every ounce of strength she could summon to control her rage.

"You say you want our relationship to be strictly professional—which I presume means that once the interview is taped and aired, we will not be seeing each other again," he said. "Am I correct?"

There was a pause. "Yes," she said.

He nodded. "So be it, then, if that is what you really want." He looked at her questioningly. When she did not respond, he went on. "You'll have my full cooperation regarding the interview, as long as my conditions are met."

"I don't see any problem with that." She was sure Petersen would not object to giving him final approval.

He continued to stare at her, then opened his mouth as if he wanted to say something, but decided against it. They sat in uncomfortable silence for what seemed like an eternity. It was Meredith who finally broke that silence.

"If there's nothing else we need to settle, I'll be leaving," she said. "I have another appointment and I'm already late."

He nodded.

She rose to her feet slowly. "If you're free Wednesday evening, we could meet then."

He nodded again. "I will call you," he promised.

"Fine."

It was not until she was in the elevator that Meredith stopped to think about what had taken place in Alexander's office. It was a strange meeting. She had expected him to be

difficult. She had even expected him to be angry. She had
not expected what had actually happened. He had made it
quite clear what he expected—what he demanded—in
exchange for the interview, but he had agreed to do it. She'd
expected him to agree to meeting with her and then tell her
to her face that it was off. But he had not only consented, he
had promised her his full cooperation. Why? she wondered.
She couldn't help but be suspicious of him.

What was his game?

In the weeks that followed, Alexander and Meredith met
several times to talk about the interview. In the beginning,
those meetings, though conducted in the most elegant
restaurants in Manhattan, could have been likened to an
armed truce. They were strained and difficult. They could
not seem to agree on anything. Gradually, however, they
began to relax with each other, and the discussions became
more pleasant. Alexander was charming and attentive, but he
never asked her to go back to his apartment with him after
dinner, never made so much as a suggestive remark. He's
been a perfect gentleman, Meredith thought, dismissing all
of her suspicions. All I had to do was make him realize that
my interest in him really is professional. She found herself
beginning to genuinely like him.

Just as the blasting cold winds of winter finally gave way
to the promise of the renewal of spring, so the antagonism
between Alexander and Meredith gave way to a growing
mutual admiration and affection. The sexual tension that had
always existed between them was still there, but it was no
longer their sole connection. They had come to terms with
it, learned to deal with it. For Meredith, this meant being
able to admit, if only to herself, that she *was* strongly
attracted to Alexander, even though she had resolved never to
do anything about it. For Alexander, it meant keeping his
physical passions in check, sublimating his desire as he felt
his way through a somewhat confusing relationship.

In early April came the official announcement from
Intercontinental Broadcasting president Austin Ferris that
IBS's fall lineup would include a weekly interview show,
Manhattan Observer, hosted by Meredith Courtney. He
confirmed that three segments of the new show would be

aired on a monthly basis during the months of June, July, and August, then would go to a weekly format in September, at which time Meredith would officially leave *World Focus*. Replacing her would be Casey Rinaldi, a newscaster who was currently a regular contributor to the show. Austin Ferris also confirmed rumors that the first segment of *Manhattan Observer* was to be an in-depth profile of Alexander Kirakis, which, he said, was "already in the works."

"It's started already," Meredith told Alexander over dinner at the Rainbow Room. "The gossip columnists all think we're having a red-hot affair."

Alexander looked at her. Even in the subdued light, his black eyes seemed to glow. "Does that bother you?" he asked, resting his fork on the edge of his plate.

"It did at first," she admitted. "I didn't like the idea of anyone thinking I had slept with you to get the interview."

"And now?" He finished a glass of wine.

"I've developed a kind of immunity to it," she said with a wary smile. "I think I've finally gotten used to it."

He smiled. "I would never have thought of you as a woman who would be terribly concerned about what anyone thought of her," he said, mildly amused.

"As a rule, I'm not," she responded. "But when I was first getting started in this business, getting my career off the ground—" She stopped short. "Let's just say things happened that made me just a little defensive about it."

"Tell me about it," he urged.

She shook her head. "It's a long story."

"I have time."

"It's not important," she insisted.

"Obviously it is, or it would not continue to bother you." He reached across the table and took her hand. "You still don't trust me, do you, Meredith?" he asked in a gentle voice.

"Trust has nothing to do with it," she said. "It's history, and it wouldn't interest anyone except possibly another newscaster who found herself in a similar situation."

"You're wrong." His eyes met hers. "It would interest me."

She hesitated for a moment. Realizing his interest was genuine, she began to talk. She found herself telling him things she had never told anyone, and even as she was saying the words, she was not sure why she was doing so. She talked about the frustrations and the obstacles she'd had to overcome in the course of her career, the skepticism she'd encountered from her male counterparts, and the jealousy and rivalry from the women. She saw only a patient understanding in Alexander's eyes as she spoke.

"We have a great deal more in common than you might think," he told her. "I, too, have had many obstacles to overcome, many prejudices to deal with."

She gave him a puzzled look. "You?"

"It was never easy, being the son of Constantine Kirakis," he said simply.

"I would have thought it made your life easier."

"In some ways, perhaps. I did grow up with every possible advantage. But until I officially became chairman of Kirakis, everything I possessed had been given to me," he said, his voice low. "My personal fortune is an inherited one. Even the chairmanship of the Kirakis Corporation was handed down to me, like a family heirloom." He shook his head. "To many, I realize this would be regarded as an ideal situation, even an enviable one, but I've found that with the privilege comes the pressure."

"What kind of pressure?" Meredith asked.

"Mainly that of constantly being compared to my father, of answering the criticism that I was content to rest upon my father's laurels. That, among other things, created the animosity between the media and myself that is today a blood feud." He paused. "That is one of the reasons I agreed to this interview."

Meredith looked at him, not sure she understood.

"I had been considering possible ways to improve my relations with the media and in the process change my public image when your offer came to appear on your program," he explained. "I was familiar with the program, of course. I had seen several of your interviews, liked what I saw, and—"

"Wait a minute!" Meredith interrupted, not bothering to conceal her surprise. "You set me up, didn't you!"

"Are you angry?" he asked, a twinkle in his eyes.

Meredith laughed. She could have cheerfully strangled

him. "I'd be furious—if it weren't so funny," she answered. "We really are two of a kind, aren't we? Here I was, using you to further my career and worrying about the possibility that you might change your mind about doing the interview, and all the time, you were using me and my show to change your image! I've always considered myself a pretty good judge of character, of being able to figure out what's going on in my subject's head, but you had me completely fooled. You've really outdistanced me, Alexander."

"I doubt that," he said easily.

"Even now, I have no idea what's going through your mind, what you're really after." She paused. "What is it you really want?"

Alexander only smiled.

Meredith sailed through the crowded lobby of the IBS Broadcast Center, waving to the security guard on duty at the front desk as she pushed her way through the heavy double doors facing West Fifty-second Street. As she stepped out into the brisk night air, she paused for a moment to turn up the collar of her blue wool melton coat for more warmth. She walked toward the limousine parked at the curb, assuming it was the network car waiting to take her home. Abruptly, the back door opened, and Alexander emerged. "Good evening," he greeted her with a devastating smile.

She stopped in her tracks. "Alexander—what are you doing here?" she asked as he took her arm and ushered her into the car so quickly that she did not have time to protest.

"I've come to abduct you," he said in an unusually cheerful voice, sliding in beside her. "I'm going to whisk you off to a secluded, terribly romantic hideaway where no one will ever find us."

"Be serious!" Meredith scolded, laughing.

"I am serious," he insisted, closing the door as he signaled the driver to proceed.

"Where are we going?" she wanted to know.

"I had a meeting over on West Fifty-seventh this afternoon," he told her. "I thought I would take you home."

"But I have a car—" she began.

He shook his head. "It's all been taken care of," he assured her.

"But—"

"You protest too much," he said with mild amusement as the car inched along in the start-and-stop traffic on Broadway. As they approached Times Square, Meredith glanced absently at the flashing neon signs and suggestive advertisements that seemed to be everywhere, at the litter and trash that whirled about in the brisk wind. She shut out the noisy turmoil coming at them from all sides. "I hate to tell you this," she said slowly, turning to look at Alexander, "but we're headed in the wrong direction."

"Oh? Are we?" he asked, feigning innocence. "Well, as long as we're already going this way, I know of a marvelous little place, very quiet, very intimate, where we can have dinner."

"And discuss the interview?" she asked, smiling.

"Of course," he agreed with a quick nod.

In the past few weeks, they'd dined together almost every night. She had accompanied him to the opening of an art exhibit at a prestigious Madison Avenue gallery when he insisted he had something important to discuss with her. The "something important" had been a suggestion that she take her camera crew out to Kennedy Airport and get some footage of his private plane, a recently acquired Boeing 747. The interior, he told her, had been remodeled and turned over to a top decorator who had transformed it into a flying palace. He was keeping his promise to maintain that professional distance between them, as she'd demanded at the onset of their association. Or he was trying to. He still wanted her. He wanted her more than ever. Meredith wondered how much of his fascination came from her continuation to deny him sexually when most women would have been eager to become his lover.

She looked at him now, seated beside her in the darkened car, and she found herself as intrigued by him as she had been the first time she saw him that afternoon at La Bella Fontana. As wary of him as she had been that night at the Rainbow Room. And as drawn to him as she had been when she met him at the polo match. Alexander Kirakis, she concluded, was a complex man—an enigma, a puzzle defying solution. He could have been likened to a magnificent diamond, cool and polished on the surface, brilliant and fiery underneath. Meredith found herself wondering if she would ever really know him, if they would ever get that far.

"Well, what's it to be?" he asked, breaking the silence. "Shall we have dinner?"

She managed a slight smile. "But I'm not dressed for dinner," she protested weakly. "I'd have to change—"

"You don't need to change," he assured her. "You look lovely."

She smiled. "Thank you, but I really am *not* dressed for dinner," she pointed out. "So if you don't mind—"

Alexander smiled, raising his hands in a gesture of surrender. "All right." He signaled his driver, giving him Meredith's address.

"I won't be long," Meredith promised as they entered the apartment. Dropping her shoulder bag on the couch, she took off her coat. "Make yourself a drink. By now you should know where everything is."

He nodded. "Take your time. I'm in no hurry." For dinner, that is, he thought.

As she disappeared into the bedroom, Alexander went over to the bar and poured himself a brandy. Lifting the glass to his lips, he stared thoughtfully at the painting of that American actress and her child. It intrigued him and yet it disturbed him as well, though he was not sure why. He still couldn't put his finger on it, but something about her seemed strangely familiar. In some ways, she reminded him of Francesca. In others, she was like any one of a dozen women he'd known over the years. Perhaps that was it. She was the kind of woman he'd always been attracted to—before Meredith. Dark, voluptuous, sultry. He kept staring at the painting, not sure what it was about her that troubled him so much.

"Is something wrong?"

Startled, Alexander whirled around. Meredith stood a few feet behind him, looking even more beautiful than she had when he picked her up at the Broadcast Center. "What?" he asked, slightly confused.

"Is something wrong?" she repeated.

He smiled at her concern. "Not anymore."

* * *

"Do you always walk like this?" Meredith asked breathlessly as she hurried to keep up with Alexander's long, quick stride. When he'd phoned her that Saturday morning, asking if she'd like to take a walk with him, she'd had no idea that he planned to spend the entire day exploring Manhattan on foot.

"No," he admitted. "Not as often as I would like." He reached out and took her hand. "Because I am often required to spend long hours locked away in my office, I welcome the opportunity to spend a day—or even an afternoon—outdoors."

No wonder he's in such good shape, Meredith thought wryly. Only a professional athlete could possibly keep up with him.

"I go to my place on Long Island as often as possible," he told her as they paused to admire a glass sculpture in the window of a gallery on Madison Avenue. "My polo ponies are there, and I need as much practice time as I can manage." Then he turned to look at her. "I will take you there one day soon."

Meredith only smiled. If anyone else had said that to her, she might have dismissed it as an idle remark, but coming from Alexander, she had the feeling that it was a promise he had every intention of keeping.

They walked north on Madison Avenue to Fifty-ninth, then headed west toward Central Park. As they walked through the park, Alexander glanced up at the formidable-looking gray clouds that filled the sky. Thunderstorms had been predicted for the late afternoon hours, but he'd had no intention of allowing the possibility of bad weather to interfere with his plans to spend the day with Meredith. "We should stop for lunch soon," he said, looking at his watch. "Where would you like to go?"

"It doesn't matter to me," she answered, thoroughly enjoying herself. "Whatever you're in the mood for."

He turned and smiled, tempted for a moment to tell her what he was in the mood for. He nodded slightly with a twinkle in his dark eyes. He reached out as if to take her hand, then withdrew abruptly. Not yet, he reprimanded himself.

"The Plaza is close," he said. "Shall we go there?"

"Sounds wonderful."

They walked around the Pond, past the Dairy, and along the striped red brick Chess and Checkers Pavilion that had served as a special recreation center for the children of Manhattan before the playgrounds were constructed. "I think we'd better start back," Meredith said in a worried tone, looking up at the overcast sky. Extending her left hand, she felt a few droplets of water falling from the air. "It's starting to rain."

"It will amount to nothing," Alexander insisted confidently.

She gave him a wry smile. "You're sure about that, are you?" she asked, unconvinced.

"Absolutely."

At that moment, the sprinkles turned into a light shower. Meredith began to laugh. "You were saying?"

Alexander grinned, his black eyes glittering wickedly. "I was saying that it definitely looks like rain and we should adjourn to the Plaza immediately," he said with mock dignity. He grabbed her hand and they started running along the Pond. By the time they reached the southeast corner of the park, the shower had turned into a downpour. Still holding hands, they made a mad dash across Central Park South toward the Plaza. They did not stop running until they reached the top of the wide concrete steps leading up to the main entrance facing Fifth Avenue. They stood looking at each other, both of them soaked to the skin, and started to laugh uncontrollably.

"Do we dare go inside?" Alexander asked.

"The question is, will they allow us to go inside?" Meredith giggled.

"Of course they will!" He tossed his head imperiously, stepping closer to her as he moved out of the path of two bellboys armed with luggage retrieved from a white Rolls-Royce parked near the entrance.

"You're sure about that?" Meredith teased.

"Absolutely."

"Now where have I heard that before?" She stepped forward and lost her balance. Alexander caught her, grasping her elbows to steady her. Their eyes met, and their gaze held for a long moment. Then, suddenly, impulsively, Alexander reached out with one hand and tilted her face upward to meet his own. His lips met hers, gently at first, then with an unmistakable urgency as he wrapped his arms around her. She returned his kisses eagerly, both of them oblivious of the curious looks of the Plaza doormen and passersby.

Soon, Alexander thought. Very soon.

"I take it your father was a powerful influence in your life," Meredith concluded over lunch. Thank God her clothes had finally begun to dry; she'd had the feeling everyone in the restaurant was staring at them.

Alexander smiled. "He was the single most important influence in my life," he answered without hesitation. "My mother always said—and without much pleasure, I might add—that Father began grooming me for the succession almost from the day I was born. She often complained that I didn't have much of a childhood. She said he regarded the corporation as his kingdom and me as the heir to the throne."

"I imagine that must have been difficult for you," Meredith commented sympathetically. "A small child carrying such a tremendous burden."

Alexander shook his head. "I never thought about it, because I never knew anything else," he admitted. "My brother died just before I was born, and I was next in line. The last of the line, in fact. Mother couldn't have any more children." He took a bite of his salad. "For as long as I can remember, I knew that one day I would take my father's place as chairman of the board. Oddly enough, even when I was very young, I looked forward to that day."

"Then you never felt it was a role that had been forced on you?" Meredith reached for her glass.

"Not at all. It was simply the role for which I had been born. I never questioned it," he said. "I would have done anything to please my father. I remember one night when I was very young—no more than seven—I sneaked down to his study very late, while he and my mother were out at some dinner party. I sat at his desk and tried to imagine what it would be like to be him." He gave a low chuckle. "Unfortunately, I fell asleep there."

Meredith giggled at the thought. "What happened?"

"When they returned home, Father came into the study and found me. He wasn't angry—actually, he was amused. He made some comment about how he would have to find a suitable place for me in his offices, and he carried me up to my room. I remember thinking how strong he was, how much I wanted to be like him." There was an odd look in his eye, something Meredith couldn't identify.

"The two of you must have been close," she said.

Alexander nodded. "We were—until I came to the States. I don't think he ever quite forgave me for it," he said with a sigh. "I wanted to work with him, but I just couldn't see myself living in his shadow. I could never have proven myself that way, and I knew it."

"Surely he realized that," Meredith offered.

"I think he did, just before he died," Alexander said thoughtfully. "Though I never quite understood why he was so set against my coming here. It was almost as though he had a personal reason—not even remotely connected to the business—for trying to keep me in Greece."

Meredith frowned. "I know the feeling."

Alexander looked surprised. "You also had an overbearing father?"

Her laugh was hollow. "The worst kind," she said. "One without power or money. He used his role as the family breadwinner to control his wife and children." It was the first time she'd expressed the feeling to anyone other than herself, and it brought back painful memories of a life she'd turned her back on a long time ago. "I grew up in a small town in the Midwest, one of those places where half the town's related and everybody knows everybody else's business."

Alexander smiled slightly. "Rather like some of the villages in Greece."

Meredith smiled too, but her heart wasn't in it. "My father was in the construction business. He'd had a lot of close calls on the job," she recalled, remembering all the nights he was late getting home from work, nights she sat by the window crying because she was sure something had happened to him and he wouldn't be coming home at all. "We were so close. I was Daddy's little girl. Until I grew up, that is."

"What changed then?"

"I did—much to my father's disappointment," Meredith answered, fingering her napkin absently. "When I started to think for myself, it was a different ball game. Dad didn't like anyone to disagree with him. There were conflicts—big ones. Then, when I was fifteen, there was an accident on the job he was working on. He was permanently disabled and had to retire. He started to drink, and things got worse."

Alexander said nothing. He waited for her to go on.

"When he drank he was verbally abusive. I finally got out. I went to live with my aunt, my mother's sister, in Chicago." Even now, the memory was painful for her. How many years had it been? Fourteen? Fifteen?

"Did you ever go back home?" Alexander wanted to know.

She nodded. "Three years after I left—for my father's funeral," she said. There was regret in her voice. "He had a massive stroke. Mom said it was all over very quickly. After that, I closed the door on my past. I promised myself I would never live that way again. I'd always be able to take care of myself."

"So," Alexander said, taking a deep breath. "We both cared deeply for our fathers in spite of difficult relationships with them."

"So it would seem," she said quietly.

Alexander reached across the table and covered her hand with his own. "You see?" he asked in a low, gentle voice. "We have much more in common than either of us could have realized."

FIFTEEN

꧰꧰꧰꧰꧰꧰꧰꧰꧰

Alexander stared absently at the reports on his desk, unable to concentrate. There were reports on possible acquisitions for the corporation, contracts waiting for his signature, financial statements requiring his immediate attention. He ignored them all. Next to the phone was a stack of messages he had not bothered to return. He had instructed his secretary to hold all of his calls so he could catch up on his paper work uninterrupted, but so far he had not touched any of it. His thoughts were of Meredith, of the changing state of their relationship. Where were they headed? he asked himself, as he had so many other times in the past few months. What was their future?

He got to his feet and prowled the length of his office in frustration. This was a situation he had never been in before, a situation he had never expected to be in. Meredith's importance to him had steadily increased over the past months, and no one was more surprised by this development than Alexander himself. In the beginning she had represented a challenge to him: a woman who was both beautiful and intelligent, a woman who seemed totally uninterested in him. He had set out to change her mind, to make her want him as much as he wanted her. His plan had backfired. She still had not come around, had not surrendered to him, but he was beginning to think he was falling in love with her. When he was with her, he was happier than he would have ever believed possible. She understood him. They understood each other. She was his Doppelgänger, his alter ego, the woman he'd once thought he would never find. If only he could make her realize. . . .

The buzzing sound of his intercom interrupted his thoughts. He went over to the console table and pressed the button. "I specifically told you to hold all of my calls, Stacey," he said irritably.

"Yes, sir, I know, but Gerald Desmond is calling from Rome," she said. "He says it's *very* important."

Alexander hesitated for a moment. "Very well," he said finally. "Put him on."

"Yes, sir."

Alexander picked up the phone. "Yes, Gerald, what is it?" he asked, annoyed.

"Alexander, are you still interested in taking over Manetti Motors?" the voice on the other end asked.

This got Alexander's attention. His interest in Manetti Motors had never been a secret. He'd had his eye on the Italian-based automobile manufacturer for the past three years, even before he became chairman of Kirakis. He had always regarded it as a prime acquisition for the corporation, but it had never been available, either for a takeover *or* a merger. "You know I'm still interested," he said.

"Well, I thought you'd like to know that the word on the street is that Carlo Manetti needs a large amount of capital—and fast," Desmond told him. "He's taken out several large loans from banks here in Rome. The rumor is that he's got some hot new design that's going to blow everything else off the streets, but he needs money—and a lot of it—to get this project off the ground."

"I see."

"He's still dead set against merging or selling out, but if you work it right, you may be able to buy into the company without his realizing it," Desmond suggested. "Can you come to Rome?"

Alexander paused. "Now is not a good time."

"Maybe you could send someone else, then. Talk to

Carlo. If he's still not receptive to letting you in, back his project anonymously.'' There was a long pause on the other end. ''Personally, I think you'd have better luck with him yourself, in person, but if that's not possible—''

Alexander thought about it for a moment. He had waited a long time for an opportunity like this. He made his decision. ''I will fly to Rome in the morning,'' he said finally.

Tonight, he had to talk to Meredith.

By the time Meredith got home, she felt totally drained. Get used to it, she told herself as she entered her darkened apartment. For the next three months you're going to be doing a juggling act with *two* shows instead of one. She looked at the clock on her desk. Eight-thirty. She checked her answering machine for messages. Nothing urgent.

She took a shower and put on an embroidered red silk robe she'd bought while taping a segment of *World Focus* in Japan last year. She pulled some cold chicken, cheese, and fruit from the refrigerator, and had just settled down on the couch with her plate when the telephone rang. She picked it up the second ring. ''Hello?''

''Meredith, it's Casey. Are you busy?''

''Sure, I've got a hot date with some leftover chicken,'' she said lightly. In the past year, Meredith and Casey Rinaldi had developed a close friendship. ''What's up?''

''I've been going over these files you gave me this afternoon—you know, the prospective interviews for upcoming shows—and I'd like to discuss some of the material with you. Are you going to be home tonight?''

Meredith hesitated for a moment. ''Sure. Come on over.''

''Great. I'll be there in about twenty minutes, okay?''

''I'll be here.''

She replaced the receiver slowly. This was one of those rare evenings that she had not brought work home with her, and she had been looking forward to relaxing and to an early bedtime. So much for that idea, she thought.

She had just finished her dinner when the doorbell rang. Casey was early, she thought as she went to answer it. She removed the safety chain and opened the door. ''Where were you calling from, the corner deli—'' She looked up and saw that it was Alexander.

"Good evening, Meredith," he said, smiling.

She gave a little laugh. "I thought you were someone else," she said, stepping back so that he could enter.

"Obviously." He walked across the room and turned to look at her again. "You're expecting someone?"

She nodded as she closed the door. "Casey Rinaldi. She's going to be my replacement on *World Focus* in the fall," she said. "We have some things to go over."

"I won't stay long, then," he told her.

"Sit down. Can I get you something? Wine, or—"

He shook his head. "I have to go to Rome on business," he said.

"Oh?" Meredith paused. "When?"

"I'll be leaving in the morning. I expect to be gone at least a week, possibly longer," he said quietly. "I had to see you before I left."

She nodded. She was going to miss him. Five months ago she would have been happy to see him fly off to Rome and stay there. Now she found herself not wanting him to leave at all.

"I came to ask you to go with me."

She turned to look at him. "Sure," she said lightly.

"I'm serious. Have you ever been to Rome?"

She smiled. "No, but—"

"You would enjoy it. Rome is famous for stealing hearts," he told her.

She nodded. He should be right at home there, she thought. She sat next to him on the couch. "There's no way I can just pick up and fly off to Rome. It's just not possible."

"All things are possible for us, Meredith," he said seriously. "You and I—we can make it possible."

She smiled. "You don't have an irate producer to contend with," she explained. "I can imagine myself calling Harv Petersen and telling him I want to take off with you and go to Rome for a week. The Broadcast Center is in chaos now. I'm trying to cope with doing two shows simultaneously and help Casey prepare herself for taking over *World Focus* in September. Harv is becoming more ratings-conscious every day." Meredith shook her head. "If I were to ask him to give me a week off right now, I couldn't even repeat some of the words he'd use!"

"Tell him it's to be part of your profile for the new program. Bring a cameraman along, tape in Rome," he suggested.

She looked at him. "You think of everything, don't you?"

"Right now, I'm only thinking of ways we can spend time together," he replied. "We've grown so close in the past few months, Meredith—"

"Right. And I think what we both really need right now is a little time apart," she said.

He looked surprised. "Why?"

"Things have changed so much between us," she said quietly. "I think we both need time to think, to decide where we want to go from here."

"I think we both know where we're going."

"We know where we're headed, but is it what we really want?" she asked.

"It's what I want," he said simply.

"I'm not so sure. Not yet."

He stared at her intently. "What are you feeling right now?" he asked.

"Confused," she admitted. "I care, yes . . . more than I want to, but . . ."

"Why more than you want to?"

She hesitated a moment before replying. "There was a lot wrong between us," she reminded him. "True, it's all in the past now, but—" She took a deep breath. "I suppose what I'm trying to say is I'm afraid to let myself get too involved."

"What are you afraid of?"

"Of not being able to make it work," she said honestly. "I've worked so hard to build my career, to get where I am today. It demands a great deal of my time—"

"I'm not asking you to give that up," he said softly. "But it cannot be your entire life. No one knows that better than I."

"For both of us—our professional lives are so demanding, so time-consuming—" she began.

He placed his hands on her shoulders. "You worry needlessly," he told her. "Your ambition is one of the things that first attracted me to you, one of the things I admire most. You're strong, and I've known so few strong women in my life. Don't you see? We are so much alike, we have so much in common—we belong together! As a team, we could be much more powerful than we can ever be as individuals.''

Her laugh was weak. ''You frighten me sometimes,'' she confessed. ''You move too fast. It's like being in the eye of a storm. I need time . . .''

He paused for a moment, then nodded. He stood up and buttoned his coat. ''Perhaps you're right, then. Perhaps we both need time to think,'' he said finally. She walked with him to the door and opened it. He turned to face her again. ''Think about what I have said, *matia mou*,'' he told her. ''Think about where we go from here.'' Impulsively, he leaned forward and kissed her gently. Neither of them saw Casey, who spotted them as she stepped off the elevator and discreetly slipped around the corner, waiting for Alexander to leave.

Meredith pulled away from him abruptly, afraid to let it go too far. ''I think you'd better go,'' she said.

He put his hands on her arms. ''Are you sure that is what you want?''

She nodded, not trusting her voice.

''Very well.'' He released her, leaving the apartment without looking back until he was in the elevator. After the doors closed and he was gone, Casey emerged from her hiding place.

''How long have you been out there?'' Meredith asked, amused.

''Long enough,'' Casey said as she came into the apartment. ''You know, he's really better-looking than his photos.''

''I suppose so.''

''Uh-huh.'' Casey eyed Meredith's robe speculatively. ''When I saw the two of you there in the doorway I thought I was interrupting something.''

''You wouldn't have been.''

''That's not the way it looked to me,'' Casey said in a disbelieving tone.

''There wasn't anything happening between us,'' Meredith insisted. ''He just kissed me, that's all.''

''Ha!'' Casey laughed. ''Listen, if I could feel the charge

out there, I know damn well that you felt it. There was
enough electricity in that kiss to power Manhattan for a
year!''

"He's an old hand at sweeping women off their feet,"
Meredith said lightly.

"I can see why," Casey said with an appreciative smile.
"There ought to be a law against men looking that good."

Meredith grinned as she closed the door. "Better be
careful, Case," she warned. "He'll turn you into a pillar of
salt."

"Oh, yeah." Casey looked at her skeptically. "You seem
to be holding up pretty well—under the circumstances."

"There's a trick to it," Meredith explained with mock
seriousness. "I never look him directly in the eye."

Casey paused. "Listen, if you weren't just getting out of
bed, then you must have been contemplating getting into
bed," she said. "Listen, if you'd rather not do this
tonight . . ."

"Oh, no," Meredith said, distracted. "To tell you the
truth, you couldn't have come at a better time. I need
something to take my mind off . . . things . . . right now."
She paused. "I'd almost forgotten you were coming."

Casey grinned. "Yeah, I guess a man like that could make
you forget a lot of things," she said with a wicked grin.

"Alexander had nothing to do with it," Meredith insisted.
"I just forgot, that's all."

"Sure." Casey didn't look convinced. "Why don't you
just admit you're wild about him?"

Meredith didn't respond. *How long can I keep denying it?*
she wondered.

Rome.

Carlo Manetti had long been regarded as something of a
maverick in the business world. He was a brilliant, aggressive man who had started out much the same as Constantine
Kirakis had: he had nothing but a dream and a fierce, driving
ambition. Manetti's goal was to become the biggest
automaker in Italy. He paid his college tuition by working in
a motorcycle assembly plant, and eventually became an

engineer with one of the larger automobile manufacturers. From there his rise had been swift, and within a few years he was promoted to vice-president. Twenty years ago he had walked away from the security of that position to form his own company, which he did with all the money he had saved and one idea. That idea, which became his much-praised Rinnegato sports car, had made Carlo Manetti a wealthy man. Today he was exactly what he had always wanted to be: the biggest and the best. The Italians called him *che si è fatto da se*—a self-made man. He was a widower with one child, a daughter who, Alexander learned, was studying painting at the Ecole des Beaux Arts in Paris.

Alexander had been interested in acquiring the Manetti plants in Rome, Milan, and Florence for several years. Manetti was doing much better than the Kirakis-owned auto manufacturers in Germany and England, and Alexander regarded it as an excellent acquisition for the corporation. He had made two previous offers, but Manetti had turned them both down cold. His plants were not for sale at any price, he insisted. He had no desire to become part of the Kirakis empire. Alexander had not been dissuaded by his refusals. To him, the fact that Manetti was not interested in a merger was merely a minor inconvenience. Carlo Manetti, like all men, had a price. And eventually Alexander would find out what it was.

"Ah, Signore Kirakis, you are one stubborn man. *Ostinato*," Manetti said with a laugh as they talked over lunch at a restaurant near Manetti's offices. "I admire you. You go after what you want, no matter what. It is easy to see why you are as successful as you are." He took a long swallow of wine. "But this time it will do you no good. As I have already told you, Manetti is not for sale, not at any price. Not now, not ever."

"You would not be selling out, Carlo," Alexander told him. "You would still be president of Manetti Motors. You would also have a place on Kirakis's board of directors."

"I would indeed be selling out," Manetti growled. "I would no longer be in charge. My position would be little more than a figurehead. No, signore, it is out of the question."

Alexander opened his mouth to say something else, but he

stopped short. A young woman approached their table. She was tall, with a stunning figure and long, lush black hair that she wore loosely around her patrician face. Alexander stood up, but Manetti remained in his chair, grinning from ear to ear when he saw her. "Donatella," he said, greeting her warmly, "how did you find me?"

"Your secretary told me you would be having lunch here," she answered, bending to kiss his cheek. She turned and smiled at Alexander. *"Buon giorno,"* she said in a soft voice.

"Buon giorno, signorina," Alexander responded, smiling appreciatively at the sight of a beautiful woman.

"Signore Kirakis, this is my daughter. Donatella, I'd like you to meet Signore Alexander Kirakis."

"I am very happy to finally meet you, Signore Kirakis," she said in heavily accented English. "I have heard so very much about you."

"The pleasure is mine, signorina," he assured her.

"Please—you will call me Donna, no? Donatella is so formal—and 'signorina' makes me sound so very old."

"Donna," he said with a nod. "Your father has told me a great deal about you."

She turned to Manetti. "What have you been telling him about me, Papa?" she asked teasingly.

"I have said nothing that is not true," Manetti replied, not bothering to conceal his pride. "I told him that you are a beautiful and talented young woman—and that you are going to be a famous painter one day."

She turned back to Alexander. "You must not believe everything my father tells you," she said lightly. "He is quite—how do you say?—biased."

Alexander held a chair for her. Manetti ordered more wine for everyone, but Alexander noticed that Donatella Manetti barely touched the glass in front of her. As he observed the two of them together, he decided that everything he had heard was true. If Manetti did indeed have a weakness, it was his daughter. The old scoundrel was putty in her hands. Alexander was amused at the way Manetti glared angrily at the young men who smiled at her as they passed the table. A man would probably be afraid to touch her, Alexander thought. Manetti would murder anyone who even looked at her as if he wanted to do anything more than shake her hand.

"How much longer will you be staying in Rome?" Donatella Manetti asked.

"I'm leaving tomorrow," Alexander replied. "I have several important matters requiring my immediate attention in New York. It would please me if both of you would join me for dinner tonight at the Pergola."

Manetti shook his head. "My apologies, but I have already made other plans. A meeting, a very important meeting," he said.

"I am free, and I would love to join you," Donatella said quickly.

Alexander hesitated for a moment. He could imagine what Manetti thought of the idea of his spending an evening alone with his daughter. He could also imagine what Meredith would think if the gossip columns got wind of it. Some of those columnists could make even the most innocent meeting look suspicious. Still, there was no way he could get out of it without offending her.

"I do not know . . ." Manetti was clearly uncomfortable with the idea of his innocent, inexperienced daughter spending an evening with a man of the world like Alexander. Alexander sensed his fatherly concern and found it amusing. Surely Manetti knew he would not be foolish enough to jeopardize any possible chance of bringing about a merger by trying to seduce his daughter. Though Manetti had no way of knowing, Alexander would not have touched Donatella even if he were not concerned about the merger. He was not about to do anything that would risk losing Meredith, and his private affairs, no matter how hard he tried to keep them private, had a way of getting into the newspapers.

"Please, Papa," Donatella was saying. "There is nothing wrong with Signore Kirakis and I having dinner together, especially in a place as public as the Pergola."

"You need not be concerned, Carlo," Alexander assured him. "Donna will be as safe with me as a baby in its mother's arms."

"Her mother is dead," Manetti said crossly. He was not at all pleased by his daughter's obvious infatuation with Alexander.

"Papa, I loathe staying home alone while you are off at

your business meetings," Donatella said, pouting prettily.
"It would be so good to have an evening out, away from
the maximum security facility you've turned our home
into."

"One can never be too careful in our position,
Donatella," he said sternly.

"Please, Papa?" She was not about to give up.

Manetti, unable to deny his daughter anything, finally
relented. "Ah, very well." He turned to Alexander. "You
will see that she gets home safely? I will be able to trust you
with her?"

"Absolutely."

"My daughter means more to me than my own life,"
Manetti said with a warning note in his voice. "I am trusting
you with her for the evening. Do not betray that trust, or you
will regret it."

"I would not dream of letting you down, Carlo." Alexander glanced at Donatella. She was smiling.

"He's a stubborn son of a bitch, but he'll come around
eventually." Alexander carried the telephone across the
room, cradling the receiver on his right shoulder as he
talked. Settling down on the couch, he switched the receiver
to his left ear and loosened his tie. "They always do."

"You're certainly confident," she noted.

"I know Manetti—and I know that his financial situation
is much worse than he's letting on," he said simply. "He
needs money. You see, Meredith, Carlo Manetti came up the
hard way. He started with nothing and built an empire, but
he has one important weakness. He's deathly afraid of
poverty. He couldn't deal with financial failure."

"I just wish it were over," Meredith admitted. "I miss
you."

"No more than I miss you," he said. He couldn't begin to
tell her how much he actually did miss her. Since they'd
been apart, he'd realized just how important she was to him.
"Meet me at the airport when I get back?"

"Just tell me when."

"I'll send you a cable."

"And I'll be there with bells on," she said and laughed.
God, he loved the sound of her laughter! "I wish I didn't

have to go, but unfortunately I do,'' he said. "I have an appointment."

"With Manetti?" she asked.

Alexander hesitated for a fraction of a second. "With someone close to him," he replied.

"I won't hold you up, then. Good night, Alexander."

"Good night, *matia mou.*" As the receiver clicked in his ear, the realization that came to him in a flash came too late to share with her. He pressed the phone to his lips and closed his eyes.

"I love you," he said softly.

The Pergola, at the Cavalieri Hilton International on the Via Cadolo, is one of the world's most renowned restaurants. Set on the hotel's uppermost level, it offers a panoramic view of Rome. The dramatically lit entryway is adorned by two snarling porcelain panthers. The restaurant's interior is a stylish blend of window-walls of glass, intimate lighting, modern paintings, and accents of glittering brass, silver, and black. The food is excellent, but Alexander had always suspected that the Pergola's relaxing ambience had more to do with its great success than did the outstanding cuisine.

"I feel like a princess in a fairy tale," Donatella told Alexander over dinner. "For so very long I have wanted to meet you—and now, it has not only happened, but here we are, spending the evening together."

Alexander was amused. She was so young, so innocent. How many young women like her were left in the world? he wondered. Most of them lost that innocence at a very early age. But most of them did not have a father like Carlo Manetti.

Donatella chattered happily throughout the meal, telling him about her childhood, about growing up in the convents in Rome, which she likened to being in prison; about her relationship with her father, who never refused her anything; about the years she had spent attending the Ecole des Beaux Arts in Paris. "I always had trouble talking to the young men I met there," she told him. "As a result, they thought me aloof. I was seldom asked out."

Alexander smiled patiently. "A young woman as lovely as yourself? I find that hard to believe," he said.

"But it is the truth," she insisted. "You are the first man who has ever really shown me any attention—other than Papa, of course." She drained her wineglass and looked expectantly at Alexander.

"Perhaps you have had enough, Donna?" Alexander asked, not refilling her glass. He could tell she was becoming slightly giddy.

She frowned. "You are beginning to sound like my father," she said petulantly. "Please—allow me to enjoy myself for once."

"You don't need alcohol to enjoy yourself," he said gently.

"No, I need it to relax." She leaned close to him and smiled. "You see, I am going to seduce you, Alexander."

He laughed without meaning to. She did not realize what she was saying, he thought. She had had too much to drink. He put his arm around her protectively. "I think perhaps it's time to take you home," he said.

At that moment, a photographer appeared, seemingly from nowhere, and snapped their picture. Paparazzi! Alexander thought angrily. He stood up, furious, and shouted at the man in gutter Italian as two of the restaurant's employees hustled him off the premises.

"I do not want to go home yet," Donna said stubbornly as Alexander helped her to her feet. "The evening is still young. I want to go with you—back to the Excelsior."

"I'm taking you home," Alexander said and held her arm as she stumbled down the stairs to a waiting taxi.

SIXTEEN

⌐⌐⌐⌐⌐⌐⌐⌐⌐⌐

Alexander stood at the window, surveying the already congested traffic on the Via Veneto below. Rome, he decided, was the only city in the world with traffic tie-ups to rival those of Manhattan. He was going to have to get an early start if he expected to make it to the airport by his scheduled departure time. In the distance, he could see threatening dark clouds approaching the city. Severe thunderstorms were predicted. As he stifled a yawn, he buttoned his shirt and reached for his gold cuff links. He had not slept well last night. He had lain awake most of the night thinking. His evening with Donatella Manetti had made him painfully aware of how much he missed Meredith, how much he needed her. He was in love with her . . . he was sure of that now. She had been right about both of them needing time to think, to clarify their feelings for each other. The time apart had opened his eyes, made him realize just how much he did care, how strong his feelings for her had become. He wanted her, yes—he wanted to marry her! When he returned to the States he was going to ask her to marry him, and if she turned him down, he would ask her again and again until she finally realized that they were meant for each other. He knew she still had doubts, but that was all going to change. He smiled to himself. He had never been a patient man, yet he was patient with her. He had never thought of himself as a romantic, yet he had been romancing her, in the subtlest of ways, from the very beginning. And still it had taken him months to realize that he loved her.

He looked at the phone. He had thought about calling her to tell her he would be coming home, and it would be to her. He reached for the phone but changed his mind. No, this would not do. He wanted to surprise her. Everything he had to say had to be said in person. She had to know that he was serious, that he meant every word of it.

As the car inched its way through the traffic on Via XX Settembre, Alexander thought about how he was going to tell Meredith he loved her. He wanted tonight to be something special. Everything had to be perfect. He intended to really sweep Meredith off her feet. Tonight, he decided, was going to be a night they would both remember.

An idea came to him when his driver, looking for a detour to bypass the heavy traffic, turned off on Via Nazionale, a busy shopping district. As he passed a small jewelry shop, Alexander remembered that his father had often gone there when in Rome to buy gifts for his mother. The shop had a reputation for its selection of rare, one-of-a-kind pieces. Rare, unusual, and exactly what Alexander had in mind.

"Stop!" he called out to the driver.

"Is something wrong, signore?"

"No," Alexander said, getting out before the car came to a complete stop. "Wait here. I won't be long."

There was no one else in the shop when he entered. He looked at the treasures in the enormous display cases. He was admiring a stunning emerald bracelet when a young salesman emerged from the back room.

"*Buon giorno,*" he said. "May I help you?"

Alexander pointed to the bracelet. "*Quant'è questo?*" he asked.

"Two hundred thousand lire."

He thought about it for a moment. It was lovely, but not exactly what he was looking for. "Actually, I am more interested in a ring," he said. "Something different, special."

The salesman's face brightened. "Ah, yes—I think I may have just what you are looking for," he said. "Over here."

Alexander followed him over to a case on the other side of the room. Displayed beneath the glass was the most unusual selection of rings he had ever seen. Diamonds, rubies, emeralds, sapphires—all of them in unique settings and designs. All beautiful, all extremely expensive. He examined several of them more closely. A few of them came close, but none of them was exactly right. He shook his head. "No. Nothing here is what I want."

"Perhaps it would help, signore, if you were to tell me exactly what you seek," the salesman said pleasantly.

"I'm not sure myself," Alexander said slowly. "But I'll know it when I find it."

The salesman was thoughtful for a moment. "Perhaps a pin might interest you?" he asked.

"What do you have in mind?"

"An item I just received from India. Very beautiful, very special. If you would like to see it—"

"Yes, I would."

"It is in the back. I will get it."

While he waited for the salesman to return with the pin, Alexander walked around the shop, admiring the magnificent gems, when one item in particular caught his eye. He stepped forward to take a closer look. It was the most beautiful necklace he had ever seen.

The salesman returned with the pin. "Here it is, signore—"

Alexander stopped him. "How much is that piece?" he asked, pointing to the necklace.

"Six hundred fifty thousand lire."

"May I see it?"

The salesman immediately took it from the case and placed it on a piece of black velvet. "I can say without the slightest doubt, signore, that it is the most beautiful piece of jewelry in all of Rome. It is nearly two hundred years old. The stones are incomparable."

"It is extraordinary," Alexander agreed, examining it

closely. The sapphires were the exact color of Meredith's eyes.

"It is a special necklace, signore . . . for a special person perhaps?" the salesman said as Alexander continued to stare at the necklace.

"Wrap it up," Alexander told the salesman as he took out his checkbook.

Through the window of the 747, Alexander could see the deep blue of the Atlantic Ocean below. Nothing but water as far as the eye could see in every direction. How deceptively calm it looks on the surface, he thought. Rather like Meredith's eyes, so placid and blue at first glance, masking a fiery nature beneath their calm surface. How many times had he looked into those eyes and tried to imagine what she was thinking, what she was feeling?

He took the Italian leather box from his overcoat pocket and opened it slowly. The necklace was nestled in soft, midnight-blue velvet. He took it between his thumb and index finger and examined it from various angles in the brilliant sunlight streaming through the window. A year ago, if anyone had told him he would pay that kind of money for a gift for any woman, he would have laughed in his face. But now it was different. Meeting Meredith Courtney had changed everything for him. She was everything he had ever wanted, everything he'd ever longed for in a woman. He finally realized what it was like to be in love, really in love. He wanted to show her that love, and to make her love him, more than he had ever wanted anything else in his life. He knew now that he would do anything, absolutely anything, to prove how much he loved her. He was exhilarated. The money meant little to him, but to have finally fallen in love, to have finally attained what he had always believed impossible, well, he could not put a price on that.

Had that been what he had been doing wrong all along? he wondered. He had spoken of desire, of wanting her, of the two of them being right for each other. He had tried to arouse her physically. But he had not once said those magic words. He had not told her he loved her. He was not sure he realized it himself until that night in Rome. It was a delicious, heady feeling, one he could not wait to share with her.

As Meredith emerged from a network limo in front of her apartment building, the doorman rushed forward to take the heavy attaché case she was carrying. She waved him off. "It's all right," she told him. "I can manage."

He held the door for her. "If you're sure, Miss Courtney—"

"I am." She smiled politely. "Thank you anyway, Charlie."

She crossed the lobby to the elevators and rode up to the twelfth floor alone. It had been an extremely hectic day and she was exhausted. She was beginning to feel the strain of doing two programs simultaneously. Though she was doing *World Focus* on a daily basis—and most of it live—she found *Manhattan Observer* by far the most difficult and time-consuming. It was worlds apart from *World Focus,* where she was part of a team, carrying only a portion of the workload. *Manhattan Observer* was *her* show, and she had full responsibility for it. Tonight she would have liked nothing better than to have a light dinner, take a hot bath, and go to bed early. But she had a case full of notes, clippings, and photographs to study. Research for her segment on Alexander. She smiled. Hardly a satisfactory substitute for the real thing, she thought. How she would have liked to spend an evening with him now! He had been in Rome almost a week, and she found herself missing him more every day, more than she would have believed she could. He phoned her every night, usually quite late, and they talked for hours at a time. Meredith would lie awake afterward, trying to sort out her emotions. She knew she was falling in love with him. What she didn't know was if it were possible for them to have a future together.

Letting herself into the apartment, she left her attaché case by the door, dropped her shoulder bag on a nearby chair, and took off her coat. She sat down on the couch and kicked off her shoes while she listened to her messages on the answering machine. Nothing from Alexander. She hadn't heard from him all day—no cable, no calls, nothing. Maybe he wasn't coming home that night after all. He'd probably call later.

The sound of the doorbell cut through her thoughts. She went to the door and opened it, but left the safety chain on. "Yes?"

"Cablegram for Ms. Meredith Courtney," said the uniformed messenger. He held up an envelope.

"One moment." She closed the door, removed the chain, then opened it again. Scribbling her signature on the clipboard he gave her, she took the envelope, gave him a tip, then closed the door again. Tearing it open, she read it hastily:

ARRIVING JFK 10:45 PM STOP ONE HOUR LAYOVER EN
ROUTE TO MONTREAL STOP MY CAR WILL BE IN FRONT
OF YOUR BUILDING 9:30 STOP NEED TO SEE YOU STOP
VERY IMPORTANT STOP LOVE ALEXANDER

Meredith stared at the telegram. He had signed it "love." Love was a word he had never used in her presence before, not even the night he'd tried to seduce her. She had the feeling it was a word he did not use freely, an emotion he did not take lightly. That he was using it now, that he was making this stopover to see her before flying off, for whatever reason, to Canada. . . . Suddenly she realized that in spite of her efforts, in spite of her determination not to let it happen, she had really fallen in love with Alexander. And he was in love with her. There was no turning back now, she told herself. Tonight, you have to let him know you love him. Tonight, you have to *show* him you love him.

It was an unusually cold evening for May. Meredith sat in the darkened limousine, watching anxiously as the Kirakis jet came to a stop on the runway. As the door opened and Alexander appeared at the top of the ramp, Meredith made a decision. They would have only an hour together, but she had to tell him of the discovery she'd made while he was away.

She got out of the car and walked toward the plane as he came down the ramp. When he reached the bottom, they both broke into a run, almost at the same moment, falling into each other's arms. They kissed, tenderly at first, then with increased urgency until they were both dangerously close to losing control. In his embrace, Meredith felt as though a dam had burst deep within her soul, allowing all the emotions she'd kept locked away for so long to come bursting forth. Allowing herself to love as she'd never believed she'd be able to love again. For Alexander, too, it was an intense moment, discovering feelings he'd never known before: a need for her, a longing to be close to her that went beyond mere physical desire.

It was Meredith who finally broke the silence. "I've missed you," she whispered, tracing the planes of his face lightly with her fingertips, much the way a blind person would feel her way in the darkness.

"And I you." He kissed her again. "As much as I knew I would."

They walked arm in arm to the car. He held the door for her, then slid in beside her. "Your cable sounded urgent," Meredith said. "Why do you have to go to Montreal tonight?"

He frowned. "There was a fire in the corporation's offices there. The authorities suspect arson," he said gravely. "I should have gone directly to Montreal from Rome, but I had to see you—if only for an hour."

"I'm glad you did," she said softly.

"This has been a long and very difficult day," he told her. "I left the hotel quite early, but bad weather shut down Leonardo da Vinci Airport. While I was waiting to leave, I called my office and that's when George told me about the fire in Montreal." He shook his head. "I had so many wonderful plans for tonight, for the two of us . . ."

"It's all right," she said. "There'll be time for that when you get back."

He looked at her for a moment. "Come with me," he said finally. "We have a great deal to talk about . . ."

"I wish I could, but I can't," she said. "My schedule has never been crazier than it is right now. To just pick up and leave in the middle of the night . . ."

He nodded. "I understand, but it does not make it any easier to live with." He held her close. "I can only think of how much I want you with me—especially now." Their eyes met and held. "Meredith—I love you . . ."

"I love you . . ."

They had spoken the words simultaneously. They continued to gaze at one another, confounded by the strength of their emotions, then came together again. "I could forget about Montreal," he whispered between kisses.

"Just like I could forget about tomorrow's show," she said breathlessly. "We both know better than that."

"I could send George . . ." He started kissing her neck.

She ran her fingers through his hair. "It wouldn't work. It's you they need to see," she said softly, secretly wishing he wouldn't leave. Not tonight. . . .

"I could leave in the morning," he said hoarsely. "Or I could make love to you right here . . . right now . . ."

She pulled back abruptly, not sure if he were serious or not. "We've waited this long," she murmured, "can another day—"

He silenced her with a kiss. "I've waited long enough, too long . . ."

She put her arms around him and held him tightly. "I'll be here when you get back. I'll be waiting for you," she promised.

"I intend to hold you to that promise," he told her.

"You have nothing to worry about. You couldn't get rid of me now if you tried."

He reached into his coat pocket and brought out the leather case. "I bought this for you in Rome," he said softly. "I saw it in a little shop on the Via Nazionale and looking at it in the case, it just seemed to be saying all the things I've never been able to say to you. It was as if it had been created for you."

She looked at him for a moment, then took the box and opened it, gasping at the magnificent necklace inside. Though Meredith was accustomed to owning fine jewelry and was no longer impressed by the sight of diamonds and sapphires, this was unlike anything she had ever seen before.

"It's an antique," Alexander told her. "Over two hundred years old." He took it from its case and put it around her neck.

"I've never seen anything so beautiful," she whispered.

"I have," he said huskily as his lips sought hers in the darkness. The black leather box fell to the floor as they came together again.

Meredith silently hoped the next forty-eight hours would pass quickly.

A sheet of paper with three lines typed on it was in the typewriter, as it had been all morning. A cup of coffee sat on one corner of the desk, cold and untouched. A stack of mail had been left unopened. Meredith stood at the window, staring ahead without really seeing anything. In her hand was a copy of *People* magazine from the week before, opened to a photograph of Alexander taken at a restaurant in Rome. With him was a beautiful young woman identified as Donatella Manetti, daughter of Italian auto magnate Carlo Manetti. They were smiling and laughing, looking very intimate. Damn you, Alexander, Meredith thought bitterly. Have you enjoyed making a fool of me? Did you enjoy your little game, making me fall in love with you? Is this your way of getting even with me for rejecting you when we first met? You must be having a good laugh over this one!

"God, how could I have been so stupid?" she asked aloud, throwing the magazine to the floor.

She sank into her chair and took the familiar black leather box from the drawer. She opened it slowly and stared at the necklace for a long time, recalling the night he gave it to her. It had been the happiest night of her life. She had finally been able to admit to her real feelings, to tell him she loved him. She had been ready to give herself to him completely. She would have gone to bed with him that night had he not had to rush off to Montreal. He would have finally gotten what he had really wanted from her.

Meredith was determined not to cry, no matter how painful it became for her. He wasn't worth it, she reminded herself. But he's not totally to blame, she conceded. It's as much my fault as it is his. I'm guilty of being stupid in the first degree. I let myself be taken in by him. I should have known better. I knew what kind of man he was. I'd heard all the horror stories.

When she thought of how foolish she had been, allowing

herself to weaken, to surrender to his charm, his cheap words of love, it sickened her. Words of love—it was almost laughable! He really isn't one to forgive and forget, she thought miserably. I refused him the first time he tried to get me into bed, so he got back at me by making me fall in love with him. Well, he's certainly gotten even. Why did I ever listen to him?

Her secretary came to the door then. "Meredith, Alexander Kirakis is on line one—"

"Tell him I'm not in."

"He says it's urgent."

"Tell him I'm not in!" Meredith snapped irritably.

Cindy stared at her for a moment. "What about the interview? Have you forgotten your deadline—"

"I haven't forgotten anything! I'll call him when I'm ready to talk to him—about the interview," she said crossly. "Until then, I'm not in when he calls."

At the World Trade Center, Alexander held one of his rare press conferences to officially announce that plans were under way for the corporation to enter the field of nuclear research. He talked about the new atomic research facility, located in Southern California's Mojave Desert region, just east of the Twenty-nine Palms Marine Corps Base. He discussed the appointment of Dr. Barry Marchwood, one of the world's foremost authorities on nuclear weaponry and a former member of the team at the Los Alamos Scientific Laboratory in New Mexico, answering criticisms that he planned to eventually go into the development of nuclear armaments. He admitted that this was a definite possibility, but refused to comment further on the subject.

"Well, you've done it again," George chided him as they walked back to Alexander's office after the conference. "You're going to be on the front page of every newspaper in the free world by tomorrow. I can see the headlines now: 'Kirakis Promotes Nuclear Arms Race.'"

Alexander walked on in stony silence. George studied him for a moment. Alexander had been in a strange mood for the past week, ever since his return from Montreal. George knew he was concerned about the arson theory regarding the fire, but he had the feeling there was more bothering Alexander than the fire. Much more. Watching him was like waiting for a time bomb to go off. He never knew when Alexander was going to erupt. He decided to leave him alone with his problem. Alexander had made it clear he was not willing to talk about it, and George knew it would do no good to push it. He excused himself and went off to his office.

As Alexander reached his own suite, his secretary met him at the door. "A package just came for you, Mr. Kirakis," she told him. "By special messenger. I put it on your desk."

"Thank you, Stacey," he said absently.

He went into the office and closed the door. He unwrapped the small package he found on his desk and discovered the Italian leather box inside. He carefully opened it and stared at the necklace inside. She had sent it back. No note, nothing. Just sent it back. He had been so close to finally making her his wife, to realizing a dream he had always thought impossible, and that damned picture in *People* had ruined everything. He might never get her back now. Lashing out in rage, he knocked a stack of reports off the desk, scattering them across the floor. He stood for a moment, trembling in anger, then made his decision. He leaned across the console table and pressed the button on the intercom. "Stacey, I will be leaving in a few minutes. I won't be back this afternoon."

"Where can I reach you?" she asked.

"You can't."

Meredith hurried through the crowded lobby of the Intercontinental Broadcasting Building and pushed her way through the doors facing Fifty-second Street. Outside, the blasting cold winds were so strong that it was hard for her to keep from losing her balance. The weather had been crazy all month, raining one day, cold and windy the next; it certainly didn't seem like May. She knew the network limo would not be waiting for her tonight. She was not going directly home. She'd decided to get a cab and go shopping. She had spent too many evenings holed up in her apartment.

She was eager to put the past few weeks behind her, once and for all.

She didn't notice the limousine parked at the curb until the door opened and Alexander stepped out, blocking her path. "Good evening, Meredith."

She looked up at him, anger in her eyes. "It was a good evening," she said coldly, "until now."

"I think we should talk. It is very important—to both of us."

"I have nothing to say to you."

"But I have something to say to you," he insisted.

"I don't want to hear it."

"It's about the interview," he said as she started to walk away.

She stopped in her tracks and turned. "What about it?" she asked briskly.

"Do you not think it's time we taped it?" he asked, leaning against the car. "I believe you are now very close to your deadline, correct?"

"Your concern is touching," she said. "But I assure you, I have not forgotten my deadline. I'll be in touch with your office when I'm ready to tape."

"It will have to be soon," he said. "I am going to be out of town at the end of the month."

"Business?"

He shook his head. "Pleasure, for once."

"What's her name?" Meredith asked in an icy tone.

Alexander frowned. "No woman," he said quietly. "I have entered a polo match in Southampton on the Saturday before Memorial Day. I plan to be away for a week or longer."

"I'll plan on taping the interview after you return, then," Meredith said.

"I thought you might be interested in taping at least part of the match for your program," he said.

She thought about it for a moment. "Maybe. I'll let you know."

He nodded.

"Is there anything else?" she asked.

"Yes," he said finally. "I love you."

She ignored his last statement. "I have to go," she said. "I'll call your office if I decide to film the match."

Alexander watched her disappear into the crowd. He did not try to stop her. He knew it would do no good. But he had not given up. Not by a long shot. He had used the interview to bring them together to begin with, and he would use it again to get her back.

SEVENTEEN

༄༄༄༄༄༄༄༄༄

Meredith leaned against the front of her rental car, watching the polo match through high-powered binoculars as an IBS cameraman filmed the action from a mobile production unit parked nearby. Though Meredith had known that including clips of the match in the show would definitely lend an air of glamour to the program and show Alexander's fierce competitive spirit in a different light, she had come very close to calling off this taping. She did not want to be here. She had not seen him since the evening he had waited for her outside the Broadcast Center. She knew she was going to be seeing a great deal of him, like it or not, until the taping was completed, but after that, she fully intended to forget she had ever known him.

Though Meredith was far from an expert on the game—this was the first match she'd attended since the one she'd covered at the Los Angeles Equestrian Center—she had picked up enough knowledge from past conversations with Alexander to know what was going on. He looks like a gladiator riding into battle, she thought as she fixed her binoculars on him. He rode a magnificent bay gelding that appeared to be larger than the other players' mounts. She remembered his telling her once that he preferred very fast horses that were somewhat larger than the standard polo pony. He always played the number one spot—the main offensive position—and selected his mounts for their speed and their ability to take the full force of an opposing back crashing into him. First and second positions are offensive, third and fourth are defensive, Meredith recalled. First position players need speed.

It was now the beginning of the fourth chukker, the "fatal fourth" as Alexander called it. He said it was the decisive chukker in a match. He liked to play his best ponies in those first four chukkers, convinced that if his team remained tied with the opposition until the start of the fourth, victory would be theirs, even in the face of the strongest opposition. He took the game as seriously as he took his business affairs, and he demanded as much of the players and ponies on his team as he did of his corporation acolytes. Meredith watched, caught up in the excitement, as Alexander, wielding his mallet like a weapon, swung out forcefully in an off-side forward shot, sending the ball blasting down the field like a guided missile. The back for the opposing team, a well-known player Alexander had once described as a "push-and-shove specialist," collided with Alexander's mount, but the bay had been braced for the hit. Meredith winced.

Polo, she decided, turning her sights briefly to the stands, was definitely a rich man's game. She scanned the crowd of poised and elegantly turned-out spectators, the women in their Halstons and their Geoffrey Beenes and their Oscar de la Rentas, and the men looking as if they had just stepped from the pages of *GQ*. People bred for this way of life almost as carefully as the horses had been—bluebloods, all of them. But it was much more than that. It was a power game, a test of courage and intellect. A game for only the most perfectly conditioned athletes. It demanded control, courage, and a calculating daring. It was, she realized, Alexander's game. He had been born for it.

The play was fast and furious during the fifth and sixth chukkers. Alexander made several blasting backhand shots with ball-rocketing accuracy as his opponents failed repeatedly in their attempts to block each shot. The cunning strategy and deadly energy he unleashed on the polo field could be likened to the brilliant board-room maneuvering he was known for, Meredith thought wryly. He changed mounts for each of the six chukkers and kept four mounts in reserve because he rode more aggressively than any of the other players and was therefore harder on his horses. Through the binoculars Meredith could see the clenched jaw, the warlike scowl on his face as he charged one of his opponents, clearly intending to unhorse the other player yet stopping just short of a clear violation of the USPA ruling that expressly forbade any player to intimidate another rider to the point of causing him to pull out. She was intrigued by the fierce manner in which he competed, playing the game as he did everything else: to win. It was easy to see why he was a champion. He was a consummate horseman who had established an unspoken communication with each of his ponies. Coupled with his cool, calculating manner, it made him virtually unbeatable.

A burst of cheering from the stands signaled the end of the match as the eight riders all headed back. Meredith lowered her binoculars and looked on with interest as Alexander was presented with a large silver cup. She signaled the cameraman to stop filming. As he looked up, Alexander saw her. He dismounted in one swift, fluid movement and headed in her direction. Extricating himself from the crowd, he picked his way across the divot-marred polo grounds, leading his pony behind him. As he approached the mobile production unit, he removed his helmet. Underneath, his thick dark hair was tousled and damp with perspiration.

"I'm glad to see you," he said, smiling. "I must admit, though, that I'm surprised."

"Why?" Her eyes met his defiantly. "I do have a show to do, remember?"

"I see." He paused. "In that case, I hope it hasn't been a wasted trip."

"Not at all." Her smile was cool. "We have more than enough footage."

"Then you'll be leaving soon?" he asked.

"As soon as we can pack it all in."

He hesitated for a moment. "I have to speak privately with you, Meredith," he said, lowering his voice.

"About the interview?"

"About us."

"There is no us. Not anymore. I'm beginning to think there never was."

"You don't believe that any more than I do," he said.

"I've said all I have to say on the subject." She started to turn away.

He grabbed her arm. "Well, *I* haven't," he snapped without raising his voice. "You are going to hear what I have to say, one way or another. Now, do we talk privately or do I say it right here and now?"

She hesitated for a moment. She knew him well enough to know that he was not bluffing. She had no desire to discuss their private affairs in front of the cameraman or anyone else. "All right," she said finally. "Where and when?"

"Right now," he said. "Come with me."

Meredith turned to the cameraman. "Wrap it up," she told him. "If I'm not back by the time you're finished, go ahead and leave."

He nodded.

Meredith walked by Alexander's side in an icy silence as they crossed the grounds in the direction of the stables. Alexander's mount trailed along slowly behind them, head lowered in exhaustion, sweating profusely. Alexander turned around and patted the animal's neck affectionately. "I'm afraid I've been a bit too rough on Spartacus here this afternoon," he said. "I think I'll have to put him out to pasture for a day or two." As they entered the stables, he handed the reins over to a young groom. "Take good care of my friend here," he instructed.

"Yes, sir, Mr. Kirakis."

They walked in silence down the long, wide aisle lined with box stalls. At the sound of their footsteps, some of the horses began to whinny and move about in their boxes. Alexander walked on, with the fast but graceful stride with which he normally moved, and headed for the section in which his own horses were kept. He checked each of them, making certain they had been tended properly and giving each horse a few sugar cubes. Meredith was surprised by the gentleness with which he treated the animals.

"Hadrian will be out of commission for a while,"

Alexander said. "He was injured this morning. I'm told it isn't serious, but I refuse to ride him again until he's in perfect condition. Ceasar here is in a foul temper today—be careful, he may try to nip you. Atilla will have to be retired soon. He's getting on in years—"

"You didn't bring me out here to tell me about your polo ponies," Meredith snapped irritably. "Would you please just say whatever it is you want to say and get it over with? It's a long drive back to Manhattan and I'd really like to go."

He smiled. "I suppose I should be encouraged by your anger," he said easily. "After all, anger *is* better than indifference, isn't it? At least you feel something for me, even if it isn't what I would like."

"Do you enjoy taunting me?" she asked.

His face was suddenly serious. "No," he answered honestly. "I'm not enjoying any of this. It doesn't please me at all that you won't see me or speak to me—or allow me the opportunity to explain about that damned picture!"

"You don't owe me any explanations," she said coldly.

He looked at her. "All of the things we said to each other that night at the airport . . . that means nothing to you now?"

"It meant a great deal to me. Obviously it meant nothing to you."

He stepped forward and put his hands on her arms. "I went to Rome to meet with Manetti. I met his daughter when we were having lunch one day," he said quietly. "I invited both of them to dinner. Carlo couldn't make it, but his daughter accepted the invitation. There was no way I could get out of it then without offending her."

"You didn't look too miserable in that picture."

"Donna Manetti is very young and very inexperienced," he said. "She has led a very sheltered life. She had a schoolgirl crush on me—"

"Some schoolgirl!" Meredith's laugh was hollow.

"Let me finish. Of course we had wine with dinner, but she had too much. When that picture was taken, she was pretty well out of it. I was trying to convince her to let me take her home."

"Whose home?" Meredith asked sarcastically.

"I didn't sleep with her, Meredith."

"It doesn't matter if you did or not." She was deliberately avoiding his eyes, not wanting him to see the pain in hers.

"Doesn't it?"

She did not respond.

"Look at me, Meredith," he insisted. "Look at me and tell me it really doesn't matter, that you don't care. Tell me what we had together before all of this happened means nothing to you."

She looked up. "All right!" she snapped. "It does matter to me! I do care about what did or did not happen in Rome! Is that what you want to hear?"

"Yes! I want you to be jealous!" he admitted. "I want to know that it matters! I want you to love me just as I love you!" His eyes met hers, and their gaze held. He leaned forward and kissed her tenderly. Meredith drew back and looked at him.

"I was so sure I knew you."

"You know me better than anyone else ever could." He kissed her again.

"I feel like a moth that's flown too close to the flame," she said.

His smile was sad. "The question is, which of us is the moth, and which is the flame?"

"I don't want to get burned again."

"Give it a chance, Meredith—give us a chance," he urged. "It will work. We belong together."

"I used to think we did."

"I have a house near here," he said. "I was planning to stay on for the rest of the week. Come with me. Give me a chance to prove to you that my love for you is real."

"I can't—I have obligations . . . to the show, to the network—"

"I have obligations as well," he said, "but our first obligation is to each other."

"Tell that to my producer," she said wearily.

Alexander thought about it for a moment. "Call him when we get there," he said. "Tell him I've given you permission to film the interview itself at Southampton, since I will be there for the week. Tell him you'll be there all week, working out last-minute details with me. He can send a camera crew up on Thursday or Friday. That will give us a few days alone.''

"I don't know . . ."

His gaze was direct. "I love you, Meredith. I don't want to lose you."

"I don't have any other clothes, or—"

"There are shops in the village."

She hesitated for a moment. "You have an answer for everything, don't you."

"Everything," he said, taking her hands in his, "except the one thing that matters most to me."

Alexander's home in Southampton was an elegant, fifteen-room Georgian mansion set on ten acres of carefully tended grounds overlooking the Atlantic Ocean. The house itself was a gracious expanse with eleven-foot ceilings, French doors, and tall casements that opened onto a broad terrace and a magnificent view of the grounds. It had a fully equipped spa with sauna, steam room, and whirlpool, an indoor pool, wine cellar, curved solarium, and music room. There were stables for his polo ponies and separate servants' quarters to the rear of the main house. Meredith was surprised to find that the interior was nothing at all like the stark, modern decor of his apartment at the Olympic Tower. The marble fireplaces in the living room, library, and master suite, the leaded windows, the ornate moldings, and planked flooring were reminiscent of another era, as were the comfortable, overstuffed couches and chairs, the antiques that seemed to be everywhere, the Impressionist paintings adorning the walls. A grandfather clock that was over a hundred years old stood in the library and kept perfect time, as well as a hand-carved table Alexander told Meredith had been made by gypsies.

"I like to think of this place as my private retreat," Alexander said, watching as Meredith walked around the library, admiring the antiques and paintings. "I come here when I need to escape the demands and pressures of Manhattan—or when I simply feel the need to be alone."

Meredith looked at him and smiled. "It's funny, I've never thought of you as a man who would want to be away from his work for very long," she said.

"As a rule, no, I would not," he told her. "But I've found that even the most dedicated of us needs to get away, to take time for ourselves occasionally. There was a time —when I first became chairman of Kirakis, and even for a time before that—when I tried to make the corporation my life. I tried to convince myself that it was all I wanted, all I needed."

"But it didn't work," Meredith concluded.

"It never works, *matia mou*," he responded with a tired smile. "The corporation is very important to me, yes. It is my birthright, the legacy left to me by my father. But I know now that it can never be my whole life, just as your career cannot be yours." He poured a glass of wine and offered it to her. "You'll like this. It is from my own vineyards."

"You're also in the wine business?" she asked, surprised.

"I own a château in the south of France—in the Côtes-du-Rhône region," he answered. "Regretfully, I haven't been able to spend as much time there in the past few years as I would have liked. I used to go every year in time for the harvest. I enjoyed working in the vineyards."

Meredith laughed without thinking. "I'm sorry," she apologized. "It's just that it's hard for me to imagine you doing any kind of physical labor."

"Actually, I found it fun," he said, pouring another glass of wine. "I was quite young—barely fourteen—when my father acquired the vineyards. I'd always had a special fondness for France—inherited from my mother, I suppose —so naturally I jumped at the chance to spend time there. My mother hated the idea of her son working in the vineyards, but I enjoyed it, and my father felt it would be a learning experience for me. He was right."

"You must miss them both very much," Meredith said hesitantly as he refilled her glass.

He nodded. "Losing them has made me realize the importance of family, of having someone to share things with," he said quietly.

Meredith's eyes met his, and she felt an involuntary shiver coursing down her spine. Was it from the wine, she wondered, or was it the way he was looking at her? She knew she was blushing, but she was unable to prevent it. "I suppose everyone needs someone," she murmured, then she fell silent, deliberately avoiding his eyes.

He noticed her empty glass. "More wine?" he asked.

She shook her head. "I think I've had enough," she said. "I'm beginning to feel a little light-headed now. Besides, it's getting late . . ."

Alexander nodded. "Forgive me, *matia mou*. I have been enjoying myself so much I have lost all track of time," he said. "You must be exhausted."

"Just a bit," she confessed.

He smiled. "Come . . . I will show you to your room."

The bright sunlight streaming through the bay windows woke Meredith the next morning. She sat up in bed and stretched, realizing she'd forgotten to draw the drapes the night before. She looked over at the antique clock on the dressing table. It was almost noon. She wondered if Alexander were still sleeping.

She heard a light tapping sound at the door. Before Meredith could respond, a maid entered. "Mademoiselle, I am Danielle," she said in a heavy French accent. "Monsieur Kirakis instructed me to look in on you, to ask you what you would like for breakfast, and to tell you he had these sent up for you from the village." She gestured toward a stack of boxes on the chair. "The clothes you will need. I hope the sizes are correct."

Meredith couldn't hide her surprise. "Yes," she mumbled. "Thank you."

"And breakfast, mademoiselle?"

Meredith thought about it for a moment. She didn't have much appetite this morning. "Something light," she said. "Maybe a croissant with butter and jam and some coffee."

"*Oui, mademoiselle.*" The woman turned to leave.

"Danielle?" Meredith said. "Alexander—Mr. Kirakis —is he already awake?"

"*Oui, mademoiselle.* He is an early riser by habit. He has been down at the stables since shortly after dawn," Danielle told her. "He asked that you join him there after you've had breakfast."

Meredith nodded. "I will."

"Would you like your breakfast served here, or will you be coming downstairs?" Danielle asked.

Meredith smiled. "I'll come down. Thank you."

She opened each of the boxes and examined the contents. Jeans, pants, cotton shirts, even riding boots. Even the sizes were correct. She smiled to herself. He thought of everything.

She finally chose a pair of jeans and a pink cotton shirt. As she dressed, she tried to remember how long it had been since she'd been on a horse. Would she be able to ride as well as she once had?

I'll soon find out, she thought.

She found Alexander in the paddock, mounting a magnificent black gelding. He looked so different now from the impeccably attired chairman of the board of the Kirakis Corporation. He wore gray pants tucked inside black riding boots and a white cotton shirt, the sleeves rolled almost to his elbows. His dark hair was blowing in the wind, and he looked more at ease than Meredith had ever seen him.

"Good morning," she greeted him as she climbed up on the fence.

He turned and smiled. "Good afternoon, *matia mou*," he responded. "Did you sleep well?"

"Too well, I think," she said as she perched on the top rail. "But I hear you've had a busy morning."

"I'm accustomed to getting up early, no matter what time I retire the night before," he said, reining in the prancing, spirited horse. "I had hoped you would go for a ride with me."

"I'd love to."

"Have you ever ridden before?" he asked.

Meredith laughed. "Where I come from, you learn how to ride around the same time you learn to walk. It's been a while, but I'm told it's something you never forget."

"If you're sure," he said. "My horses are all quite spirited. For me, a horse—like a woman—without spirit has no appeal."

She smiled knowingly. "Trying to tell me something?"

"What do you think?"

"I think you're about as subtle as a sledgehammer," she said, laughing.

He signaled one of the grooms. "Saddle Apollo for Miss Courtney," he told the boy.

"Yes, sir."

Alexander turned to look at Meredith. "Miss Courtney," he repeated in a low voice so that only she could hear him. "But not for much longer."

Meredith was surprised at how easily it all came back to her once she was in the saddle. She had almost forgotten how much she'd enjoyed riding. She and Alexander rode all over the grounds that morning, winding up with an exhilarating gallop on the beach. Afterward, they dismounted and led the horses along the surf, enjoying the privacy and the splendid view. Meredith was glad she had come, glad she had given him a chance to explain. She believed his story because she wanted to believe it and because she was convinced now that he really did love her.

"This is the real reason I decided to buy this property," he told her as they walked along the white sand beach, several hundred yards from the house. "The house itself is exactly what I had in mind when I began looking at property here. I'm quite satisfied with it. But when I saw this beach—it reminds me so much of the beaches on my island in Greece—I had to have it. Even though I've been away from the island for many years now, I find I still miss the peaceful times I spent there growing up. The first time I came through those doors"—he pointed toward the house—"the first time I saw this beach, it was like being home."

"I know how you feel," Meredith told him. "When I lived in Southern California, I always loved walking on the beach at dawn, swimming in the ocean, smelling the salt water in the air—"

"When you lived with Nick Holliday," Alexander broke in, staring out at the ocean. "Were you planning to marry him?"

She looked at him, surprised. "No, I wasn't."

Alexander picked up a piece of driftwood and threw it

several yards down the beach in front of them. "You must have loved him."

Meredith hesitated for a moment. "Yes, I did," she said softly. "Once. But then everything started to go wrong between us, and . . ." Her voice trailed off.

"You had no desire to get involved with anyone else," he concluded.

"For a long time I thought I didn't really need anyone," she admitted. "But now . . . I see I was wrong."

Alexander stopped walking and turned to face her. "I'm very pleased to hear that," he said, his eyes meeting hers. "I want to be your future, Meredith—and I want you to be mine. It would not be easy for me to have to compete with someone from your past."

"There is no one from my past, Alexander."

He took her in his arms, and when their lips met, there was a rightness between them that couldn't be denied. Meredith wrapped her arms around his neck and clung to him, finally allowing herself to respond to the passion that had always existed between them.

"I had no idea it would get so cold." Meredith stretched out on a pile of oversize pillows in front of the fireplace, basking in the warm glow of the fire, the only light in the room.

"The nights are sometimes quite cold, even at this time of the year." Alexander brought a bottle of Dom Perignon and two glasses, and joined her on the floor.

She smiled when she saw the bottle. "Are we celebrating your victory at the match?" she asked casually.

"No," he said quietly. "We're celebrating us . . . being here together." He eased the cork out of the bottle, his eyes still on her. Suddenly it popped, and they were both caught in a shower of champagne. Startled, Meredith looked down at her silk shirt, soaked and clinging to her breasts in a way that made it seem almost transparent.

"I think you just wasted an entire bottle of champagne," she said, her cheeks flushed.

"On the contrary," he said, smiling at her. "I think it looks quite becoming on you."

They stared at each other, and it was as if they were

making love with their eyes. He moved closer, and slowly, deliberately, he unbuttoned her blouse and slipped it off her shoulders. She wore nothing underneath. He kissed her tenderly as they lay back on the pillows. Slowly, sensuously, he licked the rivulets of champagne that trickled down the cleft between her breasts, raising his head only momentarily to kiss her again. His lips caressed the firm, warm swells of flesh, moving fleetingly across her nipples as he began to tease them with his tongue. He raised his head from time to time to kiss her lips again and again. "I love you," he whispered as he unzipped her jeans and pulled them off. "Let me show you how much I love you . . ."

"Oh, yes," she gasped. "Make love with me, Alexander . . ." She unbuttoned his shirt and fumbled with his belt as his mouth sought hers in the heat of their finally unleashed desire. She stroked his hair as he nuzzled her breasts. His hand moved between her legs, touching her, exploring. Their bodies entwined as they lay on the heap of pillows embracing, arousing each other with their kisses and caresses. Meredith slid her hand between their bodies and found his swollen shaft, stroking it gently, then more passionately. He lay back, moaning with pleasure as the excitement within him grew, becoming almost unbearable. "I do love you," she told him. "It's taken me so long to realize it . . . but I do . . . so much . . ." She lowered her face to his and kissed him longingly. He touched her again, caressing her, bringing her to a sharp orgasm with his hand. She rolled over on her back, trembling violently as he entered her. Once inside her, he moved deeper, faster, thrusting his hips as hers rose from the floor to meet him. She felt him tremble violently in her arms as he reached his orgasm, and just at that moment, she climaxed with him again in a final burst of excitement. The room seemed to spin as he fell limp on top of her, his breathing labored as he kissed her again.

They lay very still for a long time afterward, Alexander's face buried in her neck as he whispered endearments. Finally, he raised himself up on his elbows and gazed down at her face, glowing in the dim light of the dying fire. "I've never made love before," he whispered, fondling a lock of her hair. "I've never really made love until tonight. I never imagined that there could be such a difference between sex and making love."

His wonder at these newly realized feelings was reflected in his face, in the glow of his intense black eyes. He'd never believed it was possible to feel this way. It was as though his life had not been truly complete until she became a part of it. She'd taught him to laugh. He hadn't realized until then that laughter was within him. She'd made it possible for him to think of something other than business, to enjoy the simplest things just by being with her.

"Neither did I," Meredith said softly, savoring the feel of him, the male smell of him. Never would she have believed she would find such joy with a notorious scoundrel like Alexander Kirakis, but she'd seen a side of him no one else knew existed. In his arms, she'd been swept away by emotions so strong they took her breath away. "All these wasted months," she whispered. "It was inevitable, wasn't it."

He laughed. "I tried to tell you, my love, but I've found you to be an extremely stubborn woman at times." He kissed her forehead, the tip of her nose, her lips. "It doesn't matter now. It was worth waiting for, wasn't it?"

"Definitely." She looked up at him, her blue eyes shining.

He held her close, nuzzling her neck. "I wish I could hold you forever and never let you go . . ."

When Meredith woke the next morning, she was in bed with Alexander, lying on her side, facing away from him. He was embracing her from behind, his body pressed tightly against hers as he nibbled lightly at her neck. She barely remembered him carrying her upstairs last night. They had made love over and over, then, when they were both spent and unable to go on, he had brought her up to his bedroom and they'd fallen asleep in an embrace. It had been the most incredible night of her life.

"Good morning," he muttered. "Did I wake you?"

"I don't know," she said in a half-teasing voice. "Were you trying to?"

"Only for the past half hour," he admitted.

She rolled over on her back and looked up at him. He pulled himself up on one elbow and smiled down at her. "Last night," Meredith said softly, "was like an incredible, beautiful dream. I was almost afraid to wake up."

Alexander smiled. "I assure you, it was quite real." He kissed her tenderly. "I've been awake since dawn, just lying here, trying to think of at least one good excuse for not taking you back to Manhattan, but all I can think of are all the reasons why we must go back." He touched her hair. "I've never been a superstitious man, but I find myself afraid to take you home, afraid of breaking the spell."

She kissed him. "Nothing could break the spell you cast over me last night," she told him. "You couldn't lose me now if you wanted to. I love you."

"But there's a part of me that worries I'll lose you after fighting so hard to win your love."

"Nothing could change how I feel about you now, Alexander."

He pulled back the sheets, uncovering her, and his hand moved slowly over her breasts, stroking them as his tongue made tiny circles over the sensitive area just behind her ear. "Perhaps we could stay here just one more week?" he whispered as he began stroking her nipples with his index finger. He kissed her hungrily. "Just one more week . . ."

"I want to," she said, her excitement growing. "But I can't. I have a show to do . . ."

He lowered his head to her breast, sucking gently at her nipples, tantalizing her. He raised himself up again and kissed her lips. "Surely they can find someone to replace you for one week."

"I'm irreplaceable," she said with a grin.

"I know that, but the network can surely find someone to do your show," he muttered as he reached between her legs.

"No . . . maybe . . ." She began to moan with pleasure.

"Of course they can," he said insistently. His mouth came down on hers. They kissed again and again. "I could tell them I'm not feeling well," she murmured. "Or I could say I'm working out some of the details of the show . . ."

He grinned. "Getting to know your subject?" he asked as he started kissing her neck.

"Of course," she said, dizzy with desire. "But I don't

think we'll tell them just how well acquainted we've become.''

''I would hope not.'' He kissed her full on the mouth again, then pulled back. ''It isn't, after all, the kind of thing one discusses on nationwide television.''

''Definitely not,'' she agreed, reaching for him. He eluded her grasp as he moved lower, kissing her breasts, her stomach, her thighs, slowly working his way to her pubis. Meredith began to quiver with excitement as he parted her outer lips and began licking her clitoris. She reached a violent orgasm almost immediately, having been aroused from the moment he had awakened her with his kisses. Then, pulling away abruptly, Alexander reared over her, thrusting himself into her, taking her swiftly, silently, until his whole body convulsed with release. When it was over he held her tightly as he kissed her neck. ''Do you have any idea what you do to me?'' he rasped.

''Yes,'' she said softly, ''because you do the same thing to me.'' She held him close, not wanting to ever let him go.

''We could stay here all week and never leave this room,'' he breathed.

''It sounds heavenly,'' she whispered, stroking his hair.

''I can never be without you again, Meredith.''

The urgency in his voice surprised her. ''You won't be,'' she promised. ''I'll never leave you.''

''Not good enough.'' He pulled himself up on his elbows and looked into her eyes. ''I want to make a commitment to you. I want a commitment *from* you.''

She looked up at him expectantly, waiting for him to go on.

''I want to marry you, Meredith,'' he told her. ''I want to make you my wife.''

''You'll have to wear this,'' Alexander told Meredith as he took one of his silk robes from his closet and tossed it on the bed. ''I'm afraid your clothes are scattered on the carpet downstairs.''

Meredith sat up, pushing her hair away from her face with one hand. Until this moment, she had not given a thought to the way they had hastily discarded their clothes last night, leaving everything behind when he carried her up to his bed.

She reached for the robe. "I would have loved to see the maid's face this morning when she went into the library," she said, giggling. "Or is she accustomed to this sort of thing?"

He turned to look at her, his face serious. "I've never brought anyone here—until now," he said quietly.

She got off the bed and slipped the robe on, tying the wide sash around her waist. She crossed the room to him, wrapping her arms around his waist. "Are you sure you want to be tied down with a wife?" she asked in a playful tone. "Won't you regret having to give up your playboy ways? Marriage will definitely cramp your style."

"I'll have everything I want—or need—with you," he assured her. "And as for giving up my so-called playboy ways, I do so without regret, *matia mou*. You are the only woman I want, will ever want." His hands moved up her neck, under her hair, as he kissed her longingly.

She pulled away from him and smiled. "I think I'd better go get dressed," she said gently.

He looked at her for a moment, smiling appreciatively. "The robe looks beautiful on you," he commented as he put on his shirt. "But then, you would look beautiful in anything—or nothing . . ."

Meredith smiled and blew him a kiss. "I won't be long," she promised. She left him and went down the hall to her own room. She thought about it all as she showered and dressed. Alexander wanted to be married right away; he'd made that quite clear. As much as she wanted to marry him, Meredith also wanted a traditional wedding with all the trimmings. I'm only going to do this once, she thought, so why not make it a day to remember?

She stared at the face looking back at her from the mirror, surprised by what she saw. It seemed as if she had been transformed into a different woman overnight. The tousled hair, the flushed cheeks, the excited eyes, all the telltale signs of a woman in love, she thought. A face suddenly alive with passion, rosy with the afterglow of a night of unrestrained lovemaking.

The next three days passed quickly, much more quickly than either Alexander or Meredith would have liked. No one could have been more surprised than they were to find themselves in no hurry to return to the demands and obligations of the high-pressure worlds in which they lived back in Manhattan. They had become too absorbed in each other, in their newly consummated love, to give a thought to the world that still existed outside their sanctuary in Southampton. From the night they made love for the first time, they enjoyed an idyllic existence in a world far removed from the supercharged pace of Manhattan. They spent every moment together. They went for long walks, talking, sharing dreams, exploring the depths of each other's souls. They swam in the ocean and made love on the beach in the moonlight. They went riding every morning and sometimes again in the evening as well. They lunched on the terrace and had romantic candlelight dinners in the sumptuous dining room. After dinner, they turned out the lights and listened to music in front of a roaring fire in the library. Alexander, Meredith discovered, loved classical music and owned an extensive collection of tapes as well as a state-of-the-art stereo system that made the music sound as if it were being performed live. They invariably ended up making love on the floor before the fireplace, and afterward, Alexander carried her upstairs to his bedroom where they would fall asleep locked in each other's arms.

In Alexander, Meredith found everything she wanted, everything she needed. He was handsome and charming and wealthy, but that was only the icing on the cake. He was also gentle, affectionate, and surprisingly romantic, a wonderful lover. He was patient and understanding. He was the first man she had known—including Nick—who loved her unconditionally and didn't try to change her. He not only accepted her ambition, he encouraged it. He had said it all himself: a woman without spirit had no appeal for him. It's almost too good to be true, she thought, elated.

The IBS crew arrived to tape the interview and the remaining clips for the show early on Friday morning. While they set up their equipment in the library, Meredith went upstairs to see what could be keeping Alexander. She found him in front of the full-length mirror in the bedroom, straightening his tie. "They want to do the outdoor segments first," she said as she entered the bedroom and closed the door.

He turned to look at her. "I have never allowed media people on the grounds—let alone inside the main house—in the past," he said simply. "I'm only doing so now for you."

She crossed the room and took his hands in hers, giving him a light peck on the cheek. "I know you've never been crazy about the idea of doing it this way," she said softly. "I know you only agreed to taping the interview here so we could have some time alone."

"And to insure the success of your program," he said.

"And to convince me that we really love each other." She reached up to fix a stray lock of his hair.

His eyes met hers, and his expression was serious. "Do something for me," he said in a low voice.

"Anything," she responded without hesitation.

He put his arms around her. "Marry me—this weekend, before we return to Manhattan," he said huskily. "I don't want to wait a moment longer than is absolutely necessary."

"Neither do I," she insisted, keeping her voice light. "But then, we're not really waiting, are we?"

The IBS crew filmed a tour of the estate, following Alexander and Meredith as they walked on the grounds, in the stables, and inside the main house. For the cameras, Alexander showed Meredith his polo ponies and talked about his very private reasons for buying this particular estate.

"It's going to be a smash," Meredith told him during a break in the taping. "You wanted to change your public image, and this is going to do it. When this show is aired, the public will see a side of you no one ever dreamed existed."

The interview itself was taped in the library. Meredith had convinced Alexander that it would definitely be to his advantage to discuss his feelings about growing up in the shadow of his legendary father, to talk about the pressures and the disadvantages of having to live up to that image. She knew that it was an extremely personal approach and it would be difficult for a man as private as Alexander had always been to discuss such intimate feelings on television, but she also knew it would get the results he wanted. It would show the very human side of a man who seemed virtually invincible to the world at large. Had anyone else been doing the interview, Meredith knew that such a discussion would have been out of the question, but because they were lovers, because he trusted her, it would be easier for him to open up, to talk about such deeply personal feelings in spite of his reservations, even with the cameras rolling.

The taping was completed late in the afternoon. Though Meredith normally enjoyed taping interviews, she was as relieved as Alexander as they watched the IBS mobile production van drive away. She turned to Alexander, who stood beside her on the lawn, and wrapped her arms around him. "Now, where were we, before we were so rudely interrupted?" she asked playfully.

"I believe we were planning a wedding." He held her close.

She kissed him. "I've been thinking about that," she began slowly. "How would you feel about having a formal wedding?"

He looked at her suspiciously. "Translate," he said carefully.

"Something lovely and romantic. A celebration with our closest friends around us—maybe an outdoor wedding, right here," she suggested. "We could be married this summer, August at the very latest . . ."

He studied her for a moment. "This means a great deal to you, doesn't it."

She nodded. "This is a once-in-a-lifetime occasion, and I want it to be absolutely perfect."

"All right," he agreed, though somewhat reluctantly. "On one condition."

"Always the negotiator!" Meredith teased. "Okay, what's the condition?"

"That we live together *now*—that you move into my apartment as soon as we return to Manhattan," he said promptly.

She laughed and kissed him again. "Try and get rid of me!"

* * *

In her office at the IBS Broadcast Center, Meredith stood at the window, staring blankly at the traffic on Fifty-second Street below. She had just come from viewing the tapes of her show on Alexander. The finished product had turned out to be even better than she had anticipated. The man in those tapes was a world apart from the man whose name had appeared in so many scandalous headlines over the past few years. The man in those tapes was the man she knew, the same man she had fallen in love with: strong, ambitious, powerful, a man accustomed to his immense wealth. But beyond that, he was a man who could also be gentle and compassionate, with a fierce sense of pride, of family honor and tradition. A man who, in spite of his position and power, was very human, very down to earth. She smiled to herself. Alexander would be pleased.

They had both gotten a great deal more than they had bargained for when they agreed to the interview. He'd been looking for an effective means of changing the public's perception of him. She'd been after the interview of the year, the one that would boost her own career. In the process, they had both found something far more important: each other. In spite of the conflicts, and the roadblocks that had been thrown in their paths, Meredith realized now that they had been drifting toward one another from the moment he had held her in his arms at the Rainbow Room. Had she been a believer in fate, Meredith might have conceded that their romance had been preordained. But she knew better. In this case, it was Alexander who had orchestrated their destiny, Alexander who had made it happen.

The love she and Alexander shared was so different from what she'd had with Nick that it was impossible for her to believe that she could have loved them both so deeply. With Nick, it had been gentle and relaxed and comfortably solid. With Alexander, it was unbridled passion and uninhibited lovemaking, an unspoken communication that was almost telepathic. They came together like two stars colliding in the heavens. It seemed to her, now that she'd had time to catch her breath and think about it, that they had not really been able to resist the force that pulled them together. They had been drawn by something stronger, more powerful than each could have thought possible. With Alexander, life was exciting and volatile and unpredictable. Meredith knew in her heart that there was nothing they could not accomplish.

Leaving her office, she walked alone down the long corridor from her office to the *Manhattan Observer* set. She glanced at her watch as she pushed open the heavy door leading to the studio, now in total darkness. Nine-thirty. She'd had no idea how long she'd been holed up in her office. She had fallen behind in her correspondence, and had been struggling to catch up since returning from Southampton. She had no idea what time Cindy had finally gone home. Only a skeleton crew remained, just the technical personnel necessary to keep the news center operating and the network on the air.

Meredith fumbled in the darkness until she found the bank of switches that abruptly lit the studio with a blaze of brilliant light. Stepping over coiled wires and heavy cables, and maneuvering her way through a maze of camera equipment, she made her way up to the newly decorated set. She'd been impressed with the charcoal-gray carpeting, the royal blue upholstered armchairs, and the magnificent mock window backdrop of Manhattan at night when it was first completed, but now it was just another cold, empty, unbearably lonely place. As she stepped up onto the platform, she paused to stare at the four black-and-white blowups resting on specially designed easels flanking the set: a formal portrait of the chairman of the board in his office; the polo champion astride his favorite pony; an informal shot aboard his yacht, the *Dionysus;* and one of father and son, the last photograph taken before Constantine Kirakis's death in 1982. Meredith was filled with pride as she stared into the smiling face of the victorious polo player. She was thinking of that afternoon after the match at Southampton.

He was right: together, as a team, they would be much, much stronger than they could ever be individually.

Windows on the World is a dazzling showplace in the sky, towering high above Manhattan on the one-hundred-seventh floor of One World Trade Center. Literally encompassed by an acre of glass, the many dining rooms, lounges, and private rooms afford a spectacular view of the city from every direction. The incredible show outside is rivaled only by the stunning interior. Against a backdrop of muted tones of gold, beige, and pale rose, the lavish accents of mirror, brass trimmings, and wood paneling are offset by an abundance of fresh flowers and greenery. The ambience is elegant yet warm, from the mirrored reception chamber with its large, semiprecious geodes to the white-uniformed waiters with their flashing gold epaulets. During lunch hours, the magnificent, multitiered dining room is a private club, but in the evening the restaurant, the Hors d'Oeuvrerie, and the City Lights Bar are open to anyone who wants to enjoy the incredible view and cuisine.

Although Meredith had dined at Windows on the World many times in the years she'd lived in New York, she still found it as breathtaking now as she had the first time. Now, sitting across from Alexander at a table in one of the private dining rooms, she found it impossible to see anything beyond the open adoration in his glowing black eyes. How long had it been since a man had been able to make her feel this way just by looking at her? She wondered how she could ever have doubted his love for her.

"Tonight we celebrate," Alexander said as the captain approached their table with a bottle of Dom Perignon and two glasses. He was still amazed at how she managed to look even more beautiful to him with each passing day. Tonight she wore a low-cut, sequin-and-bead-covered evening dress and the necklace he'd bought for her in Rome. Her hair hung loosely about her shoulders, the way he liked it.

She smiled. "And what are we celebrating this time?" she asked. They'd been celebrating something every night since they had returned from Southampton. Last night, they'd celebrated living together for three weeks.

"Us, as always," he said with a mischievous smile.

The waiter put a glass down in front of her. She reached for it, then stopped short. There was only a little champagne in it. "May I have a little—" she began. Then she saw it. At the bottom of the glass was the most beautiful ring she had ever seen, a large, marquise-cut sapphire surrounded by small, pear-shaped diamonds. The wide platinum band was intricately carved in a pattern similar to that of her necklace. Plucking it from the glass, she looked up at Alexander. "It's exquisite," she gasped.

"Your engagement ring," he said, beaming. "Read the inscription inside."

Engraved on the inside of the band were the words *Now and forever*. She smiled. How like Alexander it was—direct and to the point. She couldn't take her eyes from the ring.

"I've never seen anything like it," she said softly.

He smiled, his black eyes shining. "You won't," he said as he took her left hand. "It is one of a kind." He took the ring and slipped it on her finger. "Like you, *matia mou*, it is beautiful and rare."

She looked down at the ring, then at Alexander again, her eyes misting. She loved him more than she had ever believed possible.

When they returned to his apartment that night, an urgent message waited for Alexander. "It's from Muhammed Kafir at the corporation's offices in Istanbul," he told Meredith. He looked at his watch. "I have to call him back."

"Now?" Meredith asked, surprised.

He frowned. "It must be important for him to have phoned me here at this hour," he reasoned. "It is almost eight A.M. in Istanbul. For Kafir to be in his office so early, it must be urgent."

Meredith forced a slight smile. "I'm getting used to it," she said, kissing his cheek. "Don't be too long, okay?"

"No longer than is necessary," he promised.

She went into the master bedroom and switched on the bedside lamp. Undressing slowly, she slipped on a sheer white silk robe and pinned her hair up on her head. She turned down the sheets and closed the heavy, midnight-blue drapes.

She walked barefoot across the thick white carpet to the heavy, carved mahogany door leading into their private bath. Normally, one of the maids would have drawn her bath for her in the magnificent sunken marble tub, but tonight Meredith drew it herself. It was late, and the household staff had retired to their own quarters for the evening. Besides, she wanted to be alone with Alexander once he'd finished with the man in Istanbul. She wanted tonight to be something special for both of them. It wasn't every day one became engaged.

She took off her robe and hung it on one of the large brass hooks on the back of the door. She loved the feel of the soft royal blue carpet under her feet as she walked naked to the pale gray marble tub. Submerging herself in the billowing cloud of bubbles, she lay her head back against the blue satin pillow at one end of the tub and relaxed in the splendor of her opulent surroundings. From the mirrors on the wall behind the tub to the large, perfectly tended palms in identical white porcelain pots on either side of it, from the ancient statues flanking the six-foot marble dressing table to the gold-framed mirrors and perfect lighting, it was yet another example of the life-style afforded by Alexander's seemingly unlimited wealth. For the first time in years, Meredith found herself thinking of the small, plain bedroom in the frame house where she had grown up. Her family had never been poor, but they had never been rich, either. Comfortable had never been quite enough for Meredith. Even when she was young, something deep within her soul had always demanded more. Now she was on the brink of having everything she had ever wanted: success, wealth, recognition, a man she truly loved. It would seem that the world was hers for the asking. But could she really have it all?

Stepping out of the tub, she took a large, thick bath sheet from the warming rack and dried herself carefully, then put on her robe. Returning to the bedroom, she removed the large pins from her hair and shook it down around her shoulders, then brushed it vigorously. She looked at the clock on the bedside table. It was past midnight. Alexander was probably still on the phone. She switched off the silver and crystal lamp and went to the window. Parting the drapes slightly, she peered out at the glittering lights of Fifth Avenue below. Their kingdom, Alexander jokingly called it. And looking at it now, it actually seemed as if it were true. The city belonged to them. The world was at their feet. It was a heady, wonderful feeling, yet it made her think of something she had once asked Nick, in another lifetime it seemed now. Could anyone ever really have everything—and hold onto it? She looked down at the ring on her finger and thought of the inscription. *Now and forever*. If it were possible for anyone to have everything they could possibly want, she and Alexander would.

At that moment, she felt his strong hands on her shoulders. "Did you get through to Istanbul?" she asked, still gazing out at the myriad of lights that glittered like a treasure chest filled with shimmering jewels.

"Yes." He looked down at the ring. The sapphire seemed to glow like a blue-white flame in the darkness. "Do you like it?" he asked.

"I love it." She turned to face him. "But not as much as I love you."

He smiled down at her, touching her face gently. "I have made a discovery in the past few weeks."

"Oh?" She looked up at him questioningly. "And what would that be?"

"The power of love," he answered, fingering a strand of her hair. "It is, without a doubt, the strongest force on earth."

She put one arm around his neck and rested her head on his shoulder. "Are you trying, in your subtle way, to tell me that I'm more important to you than your empire?" she asked playfully.

He smiled. "Yes," he answered without hesitation. "I never thought I would ever say this to anyone, but yes, you are."

She kissed his neck. "I love you so much it scares me sometimes," she confessed, snuggling closer. "I just wish we could always be together like this, that we'd never have to be apart again."

"I've been thinking exactly the same thing," he said, stroking her hair. "Unfortunately, it is going to happen very soon."

She looked up at him, perplexed.

"What are you talking about?"

"Relax," he said, amused by her reaction. "I have to fly to London on Thursday. Think you can get away from your television duties and go with me?"

She hesitated for a moment. She would love to go with him, but she couldn't. Not this weekend. She had business of her own to take care of. "I can't," she told him. "I have to fly to Dallas on Friday to check out a prospective interviewee."

"Could you put it off for a few days? Once my meeting is out of the way, we could have a wonderful time together in London."

"I wish I could, but I can't," she insisted. "This was set up for me weeks ago. To have to reschedule it now could mean a long delay."

"How long will you be in Dallas?" he asked.

"I'll be back on Sunday."

He smiled. "Excellent. I will also be returning on Sunday," he said. "We will have to plan something romantic for our reunion."

"Wherever we are will be romantic, as long as we're together," she said simply.

Alexander held her close. "I am not looking forward to being apart from you for even one night," he said softly.

At the Dorchester Hotel in London, Alexander stood alone at the windows in his suite, contemplating the beautiful landscape of Hyde Park stretched out before him. It had been a long, hectic day, but his meeting had been an unqualified success. Normally, he would have taken a great deal of satisfaction from a day of successful negotiations, but tonight, nothing gave him any real comfort. He thought of Meredith, of how much he missed her and wanted to be with her. He smiled to himself, thinking it ironic. How many women had he used and discarded in the past? How many times had he walked away from a woman without giving her a second thought? He'd had any of them whenever he wanted, and on his own terms. He could have married any of them and had a simple, uncomplicated relationship with someone who would have been at his beck and call. He had fallen in love with a woman who was independent and ambitious, a woman whose needs and drives were as strong as his own. A woman who was in no special hurry to marry even though she'd made it quite clear that she loved him, that there was no one in her life but him. And though he knew that she was never going to be the so-called perfect corporate wife, he knew that his life with her would always be exciting, unpredictable, and thoroughly satisfying. To Alexander, for whom women no longer held any mysteries, Meredith had proven to be a constant surprise. She was bright and beautiful and determined. He'd been intrigued by her independence and her self-assurance, but even more so by the unexpected vulnerability that lay hidden beneath that polished surface, the smoldering sensuality that had been released that night at Southampton.

Meredith, Alexander had quickly discovered, was a complex person. He still found it difficult to reconcile the poised, professional newscaster with the eager woman who shared his bed. On TV, she was skilled, efficient, and hard-hitting. In public, she was elegant, the perfect hostess, the perfect consort. But when they were alone, she was fiery and passionate, uninhibited in her lovemaking and sharing his other passions with equal enthusiasm. She was a consummate horsewoman. She'd been more than a match for him on the tennis court. When he had taken her skeet shooting, he'd been surprised to find that she could not only handle a gun, but was a crack shot. He had also found her surprisingly knowledgeable about business. How many times in the past weeks had their pillow talk consisted of a long discussion of a company he wanted to take over or a problem he was trying to resolve within the ranks of his own corporation? Alexander, who trusted few men—even within the upper echelons of the Kirakis Corporation—found it helpful to confide in Meredith. She was going to make a wonderful wife, he thought, a wonderful mother.

Meredith sat in the back of the limousine, watching anxiously as the blue and white corporate jet came to a slow stop on the runway at Kennedy Airport. In the darkness, she watched as the lights on the plane went out. The past three days had seemed endless for Meredith.

She got out of the car and walked around to the front of it. She watched as the ramp was rolled over to the 747 and the door opened. Alexander appeared almost immediately. He waved when he saw her, coming down the ramp so fast that Meredith was afraid he was going to fall. She rushed forward and embraced him, her lips at his neck.

"Do you have any idea how much I've missed you?" he asked hoarsely, holding her close.

"As much as I've missed you?" She kissed him eagerly.

"The past four days have seemed like four years," he whispered, stroking her hair.

They walked, arms around each other, back to the waiting car. Alexander helped Meredith into the back seat, then slid in beside her. "I didn't make any reservations for dinner," Meredith said. "I wasn't sure what you'd be in the mood for."

"You," he said in a low voice as he took her in his arms. "I am in the mood for you."

She laughed. "Aren't you hungry?" she asked innocently.

"Ravenous," he muttered, nibbling her ear.

She giggled as the driver slid behind the wheel and started the engine.

Alexander released her just long enough to press the button that raised the one-way glass, sealing the driver off from the back of the car. "Now he can't see or hear us," he growled, taking her in his arms again.

"I think we'd better go straight home," Meredith said in a teasing voice. "It would be dangerous to have a man in your condition out on the streets of Manhattan."

"I don't think I can wait until we get home." His mouth sought hers in the darkness.

Meredith took his face in her hands and kissed him with an urgency that matched his own. His hands moved down the length of her body, caressing her through the lightweight fabric of her summer dress. Her nipples hardened at his touch, and a hot, delicious sensation swept through her body as he slid his hand under her skirt and began stroking her inner thigh. "No," she whispered. "Not here . . ."

"I want you . . . now . . ." he breathed.

"I want you, too . . . but . . . maybe . . ." She withdrew slowly, her eyes shining in the darkness. "Maybe . . . I have a better idea . . ."

He smiled, reaching for her again. "And exactly what do you have in mind?" he asked in a low, suggestive voice.

"I'll show you." She slid down to the floor of the car and

started making love to him, caressing him, kissing him until he began to moan. She started moaning with him, moving faster until she felt his spasms of pleasure making his whole body convulse violently.

It was more than a reunion. It was a celebration.

Meredith walked briskly down the corridor toward the *Manhattan Observer* set with her secretary trailing behind as she attempted to scribble shorthand notes on a steno pad. "Type a memo to Harv Petersen detailing my ideas for a show on European fashion designers," Meredith told a beleaguered Cindy. "And get those letters off that we worked on yesterday."

"Done," Cindy said quickly. "Anything else?"

"Nothing that I can think of right now," Meredith said as they entered Studio D, where *Manhattan Observer* was videotaped. Two propmen, working under the direction of Stephen Massey, the set designer, were removing the large photographs of Alexander from the easels flanking the set. Now that the interview with Alexander had been taped, they would be replaced with blowups of her next subject. Meredith paused to admire the formal portrait that leaned against the wall. It was a flattering picture, but she decided it would be impossible to get a bad photograph of Alexander.

"What do you want us to do with these, Meredith?" Stephen asked. "I thought, under the circumstances, you might like to keep them."

"I would," Meredith said as she stepped up onto the platform. "Have them taken to my office."

Stephen turned to the two propmen. "Okay, you heard the lady, guys." He gestured toward the door. "I'll show you the way."

After they left the studio, Meredith settled into one of the chairs and looked over her notes while Cindy excused herself and went for coffee. It was so quiet, Meredith thought. So unlike the taping sessions, when the lights were bright and people were bustling about, making sure everything ran smoothly. So unlike the day the opening segment of her interview with Alexander was taped.

"I thought I'd find you in here."

Meredith jerked around to see Casey standing in the

doorway. "Hi, Case," she said with a tired smile. "We seem to be missing each other lately."

"The powers that be believe in killing time by working it to death," Casey quipped as she came forward. "At least our jobs are secure. They can't fire us—slaves have to be sold."

Meredith smiled. "That bad?"

"Worse." Casey stepped up onto the platform and slumped into the empty chair. "So tell me, how's life at the top?"

Meredith gave her a quizzical look.

"You and Alexander."

Meredith gave a little laugh. "I'll let you know when I find out." She made some notes in a steno book.

"Meaning what?" Casey asked, puzzled.

"Meaning," Meredith began, looking up from her notes, "that if Alexander and I hadn't decided to go ahead and live together now, we probably wouldn't see very much of each other. Do you have any idea how hard it is to plan a wedding with schedules like ours? We've changed the date twice already. I'm tempted to forget the whole thing and just head over to City Hall."

Casey chuckled. "Can't say that I blame you for wanting to show off with a big wedding," she admitted with a mischievous grin. "If *I* were marrying a man like Alexander Kirakis, I'd probably want to show off a bit myself."

Meredith only smiled. She was looking at one of the blowups of Alexander still leaning against the wall. I'm not showing off, she thought.

Just realizing a dream I never thought could happen in the real world.

EIGHTEEN

〰〰〰〰〰〰〰〰〰〰

Meredith curled up next to Alexander on the black leather couch as they watched the special together. Having already seen the edited tapes in their final form, she was more interested in Alexander's reactions than in what was happening on the television screen. She watched his face as he stared at the screen thoughtfully, looking for clues as to what he was thinking and feeling. He had not exercised his right to view the tapes before they were aired; he had left everything in her hands.

"Well, what do you think?" she asked finally, unable to stand it any longer.

He turned to look at her and smiled. "Your instincts are right on target, as I knew they would be," he told her. "I'm not disappointed." Indeed, he was very pleased. The interview itself, along with the selected background material and the film clips of the polo match, the tour of the Southampton estate, and the footage filmed at the Kirakis Corporation's offices at the World Trade Center had been combined to create a portrait that was strikingly different from the public image he had lived with since his Harvard days. It was a positive contrast to the notorious playboy reputation he was so eager to shed.

"Not disappointed?" She sat up and looked at him. "Is that all you have to say about it? I expected a little more enthusiasm . . ."

He laughed. "You did a marvelous job, my love," he assured her. "Even my father would have been pleased, had he been here to see it."

"Do you think it's going to improve your image?" she asked, genuinely interested in his response.

"If it doesn't, I doubt that anything will," he said with confidence. "Except perhaps our marriage—"

She drew back, a look of feigned anger on her beautiful face. "So that's why you want to marry me—to change your image!" she declared. "I'm nothing but a public relations ploy, just something to make you look respectable?" She started to laugh.

"You know better than that," he growled, pulling her close. "I want to marry you because I love you. That is the only reason—and don't you ever forget it!" His mouth came down on hers hungrily. Meredith put her arms around his neck and lay against him, returning his kisses. Over her shoulder, he caught sight of the portrait of Elizabeth Weldon-Ryan, hanging over the piano.

Why does she look so familiar? he wondered.

"Three weeks?" Meredith asked, surprised. "What am I going to be doing in Paris for three weeks?"

Harv Petersen leaned back in his chair and lit a cigar. "Seems to me that it was your idea to do a show focusing on the new breed of fashion designer," he recalled. "What better way to do that than by spending time in Paris, taping interviews and viewing the new fall collections of some of those young rising stars?"

Meredith nodded slowly, visualizing what Petersen was proposing. He was right; it had been her idea. And it would make one hell of a show. After all, how often did the average American television viewer get to glimpse the dazzling world of the top French fashion designers? How many of them would ever get to see those exclusive showings of the designers' fall collections? "How soon would I have to leave?" she asked carefully.

"Is Monday too soon?"

"Monday!"

"Look—we've already made all the travel arrangements." Petersen shuffled through a stack of papers on his desk and produced a typed itinerary. "Barrie tells me some of the shows are scheduled as much as a week apart. The first is a week from today. Leave any later than Monday and you'll miss it."

She nodded again. "Do you really think it's going to take three weeks to do all of this—the interviews and all?" she asked, looking over the papers he had given her.

"If you're lucky," Petersen answered. "You know how Murphy's Law applies to filming schedules."

"Tell me about it," Meredith muttered, rolling her eyes upward.

"You don't want to go, do you," he asked, sensing her reluctance.

"Of course I do," she insisted. "It's just the timing. I do have other commitments here . . ."

"Don't worry about doing *World Focus*," he assured her.

"I was thinking of something else," she admitted.

Petersen nodded, stubbing out his cigar. "Your wedding," he concluded.

Meredith looked up at him and frowned. "With our schedules, it's been hard for Alexander and I to make any plans at all—beyond making the announcement to the press."

Petersen smiled. "Lately, it's impossible to pick up a newspaper or magazine without reading about your engagement. You've become quite a media celebrity," he commented. "I do understand your predicament, but frankly, Meredith, I don't see how we can put this off, not if you want to do the show at all."

She nodded. "All right," she said with a sigh. "Next week it is, then."

She thought about it as she walked back to her office. Doing a show on the new faces of the international fashion scene was a project that had been close to her heart since she first suggested it three months earlier. How was she going to tell Alexander that she would be spending the next three weeks in Paris?

* * *

"I wish there were some other way," Meredith told Alexander as they walked together through the busy terminal at Kennedy Airport. "I just can't get out of it. After all, it is my show—and my idea."

"I understand that," he said crossly, looking straight ahead into the crowd. His anger was evident. "What I'm unable to understand is why it must be now and why the taping will take three weeks."

"We've been through this before," Meredith said wearily. "I'm going after tapes of the shows featuring the fall collections of the year's hottest names in fashion. To get those tapes, I have to go now."

"And this will take three weeks?" He wasn't convinced.

"The shows are spaced apart. You remember it took longer than that to tape your segment," she reminded him.

"That was different," he insisted. "The tapes you used were done at different times in different places. It would have been impossible to tape all of it within a few days—or even a week."

"Exactly. And I'm facing a similar situation now," she responded. "Some of these shows will be a day or two apart, others a week or more apart." Grabbing his arm, she stopped walking and looked him in the eye. "I hate the idea of being away from you. If I could finish this project any other way, I'd do it. I think you know that."

He looked at her for a few seconds, then nodded. Reaching into his pocket, he took out a key and pressed it into her hand. "I can't be with you, but I can make certain that you're properly taken care of while you're in Paris," he said, his eyes meeting hers.

She looked down at the key in her hand, then up at Alexander again. Her smile was taunting. "Is this a question or a statement?" she asked, knowing that he was not really giving her a choice.

"It's the key to my apartment on Avenue Foch," he answered.

"But Alexander—" she began.

"No buts, *matia mou.*" He smiled. "As far as I'm concerned, you are already my wife. The apartment is as much yours as mine."

She paused, realizing it would do no good to argue with

him when his mind was made up. "All right," she said
finally. "When you put it that way, how can I possibly
refuse?"

"You can't, so don't try." He took her hand and squeezed
it. "I've arranged for a car and driver for you. He will meet
you at De Gaulle Airport and will be at your disposal during
your stay in Paris."

"But the network's already made travel arrangements,"
she protested.

"Let your crew use whatever they have provided," he said
with gentle insistence in his voice. "You're to use my car
and driver—so I'll know that you'll be in good hands."

She looked at him for a moment, then kissed him lightly.
"Do you have any idea how hard it is for me to say no to
you?" she asked as they started walking again.

He put an arm around her. "I want to make it impossible," he said with a wicked grin.

Meredith laughed. "You're definitely on the right track,"
she assured him, digging into her bag for her passport as they
approached customs. "I guess this is where we say good-
bye—"

Alexander shook his head. "I'm going with you—to the
plane," he told her.

She gave him a puzzled look. She started to ask him how
he had managed that, but she knew Alexander. He could
arrange anything he wished by pulling the right strings in the
right places. His contacts and resources constantly amazed
her.

"You may insist upon using a commercial airline, but that
does not mean it must be inconvenient for either of us," he
said simply.

"You're full of surprises, aren't you." She paused to
present her passport to a uniformed customs official who
glanced at it and returned it to her.

Alexander only smiled. "The best is yet to come, *matia
mou*," he promised.

New York City.

Alexander was alone in his office at the World Trade

Center staring absently at a stack of reports on his desk. His mind was definitely not on business today, he thought ruefully. Meredith had been gone almost three weeks. When he spoke to her on the phone last night, she'd said she would be coming home on Friday. "I'll meet you at the airport," he'd told her, "and then I am going to spirit you off to some little church in the country where we can be married immediately." Meredith had laughed, thinking he was joking, but he had been serious. He wanted to marry her the minute she returned from Paris. He was not about to wait another day.

He opened the drawer and took out a small, midnight-blue velvet box. Opening it, he stared thoughtfully at the matching rings inside, their wedding rings. Meredith had chosen them herself: simple platinum bands with their initials engraved on them. They had been delivered yesterday. He hadn't told her about them on the phone. He planned to surprise her when he met her at the airport.

He smiled to himself, recalling the conversation he'd had with George that morning. He had been unusually abrupt with members of his staff for the past week, and George had taken mercy on them and offered Alexander a solution to his problems: "Why don't you just drop everything, fly over to Paris, and carry her off to some isolated spot and marry her? She couldn't possibly resist anything so blatantly romantic. Women love that sort of thing, and I'd be willing to bet that Meredith's no exception." Alexander had only laughed then, but the more he'd thought about it, the more sense it had made. He was intrigued with the idea of literally sweeping her off her feet, spiriting her away in the middle of the night to some secluded, romantic hideaway where they could be married privately but still have a lovely ceremony. But where? He thought about it. Only one place on earth fit the bill, one place where he could be assured of absolute privacy. He made his decision, then reached for the phone and dialed George's extension. "I need you in my office —now."

Five minutes later, George stood before him, looking concerned. "What's wrong? Did the Hammond Transcon deal fall through? I talked to Chuck Hammond this morning, and—''

Alexander cut him off. ''This does not concern business —at least not in the way you think,'' he explained as he reached for his briefcase. ''I am going to be away for a while, and you will be in charge here in my absence. I will check in from time to time, but no one will be able to reach me.'' He put on his jacket.

George gave him a puzzled look. ''I don't understand,'' he began, baffled. ''Where—how long will you be gone?''

''A month. Perhaps longer.'' Alexander took the box containing the rings from the drawer and put it in his pocket.

''A month! Where in God's name are you going?''

''To a wedding.'' Alexander started for the door.

''To a wedding? Whose—''

Alexander grinned. ''My own. Thanks to you, my friend.'' And he hurried out of the office, leaving George staring after him, a look of utter bewilderment on his face.

It was almost two in the morning when Alexander's private jet landed at Charles de Gaulle Airport. He was met by a French official who saw to it that he was whisked through customs as quickly as possible and escorted to his waiting limousine. The thirty-minute drive into Paris seemed like an eternity to Alexander, even though he had made this same journey many times before and normally in much heavier traffic. He sat alone in the back of the car, staring into the night without really seeing anything. He thought about Meredith, about how surprised she would be to see him. She had no idea he was coming. He had purposely neglected to phone her or wire the time of his arrival because he wanted to surprise her. He looked at his watch. Three-fifteen. He smiled to himself. She was definitely going to be surprised. He reached into his pocket and took out the small velvet box. He'd had time to do nothing but think during the flight from New York to Paris. He knew exactly what he was going to do, where he was going to take her. He knew where they would be married and when. It was going to be beautiful, a wedding neither of them would ever forget. A honeymoon they would never forget.

It was three-thirty when the car entered the underground

garage below the apartment building. Alexander did not wait
for the driver to open the door for him. He got out of the car
and ran to the elevators, impatient that it took so long to get a
car going up. He rode alone to his floor, digging into his
pocket for the key. When he let himself in, the apartment
was in darkness. He went to the master bedroom, where
Meredith was sleeping soundly. He took off his jacket and
draped it across the back of one of the Louis XV chairs, then
crossed the room silently and knelt on the floor beside the
bed. As he lowered his head to hers and kissed her gently,
her eyes opened suddenly and she jerked up, startled.

"Alexander!" she gasped, seeing his face clearly for the
first time. "How did you—"

"Don't ask foolish questions," he growled, kissing her
again. "Just show me you're happy to see me."

"I am," she whispered, wrapping her arms around him
tightly. "Oh, God, I am . . ."

He pulled back the sheets and took her in his arms. "I've
missed you so much," he whispered hoarsely as their bodies
came together, their passion ignited once again. His hands
were setting her on fire. She clutched at him, ripping the
buttons from his shirt in her eager attempt to undress him.
He pulled back, laughing, and lifted her nightgown over her
head and tossed it aside. Then he tore off his clothes and
came to her again. Their arms and legs entwined, their
bodies seemed to fuse together in the heat of their desire.

Afterward, they lay in each other's arms in the darkness,
the only sound in the room that of their own breathing.

Meredith broke the silence. "I don't know what possessed
you to just drop everything and come here," she began, "but
I'm glad you did."

"I couldn't stay away," he admitted, looking into her
eyes. "I missed you so terribly, I couldn't stand it a moment
longer. I had to be with you."

"I would have been home on Friday," she said softly as
she snuggled against him.

"Neither of us is going home on Friday," he said, his
face serious.

She looked at him questioningly. "I don't—" she
started.

"Don't say anything. Just listen." His tone was firm.

"I've been thinking, and I've decided we have waited long enough."

"Alexander, I know what you're getting at, but I can't—"

He put a finger to her lips. "You don't understand, *matia mou*," he said gently. "You have no choice. You have been kidnapped." He touched her cheek lightly with his fingertips.

"What?" She started to laugh.

"Tomorrow we are leaving Paris," he continued, "but we are *not* going to New York. We are going to Greece."

NINETEEN

━━━━━━━━━━━━

"Harv, you're about as romantic as a case of smallpox," Meredith scolded. The transatlantic connection was terrible, but she didn't have to hear her producer clearly to know that he was less than thrilled with the idea of her being away from the network for a month. Oddly enough, Meredith was not concerned. Only one thing mattered to her right now: being with Alexander, finally becoming his wife.

"You do have responsibilities here—in case you've forgotten," Petersen reminded her. Even with the poor quality of the connection, his anger came across loud and clear.

"I haven't forgotten anything," she assured him. "But I think you may have forgotten that I have a life away from the network. IBS is not my whole life."

"Come off it," Petersen growled. "It's impossible for me not to know that you have a private life, especially when it's not so private anymore. Hell, you're plastered all over every tabloid in town!" He paused and took a deep breath. "Look, Meredith, I'm not condemning you for it. I'm just saying now is not the right time—"

"The right time?" Meredith gave a harsh laugh. "Harv, this is something that happens to a woman once in her lifetime—if she's lucky! I can't schedule it as though it were a vacation! Alexander just dropped everything to fly over here for this. If he can leave all his responsibilities behind—"

"I don't think you understand—"

"No, Harv—*you're* the one who doesn't understand," she said firmly. "I'm getting married. I'm going on my honeymoon. I'll be back. I don't know exactly when at the moment, but I'll let you know."

"Meredith, you can't just—"

"Good-bye, Harv. I'll be in touch." Smiling contentedly, she replaced the receiver and went out to the terrace to join Alexander. He leaned against the railing, staring thoughtfully at the street below. He turned to face her as she approached.

"How did he take it?"

She smiled as she put her arms around him. "Let me put it this way: I may not have a job when we get back to New York," she said. "To say he's upset would be in the nature of an understatement."

"We could always buy the network," he suggested.

She laughed and kissed him. "Be serious!" she scolded.

"I am serious," he insisted, kissing her forehead. "The corporation already owns a television network in France and one in Japan. Another in the States would be a wonderful acquisition."

"Thank you for the vote of confidence," she teased. "You think the only way I can stay in broadcasting is if my husband happens to own the network?"

"We both know better than that." He kissed her again. "Not having second thoughts, are you?"

"Not on your life!" she said. "You started this. Now you've got to marry me."

"I most certainly do," he agreed, pulling her closer. "As quickly as possible."

"You still haven't told me. Where are we going on our honeymoon?" she wanted to know. "And why is it going to take a month?"

"Where we're going, *matia mou,* is to be a surprise," he answered easily. "And it will take a month because I want to be alone with you for as long as possible."

"How can the corporation survive without you that

long?'' she asked, running her fingers through his tousled hair.

"George will be able to keep things under control, and I'll check in with him from time to time. He won't be able to reach me, however. I want to be certain that no one interrupts us.''

"You, my love, are absolutely incredible!'' she said, laughing.

"So are you.'' His eyes met hers and their gaze held. "Just one more reason why we belong together.''

Alexander was adamant in his refusal to let anyone know where they were going or what they were planning. He had been against Meredith's decision to tell Harv Petersen they were getting married, but he knew she was right. She couldn't just take off for a month without offering an explanation. Petersen knew they were getting married, as did George, but no one knew where or precisely when. Alexander had convinced Meredith that it would not be wise to let anyone else know what they were planning.

They left Paris in the middle of the night—again, at Alexander's insistence. This way, he maintained, they were less likely to arouse the suspicions of the reporters who seemed to follow them everywhere during daylight hours. Their private jet landed at Hellenikon Airport in Athens at four in the morning, and a limousine waited to take them to Piraeus, where they would board the *Dionysus* for the trip to the island. It seemed to Meredith that Alexander had covered all the bases, making a good many plans in a very short time. It did not surprise her. Alexander was nothing if not thorough.

As the limousine slowed to a stop on the dock where Alexander's yacht was anchored, the ship's crew stood at attention on the deck in their immaculate white uniforms, waiting to bring Alexander and his bride-to-be aboard. As they walked up the ramp, they were greeted by the yacht's captain, Nicos Catapodis, who spoke to Alexander in rapid Greek as he escorted them to the master stateroom. He welcomed Meredith aboard in polite but broken English, then left them alone. After he was gone, Alexander took Meredith in his arms and kissed her tenderly. "I should show you around," he whispered as he tangled his fingers in her hair, kissing her again and again. "But what I really want is to stay right here, with you."

She returned his kisses eagerly. "Lock the door," she said softly. "You can show me around later."

He smiled but said nothing. He released her and went to lock the door so they would not be disturbed, then crossed the room and took her in his arms again.

"It's magnificent!" Meredith declared in awe as she and Alexander crossed the lawn to the villa. "I've tried to picture it in my mind so many times, but never did I imagine anything so incredibly beautiful."

"My father had it built as a setting for my mother," Alexander told her as he put one arm around her possessively. "It had to be a palace befitting the queen he thought her to be." He paused as they started up the stone steps to the main entrance. "And, as in all monarchies, there had to be a succession, so now I bring my own queen here."

They paused to kiss before entering. Helena had assembled the entire household staff in the reception hall to meet Alexander's bride-to-be, and she found it amusing, in light of the comment Alexander had made about making her his queen, that the servants seemed to regard her as if they had been presented to royalty. She was impressed with Helena, and as she studied the short, stocky, gray-haired Greek woman, she found herself trying to imagine Helena as Alexander's governess. She tried to picture Alexander as a child, running at Helena's heels, and it made her wonder what a child of theirs would be like.

"The arrangements for the wedding ceremony have been taken care of," Helena told Alexander. "The chapel is being made ready at this very moment."

"Excellent," Alexander responded. "I trust there will be no unnecessary delays, then."

"Certainly not," Helena said without hesitation. "Everyone involved is aware of how important this is to you."

"I am pleased. Thank you, Helena."

"What was that all about?" Meredith asked as they climbed the winding staircase.

Alexander smiled. "You will see, *matia mou*. Soon enough."

The master bedroom suite was unlike anything Meredith had ever seen before. Decorated in shades of blue and green, it was a large, airy room with thick carpeting, rich fabrics, enchanting bay windows, and French doors leading out to a large balcony overlooking the Aegean Sea. The magnificent canopied bed was curtained in pale blue and green, with hand-embroidered linens and heavy, royal blue quilts. The chairs in the room were upholstered in the same shade of royal blue. The sitting room and dressing rooms were done in the same colors, but the adjoining bath, similar in many ways to the one in Alexander's Olympic Tower apartment but larger and even more splendid, was done in shades of beige and mauve, with a white marble tub and white furniture. Lush ferns and palms were in every corner of the softly lit room.

"It's easy to see why you love it here," Meredith said as she stood on the balcony, admiring the unmatched view from all directions. "If I had grown up in a place like this, it would be hard for me to ever leave it."

"I haven't been able to spend nearly as much time here as I would like," Alexander admitted, pausing to look out at the blue-green Aegean. He turned to look at her again. "Perhaps we will bring our children here one day."

The wedding ceremony took place at sunset on a balmy, late-summer evening in a small, whitewashed chapel on the island, high on a bluff overlooking the sea. Meredith wore a simple, off-the-shoulder white silk dress with a four-strand pearl choker that had once belonged to Melina Kirakis. Her thick blond hair hung in loose waves around her shoulders, adorned with tiny clusters of orange blossoms to match those Alexander wore on the lapel of his dark blue suit. Standing before the altar, Meredith turned to look up at Alexander, and his dark eyes seemed to glow in the candlelight. "You look beautiful," he whispered. "Are you as happy as I am at this moment?"

She nodded, not trusting her voice.

The solemn, bearded, black-robed priest stood before

them at the altar as the chanting began, the priest throwing phrases to his young acolyte, who in turn responded quickly. Only one omission had been made from the traditional ceremony, because both Alexander and Meredith considered it inappropriate: the solemn Byzantine phrase, "Woman must fear man." Alexander had chosen his personal pilot, James Woodhill, to serve as the *koumbara*, or sponsor. He stood behind them during the ceremony with the coronets, delicate bands of white flowers connected by a long, white ribbon. Holding them over the heads of the bride and groom, he switched them back and forth three times before placing them on their heads. He produced the rings, also exchanged three times before being placed, correctly and forever, on the third fingers of their left hands. After that, he brought out a goblet of solid gold. Alexander kissed it, then passed it to Meredith, who did the same. Afterward, they both drank wine from it. They joined hands, and the priest, taking Alexander's free hand, led them around the altar three times, concluding the ceremony. Under a shower of rice and rose petals thrown by Helena, the only other person permitted to witness the ceremony, Alexander kissed his bride.

At last, she was his wife.

Traditionally, Greek weddings are large, family affairs followed by a grand feast and celebration that will sometimes last for days. Alexander and Meredith, having chosen to keep their marriage ceremony private, decided to celebrate privately. They returned to the villa, where they celebrated their marriage with caviar and champagne in their bedroom suite.

"Do you regret not having had a big wedding with lots of guests?" Alexander asked Meredith as they stood on the balcony under a star-filled summer sky, finishing the last of the champagne.

Meredith lay her head against his shoulder and smiled dreamily. "No regrets at all," she said softly, drawing his arm around her waist. "Nothing could have been more beautiful—or more romantic—than our wedding day has been. I wouldn't have wanted it any other way."

He looked down at her for a moment. "I wonder," he began thoughtfully, "is making love with one's wife different from making love with a lover?"

She smiled. "There's only one way either of us is going to
find out," she said pulling away. She took his hand and led
him back into their bedroom. Taking his glass from him, she
placed it next to her own on a table next to the bed, then put
her arms around him, kissing him deeply. "I always knew
my wedding night would be special," she whispered, loosening his tie, "but I never knew just how special it would
actually be."

"Neither did I," he said hoarsely as his lips moved down
her neck, over her right shoulder. Slowly, he unzipped the
back of her dress, his hand lingering for a moment on her
bare back. He pulled the dress down around her waist,
exposing her breasts, caressing them lightly with his fingers,
gently pinching her nipples. Finally, he lowered his hands to
push the dress away from her body, allowing it to fall in a
heap at her feet. His hands moved in slow circles over her
hips, her buttocks, as her trembling fingers unbuckled his
belt and fumbled with his zipper.

"Make love to me . . ." she whispered urgently.

"Patience, *matia mou*," he muttered as he started kissing
her neck again. He lowered her to the bed and finished
undressing, then lay on top of her, resting his weight on his
arms as he kissed her again and again, his lips seemingly
everywhere on her body. She touched him, arousing him
with her hands. He rolled over on his back, pulling her over
on top of him, holding her as she covered his face with light,
feathery kisses. She could feel his hardness pressing against
her as he caressed her, their bodies melting together in the
heat of their desire, making love as they always had, as if it
were the first time. They became one, physically and
emotionally, consumed in the fire of their love. Afterward,
when they were both too exhausted to move, they lay awake
in each other's arms, talking, making plans for the rest of
their honeymoon, dreading the day when they would have to
return to the real world awaiting them in New York.

Long after Alexander had drifted off to sleep, Meredith
was still wide awake, thinking, unable to will herself to
sleep. Finally, she got out of bed and put on her robe, trying
not to wake Alexander. She went out onto the balcony and
leaned against the railing, staring absently at the shimmering
Aegean. She held out her hand and stared long and hard at

her wedding ring, the platinum band gleaming in the moonlight. She hadn't dreamed it. It was real. They were really married.

She was Mrs. Alexander Kirakis.

They spent another week on the island. During the day, they went horseback riding and walked on the white sand beaches and swam in the Aegean. They went sailing and explored the game reserve. At night, they dined alone on the balcony off their bedroom and enjoyed the solitude, then made love well into the night. Meredith became convinced the island had to be the closest thing to heaven on earth. "Anyone who doesn't believe the Garden of Eden really existed should come here," she told Alexander the night before they were to leave. "I wish we could stay here forever."

"You'd tire of it eventually," he said with a knowing smile. "You are not the type who can remain quiet for long."

They left the island aboard the *Dionysus* in the early hours of the morning, and this time Meredith was given a tour of the entire yacht. It was a two-thousand-ton ship that had begun its seagoing life as a Canadian frigate. It had cost Constantine Kirakis over seven million dollars to turn it into the floating palace it was today. A brilliant white vessel with lovely rakish lines flowing back from its high, slender bow, it had deck space for two hydroplanes, speedboats, a hydrofoil, and a sailboat in addition to the many lifeboats. A vast air-conditioning system was sandwiched in between the decks, and a highly sophisticated alarm network, set off by open portholes or a sudden rise in temperature, was monitored constantly in the wheelhouse. Another circuit maintained the water in the freshwater pool on the deck just a few degrees below air temperature so that guests would feel pleasantly refreshed when they dived in. The bottom of the pool fascinated Meredith. It was a mosaic scene from Greek mythology, featuring, appropriately, the god Dionysus. Alexander's office was equipped with a forty-line radiotelephone system, a shortwave, and scramblers so that he could conduct his business even at sea. All this electronic gadgetry made the ship's power requirements so great that four diesel generators ran nonstop just to keep it all in operation.

The rooms were luxurious. The doors were all finished in Japanese lacquer and the fireplaces inlaid with lapis lazuli. A celebrated French artist had been commissioned to paint murals on the walls of the ship's magnificent dining room. Top decorators had been flown in from all over the world to decorate each of the nine guest cabins to Melina Kirakis's specifications, emphasizing luxury and good taste. The master stateroom was the most splendid, with its antiques, valuable paintings and sculptures, and rich fabrics. The furniture was all black mahogany, and the color scheme was in shades of blue and green. "It's the most beautiful room on the ship," Meredith told Alexander, "and I'm glad, since we seem to be spending most of our time here."

They set out on an extended cruise of the Mediterranean, anchoring whenever the mood struck them. Their first stop was Rome, where they walked the streets, enjoying the timeless beauty of the Eternal City, lunching at outdoor restaurants whenever possible. They visited the great museums, and Meredith discovered her husband's passion for Italian Renaissance art. He seemed intent upon indulging her every whim. If she admired a piece of jewelry or a dress in a shop window, he did not hesitate to buy it for her. If she expressed a desire to see something in particular, it was immediately arranged. "You're spoiling me," she warned him.

"And you are making me very happy," was his answer.

From Rome, they traveled by car north to Venice, Milan, and Portofino. They boarded the *Dionysus* again at Portofino and sailed south to Sardinia. Meredith fell in love with Sardinia's Costa Smerelda on sight. They stayed in a magnificent rented villa located halfway between Cagliari and Villasimus, a beautiful old stucco house with juniper beams inside, built on several levels, a fireplace in each of the rooms. A free-form staircase led to the upstairs, and the rustic furniture seemed to blend perfectly with the interior of the villa. The hand-woven fringed wool draperies and multicolored cerasarda tiles were made right there on the island, Alexander explained, as were the primitive paintings adorning the walls. With no servants to take care of the domestic chores, Meredith tried to cook, and Alexander was both amused and touched by her efforts. "You will never be a great chef, *matia mou*," he told her after a particularly disastrous meal, "but it does not matter. If I had wanted a cook, I would have married one."

More often, they had dinner at a charming little inn near Villasimus. It had no glamour, no crystal chandeliers, no expensive wine list, and yet Meredith discovered that Alexander was as at home there as he was at Maxim's or Lutèce. He whirled her around the small dance floor and played darts with some of the locals, who found him a formidable opponent. He seemed relaxed, thoroughly enjoying himself, and Meredith began to see yet another side to the man she had married. They would invariably leave the inn shortly after midnight, returning to the villa, where they would make love under the eiderdown quilts while a fire blazed in the stone fireplace in the master bedroom. The evenings were surprisingly cool for late August, but Meredith never noticed, because their lovemaking always left her warm inside. Warm and totally satisfied.

They rejoined the *Dionysus* at Cagliari and spent three days cruising the Mediterranean before leaving the yacht for the last time at Monte Carlo, where Alexander's white Excalibur awaited them. After two days of enjoying the casinos and the nightlife in Monte Carlo, they set out driving along the Côte d'Azur, stopping along the way in Villefranche, Nice, Antibes, Cannes, and St.-Raphaël before going on to St.-Tropez, but Alexander had no difficulty in securing the most luxurious suite at the most elegant hotel in the city. "The view seems to get more spectacular with each stop we make," Meredith remarked, enthralled with the view of the Mediterranean from their bedroom.

Alexander smiled as he started unbuttoning her blouse. "Perhaps," he whispered, kissing her as he removed the green silk shirt and dropped it to the floor, "but nothing could possibly be more beautiful than what I am seeing right now . . ."

In the morning, they ventured out into the village, and Meredith was surprised to discover that it was so small. St.-Tropez, she learned, had been a peaceful little fishing village until the early 1950s, when its quiet charm first began to attract the attentions of the very rich. It had been those rich, glamorous people, known then as the International Set, who had turned it into one of the world's most fashionable resorts. The old houses, jammed together within the ramparts, had been built so close together that there was little room left for expansion. As a result, it was still possible to see St.-Tropez as the French painters and writers like Colette had seen it, but only in the autumn, after the last of the tourists had disappeared for the season, could the little port finally cast its spell.

Alexander and Meredith biked to the Plage de Pampelone, the most appealing of St.-Tropez's nearby beaches, and Meredith was amused by Alexander's claim that the farther from the village one traveled, the fewer clothes would be seen on the beaches. They explored a small, overcrowded antique shop and posed for a sidewalk artist, who presented them with an astonishingly good charcoal portrait when he was finished. They strolled along the docks, watching the boats coming and going out in the harbor as the sunlight danced across the water.

As they drank pastis on the sun-dappled terrace of Chez Senequier, Meredith decided that Alexander's instincts had been right. This was exactly what they needed. He seemed more relaxed at this moment than she had ever seen him. In the weeks they had been honeymooning, he had been able to leave his enormous responsibilities behind, and it showed now in his face and his manner. Meredith was not surprised by the drastic change; his life in New York had been far more stressful and demanding than her own. His time was almost completely dominated by the Kirakis Corporation. How many times had they walked out of a restaurant halfway through dinner because someone had managed to track him down with an urgent transatlantic call or a business-related emergency requiring his immediate attention? Even at Southampton, they were often unsuccessful in their attempts to cut themselves off from the outside world. She had begun to feel as though they would never have any real privacy, and now that they had, she hated to give it up.

"I wish we didn't have to go back at all," she said.

Alexander leaned back in his chair and smiled indulgently. "Would you like to stay on another month?" he asked.

"I would love to," she said without hesitation. "But if

I'm not back in Manhattan by mid-September, Harv Petersen will probably send out the National Guard. You have no idea how irate he can be when his shows are behind in their production schedules."

He gave a small sigh of resignation. "Ah, but it was a marvelous idea—while it lasted," he said as he finished his drink. He signaled the waiter for another.

Meredith was silent for a moment. "What have you got in mind for this afternoon?" she asked finally.

"Nothing. I thought I'd leave that up to you. Why do you ask?"

"Have you ever been to a fortune-teller?" she asked.

He looked at her oddly. "Why on earth would you ask me that?" he asked, amusement in his voice.

She smiled. "Just curious, that's all." She paused. "When we were coming back from the Plage de Pampelone this morning, I noticed a little place just outside town. The sign in the window advertised fortune-telling."

He stared at her for a moment. "And you would like to visit this fortune-teller?"

"I think it might be fun, yes."

He paused. "Very well. Why not?" he responded with a shrug.

The bungalow was on the outskirts of St.-Tropez. It was small and looked to be at least two hundred years old. The hand-painted sign in the front window was simple and direct: MADAME ROSE—DISEUSE DE BONNE ADVENTURE. The parlor was small and dimly lit by an assortment of candles scattered through the room. The furniture was old and well worn. The large, multicolored rug on the floor was hand-woven and quite old, with a beautiful, intricate design in a kaleidoscope pattern of vivid colors. The rectangular table in the center of the room was covered with a heavy red linen tablecloth that hung all the way to the floor, and two large candles in ornately carved holders stood on each end.

"There doesn't appear to be anyone around," Alexander said in a low voice. "Where do you suppose they could have gone?"

"They're probably out in back—disposing of the bodies," Meredith said.

At that moment, a small, wizened old woman came into the room, bent over and moving in a slow shuffle. She was dressed in the traditional gypsy fashion, and her head was covered by a long black scarf so that only her thin, heavily lined face showed. She motioned them to sit down as she took her place at the table. She looked at Alexander, then at Meredith. Her dark eyes moved back to Alexander and she studied him for a good ten seconds. "Show me your hands," she said in French, in a voice that was surprisingly authoritative for one so old.

Alexander glanced over at Meredith, then extended his hands across the table.

"Palms up," she told him.

He turned his palms upward, and she leaned forward, peering intently at his hands with narrowed eyes. She looked up at him and nodded. Then she reached into a drawer and brought out a small bundle wrapped in a blue silk handkerchief. Folding it back carefully, she revealed a deck of brightly colored Tarot cards. She selected a card from the deck and placed it in the center of the table. "This will be your card," she told him. "The King of Swords. The king is very strong, very powerful. He is a firm friend as well as a powerful enemy." She handed him the deck of cards. "Mix them thoroughly so that the cards will pick up your vibrations—and always shuffle to the left. This is extremely important."

Alexander suppressed a smile. He shuffled the cards as instructed, cutting them into three piles and placing them to his left on the table. The old woman took ten cards from the first stack and placed the first card on top of the King of Swords, crossing it with the second card. She then positioned the remainder of the cards on the table so that they formed a cross and a staff. She looked up at Alexander. "You must concentrate," she said quietly. "Think only of the question you wish to have answered."

Alexander nodded slightly, a look of skepticism on his face. Meredith looked on in silence, intrigued.

Madame Rose studied the cards thoughtfully. "You face troubles, do you not?"

Alexander shook his head.

"In spite of your position of vast wealth and influence,

you will face serious financial problems in the near future,"
she said slowly, her eyes never leaving the cards. "If you are
wise and act cautiously, you will triumph. You will weather a
good many storms. Peace will come—at a price."

Alexander glanced at Meredith. She was transfixed.

"The Queen of Swords occupies that position which deals
with your past," the old gypsy went on. "She represents
a beautiful dark woman of great presence. There is such a
woman in your past?"

Meredith smiled knowingly. "Could be any one of a
hundred," she said with a smile. Alexander shot her a quick
glance.

"She carries a deep sorrow within her heart," Madame
Rose went on. "She is very unhappy. Those she loves have
been taken from her, perhaps separated from her by time and
a great distance."

Alexander shook his head but did not comment. She was
way off base. There was no such woman in his past.

"The Knight of Swords," the gypsy was saying, "represents a young man from the more recent past. He is a brave,
dashing young man, but very impetuous, torn by a great
inner conflict. This is perhaps yourself as a youth?"

Alexander's gaze was level, but again he said nothing. She
had obviously been reading the gossip columns.

"This card," she said, gesturing slightly, "indicates an
influence about to enter your life. It is reversed—he is to be a
most powerful man. If crossed, he will also be a dangerous
one." Her fingers moved slightly from one card to the next.
"You must be cautious in accepting any assistance he may
offer you. He will appear to be an ally, but there is much
treachery and deceit behind that offer. He wishes to steal
away what is rightfully yours."

Alexander tried not to smile. The old woman really knew
how to weave a tale.

"There will be much concern as a result of your dealings
with this man," the gypsy warned. "A will or an inheritance
may be challenged by this one." She looked up at him, her
ancient face illuminated in the candlelight, and her dark eyes
seemed surprisingly bright and alive. "Soon you will em-
bark upon a long journey, a journey that will take you to
places and reveal things you will not believe possible." She

looked over at Meredith. "This is the Queen of Wands —your card. You must stand by him, for the love you share will be the only stable influence in his life in the months to come. This is most important."

Meredith pushed her hair back away from her face. Something about this place, this woman, and her predictions was almost eerie. It felt creepy. She didn't believe in this sort of thing, and yet the old woman was scaring her.

"The emperor occupies that position governing the final outcome," Madame Rose continued. "Extreme care must be taken if you do not wish to be defrauded. You must fight to maintain control, but beware, for there is the possibility of serious injury if you engage in physical battle with your foe." She straightened up in her chair. "It would be most unwise of you to ignore the warnings, monsieur. The signs here are very strong."

Alexander nodded but still did not speak. He reached into his pocket and pulled out a handful of francs, giving them to the old gypsy. He looked at Meredith. "Do you want to give it a try?" he asked.

Meredith shook her head. "I think I've seen enough of the future for one day," she said. Though Meredith could not speak with Alexander's fluency, she had understood most of the fortune teller's predictions.

He nodded again and got to his feet. Speaking briefly to the gypsy in flawless French, he turned and steered Meredith toward the door. Outside, he started to laugh. "Didn't I tell you? This fortune-telling business is nothing more than an elaborate con game," he said as he helped her into the Excalibur.

"She wasn't even close?" Meredith asked.

He smiled. "What do you think?" he asked as he slid behind the wheel.

"I think you weren't impressed."

"The few areas in which she was correct were facts she could have acquired from any newspaper or magazine," he maintained as he drove back to the Hotel Byblos. "The bit about the dangerous adversary was a wonderful touch, I'll give her that. And as for the mysterious dark woman from my past"—he laughed aloud—"I think that may be a standard for all fortune-tellers. All men have a beautiful dark woman in their pasts and all women are going to fall in love with a dark and handsome man.''

''Why not?'' Meredith asked. ''I did.''

''We did not need a fortune-teller to reveal that to us,'' he reminded her. ''If you will recall, I predicted our future together the day we met.''

''So you did.'' She paused. ''You're sure that she couldn't have been talking about one of those wildly exotic women from your past as a carefree bachelor?''

''A woman separated from her loved ones by great time and distance?'' He laughed. ''There was no such woman.''

''Maybe you just didn't know—''

He turned to look at her, suddenly concerned. ''Does it bother you, *matia mou?*'' he asked. ''My past, I mean?''

''I wouldn't be human if it didn't,'' she admitted. ''But I'm learning to deal with it.''

''There is no one else,'' he assured her. ''Not anymore.''

TWENTY

When Alexander and Meredith left St.-Tropez, they drove
west along the coast to Marseille, then north along the
Rhône to Arles and Avignon, stopping for a few days at the
Kirakis château, fifteen kilometers northeast of Avignon.
"You know, I keep trying to visualize you out here working
with the laborers," Meredith told Alexander as they walked
through the vineyards, "but hard as I try, I can't picture you
engaged in any kind of physical labor." She looked up at
him with an impish smile and added, "Outside the bedroom, that is."

"Wicked woman," he said in a low, husky voice as he
pulled her close. "Don't you know the difference between
labor and pleasure?"

She wrapped her arms around him. "I should," she
responded in a playful tone. "I've been with you long
enough."

They left the château with every intention of drifting on
nonstop to Lyon, where they'd made advance reservations
for a night at the Hotel Royal on Place Bellecour, but neither
of them had anticipated the sudden appearance of the
mistral, the cold, dry, and extremely fierce wind that often
ripped through the Rhône valley. Several times the force of

the winds challenged Alexander's control of the Excalibur, until finally he decided it would be unwise to attempt to go any further. "We will stay in Montélimar until the winds have died," he told Meredith as they drove along the Avenue d'Aygu. "There is a wonderful château hotel on the Place Max Dormoy, the Relais de l'Empereur—only forty rooms, very intimate, quite delightful. We will go there."

"Does this sort of thing happen often?" Meredith asked, still shaken by the strength of the winds that had more than once sent them weaving crazily on the roads leading to Montélimar.

"More often than anyone in the valley would like," he answered. "It has been said that when the mistral rages, the people of the Rhône valley rage also."

Meredith had long ago ceased to be surprised by the ease with which Alexander was able to secure the best suites in the best hotels wherever they went. She was, however, still impressed by the easy, relaxed manner with which he seemed to be able to deal with everyone he met. Now, as she observed him chatting casually in his impeccable French with the hotelier, Monsieur Roger Latry, and his charming wife, it seemed as if they were friends of long standing. "I've stayed here many times in the past," Alexander told her as they were escorted to their room. "Monsieur Latry has an extraordinary talent for making all of his guests feel comfortable and at home. I'm given my usual room —number fifteen—when I stay here. I think Monsieur Latry's daughter—the lovely young woman at the front desk—thinks I'm superstitious because I always request the same room."

Meredith paused for a moment to admire an old, stained-glass window. "There seem to be references to Napoleon everywhere I turn," she commented. "The window, the paintings, the artifacts . . ."

Alexander laughed. "The emperor of the hotel's name is Napoleon himself," he explained as they entered their room. "I'm told he stayed here, in this same room, on four separate occasions—with four different lovers." He gave the bellman a generous tip, then closed the door.

"And what about you?" she asked, teasing him. "How many lovers have you brought here?"

"You, *matia mou,* are the first." He took her in his arms. "In the past, I have always come alone—except once . . ."

"And who was with you then?"

"My mother," he answered with a grin. "It was my first trip to the south of France. I was fourteen at the time."

"And I'll bet you charmed all of the mademoiselles even then," she said, kissing the tip of his nose.

"Actually, I was a shy, awkward adolescent," he insisted.

She kissed him again, this time full on the lips. "I find that very hard to believe."

"Hmmm . . . it seems that my reputation is much worse than even I had realized," he remarked as he held her close, looking down at her with a wicked gleam in his black eyes.

"Well, why don't you stop fighting it and start living up to that reputation of yours?" she teased.

His smile was devilish. "I can't think of anything I would rather do."

The mistral lasted three days, and for the last two was accompanied by torrential rains. Alexander and Meredith waited out the storm at the hotel, and during that time never left their room. When they were hungry, which was not often, they called for room service. On the morning of the fourth day, the rain stopped and the winds calmed considerably. When Meredith awakened, Alexander was already up and dressed, standing at the windows contemplating the sunrise.

"Has it stopped?" Meredith asked as she sat up, pulling the sheet up to cover herself. She shook her head so that her hair fell back, away from her face.

He nodded, turning to face her. "We should plan on getting an early start," he said quietly. "It's a long drive to Paris."

She smiled at him, extending one arm. "You sound disappointed."

He crossed the room and sat beside her on the bed. "I wouldn't have complained if it had lasted a few more days," he admitted, kissing her tenderly. "I rather enjoyed this enforced hibernation of ours."

Her eyes met his. "So did I," she said softly. "But we both knew we couldn't stay here forever, darling. And I have

a show to do and a by now hysterical producer to pacify
—thank God the taping was already finished when you
kidnapped me from Paris—and *you* have the corporation to
think about.''

He forced a smile. ''As always, you're right, *matia mou*,''
he said with resignation. ''But that doesn't make it any easier
to give up this idyllic existence of ours.''

''Our existence will always be idyllic—as long as we're
together,'' she promised. ''And as for these romantic
getaways you seem so good at staging, we have the rest of our
lives to plan repeat performances—as you've said yourself
more than once.''

''The first time I came here, I was twelve years old,''
Alexander told Meredith as they walked along the Seine in
the twilight. ''My mother was ill. She was a semi-invalid for
most of her life and was never allowed to travel alone. My
father always accompanied her when she wished to travel.
Then, when I was old enough, I took her place when he was
occupied elsewhere.'' They paused on the extraordinarily
beautiful Pont Alexandre III, the most elaborate of the
bridges crossing the Seine, its splendid wrought-iron lamp-
posts illuminating its Second Empire design, and savored the
view of the Grand and Petit Palaces facing Les Invalides.
''Mother loved everything about France,'' Alexander said.
''She transferred that love to me. Of all the cities I have
visited in my life, Paris has always remained my favorite.''
Pausing for a moment, he reached into his pocket and took
out a coin, tossing it into the water. Meredith looked at him
questioningly but said nothing.

''Old habits are hard to break,'' he said lightly. ''This
was a tradition for Mother and myself, much the same as the
custom of tossing a coin into the Fontana di Trevi in Rome
has always been for tourists. When I was twelve, Mother told
me if I threw a coin into the Seine and made a wish, it was
sure to come true. I never told her I didn't believe it; I just
went along with it for her. I still do it out of habit—and, I
suppose, because for some crazy reason it makes me feel
close to her in spirit.''

''What was she like, Alexander?'' Meredith asked, sensing that he wanted to talk about her.

"Very much like you in so many ways," he answered with a sad smile. "Strong, spirited, determined. She was an incredible woman, beautiful and feminine, yet so very courageous. In spite of her condition she led a full, happy life. Mother was a survivor. She never had a career of her own—God forbid that a daughter of the aristocracy should work at anything except being beautiful and cultured—yet when my father had to leave her behind in New York during the war while he went off to serve in the Royal Hellenic Navy, she ran the corporation from New York, making all the major decisions and reporting to him as often as she could. It was quite an accomplishment for a woman who had never had any previous business experience—unless one could call being Madame Constantine Kirakis a career."

"Ah, yes," Meredith said slowly, recognition registering on her beautiful face. "Your mother was the rich girl who married the poor boy from the wrong side of the tracks and lived happily ever after," she said.

Alexander nodded, staring thoughtfully into the water as he leaned against the railing. "In the beginning, Mother's family and Father's might as well have been on two different planets. Supposedly, her family was related to all the crowned heads of Europe. Theirs was old money, as some call it. Mother had maids to do everything for her, even dress her if she wished. Father, on the other hand, was the flip side of the coin—son of a stevedore, youngest of thirteen children, he grew up on the docks in Piraeus where there was never enough money, never enough food on the table. Their existence was a constant fight for survival. When it comes down to children being forced to fight one another for that last crumb of bread just to survive, it does something to them. It is a way of life that can either break a man's spirit or make him hungry for more. Father was a fighter. He wanted more, and he went after it."

"Like you," Meredith concluded.

Alexander looked at her and smiled. "The battles in which I have engaged in the past are of a different nature," he said easily. "I have never had to fight for survival, though there have been times when I felt as though I were fighting for my life."

She put her arms around him. "For what it's worth,

darling, you'll never have to fight alone again," she said softly. "I'll always be here for you, right beside you, all the way."

He held her close, kissing her tenderly. "You are what I have always needed, the one element that has always been missing from my life," he told her.

"Not anymore," she whispered. "And never again."

When the Kirakis Corporation's 747 landed at Kennedy Airport, word of Alexander Kirakis's sudden marriage to Meredith Courtney had already leaked to the press. Reporters and photographers had gathered just beyond the gates where they were expected to arrive, eagerly awaiting the newlyweds' return from their honeymoon. Alexander, who had long ago developed a sixth sense for detecting the presence of the paparazzi even before they were in sight, knew they were there even as he and Meredith disembarked from the plane. "Are you ready to face the mob?" he asked as they walked down the ramp together.

"Face them?" Meredith laughed. "I'm one of them, remember?"

"Not this time, my love," he reminded her. "Today you're their prey."

"Perhaps, but having spent so much time on the other side of the mike, I know how to handle them," she said confidently.

They were met at the bottom of the ramp by an airport official who offered profuse apologies for the inconvenience the press had caused them. He escorted them to another part of the airport where they were rushed through customs and taken to their waiting limo by a small platoon of security guards. It was not until they were in the car and about to leave that the reporters caught up with them, surrounding the car, making it difficult for them to make their getaway. Meredith was temporarily blinded by the continually popping flashbulbs as the car inched its way through the crowd. They shouted, calling her name, calling Alexander's name, clamoring for a statement or a photograph. She moved closer to Alexander, who put one arm around her protectively and persistently refused their requests as the car moved away from the mob and headed for the exit.

"How the hell did they find out?" Alexander asked irritably. "Only two people knew what we were planning —and they were sworn to secrecy. Unless your producer . . ."

Meredith gave him a tired smile. "No, Harv wouldn't have done it," she assured him. "But you'd be surprised at the sources a good reporter has at his or her disposal." She rested her head on his shoulder. "Hotel clerks, waiters who might have overheard part of a conversation over dinner, shop clerks—"

"Or an old gypsy fortune-teller in St.-Tropez?"

She laughed. "Or an old gypsy fortune-teller in St.-Tropez."

It was a cold, gray morning in mid-December, and visibility from the floor-to-ceiling windows in Alexander's office in the World Trade Center was near zero, but he had not taken notice of it. Even now, three months after returning from his honeymoon, he found himself still catching up on all the paper work that had accumulated in his absence. He met with George on a daily basis to discuss reports, contracts, possible acquisitions, and joint ventures being considered by the corporation. He was pleased with how well George had handled things in his absence.

"In the future, we shall be working together even more closely than we have in the past," Alexander told George. "It relieves me to know that I'm able to leave the office for extended periods of time and know that the corporation will be in good hands. In fact, I'm looking forward to getting away with Meredith from time to time without being interrupted by business matters."

George grinned. "Next time, give me a little advance warning, okay?" he asked. "I had a few shaky moments right after you left. If you look closely, you'll find a few silver threads among the gold." He ran his fingers through his sandy-blond hair.

Alexander laughed. "You have my word—no more last-minute weddings," he promised.

George paused for a moment, lighting a cigarette. "Meredith's off on assignment again, isn't she?" he asked, taking a drag.

"For a few days." Alexander frowned, twisting the platinum wedding ring on his finger absently as he spoke. "This is the second time since we've been back. Some important interview she's after." He got to his feet and moved around to one side of his desk, turning to the windows for the first time but only vaguely aware of the fog. "Have you seen the new issue of *People* magazine?"

George's face brightened. "The big spread on the newlyweds?" He grinned. "Very flattering. Meredith managed to change your image more than either of you anticipated, didn't she?"

Alexander smiled. "When I married Meredith, changing my image was the last thing on my mind," he said quietly, pausing to look at the silver-framed photograph of his wife on one corner of his desk.

"Maybe, but it couldn't have succeeded more brilliantly if it had been planned that way," George pointed out. "Manhattan's royal couple—I think that's what they're calling you now. The emperor and his lovely consort. Six major periodicals have done stories on you two since the wedding. The public is eating it up. They've forgotten all about your notorious past. They love romance, and you and Meredith have given them the love story of the decade. A modern fairy tale, no less."

Alexander shook his head, still smiling. "Perhaps I should have made you vice-president and director of public relations," he said.

"You make light of it, but your new wife is an asset, Alexander. A real and important asset. Take advantage of it," George advised.

"Take advantage of it?" Alexander echoed with mild amusement. "I thought that was exactly what I had been doing!"

"You know what I'm talking about," George insisted. "Make public appearances. Go to all those charity balls you've avoided in the past. Pull out all the stops."

Alexander laughed. "I'm definitely in favor of showing off my wife," he responded easily, "but as you have already said yourself, my marriage has already improved my image. Why go to so much trouble—"

"Because most of the key members of the international business community still see you as untrustworthy—a ruthless, cold-blooded bastard," George said honestly. "They're afraid of you."

Alexander turned to face him. He was smiling. "Good," he said, obviously pleased. "Let's keep it that way."

Rome.

Carlo Manetti was worried. The Fates, once so very good to him, seemed now to have suddenly turned on him. Business was not good these days; in fact it could not get much worse. Sales of Manetti's once popular sports cars were down. A writer for *Oggi* had callously proclaimed in print that Carlo Manetti had "lost his Midas touch." While most dismissed the claim as idle speculation, Manetti himself had begun to believe it.

He had ultimately been forced to take drastic action. He closed his assembly plants in Verona, Florence, and Naples, putting thousands of Italian auto workers out of jobs. He cut back on production—and personnel—at the remaining plants in Rome and Milan, and made severe reductions in the executive branch of the company. As time passed and the situation seemed to worsen instead of improve, Carlo Manetti began to feel like a condemned man awaiting his fate on death row. Still, he kept up a brave front. He faced his bankers, to whom he was more deeply in debt with the passing of each day, with a smile, knowing how important it was that he radiate optimism for the future of his troubled company. Publicly, he told reporters that his predicament was "only temporary, nothing to worry about." Privately, he drank too much and slept too little, and seemed to have aged ten years overnight. He was short-tempered and impatient. His daughter, who knew him better than anyone, grew concerned, but when she tried to talk to him, he immediately shut her out.

His last trip to Milan had offered hope for the economic recovery of Manetti Motors. His automotive engineers, among the best and the brightest in all of Europe, had designed a new sports car they were predicting would outdistance even his fabulously successful Rinnegato, both in sales and in popularity. It was, Manetti conceded, a magnificent vehicle, a truly exciting design. Manetti was enthusiastic, but he worried aloud that it would almost certainly be an expensive car to produce and would therefore carry an unusually high price tag.

"Of course, Signore Manetti," one of the young engineers agreed, "but this one is destined to become a status object—given the right advertising campaign, of course. It will be like the Ferrari or the Rolls-Royce. Everyone who is anyone will want to own one."

"I suppose," Manetti said slowly. "But it will require a rather large monetary investment on my part also, is that not true?"

"That is to be expected when you are producing a car of the caliber of this one, signore," the other engineer said reasonably. "But it will pay off, we are certain of that."

"I will consider it," Manetti promised. "Now is not the best time, as I am sure you already know, but I will consider it."

"There could not be a better time, signore," the first engineer disagreed. "You are in financial trouble, no? This car will bail you out."

Manetti frowned. To say that he was in trouble was looking at things on the bright side. "I will consider it," he repeated. "I shall get back to you in a week or so."

Though Carlo Manetti would never have admitted it, he believed with every fiber of his being that his company's survival, his survival, depended upon the success of this new model.

If he could only raise the needed capital to get it from the drawing board to the showrooms. . . .

New York City.

The water was warm and fragrant, the huge marble tub filled with billowing clouds of bubbles. Meredith lay back against Alexander's shoulder, content in his embrace as she sipped ice-cold Dom Perignon. This, she thought, has to be the very best way to unwind after an exhausting day. She held the glass to his lips. "More champagne, darling?" she asked.

He shook his head. "I think I've had enough for tonight," he said quietly.

"You've had enough of something, but I'm not sure it's the champagne," she said, looking up at him with concern in her pale blue eyes. "Feel like talking about it?"

"It's been a long day, *matia mou*—a long and exceptionally difficult day," he told her. "No major crises, just a large number of minor problems, all cropping up at one time. And if I did not have enough to contend with, I received a call late this afternoon from one of my people in Rome concerning Carlo Manetti. His company is facing serious problems and the Italian press is out in force, blaming me for his predicament. They seem to think it's part of my plan to take over his company." His smile was tired. "It's ironic. Carlo and I have been adversaries for many years. There was a time I might have tried something underhanded to gain control of his company, more to prove a point than anything else. But this . . . I knew nothing of this until today."

"Carlo Manetti," Meredith repeated slowly, recognition registering on her face. "The rich Italian auto magnate with the sexy schoolgirl daughter who has the hots for you."

"Had," Alexander corrected.

"What makes you think she's gotten over you?" Meredith asked in a teasing voice. "It hasn't been that long."

Alexander's laugh was hollow. "Take my word for it, darling, the only thing Donna Manetti feels for me now is a deep, all-consuming hatred," he assured her. "I will never forget the look on her face the last time I saw her, when I sent her home after that episode in the restaurant. She probably wanted to kill me. She was trying so hard to be a temptress, and I treated her like the child she is."

"That doesn't mean she doesn't still want you, my love," Meredith said knowingly, touching his face with her fingertips. "As angry as I was with you because of her, I never stopped wanting you."

"And what about now?" he asked in a low voice.

Her eyes met his. "Now? I want you more than ever," she said simply.

He smiled as he took the glass from her and put it aside. Then he took her in his arms again and kissed her hungrily. She lay back against the side of the tub, safe in his arms as he ignited the fires of her passion. Their bodies came together, fused with desire. Alexander looked down at her, her face bare of any traces of makeup, her long hair plastered against her head and neck, and he was totally amazed.

Even at this moment, she was the most beautiful woman he had ever seen.

Though Meredith had been a celebrity in her own right before their marriage, she quickly discovered just how much her social position had changed since becoming Mrs. Alexander Kirakis. Before, she had received preferential treatment in all the best shops in Manhattan. She had been given the best tables in the best restaurants—but only if she had a reservation. Her designer clothes were free if she wore them on the show. Now, people came to her. Designers in New York, Paris, and Rome were ecstatic when she showed a preference for one of their designs. They arranged fittings at her convenience. Some of them had designed suits, dresses, and gowns especially for her. When she wanted anything from any of Manhattan's more prestigious shops, she had only to have her personal secretary put in a call to have a selection of the particular item brought to the Olympic Tower for her inspection. Whenever she and Alexander traveled, she received the same courtesy at whatever hotel they stayed. She no longer used commercial airlines. Alexander seemed to delight in spoiling her. At least once a month, a representative from one of the city's leading jewelers came to their apartment with a large selection of rings, bracelets, necklaces, and earrings, and Meredith had only to admire a piece to own it. She had more jewelry than she could use, a closet full of furs, and another—as large as the bedroom in the apartment she'd had before her marriage—filled with her clothes, shoes, and accessories.

But as Alexander himself had once observed, with the privilege came the pressures. In the year she had been Alexander's wife, she often found herself defending him to those in international business circles who regarded him as ruthless and his business practices as unethical. She tried to be diplomatic whenever someone attacked him for his alleged involvement in the Manetti affair in Rome. To all of the criticism, she responded that how her husband chose to run the Kirakis Corporation was his own business. She did not tell him how to conduct his business dealings, and he did not tell her how to do her show.

Oddly enough, Meredith realized as she sat at her dressing table, alone in their bedroom, not one of them ever approached her about any of his former lovers. Nor did they ever mention her live-in relationship with Nick Holliday to him. She put down her hairbrush and looked up thoughtfully at the portrait of Elizabeth and David that now hung in the bedroom. She'd been thinking of having it moved again, this time to one of the guest rooms where Alexander was not likely to see it often. He was clearly not comfortable with it. At first he'd seemed intrigued by it, but perhaps disturbed would better describe how he felt. Did Elizabeth remind him of one of those dark, sultry women from his past? she wondered. She doubted she'd ever know. He flatly refused to discuss it.

Zürich.

The large-scale expansion of the Kirakis Corporation's operations in Switzerland had made it necessary for Alexander to seek financial assistance from outside sources, so he had arranged a meeting with six members of a Swiss banking consortium to discuss his plans and, he hoped, to obtain their support for his projects. Though the meeting had been set up weeks in advance, and Meredith had planned to make the trip with him, her television commitments had forced her to change her plans at the last minute. Alexander flew to Zürich alone, hoping to secure the loans he needed and wanting to get back to New York as quickly as possible but not sure he could accomplish both without compromise.

Though the meeting was scheduled to take place at his offices on the Ramistrasse, Alexander arranged to be away from the office when the bankers arrived. He intended to be late for that meeting, recalling something his father had once told him: "Do not let them know that you are too eager, Alexander. They are like the piranha. They can smell your blood, your fear." He decided a ten-minute delay would make him appear responsible without seeming too eager, so he waited exactly that length of time before returning to the offices. He needed these men, he thought as he rode up in the elevator alone. But he could not afford to let them know just how much he needed them.

As he entered the conference room, he paused for a moment, his black eyes sweeping across the room, taking in the annoyed looks of the five men who awaited him. He apologized for being late. "I have been on the phone with one of my associates in Istanbul," he explained. "You know, of course, that we have been drilling in the Java Sea."

They all nodded.

"Why have you asked to meet with us, Herr Kirakis?" one of the others asked, voicing the curiosity of the entire group.

Alexander flashed an easy grin. "I would think that would be obvious to all of you."

"Surely you are not considering asking for a loan . . ." the banker said.

"That is precisely what I had in mind." Alexander paused. "There is a problem with this?"

"No, of course not," the man responded quickly. "It is just that the Kirakis Corporation has always done its own financing in the past, and—"

"Correction—we have *usually* done our own financing," Alexander said politely. "Except in cases where we were planning a large-scale expansion of our holdings—as we are now."

"I see."

Alexander studied the men collectively for a few seconds. "Many of you knew my father, didn't you?" he asked. "Perhaps you were involved in business deals with him at one time or another?"

Three of the men nodded.

"If you knew him at all, you know that he was a brilliant businessman," Alexander reasoned. "He was the man who made Athena Maritime the greatest merchant fleet in the Eastern Hemisphere—no, in the world. The Kirakis Corporation was born of Athena's success, as you are all aware. Oil, diamond mines, automobiles, aircraft—''

"You have our attention, Herr Kirakis," one of the men cut in impatiently. "We are all definitely interested in what you have in mind. What, exactly, are you leading up to?"

"Expansion. Growth. Large-scale growth." Alexander's eyes moved from one man to the next, slowly, deliberately, as if he were appraising them. "Gentlemen, when I took my father's place as chairman of the board of Kirakis in 1979, its assets in Europe, North and South America, Asia, and Africa amounted to roughly nine hundred million Swiss francs. Today it is closer to fourteen billion."

The banker cut in again. "We are all aware of the Kirakis Corporation's impressive record. We are also aware that it has generally been able to sustain itself financially," he said.

"In the past, we have done so whenever possible." Alexander's eyes glowed like polished onyx. "But to accomplish the expansion I have in mind will require several very large loans. And naturally, whatever bank provides that assistance can expect to act as the prime bankers for Kirakis in all future transactions."

There was a loud murmur among the group as they nodded their assent.

Now he had them! Alexander could almost smell their excitement. "I plan to expand my holdings, not only in Switzerland but all over Europe. Just as I have been doing in the United States. I plan to diversify, branch out into new fields, fields untested by my father."

"For example?" one of the men asked.

"Many of the same fields we are now branching into in the United States—construction, real estate. I plan to buy or build hotels, condominiums, resorts." He paused. "I would also like to explore the avenues of nuclear energy here in Switzerland and in my homeland. Our work in the American plant looks very promising at the moment. We have also been considering further involvement in the field of solar energy. I am sure that you will all agree that energy is a major concern to all of us now. A problem that must be faced—and solved."

They all nodded once again.

"To do so will require extensive research—and the capital

to fund such research.'' Alexander savored their enthusiasm, relished it. Time to play the trump card, he thought. ''Nuclear weaponry,'' he said with quiet reverence in his voice.

''Bombs?'' one of the men asked.

''Profits,'' Alexander corrected emphatically. ''Unbelievable profits. Dr. Barry Marchwood, who serves as director of my nuclear research facility in the States, is one of the world's leading authorities on nuclear armaments. Under his direction, the Kirakis Corporation will soon be able to boast one of the largest privately owned nuclear research facilities in the world.''

The five men listened intently as Alexander went on.

''In three years, gentlemen, the Kirakis Corporation's profits are expected to triple under my plan,'' he told them. ''We shall continue to grow, to expand, and naturally, we will be seeking additional loans from our prime bankers.''

''Naturally,'' they all agreed.

''The loans you would require would be quite large,'' one of the men pointed out.

''Very true,'' Alexander admitted. ''But in light of the size and scope of the project I propose, I do not consider my request unreasonable.''

''We will discuss it and get back to you,'' he promised.

''Do not wait too long,'' Alexander cautioned, preparing his bluff. ''I would not want to be forced to borrow the money in the United States.''

At that, the man stiffened as though he had been struck physically. ''Twenty-four hours?'' he asked?

''Twenty-four hours,'' Alexander agreed. It will not take that long, he thought confidently.

The banker studied the younger man thoughtfully for a moment. He had known Constantine Kirakis for over thirty years and had done business with him on several occasions. He had been a dynamic businessman. But his son was something else again. In his thirties, Alexander Kirakis had the poise and confidence of a man with years of experience behind him. Next to Alexander Kirakis, the banker felt uncomfortably self-conscious. The younger man was so damned self-assured!

Alexander shook hands with each of them. ''I apologize

for having to depart so quickly,'' he told them. ''I have a
meeting in Paris tonight and must leave immediately.''

He walked out, leaving them staring after him.

In a magnificent villa thirty kilometers northwest of Zürich,
Julius Hauptmann was alone in his impressive oak-paneled
library. His domestic staff had been given their instructions:
he was not to be disturbed for any reason. He sat in the
darkness, thinking about the meeting that was taking place at
the Kirakis Corporation's offices. Alexander Kirakis did not
know—must never know—that he was also a part of the
consortium, the silent member. Hauptmann knew he would
have to be careful. He could not make the mistake of
underestimating Alexander. He was young, but he was
brilliant. He missed nothing. He was also a dangerous
adversary. Hauptmann had known from the start that he
would have to use extreme caution in dealing with this man.
If Alexander were to become suspicious, he would be on his
guard. It could turn everything.

Hauptmann switched on the antique brass lamp on the
corner of his eighteenth-century English desk and took a
large scrapbook bound in pine-green leather from the top
drawer. He put it on the desk and turned the pages slowly,
studying each of the clippings inside as if seeing them for the
first time. In reality he had seen all of them many times
before and knew their contents by heart. The book was filled
with photos and clippings of Alexander Kirakis. He had
memorized everything in it. Not a day passed that Herr
Hauptmann did not think about Alexander Kirakis, about
how he was going to destroy the man who had long ago
destroyed all that was important to him.

From the back of the book he took a small, well-worn
clipping from a Geneva newspaper dated February 16, 1980.
It was a brief article that had not been given the front-page
prominence of the exploits of someone as notorious and
colorful as Alexander Kirakis, but to Hauptmann it was the
most important piece in the book. The reason for everything
he did, for everything he had done in the past five years.
Even now, as he picked it up with trembling fingers, reading
it again, tears stung his gray eyes. It was a brief account of
the death of a young college student from Neuchâtel who had

hanged herself in a hotel room near the campus of the Université de Genève. The article did not give any specifics, how she had been driven to take her own life or who had been behind it, but Hauptmann knew only too well why it had happened. As long as he lived, he would never forget the morning the Geneva police took him there to identify the body. In his mind, he could still see her hanging from the pole in the small bathroom; could still remember, verbatim, the message in her note. He had been filled with a pain and a hatred so strong that it threatened to destroy him. He realized that he could not die in peace until he avenged her senseless death—in his own way.

Alexander Kirakis would pay for what he had done to his beloved Marianne.

TWENTY-ONE

⌐⌐⌐⌐⌐⌐⌐⌐⌐⌐

In her office high above West Fifty-second Street, Meredith sat at her desk, staring thoughtfully at a photograph of Alexander when the sound of light tapping at her door cut through her reverie. Her head jerked up. "Come in," she called out.

The door swung open and Casey entered, carrying a large cardboard box. "This just came for you while I was downstairs. It's from Los Angeles," she said as she placed it on Meredith's desk. "I signed for it, so I thought I might as well bring it up with me. No telling how long it would take those characters in the mailroom to get around to delivering it." She sank into a chair and blew a lock of her dark red hair out of her face.

Meredith cut through the heavy packing tape with a letter opener. "I've been waiting for this," she said as she opened the box and inspected its contents. "I was hoping it would show up before my meeting with Harv tomorrow afternoon."

"Does this have anything to do with all the trips you've been making to the West Coast lately?" Casey asked, gesturing toward the box.

"In a way," Meredith responded evasively. Everything was here. Good. She hadn't been sure Kay would be able to track it down. This box, along with several others she'd packed when she left the beach house, had been in storage for the past four years. She picked up one of the eight-by-ten black-and-white photographs and studied it for a moment, then showed it to Casey. "Recognize this lady?" she asked.

Casey sat up, ramrod-straight, not bothering to hide her surprise. "Elizabeth Weldon-Ryan?" she asked. "That's what this has all been about? The trips to L.A., the meetings with Harv—"

Meredith nodded, smiling. "Years ago, while I was still with the IBS affiliate in Los Angeles, I met her husband, Tom Ryan. He was the one who gave Nick his first big break," she began, perching on one corner of the desk. "After Nick introduced us, I came up with the idea of doing a documentary on the Ryans—how they met, how he launched her career, their final triumph—"

"And concluding with what really happened to Elizabeth and her son during the filming of her last picture," Casey finished.

"Exactly." Meredith paused. "Tom Ryan was less than enthusiastic about the project at first, but I finally convinced him to cooperate with me." She told Casey how Ryan had not wanted to confide in her in the beginning, how she'd had to win him over gradually, and how he had been on his way to see her the night he died in the accident on the Pacific Coast Highway. "The station scrapped the project because I couldn't deliver. We had a story with no clear-cut ending."

"And you think you can deliver it now?" Casey asked.

Meredith shrugged. "I certainly intend to try," she said, toying with a pencil absently. "I can't help thinking that there has to be someone, somewhere, other than Tom Ryan, who can tell me what happened during the filming of that picture. One way or another, I'm going to locate someone who knows the truth and is willing to talk to me about it."

Casey stood up. "I wish you luck," she said as she started for the door. "I think you're going to need it."

"You're probably right," Meredith muttered to herself.

Lausanne.

It was a pity, Dr. Henri Goudron thought sadly as he studied his patient. She had been so young, so very lovely—and such a promising future ahead of her! Such a terrible waste. This woman had had everything—youth, beauty, success, a good marriage, a beautiful child—and to have it all so cruelly snatched away from her one tragic night. . . .

The night they told her about her child.

Dr. Goudron was one of the most respected psychiatrists in Switzerland, and he considered himself to be highly ethical. Never would he permit himself to become emotionally involved with a patient. But this woman was something special. Everything about her fascinated him: her life, her tragic past, her brilliant career, the way she had managed to cut herself off from an unacceptable reality. She had been different for him from the moment he saw her, when her husband brought her to the Clinique de Lausanne some thirty years ago. He had just completed his residency and was recommended by the administrator to take over her case. He had spent so many hours with her in the beginning, trying to reach her, trying to establish communication with her, but after a while he had forced himself to accept the realization that nothing he said or did would snap her out of it. But he had never stopped caring about her, about making her as comfortable as he possibly could for the rest of her days. He saw to it that the staff looked after her, giving her extra-special attention, dressing her in the beautiful clothes her husband had brought her, combing her luxuriant dark hair, taking her for long walks on the grounds whenever weather permitted. He brought her fresh flowers from his wife's garden during the spring and summer months, and whenever he could, he still spent time with her himself, talking to her as though she could hear him and know what he was saying. He had tried to discourage her husband from visiting her, mainly because he knew Tom Ryan still held out the hope that she would recover, and he did not like to see the poor man continue to torment himself in such a manner.

"Ah, Elizabeth," he sighed wistfully, "I wish that somehow I could reach you. I wish I could—how do you

Americans say?—get into your head." English was such an unromantic language, he thought disapprovingly. So inappropriate for a woman who literally inspired romance, even now, in her sad condition. He looked at her and felt a painful sorrow at the bottom of his soul. "What must it be like for you?" he asked aloud.

She had not had a visitor in a very long time. The last thing Tom Ryan had said to Dr. Goudron during his last visit, just before his death, was, "Protect her . . . don't let them ever see her." By *them*, Goudron decided Ryan meant the press. Ryan had gone to such great lengths to protect her from those who might try to exploit her tragedy. Now it troubled Goudron that he had never told Tom Ryan about the other man who visited her, the man who had asked that his visits be kept strictly confidential. The first time he came to see her, only a few months after her admission to the clinic, Goudron had been ready to send him away, but the man's interest in her seemed genuine. And moreover, he had surprised Goudron with his knowledge of catatonia, of what happened within the depths of one's unconscious. For a time, Goudron wondered if the man might have been a doctor himself. He had allowed the visits and kept them a secret because he had believed at first that this man might actually be able to help Elizabeth.

But now, in his heart, that sensible, rational, and most realistic of hearts, Henri Goudron knew that it was never going to happen. For it to be possible, it would require a miracle.

The resurrection of her dead child.

Greece.

Meredith stood on the balcony off the master bedroom suite, admiring the magnificent Aegean sunset. They had not had time to visit the island since their honeymoon, and Meredith had almost forgotten how truly beautiful it was. Our own private Eden, she thought, exhilarated, swept away by the romance that seemed to permeate the air there. She was glad Alexander had insisted they get away from their demanding, fast-paced life in New York and spend their anniversary here. Things had been so hectic lately for both of them. They needed to get away, to spend some time alone.

She went back into the bedroom and curled up in bed with a small, leatherbound book she'd tucked into the bottom of one of her suitcases without telling Alexander. Elizabeth's diary. It had been among the things Tom Ryan had loaned her just before his death. She hadn't looked at it since the day he was buried. She smiled to herself. Alexander had extracted a promise from her that she would leave the network behind on this trip. It was, he had reminded her, their anniversary, and he wanted her undivided attention. In the past he had always been annoyed when they tried to get away for a few days or a few weeks and she ended up taking half her office along. But this time she felt entirely within her rights. Alexander was downstairs in his library, talking with George on the phone. Her stealing a few minutes reading time was justified.

Meredith became so engrossed in the diary, she hardly noticed that Alexander had returned. Closing the door, he crossed the room and sat on the bed beside her, kissing her lightly on the forehead. She looked up at him, startled. "Finished with George so soon?" she asked.

"There wasn't much to discuss." He looked down at the book in her hand. "What are you reading?"

"The diary of Elizabeth Weldon-Ryan."

"Interesting?" he asked.

"Fascinating," Meredith replied.

Alexander took the book from her and placed it on the table beside the bed. "We didn't come here to read—or to work."

"What were you doing down in the library—socializing?" she asked in a teasing voice.

"I was just checking in. And now that it is done, I want you all to myself for the rest of the evening." He smiled. "Make that the rest of the night. I think it's time we had a heart-to-heart talk."

"Sounds serious," she said.

"It is." His eyes met hers. "When we were first married, you made it clear you were not ready to start a family. I accepted that—then."

"And now?" she asked hesitantly, sure she knew what he was leading up to.

"I realize it has only been a year, *matia mou,*" he said quietly. "I have tried to be patient, but I had hoped to become a father while I'm still young enough to enjoy my children."

"Alexander, I—" she began.

He pressed a finger to her lips. "Don't," he said softly. "Don't say anything—yet. Just think about it. Think about how wonderful it would be to have a baby—soon." He pushed one of the pencil-thin straps of her ice blue silk nightgown off her shoulder and bent his head to kiss the smooth, golden flesh. "It would make our marriage perfect, *matia mou,* perfect." He pulled her nightgown down to expose her breasts. She lay back against the pillows as his lips moved down over the warm, soft flesh, shivering with pleasure as he flicked his tongue across her nipples. She stroked his head.

Maybe he's right, she thought.

New York City.

Three weeks passed, and Meredith still had not decided whether or not she was ready to have children. To Alexander's gentle pressuring, she responded by telling him she wanted a baby as much as he did, but those things *did* take time. She was obsessed with the story that had preoccupied her for much of her professional life: the story of the beautiful and tragic Elizabeth Weldon-Ryan. She had assigned members of her research team to begin an all-out search for anyone who might have been involved with the production of her last film, anyone who might have been present on the set at the time of David Ryan's tragic accident, anyone who might know what really happened to Elizabeth after the death of her son.

Meredith instructed her secretary to place an ad in *Variety* and in major trade periodicals and newspapers across the country, requesting information from anyone who might have been involved with the picture or known someone who was. "This is going to bring every kook in the country out from under his or her rock, but we'll just have to put up with it,'' she told Cindy. Most of the leads they received turned out to be useless, resulting in dead ends. Some were legitimate but were unable to provide her with the information she sought. The longer she pursued the story, the more frustrated she became. Tom Ryan had done a good job of safeguarding his secret. Too good. There seemed to be a conspiracy of silence surrounding the mysterious deaths of Elizabeth and her young son.

"We may never find out what really happened to her," Meredith's secretary lamented one afternoon as they sorted through the latest batch of responses. "This has been dead and buried for thirty years now. The longer you keep a secret, the easier it gets to keep it, you know."

Meredith nodded, frowning. How well I know that, she thought grimly.

Cindy sliced open yet another envelope with her letter opener. Taking out the letter, she unfolded it and started reading, halfheartedly at first, but becoming more intrigued as she continued. She reached out and touched Meredith's arm excitedly, her eyes never leaving the letter. "I think you'd better take a look at this," she said slowly.

"What is it?"

"See for yourself." Cindy handed her the letter.

Meredith took it, reading it through quickly the first time, then again, more slowly. It was from a man named William McCloskey, who claimed to have been a cinematographer on Elizabeth Weldon's last picture. He explained that he was retired now, living in Chicago, but still had in his possession footage that had been cut from the motion picture during the final editing process. He wrote that he had been on location with the picture at the time of the tragedy. To verify his claim, he had paper-clipped two old, yellowed photographs to his letter. One was of Elizabeth and her co-stars, all in costume and full makeup. The other was Elizabeth with her husband and son. On the back of each, in a barely legible scrawl, was a date: July 26, 1953. Four days before David Ryan's accident, Meredith thought, recalling what Tom Ryan had told her about it. "Take the rest of this away," she told Cindy, gesturing toward the mail piled up on her desk. "Our Mr. McCloskey included a phone number with his letter. I think I'll give him a call."

She spoke to William McCloskey for almost an hour, and at the end of that conversation, she was convinced the man's claim was a legitimate one. "Harv Petersen's been in a meeting all afternoon. I haven't been able to reach him," she told Cindy as she was leaving that evening. "Call his secretary first thing in the morning. Tell him I'll be out of the office all day tomorrow."

"Where are you going?" Cindy asked.

"Chicago."

"I'll be happy to help you in any way that I can, Ms. Courtney, though I couldn't be sure from your advertisement exactly what kind of information you're looking for." William McCloskey, a tall, slim man in his early seventies with sparse gray hair and a weatherbeaten face, sat across from Meredith in the living room of his Chicago home. "Coffee?"

"Yes, please." Meredith dug into her bag for the pocket-size tape recorder she always carried. "You said in your letter that you were part of the crew on Elizabeth Weldon's last picture when it went on location, right?"

"That's right, ma'am." He offered her a cup.

She took the coffee, stirring it slowly. "I know how her son died," she said quietly. "How did Elizabeth die? Did she have a stroke? A heart attack?"

McCloskey scratched the back of his head thoughtfully. "I'm afraid that's the one question I don't have a definite answer for," he admitted. "You see, Ms. Courtney, Elizabeth Weldon was in a state of shock. The four days preceding her son's death had been a difficult ordeal for her. The boy had fallen into that old well—I don't know why the owners didn't have those shafts sealed so things like that wouldn't happen—and for four days we worked with men from the town, trying to get to him. On the fourth day, we finally had to give up. There was a doctor there—I don't remember his name, it was some hard-to-pronounce foreign name—and he said there was no way the boy could have survived down there that long." He paused. "When they told Elizabeth, it was like something just snapped in her head. She screamed, just once. It was like the howl of a wounded animal, high-pitched and eerie. Then she collapsed. She never spoke again after that, as far as anyone knows. Just sat there, staring into space with a blank look on her face, like a zombie. She didn't talk, didn't recognize anyone—not even her husband. She didn't seem to know what was going on around her.''

''Wasn't she hospitalized?'' Meredith asked.

McCloskey shook his head. ''The town where we were filming was little more than a village, with inadequate medical facilities. Her husband arranged to have her moved to a hospital a couple of hundred miles away, where she'd get proper care. None of us on the technical crew ever saw her again after that,'' he recalled. ''Though her role in the film had been completed, we still had some outdoor footage to film—with the extras, things like that. We stayed on another two weeks after she was taken away. Oh, we heard a lot of different stories about what happened to her after that—just like everybody else—but we never knew for sure. There was talk that she'd had a stroke, or that her heart had just stopped one day, but the most prevalent rumor was that she'd committed suicide. I always thought it was possible, under the circumstances.'' He looked at Meredith and shrugged.

Meredith was unable to hide her surprise. Suicide was the one possibility she hadn't considered. Nor had she given thought to the obvious, that Elizabeth had suffered a complete emotional collapse. ''Mr. McCloskey, are you sure she died? Couldn't she still be alive somewhere—in an institution, perhaps?''

He frowned. ''I suppose anything's possible. Everyone in the business just always assumed she died,'' he said quietly. ''You see, Ms. Courtney, when Tom Ryan returned to the States, he came alone. It just looked like maybe he'd buried her over there. It was fitting, somehow. She wanted to be near her son in life, so maybe he wanted her to be near him in death, too.''

Meredith nodded slowly. ''One thing has always been rather vague about this whole business, Mr. McCloskey,'' she said then. ''It's a well-known fact that the picture was being filmed in Greece, but exactly where in Greece?''

McCloskey answered without hesitation. ''In a little village called Ioannina.''

TWENTY-TWO

𐂷𐂷𐂷𐂷𐂷𐂷𐂷𐂷𐂷

Meredith sat in the middle of the bed, her legs crossed in a lotus position, her eyes closed, her head hanging over in exhaustion as Alexander, kneeling behind her, gently massaged the knotted muscles in her neck and shoulders. "I take it your trip to Chicago turned out to be another dead end," he said, pushing the thin straps of her dark blue teddy off her shoulders as he continued to knead the soft skin.

"Not exactly," Meredith began, relaxing under his gentle manipulations. "McCloskey didn't know how or where Elizabeth died—or even if she really did die—but he did tell me something I didn't know before."

"Such as?" Alexander asked. She had already told him the whole story as she knew it, and he was convinced there were many dead ends.

"They were filming in Greece at the time of the accident," Meredith answered. "David Ryan died in a place called Ioannina. Ever heard of it?"

"Of course. It's a town on the mainland, about nine hours by car from Athens," Alexander recalled. "We—the corporation, that is—own property there. My father bought it not long after the war ended in Europe, when Ioannina was still just a tiny village. Father had a dream of turning the town into a resort community one day. He bought the land while it was cheap, and planned to build a large hotel there. Unfortunately, the project never got off the ground. His people were never able to complete the well needed to furnish water for the proposed hotel site. They tried drilling in two or three different spots, but the problem was always the same—they kept hitting the underground caves."

"Caves?" Meredith asked.

"They're quite common in that region," he explained, continuing to massage her shoulders. "Father finally decided to abandon the project. He had more urgent matters to consider at that time—my brother's health was deteriorating and Mother was pregnant again. He was needed at home, so he left Ioannina after ordering that all of the old wells be sealed over so that the village children would not fall into them."

Meredith thought of her conversation with McCloskey: *I don't know why the owners didn't have those shafts sealed so things like that wouldn't happen.* "Is it possible that he could have leased the land for other purposes?" she asked, twisting around to face him. "Is it possible that the shafts were not sealed, that something like this could have happened on his land?"

"I suppose so. I have no idea," Alexander replied. "You are thinking that perhaps my father could have been at fault for what happened to this woman's child?"

"Not exactly, but if those old wells were not sealed as he ordered—" She looked up at him. "David Ryan died in Ioannina in July 1953. He fell into a two-hundred-foot shaft—an unfinished artesian well. After four days, they gave up hope of getting him out alive. He died there. Think about it—your father had at least two unfinished wells on his property. The property was in Ioannina. David Ryan died in a well in Ioannina. You said yourself it was only a small village. What are the chances of two such sites existing there at the same time?"

"But Father ordered those wells sealed," he insisted.

"But *were* they sealed? Do you know that for a fact?" she asked.

"I have no idea," he answered honestly. "I didn't even know about Ioannina until after Father died, three years ago.

It was the one corporation project he never discussed with me, I suppose because it was such a devastating failure.''

"How did you find out?" Meredith was more than a little curious.

"Frederick Kazomides," Alexander answered. "He is now senior vice-president in charge of our Greek offices. He was with the corporation at that time and gave me all of the facts." He paused thoughtfully. "I always just assumed that Father never talked about it because it all took place during such a painful episode in his life: the war had just ended, Damian was dying, Mother almost suffered another miscarriage—"

"Is there any way we can find out if that picture was filmed near there?" Meredith asked. "If it was, maybe I have a way of cracking this conspiracy of silence after all."

"Possibly—if any records were kept," he told her. "This is very important to you, isn't it."

"Of course."

"I'm not talking about as a segment for your show," he said, his fingers lingering for a moment on her bare back. "I think you have become personally involved with this story. Am I right?"

She hesitated, then nodded. "It's frustrating—like a puzzle with half the pieces missing," she admitted.

"It goes much deeper than that," he insisted gently. "I think you have come to care about these people you have never met—the woman and her child—and the man you knew only briefly. You care about what happened to them—and why."

She nodded. "Yes . . . I do care," she said finally. "I think I knew Tom as well as he would allow anyone to know him. I liked him—in spite of himself." She paused. "Sure, I'd like to be the one to break this story. But aside from the obvious reasons, I'd like to see it—and them—finally put to rest."

He bent his head, kissing her shoulder lovingly. "I'm sure that if anyone can make that happen, you can," he said in a low voice.

She reached up and stroked his hair. "You know, I can't begin to imagine what it must be like to lose a child, especially in such a horrible accident,'' she said slowly.

He stopped kissing her and looked up.

''Alexander, I *do* want a baby. Eventually,'' she told him. ''I want several children—our children!''

''I was beginning to wonder,'' he said as he folded his arms around her and started kissing her again. ''I was beginning to wonder what I was going to have to do to get a son out of you.''

''I would love to give you a son,'' she whispered. ''A son of your own. I'd love to have a little boy with your dark hair, your black eyes . . .''

''Or a little girl, blond and blue-eyed like you,'' he suggested.

''I know how much you want a son . . .''

''Maybe we should start working on it right now,'' he said promptly as he pulled her down on the bed and removed her teddy.

She smiled, her heart skipping a beat. ''Right now?'' she asked.

''There's no time like the present.''

Meredith was in her office early the next morning and went over all of her research notes, listening to the tapes of her conversations with Tom Ryan and with William McCloskey, poring over the clippings, photographs, and journal entries. She leafed through Elizabeth's scrapbooks. Was there something she had missed? she wondered. She threw her pen down on the desk and rubbed her temples in an attempt to ease the throbbing in her head. This was frustrating. All the time she had spent pursuing this story five years ago and again now, and still she felt as though she were beating her head against a stone wall. It was as if everyone involved were sworn to secrecy, as if someone were trying to hide something.

But what?

Rome.

''Signore Manetti has secured several large loans over the past six months,'' the banker explained in broken English. ''He is, as I have told you before, pouring his capital into that new sports car of his. Unfortunately, he is more deeply in debt every day. The man's business is failing, but he seems either unable or unwilling to accept it.''

The man sitting across the desk from him smiled thought-fully. It is time to spring the trap, he thought. It had taken months, but it was worth the wait. He finally had Carlo Manetti—and Alexander Kirakis—exactly where he wanted them. He was not really interested in destroying Manetti, but the Italian had proven to be the perfect pawn. Through Manetti, he would be able to discredit Alexander Kirakis, tarnish that golden image he'd created for himself. Through Manetti, he would be able to put his plan in action to bring about the fall of the Kirakis empire. ''I want you to call in all of Manetti's notes,'' he said aloud. ''Immediately.''

The banker looked confused. ''But, signore—there is no way that he can pay—'' he sputtered.

''I did not ask you if he could afford to pay,'' the man snapped irritably. ''I only directed you to call in his notes. Were my instructions not clear to you?''

''Uh . . . of course, signore,'' the Italian answered, still somewhat confused. ''You were most explicit.'' The banker had the uncomfortable feeling that it was not the money this man was interested in, but a personal vendetta against Carlo Manetti.

''Then I trust there will be no further delays,'' he said icily.

''Oh, no, signore, certainly not!''

He smiled. ''Excellent. You will let me know, then, when it is done.'' He rose from his chair and walked out of the banker's office without a backward glance, leaving the troubled Italian staring after him.

Carlo Manetti did not know what had hit him. Everything had happened so fast that he did not realize what was going on within his own company until it was too late. My God, he thought as he left his office. I am ruined! It had taken him most of his adult life to build Manetti Motors and now it had all come crashing down around him. It seemed to have happened overnight, but Manetti was still coherent enough to realize that it had taken months of careful planning to do this. Careful planning by the one man who had never stopped trying to bring him down.

There was not the slightest doubt in Manetti's mind who had been behind this diabolical plot to destroy him. But how had Alexander Kirakis done it? Who had he blackmailed or paid off? How much had it cost him to gain his final revenge against Manetti? Manetti had always known that Alexander wanted his company, but he had never known how far the man would be willing to go to get it. Only now did Carlo Manetti realize how dangerous a rival Kirakis could be, what a threat he had been to his company.

It is ironic, Manetti thought as he paused to look up at the magnificent tower of glass and steel that had been the realization of his lifelong dream, a testament to his dedication and determination. There was a time I thought of him as an honorable man, in spite of the rivalry between us. Leaving now, he was filled with a deep, ineffable sadness, as if he were being forced to abandon a beloved brother who needed him desperately. He found himself wondering where he was going to go, what he was going to do. He could not go home; that was out of the question. Donatella would be there, and he was not ready to face his daughter. Not yet. Perhaps not ever. How could he go home and tell her that they were ruined, that Alexander Kirakis had finally won? Or did she already know? Could she have heard the news on television? Could he admit, even to his beloved daughter who knew him so well, that he had finally been beaten? No. Not yet. He found the closest bar and proceeded to get quietly drunk.

It was almost dawn when he finally returned to the villa at Porto Ercole. Donatella was waiting up for him. "Papa!" she cried with relief when she saw him come through the door. "I have been so worried about you! I—" She stopped short, now close enough to smell the liquor on his breath. "Papa—you are drunk!"

"I have been drinking, yes," he mumbled as he hung his coat on the ornate iron railing of the winding staircase. It slid off and fell to the floor. He didn't notice, or if he did, he didn't care enough to pick it up. "It numbs the pain."

"Pain? Papa, I do not understand . . ." She took the newspaper he handed her. The headlines said it all in a few words: Manetti had gone into receivership. *"Dio mio!"* Donatella exclaimed. "How—"

"Our old friend Alexander Kirakis," Manetti said in slurred words as he stumbled up the stairs.

Donatella stared after him, numb with shock. He will pay for this, she thought bitterly. Alexander Kirakis will pay for what he has done to my father.

Manetti slept most of the next day. When he finally awakened, his daughter came to his room with a tray of food and insisted that he eat. "It is not good to starve yourself, Papa," she told him as she poured the espresso. "Drink this—it will clear your head."

He sat up. His head was throbbing. "I am not at all sure I would like to have my head cleared just yet," he confessed as he sipped the espresso. "I drank last night because I wished to forget."

"And did it work?" she wanted to know.

He shrugged. "For a while, anyway."

"Was it worth the trouble?"

Manetti shook his head. "It was only good for the night, hardly worth the effort *or* the cost." He drank slowly. The espresso was very hot. "And it gave me this terrible headache."

"Do not let him do this to you, Papa," she said finally, choosing her words carefully as she sat on the bed, making sure he ate. "You have always been a fighter, a survivor. You must fight back."

"Ah, Donatella, *figlia mia,* you are still so very idealistic. Perhaps I have sheltered you too much in the past," he said with a sad smile. "I *have* been fighting back. For months now, I have fought with everything I have. Fought to save the company. But it is over. I have lost. There is no longer a reason to keep fighting."

"Impossible!" she cried out angrily.

"Accept it," he said wearily. "It is done."

"No, Papa," she said stubbornly. "It is not over. Not yet."

* * *

Donatella Manetti, concerned for her father's safety, saw to it that he was never left alone for more than a few minutes at a time. She had never seen him like this before, so withdrawn, so hopeless. If she had been concerned about the possibility that her father might be contemplating suicide before, it terrified her now. She tried to be with him as much as possible, but when she was not, she made certain that their maid, Margherita, the only remaining servant at the villa, was there. He seldom left the house these days, so it had been a simple matter to keep an eye on him.

"I feel like the Prisoner of Zenda," he grumbled when Donatella insisted upon going along the few times he did venture out of Porto Ercole. "I am too old to have a nursemaid."

Donatella did not know what to say to him. She adored her father and hated having to treat him like a troublesome child, but she saw no other alternative.

"I promise you, Papa, things will get better soon," she told him, gently insisting that she had to go with him. Not a day passed that she did not curse Alexander for what he had done. Not a day passed that she did not renew her vow of vengeance against him.

Carlo Manetti was overcome by unbearable feelings of depression and hopelessness. After years and years of being a winner, he found himself the worst kind of loser, a man who had been completely and totally defeated. He was finished. Defeat, unfortunately, was the one thing in his life Carlo Manetti could never accept. He saw only one alternative open to him.

He knew what had to be done.

"Papa, you eat barely enough to keep a small bird alive," Donatella observed as she watched him push the food around on his plate with his fork. "You must try to eat. You will make yourself ill if you do not."

"What difference does it make now?" he asked blankly.

"It makes a great deal of difference," she insisted stubbornly. "You must not give up, Papa. You must be strong and keep fighting if you are ever to defeat Alexander Kirakis."

"It is not possible, *figlia mia*," he said wearily. "Give up,

Donatella. Do not try to beat this man at his own game. You will only get hurt.''

"And what will you do, Papa? Do you have it in mind to starve yourself?'' she demanded.

"I have nothing at all in mind at this point, Donatella, nothing at all,'' he said tonelessly. He rose from his chair. "I think I would like to be alone for a while—if my keepers have no objections, that is.'' He looked at his daughter and Margherita accusingly.

Donatella stared after him as he walked out of the room. Margherita finally broke the silence. "I think maybe your papa needs a doctor, signorina,'' she said softly.

Donatella turned to her. "I think I agree with you,'' she murmured.

The revolver lay on the desk. Manetti stared at it thoughtfully for a long time before picking it up. This was not going to be as easy as he had expected. He was not as brave as he thought. Dying by one's own hand was no simple matter.

He examined the gun thoroughly, as a surgeon would examine one of the instruments he might use to save a life. Only the instrument Manetti now held in his hand was an instrument of death. Once, he had kept a gun in the house only for protection, but there was no longer anything to protect. He had been robbed, legally robbed, and there was nothing he could have done to prevent it. Alexander Kirakis was far too clever for him. He had not even seen it coming.

He held the gun with trembling hands. What did the Japanese call it? Saving face. He, Carlo Manetti, would leave this world exactly as he had come into it—a peasant. But he would retain the dignity of his ancestors. His pride would be intact, as it should be. He told himself that he was sparing Donatella, and in his troubled mind, he believed it to be true.

Manetti's last thoughts were for his daughter as he pressed the barrel of the gun to his right temple and squeezed the trigger.

TWENTY-THREE

Rome.

The limousine slowed to a stop in front of the Kirakis Corporation's office complex, and the moment Alexander emerged, he was besieged by reporters and photographers, all of them eager to prove that a link existed between himself and Manetti's suicide.

"Mr. Kirakis, could you tell us . . ."

"Signore, does this have anything to do with your bid to take over the Manetti assembly plants . . ."

"Herr Kirakis, now that Carlo Manetti is dead, will you . . ."

"Monsieur Kirakis, will Manetti's death have any bearing on your bid to . . ."

"Look this way, sir . . ."

"Could we have a statement . . ."

"Just one more picture, señor . . ."

George Prescott, following closely behind Alexander, waved them off. "No comment," he told them firmly. "No comment."

They entered the building as the security men moved in to hold off the crowd. They took the express elevator to Alexander's offices on the eighteenth floor, where a special meeting had been called with the heads of his Italian operations and government officials eager to wash their hands of Manetti's financially troubled corporation. He turned to George. "How much time do we have?" he asked quietly.

"We are early," George said, glancing at his watch. "They will not be here for at least an hour."

Alexander frowned. "I will be in my office. Call me when they arrive."

"Sure." George watched with concern as Alexander disappeared into his office and closed the door. He had been in an odd mood since receiving word of Manetti's suicide. The world at large was blaming him for the death of the Italian auto magnate, even though Alexander had had nothing at all to do with the financial state of the ailing company. George believed that Alexander was genuinely sorry about Manetti's death, and decided it would be best to leave him alone. He knew that communication with him at this moment would be damned near impossible.

Donatella Manetti stood in front of the mirror, adjusting the delicate lace veil on her wide-brimmed black hat. She felt numb, as though a part of her had died with her father. Now, as she studied her reflection in the mirror, it seemed to be the face of a stranger looking back at her. The face of an old woman, she thought. Eyes that had seen too much violence. An expressionless mouth that had forgotten the movement of laughter, the glow of a smile; a face now etched with the lines of sorrow. Certainly not the face of a woman in her early twenties.

A line from the Bible came to mind and she repeated it now, over and over, like a litany: "An eye for an eye . . . an eye for an eye . . ." But will that ever be enough? she asked herself. No, her embittered soul screamed out at her. Alexander will pay for this, Papa, she vowed.

The press turned the funeral of Carlo Manetti into a media circus. They surrounded Donatella like hungry vultures as she clung to her constant companion, Luca Agretti, like a lost, frightened child. They swarmed about her, hoping to cash in on her grief, taking pictures, blinding her with their flashbulbs. She tried to cover her eyes, but it was no use.

Finally, she turned on them in anger, cursing them and demanding that they leave immediately.

"You think only of the lire, eh?" she shouted angrily, rubbing her fingers together in an exaggerated gesture. "You have no compassion, no consideration for my loss. My father is dead, and it is the *figlio di putana*, Alexander Kirakis, who is to blame for this! Go hound him! If all you can think about is how many papers you will sell with this story, then go to the man who killed my father as certainly as if he had held the gun to Papa's head and pulled the trigger!"

The photos that appeared in newspapers all over the world showed Donatella Manetti, pale and drawn as she stood over her father's open grave, casting a handful of dirt onto the coffin.

Journalists in every part of the world speculated as to what the beautiful young heiress would do now that her father was dead and his ailing company was about to be taken over by the Kirakis Corporation of the United States. She had survived the ordeal a wealthy woman, since her father had made investments for her that were not tied up with his company. None of the reporters who watched her closely following her father's death, nor even the photographers who had felt the full force of her fury that morning at the cemetery, could possibly have imagined what was going through her mind as the young Roman Catholic priest read the lengthy graveside service in the traditional Latin.

Southampton.

Alexander had been right, Meredith thought as she watched him execute yet another of his long, cracking hits out on the polo field. One had to be obsessed to become a top player. Meredith smiled to herself. His mind was cool and his blood hot—two prerequisites for polo he had undoubtedly been born with. In the two years she and Alexander had been together, she had learned a great deal about the game that was one of his great passions. She'd lost track of how many times she'd become a "polo widow" as Alexander became absorbed in watching videotapes of past matches, observing his opponents in action, scrutinizing their horses and their individual playing styles, gauging their strengths and weaknesses, mentally planning his strategy. He never went into a match without first having developed a game plan for his entire team *and* six individual game plans for each opposing horse and player. Though he knew that he had a topflight, well-mounted team, he had never made the mistake of becoming overly confident. Alexander played to win and expected no less from his teammates.

How many matches had he won in the past two years? Meredith asked herself now. There had been the Cartier International Open in March, and before that, the Chilean Open in Santiago in December, the Argentine Open, the World Series of polo, at Palermo Park, in November, the Americas Cup at the Greenwich Polo Club in September, and her favorite of the events, the Championnat Mondial Cup in August at Deauville in France. Since they had been married, Alexander took more time away from the office, relaxed more, spent more time on the polo circuit. This year he planned to include Palm Beach—and the Piaget World Cup—on his itinerary. He played outside the country only when Meredith was able to accompany him, either on a vacation or when she could tape an interview or footage of one of her subjects. This was the second anniversary of that match that had brought them back together—after her jealousy and mistrust had nearly driven them apart for good. Meredith smiled. She'd believed then that she could not possibly love him more than she had that night they made love for the first time, but she had been wrong. It seemed to her now that their love grew stronger with each passing day.

The match came to an end with a round of enthusiastic applause from the stands. As the horses crossed the field at a canter, Meredith got to her feet and left the table from which she had viewed the match, picking her way through the crowd to join her husband as he dismounted, trophy in hand. As she gave him a congratulatory kiss, she was only dimly aware of the photographers snapping their picture in their moment of victory.

"They should have enough pictures now to give them something to talk about besides your questionable business dealings—for a while, at least," Meredith said with a laugh as they drove to the estate after the match.

Alexander paused thoughtfully. "Would it bother you if I had been behind Manetti's financial problems?" he asked finally.

She looked at him, genuinely surprised. "I knew all about the treachery and the double-dealing involved in big business long before I met you," she told him. "Your business is just that—your business. It has nothing to do with us, with what we feel for each other. You're my husband. I love you and I'll stand by you, no matter what."

He smiled as he reached out to touch her hand. Manetti's suicide had brought back memories of another time, of an episode in his life he had not thought about in a very long time, one he would never be able to forget. Meredith could have dealt with his involvement in Manetti's dilemma, had he been behind it. He did not doubt that for a moment, not now. She was strong and she was sensible, and above all, she was a pragmatist. She knew the score, that business was business and had nothing to do with their marriage.

But how would she feel if she knew about Marianne Hauptmann?

"I can't help thinking that there's more to this than meets the eye, more than a simple matter of Tom Ryan not wanting to talk about what happened to his wife in Ioannina," Meredith told Alexander as they walked together on the beach near their home. "It's as if there's some sort of conspiracy of silence surrounding the accident. There are maybe a handful of people who were there and know the truth, and they aren't talking. I get the feeling they were either paid to keep quiet—or they were threatened."

Alexander smiled, putting one arm around her. "If they were paid to keep quiet and you are able to locate them, then you simply offer them a higher price to talk," he reasoned. "But if they were threatened, as you say, then it's a different matter entirely. It's not easy to buy someone who has something more to lose than money."

She looked at him, the soft evening breeze ruffling his hair. "Are you speaking from firsthand experience?" she asked.

"I've always believed that everyone has a price," he

admitted, staring up at the star-filled sky. "But the price cannot always be translated into dollars and cents."

"But why would anyone pay them off to keep them quiet—*or* threaten them, for that matter?" Meredith was puzzled. "What could possibly be so important that anyone would go that far?"

"Maybe this fellow Ryan just wanted to protect his wife's memory, her image," Alexander suggested.

Meredith shook her head. "No," she said with certainty. "I knew Tom Ryan. I know that he ignored all the gossip and speculation surrounding the accident, so he couldn't have cared much about what anyone thought. He just didn't want to talk about it himself."

"What other reason could anyone possibly have for wanting to put a lid on it?" Alexander asked. "Why would anyone other than Ryan care who knew what might or might not have happened in Ioannina?"

"I don't know," Meredith said, shaking her head. "On the surface, it just looks like Tom wanted to keep it all hush-hush. But my reporter's instincts tell me there's more to it than that, much more. I have the feeling that it's not just the accident and the deaths of David and Elizabeth that are being covered up, but something bigger, much bigger. Someone—and not necessarily Tom Ryan—has used a great deal of muscle, a great deal of money, or both to conceal the truth."

"You make it all sound so cloak-and-dagger," Alexander said.

"I think it might be." Meredith's face was grim. "I think I may have stumbled onto something much more serious, much more complicated, than anyone previously imagined."

Alexander didn't respond. If only he had the answers to his own questions about Ioannina, about his father's involvement, if any, in the tragedy that took place there.

Perhaps then he could help Meredith find what she was looking for.

"Congratulations," George said as he entered Alexander's office on Monday morning and seated himself. "I saw clips of the match on the news Sunday night."

Alexander smiled. "It was not such an easy victory this time," he admitted.

"Looked to me like the opposition didn't stand a chance," George said easily. He took a cigarette from his gold case and lit it.

"The sportscasters were very selective in what they chose to air," Alexander responded. "They showed only the highlights of the match." He glanced over some notes he'd made on a yellow legal pad. "How does your schedule look for the next week or so?"

"Open, except for a few staff meetings."

"Reschedule them," Alexander told him. "I need someone to go to California to meet with Dr. Marchwood and see how things are progressing at the nuclear research facility. They've been having some problems lately, mostly financial. I should go myself, but I am unable to get away now, so you, my friend, are the logical choice."

"No problem," George assured him. "I'll have my secretary take care of the rescheduling."

"How soon can you leave?"

"Tomorrow soon enough?"

"Excellent."

After George was gone, Alexander picked up the copy of the Italian newspaper that had been sent to him by one of his people in Rome. On page three was a photograph of Carlo Manetti and his daughter in happier times. In the accompanying article, Donatella Manetti once again condemned Alexander and the Kirakis Corporation for her father's suicide, claiming that Alexander had been behind the arranging of the large loans he'd received, setting Manetti up for "a big fall." She was right about one thing: someone had set Manetti up. Someone had arranged for Manetti to be able to borrow large sums of money, then called in the notes when he was unable to pay. Alexander was convinced that someone had gone to a great deal of trouble to make it appear to Manetti and to everyone else that the Kirakis Corporation had been behind it. Carlo Manetti had been nothing more than a pawn for someone who wanted to get at Alexander Kirakis.

Who? he wondered.

Kitzbühel, Austria.

A man sat alone on the terrace of the Tennerhof Hotel reading the morning papers as he finished breakfast. On page three was a photograph of Carlo Manetti and a follow-up on his suicide. A smile came to the man's lips as he read the short piece. He could have felt sympathy for Manetti's bereaved daughter had the timing not been so perfect, had Manetti not suited his plans so perfectly. It appeared to the public at large that Alexander Kirakis's quest for power had become destructive.

He turned to an article in the business section that detailed the Kirakis Corporation's plans to go into the production of nuclear armaments in an attempt to overcome financial difficulties the research facility was now experiencing. The man frowned. He could not allow that to happen. Armaments meant big money. Big money meant Kirakis could easily survive setbacks in other areas of its business.

They had to be stopped.

TWENTY-FOUR

‎❧❧❧❧❧❧❧❧❧❧❧

"I can't help thinking I'm missing something, that I'm overlooking the obvious." Meredith sat up in bed, reviewing her research notes on Elizabeth Weldon-Ryan. According to the clock on the nightstand, it was well past midnight, but she was not the least bit tired. Over the past few weeks, her research had been plagued by disappointment and doubt, but now she was tackling it again with renewed determination. "If only I knew where they took her when Tom had her moved."

Alexander, lying in bed beside her, pulled himself up on one arm. "You believe she may still be alive, don't you," he said, genuinely interested.

Meredith nodded slowly. "I think it's possible, yes," she confessed. "McCloskey said that when they told her about her son, when she realized there was no longer any hope, she collapsed, but he said it wasn't a stroke or a heart attack. It was a mental breakdown. An emotional collapse. The last time anyone from the film company saw her, she was alive."

"She could have died later," Alexander offered. "Strokes can come on quite suddenly, I am told."

"But she could still be alive," Meredith said, grasping at straws.

"But that was more than thirty years ago," he said, running his fingers through his hair. "Even if she were alive then, she could be dead by now."

"It was, but if she is alive, she would be in her sixties now," Meredith said as she put her notebook aside. "She could still be alive . . . somewhere."

"And what will you do to find her?" Alexander asked. "Send out a search party? Check out every mental hospital in Europe? You said yourself that Ryan came back from Europe alone. If his wife were still alive, then he had to have left her over there somewhere. It's a large continent, my love, and a large task for one woman to take on alone."

"Not necessarily," Meredith disagreed. "Tom Ryan was an extremely wealthy man. If he left his wife in an institution, it would be a good one. One of the best. That narrows the field considerably."

"But if he wanted to protect her, if he wanted to shield her from the press, he would be very careful where he took her," Alexander reasoned, pulling himself into an upright position. "The better hospitals would be the first place anyone would look."

"Not if they thought she was dead," Meredith pointed out.

"Well, if your theory is correct, she would probably have been taken to one of the private clinics in Switzerland," he said. "I'm not sure how much they'll tell you if you do contact them, though. They are normally very tight-lipped about their patient roster. And you must also consider the possibility that she may not be in a hospital at all. For someone with a great deal of money, it would be a simple matter to buy a villa and install here there with a trained medical staff to look after her."

Meredith shook her head. "I don't think Tom would have done that. I think he would have wanted to be sure she was getting the very best care possible—in safe surroundings. I knew him, darling. The man was obsessed with guarding his secret at any cost. He wouldn't have taken any unnecessary chances. Not where she was concerned."

Alexander fell silent for a few seconds. "It would seem that Ioannina is a cursed land," he said finally.

She looked at him. "What do you mean?"

He hesitated at first. "When I was a child, very close to the same age as the Ryan child, my parents took me to Ioannina. My father was there on business of some kind. It was the first and only time I have ever been there," he told her. "There was an accident. I was critically injured and nearly died."

"What happened?" Meredith asked, her surprise jerking her around to face Alexander.

Alexander frowned. "That's just it—I don't know," he answered. "I was very young. I have no memory of the incident, and my parents never spoke of it—at least not to me."

"How did you find out about it, then?"

"I overheard my mother talking to Helena one day. She said I was never to be told of it, that the experience had been so traumatic that the doctors at Kiffisia Hospital in Athens told them I had intentionally, subconsciously blocked it from my memory, which I suppose is true, since to this day I have no memory of it all," he said. "When I was a child, even just before I left Greece to attend Harvard, I had dreams —terrifying nightmares. I always thought they were related to the accident, though they made absolutely no sense to me at all—just images of people from another era, and the terrible feeling of being buried alive. I used to be extremely uncomfortable in places like elevators, closed-in places, but I have learned to deal with it in recent years."

Meredith touched his arm. "Why didn't you ever tell me about this before?" she asked gently.

He frowned. "I have never discussed it with anyone before," he said gravely. "It has never been easy for me to talk about such things. I don't like dark areas in my brain, unanswered questions. It is not easy to admit that I have lost five years of my life. I have no memory at all of what happened to me in Ioannina—or anything of my life before that."

"Lots of people can't remember that far back," Meredith reminded him. "You were so young—"

"Most people can recall something—a person, a place, a favorite toy," Alexander said. "I remember nothing at all. It's not normal."

"You said you overheard your mother talking to Helena about it," Meredith said then. "Does *she* know?"

Alexander shook his head. "She became my governess when I was seven, more than two years later. She was questioning my mother about it when I overheard them," he said. "Mother said I was not to know, and that if Helena wanted to keep working for them, she should never mention it in front of my father."

"Why not?" Meredith asked.

Alexander shook his head. "I suppose coming that close to losing another child was also traumatic for him," he said. "They had already lost Damian, and Mother had suffered those miscarriages. I was the only child they were ever going to have. Mother could not risk another pregnancy. So, for my father, I represented not only his last chance at fatherhood, but the last hope for the future of the Kirakis empire, as well."

"I can understand how that knowledge could make a child even more precious to his parents," Meredith said sympathetically.

"I suppose. It is sad, when a couple wants children as much as they did, and have to accept that they cannot have any more . . . after all they went through." His hand lingered on her flat stomach. "I, for one, would like a large family."

"You just want to see me get fat," she said, keeping her voice playful.

"Not fat, ripe." He kissed her gently. "I think you would look even more beautiful. I know you would be more beautiful to me." His lips were on her neck as he lifted her nightgown.

Meredith's arms encircled his neck as they fell back against the pillows. She was thinking of what Casey had once said: *The ultimate expression of a woman's love is having her lover's baby.* Meredith wanted so much to give Alexander a child. "I wish you didn't have to go to Turkey," she whispered. "I wish you weren't leaving."

"I'll be back as soon as I possibly can," he promised as he tossed her nightgown aside and covered her body with his own. "As soon as I possibly can . . ."

Istanbul.

"There is much unrest in Southeast Asia, Alexander," Kafir said grimly. "A political revolution is inevitable, I fear."

Each of Kafir's words struck Alexander like hammer blows. He was totally numb. "Exactly what impact will this have upon our drilling operations in the Java Sea?" he asked. He spoke quietly, still not facing the older man as he stood at the window, staring blankly at the minarets on the horizon.

Kafir frowned. "The tracts now owned by the corporation would become nationalized. There would be no question of it."

Alexander turned to look at him for the first time. "So we would lose them," he said slowly. "What would you suggest I do?"

Kafir shrugged. "It is your decision to make, but you would be wise to sell now, to save yourself while there is still time," he advised.

"Save myself." Alexander frowned. He had established those tracts himself, one of his first ventures as chairman of Kirakis. He felt a strong attachment to them because of it.

"I will consider it," he said finally.

Kafir's jaw tightened nervously. "Do not wait too long," he warned.

"I will get back to you," Alexander promised. "You have a contact there, don't you? Someone reliable?"

The Turk nodded. "A man in Djakarta, an Englishman. I trust him implicitly."

"You've checked him out?"

"Of course," Kafir answered without hesitation. "We take no unnecessary chances. A lesson your papa taught me many years ago, Alexander."

Alexander managed a slight smile. "I should not be surprised," he said. "My father was always impressed with your thoroughness."

"Your father was a fine man, Alexander."

"Yes. Yes, he was." Alexander sat on the corner of Kafir's desk. "I want you to maintain contact with your man in Djakarta. You, in turn, will maintain that same close contact with me. Any new developments will be reported to me immediately—regardless of the time of day or night or where I might happen to be at the time. Understood?''

''Perfectly,'' Kafir replied solemnly.

''Excellent. We shall be in touch, then.'' He shook Kafir's hand. ''Do not disappoint me.'' His tone was casual, but the black eyes held a warning that caught Muhammed Kafir off guard.

''I would never do that,'' he assured Alexander.

As Alexander turned away from him, he caught a glimpse of Kafir's troubled face in the glass doors, and what he saw disturbed him.

New York City.

The antique clock in Alexander's study chimed, signaling the hour of two A.M. Meredith sat at his desk, bleary-eyed from the long hours she'd spent reading and rereading newspaper clippings, journals, and her own research notes, refusing to give up even though it was late and she was very tired. She had been putting in long hours at night ever since Alexander left for Istanbul, once again going over all the Ryan material.

After almost an hour of sorting through the clippings and photographs, she finally decided to call it a night. She was exhausted and this was getting her nowhere. She stifled a yawn as she got to her feet and began piling the materials back into the cardboard box in which she had brought them home from the Broadcast Center. As she picked up a stack of old, yellowed newspaper clippings, something caught her eye and she paused. One of the black-and-white studio photographs of Elizabeth lay on the corner of the desk, next to a silver-framed photograph of Alexander and Meredith, taken on their honeymoon, and Meredith noticed something about the two photographs that disturbed her. Picking them up slowly, she held them so that the faces of Elizabeth and Alexander were side by side, and studied them carefully. Two people, each from different worlds, different times, and different countries, yet the physical resemblance was such that it was impossible to ignore. It was striking: both had the same sharp, symmetrical features, the same coloring, the same dark, luxuriant hair. But it was the eyes, those incredible black eyes, that caught her attention. They both had the dark, flashing eyes of a gypsy. They looked so much alike that . . . no, it wasn't possible, she told herself. Alexander was the son of Constantine and Melina Kirakis. Elizabeth's son was dead. Yet words kept echoing through her mind: *I was critically injured and nearly died. . . . My parents never spoke of it. . . . So, for my father, I represented not only his last chance at fatherhood, but the last hope for the future of the Kirakis empire as well. . . . They couldn't get to him . . . after four days, they gave up hope. . . . When they told her, she screamed, just once—it was the eerie, high-pitched howl of a wounded animal. . . . The last time I saw her, she was alive.*

Meredith looked up at the painting of Elizabeth and her son. A mother and child with the same dark coloring, the same features, the same black eyes, glowing like polished onyx. In her mind she saw the paintings of Constantine and Melina, hanging in the entrance foyer at the villa in Greece, heard herself telling Alexander, half-jokingly: "You must be a throwback—you don't look like either of them."

No, she told herself. It's simply not possible.

The next morning, she placed a call to William McCloskey in Chicago. "There's one thing I forgot to ask you," she told him. "You were there when David Ryan died. Do you by any chance know where he was buried?"

"He wasn't," McCloskey answered without hesitation.

"I don't understand."

"As I told you, Ms. Courtney, the boy died in that old well because they couldn't get to him," he said. "They never did get to him, even after he was declared legally dead. The body was never recovered."

Berlin.

A man had been arrested by the Berlin Kriminal Polizei, the first in a series of arrests made following an extensive investigation into illicit financial schemes in Germany. Billions of dollars in assets had been concealed, laundered, mingled and remingled, transferred and retransferred through a complicated network of dummy corporations set up for just those purposes. Though the police had conducted their investigation over a period of several months, their first real lead had come from an anonymous phone call to the headquarters of the Berlin Kriminal Polizei at 2832 Keithstrasse. The Delikt am Mensch division, with its elaborate telephone system, was equipped with an automatic hold system that made it impossible for a caller to disconnect until the line was released electronically by the department's switchboard. This enabled the police to trace all incoming calls. Though they had been unable to learn the identity of their caller, they knew where the call had originated from.

The number was that of an office complex in Vienna.

Within the hour, news of the arrest had leaked to the newspapers. It had been rumored that the first of the men taken into custody was still vehemently protesting his innocence. He had been set up, framed, he repeatedly told police interrogators. He did not know by whom, but he knew it just as surely as he knew his own name.

The man was a senior vice-president of the Kirakis Corporation.

Paris.

The headquarters of Interpol, the clearinghouse for all information concerning international criminal activity, were located at 26 rue Armengaud in an imposing glass and steel structure that towered over the one- and two-story private residences surrounding it. In the basement computer room, Inspector Adrian Dessain was talking with the great machines that held in their massive data banks the most intimate secrets of even those most private citizens.

Adrian Dessain was a short, slightly overweight man in his late forties. When he walked, he shuffled along as if it took every ounce of his minimal energy just to make it across a room. When he spoke, it was in the same slow, unhurried manner. He was a scruffy, unkempt caricature of a man whose clothing always looked in dire need of pressing. But to those of his colleagues who had had the privilege of working closely with him, his appearance was a striking contrast to the infallible detective beneath. Dessain had a keen analytical mind and a most uncanny ability to ferret out even the most minute detail of inconsistency in a case, skillfully unraveling that one loose thread until an airtight case suddenly fell apart, revealing the truth in all its ugliness. "Unsolvable" cases suddenly became solvable when Adrian Dessain entered the picture. His scruffy appearance had been an advantage in many instances, because it had led many people, including his suspects, to believe that he was either stupid or lazy. Dessain was that rare, brilliant investigator whose mind was forever racing ahead, anticipating the next step in his procedure. Once he found that loose thread, he never failed.

Staring thoughtfully at the words and numbers on the screen, Dessain remembered an inquiry Interpol had received regarding the arrests made in Berlin three days earlier. The laundering scheme. Dessain shook his head. There was not the slightest doubt in his mind that this was just the tip of the iceberg. He was convinced that the men taken into custody were just a part, a very small part, of an international network involved in illicit financial schemes all over Europe. When Dessain had spoken with Chief Inspector Walter Mendler of the Berlin Kriminal Polizei, he had been intrigued by Mendler's account of the tip-off and subsequent arrests. He found it odd that the Berlin police had been able to track down the point of origin of that anonymous caller but had been unable to learn his identity. They had not bothered to investigate further, but Dessain was curious and decided to look into it. He made a few discreet calls and found that the offices from which that call had been made had been leased not to an individual, but to a corporation. A dummy corporation. Offices in Vienna that were never occupied. A holding company that did not appear to have any legitimate holdings. No one seemed to know exactly what kind of a business it was or who controlled it. It appeared to be privately held. No stockholders. And, apparently, no employees to speak of, either. Dessain had called the number Mendler gave him three times, and each time the call was taken by an answering service. He had not bothered to leave a message. The anonymous caller who had tipped off the Berlin police was either a part of that network of businessmen involved in the laundering operation, or he had some other reason for wanting to conceal his identity. It was the possibility of another reason that disturbed Dessain most. His highly developed instincts told him something was wrong, that this was an avenue definitely worth pursuing. Dessain was determined to find that proverbial loose thread and unravel it.

One of the men arrested in Berlin was Kurt Badrutt, a senior vice-president of the Kirakis Corporation. Dessain's fingers flew over the computer's keys as he asked questions about Badrutt and about his position within the upper echelons of the Kirakis Corporation. What he learned was most interesting.

Kurt Badrutt was one of the highest-paid executives in all of Europe. He owned a home in Wannsee, a beautiful Schinkel manor, and had recently acquired a villa on the Italian Riviera. He had been with Kirakis over twenty-two years, and there had never, in all that time, been a blemish on his business record. Until now. There was, of course, a first time for all things, but Dessain was curious. Why now? Why, after so many years of playing by the rules, would a man in Badrutt's position risk everything he'd worked all of his life to accomplish? It didn't make sense. He kept thinking about what Mendler had said, about how Badrutt had continued to protest his innocence, insisting he had been set up, framed. Was it possible? Dessain wondered. Could Badrutt have been telling the truth? And if so, why had he been set up? What reason could anyone have had for wanting to bring him down? If Badrutt were telling the truth, then someone had to be out to get him—or using him to get at someone else. The first thing that came to mind was that someone had been trying, indirectly, to damage the solid, conservative image of the behemoth that was the Kirakis Corporation. Dessain smelled big trouble. Playing a hunch —and his hunches were seldom wrong—he decided to look into the matter. First, he had to talk to Badrutt.

The next day, Dessain flew to Berlin.

TWENTY-FIVE

⌐⌐⌐⌐⌐⌐⌐⌐⌐⌐⌐

In a darkened screening room on an upper floor of One World Trade Center, a small group of executives from the Kirakis Corporation's public relations department nervously awaited the arrival of the chairman of the board. In the past, Alexander Kirakis had never attended any of the screenings of their public relations films or television spots, preferring to leave such matters in the most capable hands of George Prescott. Alexander had never taken the time to approve the advertising campaigns developed for the Kirakis Corporation or any of its subsidiaries. It was the one area of his vast international empire in which he had never taken an active role. But now there had been speculation that the problems the corporation had been facing recently had spurred his interest in what his PR people were doing to improve the corporation's clouded image.

To those who did not know, it might have appeared that all of the corporation's failures and setbacks had hit at once. The bad press Kirakis had received over the past year had certainly made it appear so. The headlines in the *Wall Street Journal*, *Fortune*, *Forbes*, and *Business Week* had all been negative. There had been stories about several incidents of drug tampering in which over-the-counter painkillers had been found to contain cyanide, the painkillers manufactured by a Kirakis-owned pharmaceutical company. Three people had died. There was the incident at the corporation's nuclear research facility, an unexplained explosion in one of the buildings housing the giant reactors. The only fortunate aspect of that incident was the fact that none of the reactors were in operation at the time. There had been the revolution in Indonesia and the threat of nationalization of the corporation's oil leases in the Java Sea. And there had been countless other mishaps the press had missed.

The low sound of the men's voices came to an abrupt halt as the door opened and a stream of brilliant light knifed through the darkness. Everyone in the room looked up to see the chairman of the board framed in the doorway. Alexander entered the screening room followed by George Prescott and Jeremy Roberts, Kirakis's director of public relations and advertising. Alexander nodded to the men in the room and took a seat. George Prescott and Jeremy Roberts seated themselves on either side of him, and Roberts motioned to one of his people to start the film. Almost immediately, the screen came to life. Alexander sat silent, motionless, as the voice-over and visual images combined to create a detailed illustration of the fifty-year history of the Kirakis Corporation and the world, emphasizing Kirakis's role in the Second World War, in the economic and technological advancements Kirakis had been involved in in recent years, as well as plans for the future of the corporate empire. Roberts was not looking at the screen, but at Alexander, searching the board chairman's face in the darkness for a hint, some clue as to what Kirakis might be thinking. But there was none. His face was expressionless, his black eyes fixed on the screen. He did not move and did not speak until the film ended and the lights came on.

"Well?" Roberts asked anxiously, unable to conceal his nervousness.

"Two dangling participles, three mixed metaphors, and a split infinitive," Alexander said irritably.

Roberts stared at him for a moment. "If you don't mind my saying so, Mr. Kirakis, I really don't think anyone's going to pay much attention to that sort of thing," he said feebly.

"They're not going to pay much attention to this piece of sanctimonious rubbish, either," Alexander said crossly as he got to his feet. "I expected to see a film dealing with the Kirakis Corporation's plans for the future—our new horizons—and what you've given me is a history lesson."

"But Mr. Kirakis—" Roberts began.

"I have seen the new layouts for our print ads and now this, and I must say that I am quite disappointed," Alexander said, his eyes glacial.

"Disappointed? But a great deal of work went into this!"

"Apparently it was not enough," Alexander responded, his displeasure evident in his voice and his manner. "This will not impress the public. It won't even interest them." He turned to George. "See what you can find for them from our past campaigns—a fairly recent television spot, some print material." He gestured toward the screen. "I don't want this aired—under any circumstances."

"It could take months to come up with a new campaign," Roberts pointed out.

"I don't care how long it takes!" Alexander snapped. "And when your people begin to work on that new campaign, it would be wise to have them bear in mind that I am not interested in telling the public what Kirakis is doing: I want to *show* them! I want to see Kirakis relief teams at work in underdeveloped countries. Show them our progress in solving the energy shortage. Show how housing shortages in various parts of the world are being remedied by our real estate and construction projects." He paused, his black eyes dark with anger. "Talk is cheap, gentlemen. I want action. The public wants action. Telling them what we have on the drawing boards will not be nearly as effective as showing them, letting them *see* us in action."

"But sir, we've put in a great deal of time and money on the film, the layouts—"

Alexander's smile was wintry. "It is most unwise of you, Roberts, to remind me of the waste of corporation capital and manpower," he said sharply. "I suggest you and your people get started on a new campaign immediately."

Roberts hesitated for a moment, then nodded. "Yes, sir," he said finally.

Jeremy Roberts and his staff watched in silence as Alexander and George left the screening room. Everyone present was aware of the reverses that had befallen the Kirakis Corporation in the past year, and they all knew that Alexander Kirakis was under a great deal of stress. They all acknowledged that the chairman of the board was a driven, ambitious man, a perfectionist who had always been difficult to work for, but no one present had ever seen him quite like this. When he left the screening room, he had looked as though he were ready to explode.

"I want to talk to you—in my office," Alexander said in a low voice as they walked to the elevators.

"When?"

"Right now," Alexander answered as they stepped into the empty car and the doors closed behind them. "I have worked out a solution to the situation in Southeast Asia."

George looked at him, unable to hide his surprise. He started to ask how that could be possible, then changed his mind. Anyone else might have resigned himself to being trapped, to having to decide whether to risk holding on to the tracts or selling out, but not Alexander. Alexander was the master escape artist of the business world. Somehow, he had always managed to have his cake and eat it too.

Alexander did not speak again until they reached his office. "Hold my calls, Stacey," he told his secretary as they entered the office and closed the doors. As he seated himself behind his desk, George noticed that he was smiling. "I've been thinking. Hammond Transcon, Barkley-Howard, Patterson Holdings Limited, and Lone Star Oil have all expressed an interest in buying a piece of the action—almost from the day we began drilling in those tracts." He paused. "I've decided to cut each of them in—for twenty-five percent."

"What?" George looked at him, not sure he'd heard correctly. "All four of them? Twenty-five percent apiece is the whole pie—"

"Not quite," Alexander said easily. "The deal I intend to offer will be identical for each of them. I'll cut them in for twenty-five percent—confidentially, of course. They won't be permitted to tell anyone of the arrangement. But they will each have to give me a royalty of fifteen percent of their profits.''

"So none of them will know the others are involved," George said slowly.

"Precisely."

"And you get back your original investment, plus a hefty royalty if the tracts prove to be as good as you think they are—*and* if they are not nationalized," George said, lighting a cigarette.

Alexander nodded.

George thought about it for a moment. "So, in other words, you retain all of the benefits with none of the risks," he concluded.

Alexander leaned forward, his hands clasped together in front of him on the desk. "Can you think of a better way to save myself—as Kafir so aptly put it?" he asked, clearly pleased with himself.

George shook his head. "No, and I don't think anyone else could, either," he admitted. "There's one problem, though. If there is a leak within our own ranks, as has been suggested more than once, aren't you running the risk that it could get out anyway?"

"I've considered that possibility," Alexander assured him. "That's why I've decided that no one can know, except the two of us. The royalties will be deposited directly into a numbered bank account in Switzerland."

George looked properly impressed. "You seem to have all the bases covered," he said easily.

"I have to." Alexander picked up a telegram lying on the desk and passed it over to George. "The consortium is concerned about our stability," he said grimly. "They're threatening to call in our notes."

At the Clinique de Lausanne, Dr. Henri Goudron left his office and climbed the staircase, walking slowly, deliberately, to Elizabeth Ryan's room at the far end of the corridor. He found her exactly as he always found her: seated in a velvet chair near the window, staring blankly into space. A nurse's aid was brushing her magnificent hair. Elizabeth was truly alone now. But, he mused, she had been alone in all of

the ways that counted since that terrible night so many years
ago.

New York City.

Over the next few weeks, Meredith turned her research in
yet another direction. She began looking into Alexander's
past, into the lives of Constantine and Melina Kirakis. She
took out the old family albums, full of photographs and
memories, that she'd brought back from Greece. She also
spoke at length with Helena over the phone, asking discreet
questions without giving a reason for her curiosity. She
deliberately avoided any mention of Ioannina, knowing that
it would immediately arouse the suspicions of the Greek
woman. Still, she had managed to learn a great deal.

In the course of her research, Meredith had encountered
one puzzling fact: there had been scores of photographs of
Damian Kirakis, literally hundreds of baby pictures. There
had not been one of Alexander. Meredith thought it odd that
the earliest photographs of Alexander had been taken when
he was five years old. Why, she wondered, were there no
baby pictures of him?

She asked Helena about it, but Helena was unable to offer
any reasonable explanation other than to suggest that they
might have been inadvertently destroyed. "I am sure it is not
significant," Helena told her. But Meredith wasn't so sure.

"It doesn't make sense," Meredith pointed out. "There
are tons of photos in the family albums that are dated from
November 1948 to September 1953—but none of Alexander. If they had been destroyed, wouldn't all of the pictures
taken in that time period be missing?"

"Perhaps you should ask Alexi about it," Helena suggested helpfully.

"You're right," she agreed. "I'm probably making too
much out of nothing."

"Why are you so interested in these old photographs?"
Helena had asked hesitantly.

"Natural curiosity," Meredith lied. "We've been discussing having children. I'd love to see what Alexander
looked like as a little boy, though I'm still having difficulty
even imagining him as a child."

"He was definitely a child," Helena assured her with a little laugh. "And a bright, mischievous child at that!"

Their conversation had been enlightening but hardly reassuring. The more Meredith thought about it, the more she was certain that the death of Elizabeth Ryan's child and Alexander's own accident in Ioannina were somehow related. It all seemed to fit: the Ryan boy had been four years old then, Alexander was also four. Both accidents had taken place in Ioannina, and she was willing to bet that both took place at the same time. Little David Ryan had supposedly died in an abandoned well; Alexander had nightmares about being swallowed up by the earth. The woman in his nightmares wore the attire of ancient Greece, he had told her; Elizabeth Ryan was filming a Biblical picture at the time of the accident. Helena had said that Melina Kirakis described Alexander's accident as "traumatic," but his mother had offered no further explanation. Falling into a well could certainly be described as a traumatic experience for a four-year-old child, traumatic enough to rob him of his memory. But how had Alexander managed to survive? And what about Elizabeth Ryan herself? Was she really dead, or was she alive and in hiding, perhaps somewhere on the Continent? Meredith had been suspicious from the moment she first noticed the strong physical resemblance between Alexander and Elizabeth, a resemblance too strong to be mere coincidence.

She could not mention it to him again until she had proof.

"Hold all of my calls until I tell you otherwise, Stacey," Alexander instructed his secretary as he entered his office. "I don't want to be disturbed for any reason."

"Yes, sir, Mr. Kirakis."

Alexander closed the door and took a deep breath. He had just come from a meeting with his board of directors. Days like this made him wish his father had not decided to let the corporation go public. Had it remained a privately held company, he would have had no one else to answer to, and while he was still in control with fifty-one percent of the stock, his life would have been simpler.

Damn them! he thought angrily. They are so narrow-minded, so shortsighted.

They had expressed doubts about the future of the nuclear research facility. They had pointed out—as if he did not already know—that it was costing the corporation more now than it stood to make in the next year, its first year of full operation. There were problems concerning federal regulations. They were under fire from the antinuclear groups, who wanted them shut down completely. And as if that were not enough, the project had been plagued by a series of minor problems and setbacks almost from the day it opened. The board thought it should be scrapped, but Alexander vetoed the suggestion. They called it throwing good money after bad. He called it progress. They did not see the potential for its future. Trying to reason with them was frustrating. He would rather be putting his energies to more productive use elsewhere.

He seated himself behind the massive black mahogany desk and massaged his temples, willing the throbbing sensation inside his head to stop. What next? he asked himself. In the past three years, it seemed as though his global operation had been hit by a series of accidents and tragedies, one right after the other. And in the past year, that tempo had increased greatly. First, there had been the fire at his offices in Montreal. There were still rumors that it had been arson, but no one had ever been able to prove it. Then there had been the bankruptcy of Carlo Manetti and his subsequent suicide. The speculation that he had been behind Manetti's financial woes had done considerable damage to his image and to that of the corporation. Alexander had never known who was responsible for forcing Manetti into receivership, but he had always suspected that whoever had been behind it had accomplished exactly what he had set out to do: tarnish the sterling Kirakis image. When the smoke finally cleared after Manetti's untimely death, the lawsuits had begun to pour in, lawsuits aimed at his French-based pharmaceuticals company after the cyanide incidents. His people in Paris had attempted to sweep it under the rug, but it was too late. The damage had already been done. Now the public was afraid of anything coming out of that plant. It had happened once; it could easily happen again, they reasoned. He had to deal with the possibility that Kafir had sold him out, and with pressure from the board to close the nuclear research facility. It seemed to Alexander that there existed a conspiracy—possibly within his own ranks—to destroy him. Whoever was behind it was obviously quite clever —and dangerous. They had done their homework; they knew which areas of his worldwide operation were most vulnerable. Alexander knew he was up against a deadly, faceless adversary, but he was damned if he would just sit back and wait to be destroyed. He was going to fight back with everything he had.

Meredith sat in the makeup chair as the makeup woman tucked a large paper napkin into the front of her dress before applying a light foundation to Meredith's face. Her skin was so flawless that she never used it except when she went before the cameras. Cindy sat in a chair in one corner of the room, reviewing Meredith's schedule verbally and making notes for the coming week. She was in the middle of reviewing her calendar for the next month when Larry Kyle, the show's assistant producer, poked his head in the door. "Well, well, the prodigal hath returneth," he joked. "Must be nice to be able to fly off to all those exotic locations on the pretense of working—while yours truly slaves away in a hot studio."

"Give it up, Kyle," she told him, trying to keep from laughing as the makeup woman applied color on the area just above her cheekbones. "I'm not going to sit here and trade insults with you. It wouldn't be fair. You haven't lost your amateur standing yet."

He laughed. "You're in good form for someone who's been on the road for the past two weeks."

"You're lucky I'm in a good mood," she told him in a menacing tone as the makeup woman removed the napkin and turned her over to the hairdresser. She paused to check her finished face in a hand mirror.

"A good mood?" He grinned. "That means that husband of yours was here when you came in last night instead of being off on one of *his* business trips. I can always tell when the two of you have been apart too long. You're downright unpleasant."

"And you're close to getting out of line," she warned with a raised eyebrow.

Larry Kyle turned to Cindy. "Did you by any chance tell

her about the nut case who's been trying to get in touch with her while she's been away?'' he asked, sticking a pencil behind his ear.

"Nut?" Meredith looked up.

Cindy nodded. "It's nothing, really," she said confidently. "Just some crank who doesn't know what planet he's on. He calls here and goes through all the trouble of getting past the switchboard, then refuses to leave a message when I tell him you're away. He just hangs up. Then, next day around the same time, there he is again, demanding to talk to you."

"Ah, the price of being a celebrity," Kyle chimed in with an exaggerated groan.

Meredith only smiled. "Didn't I tell you those ads we placed would lure every kook from here to San Francisco?"

"You're not concerned?" Cindy asked, closing her steno book.

"Should I be?" Meredith forced her most professional smile.

"Well, quite frankly, he sounds a little strange . . ."

Meredith laughed. "They're all a little strange—and usually harmless," she said confidently.

But she was more than a little curious.

TWENTY-SIX

ݎݎݎݎݎݎݎݎݎ

London.

Inspector Dessain followed the constable down the long, narrow corridor to the morgue. He was acutely aware of the eerie, hushed silence, and it sent chills down his spine. Death is all around, he thought. Indeed, it could be felt, almost like a physical presence. The constable opened a door, and Dessain stepped into a dismal gray room lined with large metal cabinets in which the corpses were kept. On a narrow metal table in the center of the room, one body, completely covered with a large white sheet, waited to be identified. The attendant came forward as they approached and he lifted the sheet to reveal its face.

"Is this the one, Inspector?" the constable asked.

Dessain nodded, feeling slightly nauseous. *"Oui,"* he said tightly. "This is the one."

He looked at the face of the dead woman one last time before the sheet was put back in place. There was no doubt. She was the woman he was looking for, the woman he had been looking for these past two weeks. "How did she die?" he asked.

The attendant frowned. "Hit and run. She was crossing

the street at Gloucester Place, not far from Hyde Park. From what I hear, the driver of the car didn't even slow down.''

Dessain looked at the constable again. "Did anyone see the car?" he asked. "The make, the color? The license plate?''

The constable shook his head. "It happened late at night," he said. "The few who actually witnessed it said it happened much too quickly for anyone to get a look at the car. He was driving very fast—''

"He?" Dessain interrupted.

"A figure of speech, sir," the constable explained.

Dessain nodded. "You are going to notify her sister now?''

"Yes, sir. Right away, to be sure.''

"You have my telephone number at the hotel and in Paris," Dessain said. "You will contact me if there are any new developments?''

"About the accident? Of course.''

The Frenchman's expression was grim. "This," he said quietly, "was no accident.''

Dessain thought about it in the taxi en route to his hotel. Though he had never met Carolyn Grayson face-to-face, he had had no trouble recognizing her. Her photograph had turned up at Interpol headquarters in Paris two weeks earlier. She was the executive secretary to Drew Douglas-Kent, a vice-president of the Kirakis Corporation and head of its operations in London. Three weeks ago she had disappeared with an attaché case full of confidential documents. Interpol had been notified because she was believed to have been involved in the same illicit business dealings that had led to the arrest of Kurt Badrutt in Berlin. Dessain had never believed it. She was a secretary, hardly in a position to be a part of such a highly specialized, delicate operation. Even if she had been acting as a courier for Douglas-Kent—or someone else—something about it just didn't make sense. Dessain had spoken with her sister, a reporter with the BBC. Lucy Grayson Taylor had told him that Carolyn had telephoned her the night before she disappeared. Carolyn had been terrified, Lucy recalled. She said she had stumbled onto something, quite by accident, that had frightened her.

She had not told her sister exactly what it was, only that it was important and that she had received threats from an unknown man over the phone. She told Lucy that she had taken the documents and was going to deliver them to the authorities. That had been the last time Lucy Grayson Taylor heard from her sister.

But Carolyn Grayson had not had the attaché case with her at the time of her death, Dessain remembered as he paid the driver and got out of the cab in front of the Royal Westminister Thistle Hotel. And Lucy Grayson Taylor insisted it was not in her sister's apartment, which she had searched from top to bottom. What, she asked, could have been so important that someone would want to kill Carolyn Grayson for possessing it?

Dessain stopped at the front desk to check for messages. There were none, so he went up to his room. As he let himself in, he thought about his investigation into the activity taking place within the upper echelons of the Kirakis Corporation, an investigation that had occupied most of his time for the past six months. He thought about the long hours he had put in at the computers, the Fortran IV and the giant IBM 370, in the basement at Interpol headquarters, studying the thick printouts the large printers produced at the rate of over a thousand lines per minute. In the beginning, Dessain had acted on a hunch when he decided to take a look at the Kirakis Corporation's holdings and activities around the world. He had checked out Kurt Badrutt thoroughly, and the man had come up clean in every respect. Dessain had spent a week in Germany, conversing with computers at banks, credit-rating organizations, and the office of vital statistics, and by the end of that week he had assembled a detailed portrait, a factual and financial identikit, of Kurt Badrutt. Badrutt was a brilliant, successful businessman with a flawless track record. He had no criminal record, not even a traffic ticket. He was married to the daughter of a German diplomat for almost twenty-five years, and had two children. He had been keeping a mistress for the past four years, a woman ten years his junior who had been a call girl for most of her life, living off the favors of rich men who were able and willing to pay her price. A bit foolish on Badrutt's part, Dessain thought, but hardly a motive for setting him up for what could turn out to be a very long prison term. No. Dessain was convinced that whoever had set him up was the same person who wanted Carolyn Grayson out of the way, and the same person who had been behind everything that was going wrong with the Kirakis Corporation. Badrutt and Grayson had been pawns. Whoever was behind their misfortune had been after much bigger game.

He had turned his attention to the Kirakis Corporation after Grayson's disappearance, two weeks ago. He'd spent weeks accessing computers all over Europe, and what he had learned amazed him. It was common knowledge that the Kirakis Corporation was the world's largest multinational conglomerate, but Dessain was sure that no one, except possibly Alexander Kirakis himself, knew just how vast the Kirakis empire really was. It was like a gigantic octopus whose tentacles of power encircled the globe. It seemed that no area of business or industry had been left untouched by its influence. The number of its employees and the sum total of its assets worldwide made it larger and more powerful than many nations, quite an accomplishment for a company that, in its infancy, back in the mid-1920s, had been the troubled Athens-based Athena Shipping Company.

As Dessain reviewed all of the information, he became fascinated with the phenomenal growth of the Kirakis Corporation over the past sixty years. The floundering Athena Shipping Company had been saved during the Depression by the genius of Constantine Kirakis and the support of his wealthy father-in-law, Damian Katramopoulos. Eventually Kirakis had branched out into other areas of enterprise. His company continued to flourish, even as war ravaged Europe, and Athena Shipping became Athena Maritime, the flagship company of what would later be the Kirakis Corporation. Constantine Kirakis had forged his empire slowly, steadily, and without too many serious problems. Then, in early 1982, he had handed the reins of power over to his only surviving son, Alexander. And that was when the trouble began.

The growth of the Kirakis Corporation in the past few years had been greater than that of the fifty-five preceding them. Alexander Kirakis, it seemed, was a dynamic businessman. And a ruthless one. He was a man especially adept at making enemies. He had accomplished a great deal, and collected a number of powerful, dangerous adversaries along the way. One did not become as powerful and influential as Alexander Kirakis without arousing a certain amount of antagonism in the process.

Dessain thought about what the computers had told him: a fire in the Kirakis Corporation's offices in Montreal, arson suspected but never confirmed; Kirakis's alleged involvement in the Manetti scandal; a nuclear research facility plagued by legal problems almost from the day it had opened; a pharmaceutical company in France bombarded by lawsuits; political unrest in Southeast Asia jeopardizing Kirakis oil drilling operations; the arrest of one of his most trusted men, another under suspicion; and now an employee was dead under questionable circumstances.

Dessain noted that Alexander Kirakis had obtained several large loans from a group of Swiss banks for the expansion of his empire, loans that were due, loans he had not been able to repay. Bankers were pressuring him. It was curious, Dessain mused. The head of a corporate empire plagued by serious problems and under pressure to repay financial obligations. Maybe I've been looking in the wrong direction, he thought. Maybe the Kirakis Corporation was *not* the intended target.

Maybe it was Alexander Kirakis himself.

New York City.

In her office at the Broadcast Center, Meredith was dictating a letter to her secretary. On the desk in front of her was a yellow legal pad scribbled full of notes for upcoming shows, prospective guests, and possible contacts; a stack of mail she had not yet had time to read; and the latest issue of *Working Woman* magazine, featuring her photograph on its cover. On the floor to the right of the desk was the cardboard box containing all of her research on the Ryan story. As she dictated to Cindy, her eyes, and her thoughts, kept wandering back to the carton. She felt as though she had opened Pandora's box, and now that it was open, it was too late to try to close it again. There was no turning back. Now that her suspicions had been aroused, she had no choice but to see it through to its conclusion. She had to find the truth, more for Alexander's sake than for her own.

A week ago, she had had a lengthy telephone conversation with the administrator of the Kiffisia Hospital in Athens. Normally, the man would have refused her request for information, patient records being strictly confidential, but since she was Mrs. Alexander Kirakis, and since both Constantine and Alexander Kirakis had made generous contributions to the hospital over the years—Constantine Kirakis had funded the building of a new wing only a year before his death, dedicated in the name of his late wife—the administrator would certainly do his best to accommodate Meredith's request.

First, Meredith wanted information on Alexander: he had mentioned that his mother once told Helena he had been hospitalized there following his accident in Ioannina. She had also asked for information on an American woman who might have been a patient there in July or August 1953, Elizabeth Weldon-Ryan. McCloskey had told Meredith that Elizabeth had been taken from Ioannina after her collapse, that Tom Ryan had moved her to a place where she would receive proper medical attention. Athens was the nearest major city. If she had been a patient there, even temporarily, it might give Meredith a lead as to where she was taken after that, dead or alive. If, Meredith thought darkly. There were so many *ifs*.

Now more than ever, Meredith's instincts told her Elizabeth was still alive . . . somewhere. And if she could find Elizabeth, then perhaps she could unlock the secrets buried in Ioannina. Perhaps she could free Alexander from the demons of his past. It was strange, Meredith thought. At first, the story had been the important thing, how she was going to break the conspiracy of silence that had surrounded the ''death'' of Elizabeth Weldon-Ryan for over three decades. It had been her dream, but the dream had suddenly turned into a nightmare. Now the story no longer mattered. She had to find out what had really happened to Alexander in Ioannina. She had to know if he was the resurrection of David Ryan, of the beautiful little boy whose body had never been recovered from that well. Could Alexander be the child who supposedly died in the well? If so, how had he survived? And why had Tom and Elizabeth Ryan been so certain he was dead?

"Will that be all, Meredith?"

Cindy's words cut through her thoughts. "What? Oh, yes—that's all. For now," she said distractedly.

Her secretary looked at her quizzically for a moment, then got to her feet and left the office. Meredith took one of the photographs of Elizabeth from the box and held it next to a framed portrait of Alexander on her desk. It was incredible. Almost like looking at a mirror reflection. If Alexander had been a woman, they probably could have passed for twins.

Suddenly, Meredith shivered. Everything she'd researched seemed to point to Alexander. It now appeared to her that her own husband was the missing piece to the puzzle she had been trying to solve for so many years, the obvious clue she had overlooked. There were, on the one hand, Tom Ryan and Elizabeth Weldon, Hollywood's golden couple in a golden era of films. On the other hand were Constantine and Melina Kirakis. Rich, powerful, a solid marriage. A dynasty cursed by personal tragedy. They had everything except the one thing they both wanted most: a strong, healthy child. An heir for the empire. Melina Kirakis, a semi-invalid who'd suffered three miscarriages before giving birth to Damian —who died at age five. And then there was Alexander. Seemingly the answer to their prayers. A child who had been through a terrible ordeal. He had survived but had no memory of who he was or what had happened to him. A man who to this day could not remember. What had really happened that summer in Greece? Meredith wondered.

Unlock the secrets of Ioannina and unlock the secret of Alexander's past, she thought. Just like Pandora's box.

Paris.

Having turned his attention to learning as much about Alexander Kirakis as he possibly could, Dessain found himself traveling across Europe once again, asking questions of computers in almost every country. In Greece, he checked with the bureau of vital statistics, the Bank of Greece, and the Hellenic Industrial Development Bank. In Paris, he accessed the great computers of the Inspecteurs des Finances, the Crédit Lyonnais, and the Assurance Nationale. He spent time in Rome and made another trip to Berlin. He collected data from various sources in London, Madrid, and Copenhagen. He checked the morgues of newspapers in every city he visited. It had been a long, time-consuming process, but the results had been well worth the effort.

By the time he had finished, Dessain knew that Alexander Kirakis had been born in Greece on November 17, 1948. His medical records showed that he had the rarest of all blood types, AB negative. He had not been able to locate the birth certificate, but Dessain conceded that even the computers made errors occasionally. Kirakis had been educated by private tutors on the family's private Aegean island until he was eighteen. He had received his M.B.A. from the Harvard Business School, and had graduated at the top of his class in 1971. He knew that the younger Kirakis adored travel, had expensive tastes, and spent large amounts of money on women and polo ponies, though not always in that order. He found that Alexander Kirakis's reputation as a world-class polo player was eclipsed only by his more notorious reputation as a womanizer.

The newspaper accounts had confirmed this time and time again. He had been involved in a series of short-lived affairs with some of the most dazzling women in the world. He'd kept a Greek mistress for almost a year before his marriage to American newscaster Meredith Courtney in 1984. Dessain discovered that Kirakis had made as many enemies in his private life as he had made in his business dealings, most of them women. Interesting, Dessain thought. Alexander Kirakis, a man more controversial than the corporate empire he ruled. A corporation plagued by tragedy and adverse publicity, forced to pay astronomical amounts in lawsuits, owing large sums to banks that grew impatient. It would seem that Alexander Kirakis was a desperate man. Desperate people did desperate things. Perhaps, Dessain reasoned, it was time he and Alexander Kirakis met, face-to-face.

Dessain was on the next Air France flight to New York.

* * *

Los Angeles.

At the Hall of Records a man sat before one of the many microfilm viewers available for public use, staring thought-fully at the data on the screen in front of him. It had been a long day, but it had also been a productive one. He'd encountered some difficulty in obtaining the medical records he'd been instructed to locate, but it had been done. Getting that information, he thought with satisfaction, meant a six-figure bonus from his employer.

His employer. He had no idea who he was working for. He had never met the person for whom he was obtaining this confidential and somewhat delicate information. He didn't even know if he was working for a man or a woman. His contact had always been a third party, a woman from whom he received his instructions. He was paid by regular deposits made into his bank account. All he knew was that his anonymous employer was very rich, very powerful, and very determined to remain anonymous.

But why was this person so interested in the medical records of a child who had been dead for over thirty years?

New York City.

Alexander had spent the entire morning holed up in his office at the World Trade Center. He was not seeing anyone, not taking any calls. He tried to work but found himself unable to concentrate. Meredith had been right, he thought as he got to his feet and stared absently at the boats in the harbor headed out to sea. He did need to get away for a while, to sort things out in his own mind, to come to grips with the realities he'd had to face in the past few weeks. He was suddenly glad she had insisted they go to Southampton. He was looking forward to spending time alone with her, talking out his feelings.

In two hours he had a meeting uptown with a group of bankers. He was not looking forward to it and would have liked to reschedule it, but the meeting was far too important to be put off for even a day. He drew in his breath. At least it was the last such meeting before they left for the weekend.

The buzzing sound of the intercom interrupted his

thoughts. He leaned across the desk and flipped the switch angrily. "Stacey, I told you I did not wish to be disturbed," he barked.

"I know, sir, but there's a gentleman out here who says he must speak with you. He's from Interpol," she said hastily.

"Interpol?" What did Interpol want with him? He hesitated for a moment. "Very well. Send him in."

"Yes, sir."

The door opened and the man entered. Somehow, he was not at all what Alexander had expected. He was a short, stocky, middle-aged man with rumpled hair and a lazy shuffle of a walk. He smiled as he crossed the room, extending his hand to Alexander. They shook hands, and he produced his identification. "I am Inspector Adrian Dessain, Interpol," he said as he returned his identification to his pocket. "I wonder if I might ask you a few questions?"

"About what?" Alexander asked impatiently.

"About certain—mishaps within your corporate structure," Dessain answered. "May I sit down? I have been on my feet most of the morning and I am quite tired."

Alexander nodded. "I do not have very much time. I have a meeting uptown in an hour or so, and—"

"This will not take long," Dessain assured him as he seated himself. "You are aware, of course, that one of your executives was arrested in Berlin as part of a crackdown on illegal business scams, are you not?"

"Of course."

"I have been to Berlin. I have spoken with him at length. He swears he is innocent," Dessain told Alexander. "And I am inclined to believe him."

Alexander's gaze was level. "Why?"

"Because I think he was set up. I think whoever set him up was actually out to get *you*, Monsieur Kirakis."

"That's an interesting theory, Inspector," Alexander said carefully.

"It seems rather obvious to me," Dessain responded, ticking off each setback that had befallen the Kirakis Corporation in the past few years. He showed Alexander the computer printouts and other information he had accumulated in the course of his investigation. "It would appear,

Monsieur Kirakis, that your empire sits on a somewhat shaky foundation.''

''We have experienced difficulties, yes,'' Alexander admitted. ''But that sort of thing happens in even the most solid companies from time to time.''

''Perhaps.'' Dessain paused. ''But does it not strike you as odd that things were relatively quiet within the Kirakis Corporation's worldwide operation until 1982—when you became chairman of the board?''

''What exactly are you saying, Inspector Dessain?'' Alexander asked.

''I believe someone would like to see you put out of business—permanently,'' Dessain responded bluntly.

Alexander smiled. ''I am sure there are a good many people who would like to see that,'' he conceded. ''But it is not likely that they will get their wish.''

''You are sure about that?''

Alexander looked at him. ''Yes,'' he said with finality. ''I am.''

Dessain closed the attaché case now resting across his knees and put it on the floor beside him. ''When Kurt Badrutt was first arrested, monsieur, Interpol received an inquiry concerning his involvement in the laundering business,'' he explained in his heavily accented English. ''From the very beginning, something about the circumstances surrounding his arrest did not seem quite right. Badrutt insisted he had been framed, and I was inclined to believe him, even then.''

''Why?'' Alexander asked. ''You said this earlier. What made you believe him?''

''Didn't you?'' Dessain wanted to know.

''Of course I did,'' Alexander answered without hesitation. ''But I've known him for many years. I knew he could not have done the things he had been accused of doing.''

''I, too, know him well,'' Dessain responded, telling Alexander of the lengthy process by which he had assembled a portrait of Kurt Badrutt. ''I am convinced that Badrutt was no more than a pawn, Monsieur Kirakis. You see, it is you who is the real target.''

''I?'' Alexander asked, keeping his voice steady.

Dessain told him everything he had learned about the

Kirakis Corporation—and about Alexander himself—in the course of his investigation. He gave names, incidents, and dates, finishing with the death of Carolyn Grayson in London. "The official ruling was that it was an accident," he said in conclusion.

"But you don't believe that," Alexander said slowly.

"I do not." Dessain frowned. "Someone wanted it to look like an accident—and did a very good job of making some people believe that it was. But I am not convinced." He paused. "You have stepped on more than a few toes in the years you have been an active part of the Kirakis Corporation, yes?"

Alexander smiled tightly. "When you are in business, Inspector, it's impossible to find great success without making a few enemies along the way."

"But rivals in business do not usually resort to murder to win a competition," Dessain noted. "No, Monsieur Kirakis, it is my guess that whoever is out to get you holds some kind of personal grudge. I came here with the hope that you might be able to offer some suggestions as to who that person might be."

"The list is quite long, I am afraid," Alexander admitted. "My personal relationships have created almost as many antagonists as my business dealings." He paused and glanced at his watch. "I must be going. Bankers do not like to be kept waiting. Time is money: that is their philosophy. But if you would be kind enough to give me a number where I might reach you—"

Dessain scribbled down the number of the hotel where he was staying. "I will be staying on for a few days," he told Alexander.

"I'm afraid I won't be," Alexander told him. "I am flying to Paris on business. I am leaving late tomorrow afternoon and probably will not be returning until early next week."

The Frenchman pointed to the card he had given Alexander. "The telephone number of Interpol's Paris headquarters is on the other side," he said. "If you think of anything, anything at all that may be useful to our investigation, please do not hesitate to contact me."

"I will do that," Alexander promised.

Dessain's eyes met Alexander's, and the Frenchman's face was serious. "Please, monsieur, do not take the matter we discuss too lightly," he cautioned. "If my hunch is correct, your business interests—even your life—may be in jeopardy."

Long after Dessain had gone, Alexander still thought about what the Interpol agent had told him. This Inspector Dessain had been thorough. He knew almost as much about what was happening within the corporation as Alexander himself did. Though Alexander would never have admitted it, he was worried. He shared Dessain's theory that everything that had happened—every setback, every accident, every crisis—had been carefully orchestrated with one objective in mind: to ruin him. Whoever was behind this plot was clever. And dangerous.

Alexander took a deep breath. Dessain had wanted names, names of those who might have cause to want to see him destroyed. It was almost laughable. How could he pick out the person who might want to ruin him from a list that was virtually endless? He would not know where to begin. He had made some powerful enemies in the business world —and a good many more in his private life who were even more powerful, more ruthless. Any one of them had the motive and the means to make it happen. But which one—or ones, since he had not ruled out the possibility that they could have banded together—had actually been behind his troubles?

Who hated him enough to go to so much effort to ruin him?

"Why don't you give up, Larry?" Meredith said, laughing as she stepped down from the familiar blue and gray set of *Manhattan Observer*. "In a battle of wits, you would be totally defenseless!"

"It's good to see you've got your sense of humor back," the assistant producer proclaimed as he shifted around on the high stool from which he had been badgering Meredith during her attempted rehearsals. "You've been in such a foul mood lately."

"Who wouldn't be, in my place?" she asked with mock

anger in her voice. "I spend fourteen hours—or more —every day in this zoo. My husband is away on business and by the time he calls, I can barely keep my eyes open—"

"You're the one who wanted to be a star, sweetheart," he chided her good-naturedly.

"Sure." Meredith picked her way through the maze of camera and sound equipment and headed back to her office. Halfway there, she ran into Casey. "If I have to put in one more season with Larry, I think I'll put in for combat pay," she lamented. "He drove me crazy during morning rehearsals."

"He drives everybody crazy," Casey said with a laugh. "Are you free for lunch today? There's a new place over on Thirty-sixth and Madison I thought we might try—"

"I can't. I'm ordering in," Meredith told her. "I want to get out of here at a respectable hour this evening."

"Is Alexander coming home?" Casey asked.

Meredith shook her head. "I wish he were," she sighed. "No, he was delayed in Paris. I have no idea when he'll be home now."

"Like a rain check?" Casey asked with a grin.

"Definitely."

As Meredith approached her office, her secretary emerged, a look of relief on her face when she saw Meredith. "I called down to the set and Larry said you had already left," Cindy began, nodding toward the door. "There's a messenger here with an envelope for you."

"Why didn't you just accept it?" Meredith asked.

Cindy shook her head emphatically. "He has instructions to deliver it to you personally," she said. "I thought it might be important."

Meredith nodded. As she entered her office, the young, uniformed messenger stood up. "Meredith Kirakis?" he asked pleasantly.

"Yes?"

"Could you sign for this, please?" he asked. "I can only give it to you."

She scribbled her name on the receipt and took the envelope. As the messenger let himself out, she closed the door. If it were so important that it could be handed to no one but her, then it must also be private. She picked up her letter opener and ripped open the envelope. There was only a single sheet of paper inside, a photocopy of a document dated September 1953. There was no note, nothing to explain it, but it needed no explanation. Its message was all too clear. Someone else had been looking into the pasts of her husband and Elizabeth Weldon-Ryan. Someone else had uncovered the truth, the proof she had been searching for to verify a connection between Alexander, the Kirakises, and possibly the Ryans. But who? Who had discovered the truth? Who else knew about this? She felt the last vestiges of blood drain from her face as she stared at the legal document from the Greek courts in Athens. A final decree of adoption.

Alexander's adoption.

TWENTY-SEVEN

᠌᠌᠌᠌᠌᠌᠌᠌᠌᠌᠌᠌

Meredith lay on the bed, her head pounding. Her worst fears had been realized when she saw the contents of that envelope. She really *had* opened Pandora's box—and released all of the demons that haunted Alexander's past. Why had she tried to revive the story? she asked herself again. Why hadn't she left the past—and the secrets of Ioannina —buried, as Tom Ryan and Constantine Kirakis had wanted them to be? How am I going to tell him? she wondered now, as a knot of fear tightened and grew within her.

She stared at the document in her hand. Though the names of the natural parents appearing on the adoption decree were unfamiliar Greek names, she knew the truth as surely as she knew her own name. Alexander was the son Tom and Elizabeth had believed died in that old well in Ioannina. Alexander was David Ryan!

How had they done it? Meredith wondered. How had they arranged for a birth certificate and an adoption without anyone knowing the truth? How had they pulled it off without arousing suspicions? And how much had it cost Constantine Kirakis to hide the truth from the world—and from Alexander himself?

Hearing footsteps outside the door, she quickly tucked the

paper back into her shoulder bag and lay back on the bed. The door opened and Alexander entered. He paused, studying her for a moment with concern in his eyes, then crossed the room and settled onto the bed next to her. "Do you want to tell me what's wrong?" he asked in a gentle voice, stroking her hair.

"I think it's bubonic plague," she said, trying to keep her voice cheerful. When she had entered the building an hour ago, and the concierge had told her Alexander was waiting for her upstairs, she had been afraid to face him, afraid he would know instantly that something was wrong, terribly wrong. Alexander knew instinctively when something was bothering her. The same feral instinct that had served him so well in business had made him sensitive to the slightest change in her mood.

"The truth," he said in a firm but patient tone. "What's wrong?"

"Seriously, I think I may have picked up a bug somewhere," she insisted. "While you were away I was putting in fourteen hours a day—sometimes more—to get the new segments ready for airing. I've been tired, not eating too well, I'm afraid—and I guess it's all caught up with me."

"I think perhaps you should take a day or two off," he said, brushing her hair away from her face.

"Harv would have a coronary if I took time off now," she said with a weak smile.

"His problems are *his* concern. You are mine—and I'm going to insist, *matia mou*. I will not have you working yourself to death."

"Don't you think you should practice what you preach?" she asked in a half-teasing tone. "How many nights have you burned the midnight oil lately?"

"It's different in my case and you know it," he said, frowning. "I am responsible for the corporation—I *am* Kirakis. I must find out who is out to ruin me—before it is too late and too much damage is done. The fate of the IBS network does not rest on your shoulders, though it may seem that way to you at times. I would rather insist you take a day or two off than allow you to collapse from exhaustion."

She looked up at him, feeling dangerously close to tears. "I love you," she said softly as her arms encircled his neck.

"No matter what happens or how things may seem, please *never* forget how much I love you."

He held her close. Something was bothering her, and it was not as minor as she was leading him to believe. If only she would tell him why she was so frightened.

Meredith read the letter slowly, then threw it down on the desk, more frustrated than angry. It was a letter from the administrator of the Clinique de Lausanne in Switzerland, responding to her request for information concerning Elizabeth Weldon-Ryan, who may have been a patient at the clinic in September 1953. Like the two she had received before it—from the administrators of institutions in Geneva and Davos-Dorf—the letter was formal, polite, but uninformative. Monsieur Michel Beauvais, the administrator, explained that, while he would like very much to help her, it was the clinic's policy to protect the privacy of its patients. He was, unfortunately, not at liberty to release any information concerning any of the patients, not even their names.

Meredith got up and walked over to the window. The streets were decked out in cheerful Christmas fashion: huge bows in shades of red and green, giant poinsettias, snowflakes, and tinsel garlands. Christmas was only weeks away, but Meredith was not in a festive mood this year. She had tried to force herself to show some enthusiasm to keep from arousing Alexander's suspicions. Christmas had always been such a happy time for them. They celebrated the American holiday on December twenty-fifth, then had another celebration on St. Basil's Day, January sixth, maintaining the traditions in which Alexander had been brought up. Meredith frowned. For so many years, Alexander had lived with Greek traditions and values. All of his life—at least all of it that he was able to remember—he had thought of himself as Greek, as the son of Constantine and Melina Kirakis. What is it going to do to him when I tell him the truth? Meredith asked herself.

Her secretary entered the office. "Meredith, this just came for you—it's marked *Confidential*," Cindy said as she handed her the envelope.

Meredith took it from her and checked the return address.

It was from a law firm in Los Angeles. As she tore it open, she realized she was almost afraid to read it. She did not think she could take another surprise so soon after the special delivery on Friday.

She read the letter quickly. It was from a man named Curtis Harmon, the senior partner of the firm. As executor of the estate and trustee for Mrs. Ryan, he explained that her interest in the Thomas Ryan estate had come to his attention. He asked that she contact him at her earliest convenience concerning the trust provided for Mrs. Ryan's care through the Kirakis Foundation of Athens. The Kirakis Foundation? It didn't make sense, but she had the feeling it would as soon as she spoke with Mr. Harmon. She looked up at her secretary. "Cindy, hold all of my calls," she instructed. "I may be tied up for some time with this."

Cindy nodded and left the office.

Meredith put through a call to Los Angeles. When she gave the receptionist her name, Curtis Harmon came on the line almost immediately. "I received your letter, Mr. Harmon," she told him, "and frankly I'm more than a little confused. I *have* expressed an interest in the Ryan estate, but what is this about a trust?"

"You mean you don't know?" he asked, surprised.

"No. I don't."

"Well, Mrs. Kirakis, the trust was set up for Mrs. Ryan in November 1953 by the Kirakis Foundation—which I naturally assumed was now run by your husband, since Constantine Kirakis has been dead for several years. The foundation originated the trust because Mr. Kirakis—Constantine Kirakis, I mean—felt responsible for the death of Mrs. Ryan's child and her unfortunate mental state following the accident," Harmon explained.

I'll bet he did, Meredith thought angrily. "What, exactly, does the trust do for Mrs. Ryan?" she asked carefully.

"In the past, it has always covered all of her expenses at the Clinique de Lausanne in Switzerland," Harmon answered. "You weren't aware of this?"

"An oversight on my part," Meredith lied. "My husband has left the foundation in very capable hands, but he has little time to keep up with what is being done."

"Of course. I understand perfectly," he said pleasantly. "My contact has always been with a Dr. Karamanlis."

"I believe he must be running the foundation now," Meredith said vaguely.

"I know he has been handling everything connected with the Ryan trust," Harmon told her. "Including the property in Bel-Air formerly owned by the Ryans."

"The property?" Meredith was confused. She knew that the house had been left to Nick Holliday in Tom Ryan's will. "I don't understand—"

"The foundation acquired it two years ago from Nick Holliday, who inherited it from Mr. Ryan," Harmon explained. "It seems Holliday's Stargazer Productions was in a bit of financial trouble, and—"

"Why?" Meredith cut in. "I mean, why would the foundation want it?" Her thoughts were racing.

"I have no idea, Mrs. Kirakis," the lawyer answered truthfully.

"You said Mrs. Ryan is a patient at the Clinique de Lausanne?" she asked.

"That's correct. As far as I know, she has been there since she was first admitted in September 1953."

Meredith tried to organize her thoughts. When she talked with the administrator of the Kiffisia Hospital in Athens, he had told her that Alexander Kirakis had never been a patient there, which hadn't surprised her at all—under the circumstances—but that a Mrs. Elizabeth Weldon-Ryan had been hospitalized for six weeks, from August 2, 1953, until September 15, 1953. It all began to fall into place.

"Mrs. Kirakis?" Harmon asked, not sure she was still on the line.

"I'm here," she assured him. "Thank you, Mr. Harmon. You have been most helpful."

"If I can be of further assistance, please don't hesitate to call," he told her.

"I won't." She replaced the receiver slowly, trying to absorb what he had told her. It all made sense now, except for one thing: how had Alexander survived when everyone thought he had died in the well? Surely someone had the answers to that all-important question. She drew in a deep breath, realizing that she was now facing the most difficult task of her life.

Tonight, she had to tell Alexander.

Alexander read the paper over and over in stunned silence. Finally he turned back to Meredith, who watched him with concern. "Where did you get this?" he asked in a tense voice.

She took a deep breath. "I have no idea. It was delivered to me at the Broadcast Center by special messenger. There was no note, nothing."

"Then someone else knows."

"Unfortunately," she said quietly. "At first, I thought someone had found it while trying to aid me in my research, but—"

"I wonder," he began slowly, his anger growing in intensity, "how many other things they lied to me about?" He threw it down suddenly as if it were a deadly reptile about to strike. "Lies! My entire life has been a lie!"

"I don't understand," she said.

"Why did they never tell me?" he asked. "They let me believe I was their own flesh and blood—"

"To them, you *were,*" she said.

He turned to look at her. "How could you know that?" he asked coldly. "You never knew them—God, *I* never really knew them, did I? I lived with them all of my life—for as long as I could recall—and I never even *knew* them!"

"I knew both of them, Alexander," she said patiently. "I've spent months getting to know them. I've read their thoughts, felt their emotions. Your mother—Melina—was willing to die to give her husband a son."

He laughed thinly. "Now *that* might have been a more acceptable solution to the problem." His voice was brittle. "They could have paid some young girl to bear his child. It certainly would have been less expensive than the route they took—and it would have been legal. Not like kidnapping—"

"Alexander—" Meredith began.

He shook his head emphatically, waving her off.

"No. Don't defend them," he said sharply. He reached

for his coat. "I think I need to be alone for a while. I am going to go for a walk."

She watched him leave, and she was filled with a deep sadness—not for Alexander, not for herself, but for Constantine and Melina Kirakis, who had given everything they had for the child they regarded as their son. God only knew the guilt that must have gone with them to their graves.

It was late when he returned. Meredith was waiting for him in their bedroom. She had collected everything she had on Elizabeth Ryan and was waiting to show it to him. No more lies, she thought as she glanced at the photographs. He feels as if he's been betrayed now. If I hide this from him, he could turn on me, too.

He had not wanted to talk when he came home. He avoided all conversation, but Meredith had been insistent. She made him listen to her as she explained how she had learned of the trust fund Kirakis had set up for Elizabeth Ryan thirty-three years ago, how she had continued to search for answers, and the one factor that linked the Ryans to his parents. She explained that she still did not have all of the answers, but she had not given up.

"So . . . *more* secrets," he said icily. "It proves that one can live with people all their lives and never really know them."

"They loved you, Alexander. They must have had a good reason for what they did," she insisted.

"Of course they did. Constantine Kirakis needed a suitable heir for his empire," Alexander said contemptuously. "He would have done anything to insure the future of that empire—even steal a child if he could not have one of his own!"

"You know better than that. They both loved you—that's obvious." She wasn't sure he'd heard a word she'd said; he was staring, mesmerized, at the portrait of Elizabeth and her child.

"Then why did they never tell me the truth?" Alexander challenged, stalking the length of the room. There was undisguised bitterness in his voice.

"Maybe they were advised not to tell you," Meredith suggested.

"Why? What reason could they possibly have had?"

"You said yourself that the experience was so traumatic that you blocked it from your memory. Maybe they were afraid that reminding you of it might push you over the edge."

"Or perhaps they were afraid I might regain my memory —might remember who I was and what had been done to me!" Alexander snapped. He looked at the photograph of Elizabeth he now held in his hand. "What must it have been like for her—and for my father—to believe for so long that I was dead? How must she have felt when they told her her child was dead?"

"She doesn't feel anything," Meredith said quietly. "She's been catatonic ever since the night they told her you were dead."

He turned to look at her. "Then she *is* still alive!"

Meredith nodded. "She's in Switzerland—at the Clinique de Lausanne," she told him. "She's been there since 1953. As it turns out, the Kirakis Foundation has not only been taking care of her expenses there, but they've been absorbing all the expenses for the upkeep of the Ryan estate as well."

"The Kirakis Foundation," Alexander said slowly, biting off each word as if he were tasting bitter fruit. "Karamanlis."

"What?" She gave him a puzzled look.

"When my father died, the foundation was turned over to his good friend and physician, Pericles Karamanlis," Alexander recalled. "He has complete control over it."

"So that's why you didn't know about the trust—" she began, the pieces falling together in her mind.

He shook his head. "No, I did *not* know, but I am willing to bet that the good doctor does." He remembered the conversation he'd had with Karamanlis just after his father's death. "Something tells me he knows everything. If I find him, I will find the truth."

"Where is he now?"

"I do not know. But it will not take long to find out."

Meredith worried about Alexander. It seemed to her that he had become obsessed with uncovering the truth, with somehow restoring his own memory. He had sent one of his people to Los Angeles to collect Elizabeth Ryan's films from the archives at Centurion Studios. He enlisted the services of private investigators all over the world in an all-out search for those among his father's employees who might have been in Ioannina at the time of the tragedy. Making a number of phone calls, he tracked down Pericles Karamanlis.

"He is living in Rafina," he told Meredith. "He has a villa there, no doubt paid for by my father. By Constantine Kirakis."

"Are you going to call him?" Meredith asked, concerned.

"No. I am going to Rafina," he said darkly. "When I confront him, I want to see his face. I want to know if he tells me the truth."

"I'm going with you," she said promptly.

The next morning, they flew to Greece.

Alexander and Meredith flew from Athens to Rafina by helicopter, landing on the lawn in front of Karamanlis's magnificent Mediterranean-style villa that overlooked the sea. As they disembarked from the chopper, Alexander looked up, spotting Karamanlis on the veranda encircling the third-floor master suite. "He knows," Alexander told Meredith as they hurried across the lawn, away from the wind created by the whirling rotors of the helicopter. "Somehow, he knows. He has been expecting us."

They were admitted to the villa by an Oriental houseboy who took them to the rotunda, a large room lavishly decorated in rich fabrics and colors. "Dr. Karamanlis will be with you shortly," the young man told them. Then he turned and left the room.

"This is beautiful," Meredith said in a low voice as she admired the three-hundred-sixty-degree view of the Aegean from the arched windows lining the semicircular wall.

"It should be," Alexander said tightly. "He was undoubtedly paid well for his silence."

Pericles Karamanlis entered the rotunda. He was smaller than Alexander remembered, and he appeared to have lost a great deal of weight. The authority that had once radiated from his strong, hawk-nosed Greek face, his clear voice, his confident manner—even the way he moved—had all but vanished. He looked frail as he crossed the room, waving to them to sit.

"It is good to see you, Alexander," he said in English in a low, tired voice. "It has been a long time, too long."

"This is my wife Meredith," Alexander said with an unmistakable coldness in his voice. "Meredith, this is Pericles Karamanlis, my father's very good friend." He did not bother to conceal his contempt.

Karamanlis was gracious as he shook Meredith's hand gently. He turned to Alexander again. "I am only disappointed that you have not come before now, Alexander," he said.

"Are you?" Alexander asked, his tone glacial.

Karamanlis ignored his sarcasm. "Sit down, please. You would like a drink, perhaps?"

"No, I would not like a drink. What I would like are some answers," Alexander said sharply. He sat down beside Meredith on the couch.

"Of course. What is the problem?" Karamanlis sat across from them, and he still marveled at how much like Constantine Kirakis the younger man was.

"I am interested in information regarding an American woman—an actress," Alexander began. "Her name is Ryan, Elizabeth Weldon-Ryan."

Karamanlis jerked backward as if he'd received a physical blow. He tried to cover up his reaction, but he was not fast enough. "So you *do* know her," Alexander said.

"I know of her. I never met her personally."

"Tell me what you know about her, Doctor," Alexander said in a menacing tone.

"I do not recall very much—one of the hazards of aging, I am afraid," Karamanlis said in a faltering voice. "She was in Greece to make a movie, I believe. Her little one was killed in an accident."

"The accident—it took place in Ioannina, correct?" Alexander's voice was low, controlled.

"I don't know—"

"Surely you must remember," Alexander prodded him. "Helena tells me you were the one who cared for me after *my* accident—"

"What has that to do with the Ryans—"

"You tell *me*, Doctor," Alexander snapped. "I was critically injured in some sort of accident in Ioannina. The Ryans' son was killed in a similar accident. We were both four years old."

"That does not mean the two are related—"

"Do not lie to me, Doctor!" Alexander exploded, leaping to his feet. He took some papers from a large manila envelope and tossed them on the table in front of Karamanlis. "Take a good look, Doctor, then tell me the truth."

Karamanlis looked them over carefully. Birth certificates, medical records. This was the moment he'd dreaded for over thirty years. It all vividly came back to him now as he studied each of the documents. Two children, born at the same time, sharing the same rare blood types. A coincidence? Perhaps to someone who, unlike Pericles Karamanlis, did not know the truth.

"Explain those if you can, Doctor," Alexander challenged.

He shook his head. "Alexander, you do not understand —" he began.

Alexander grabbed the front of his shirt and pulled the elderly man to his feet. "No more lies, Karamanlis," he warned angrily. "I have lived with lies all of my life. Now I want the truth!"

Meredith got to her feet quickly, ready to intervene if necessary.

"I do not know—"

Alexander reacted as if he might hit Karamanlis. "The truth, Doctor!" he rasped. "Or do I have to remind you that *I* now control the most generous trust left to you by my father? I should destroy you—all of you!"

Karamanlis nodded in defeat. "Sit down, Alexander. I will tell you everything you wish to know. They should have told you years ago."

Alexander sank into a chair, suddenly feeling weak. "I am listening," he said quietly.

Karamanlis rose and walked to the windows, staring out at the ocean for a moment, as if drawing courage from the sea. "I had known your papa since we were all children, growing up in Piraeus. He and I were the best of friends. We shared the same backgrounds, the same dreams. We felt a bond few friends ever share. I was there when he and Melina fell in love. When he and Melina were married, I warned her, no children. But Melina was a stubborn lady, as you must know." He explained how Melina had suffered three miscarriages and the loss of Damian. "She was pregnant when Damian died, but that was not meant to be, either."

Meredith spoke up for the first time since their arrival. "Are you saying that she had a *fourth* miscarriage, Dr. Karamanlis?" she asked, looking at the doctor with a deepening concern.

She could hear the sharp intake of breath. "Yes," he said weakly. "She was at the start of her fifth month. They had both been so sure that it was going to be all right, that the baby would arrive safely." He shook his head. "Losing that baby nearly killed Melina. It almost destroyed both of them. They both wanted a large family so much, and knowing there could never be any more children was hard on them. Melina wanted to adopt, but"—Karamanlis shook his head sadly—"Constantine would have no part of it. He was such a proud, stubborn man. He wanted children of his own, sons to carry on his name and his work—"

"Then how—"

"Adoption laws in our country are quite strict, Alexander. When Melina consulted attorneys about adopting a child, she encountered numerous obstacles," Karamanlis remembered. "Greek adoptions take time. A baby cannot be adopted until it is two weeks old. The courts consider everything when a child's welfare is at stake, everything from religion to the mutual suitability of the prospective parents and the child. They consider the reasons for the proposed adoption. It is necessary to obtain the consent of both natural parents if the child is legitimate. Her age was Melina's downfall. In that area the courts were quite firm: Constantine and Melina were too old to adopt a baby at the time."

"But with so much money . . ." Alexander's voice trailed off.

The doctor shrugged. "Sometimes it helps; sometimes it does not. At any rate, Melina discovered it could take years, years they did not have. By then, they would be that much older and their chances of success possibly worse. She was beside herself with grief.''

''So they decided to steal a child?'' Alexander asked.

''Please, Alexander—do not misunderstand. They did not plan it the way it happened.'' Karamanlis frowned. ''When the American film company arrived in Greece, your papa leased them the land in Ioannina. It was not much good for anything else, and he had considered selling it.''

''I see,'' Alexander said, clenching and unclenching his fists.

''When Constantine abandoned the hotel project, he had ordered the old wells sealed so that they would not be a danger to the village children. He did not know that his orders had not been followed,'' Karamanlis went on. ''Melina was fascinated with the idea of watching an American film being made, and talked your father into going to Ioannina that summer. He was still quite depressed over losing Damian and the other child. In Ioannina, they met the Ryans, your biological parents.''

Meredith's eyes moved from Alexander to the doctor and back to Alexander again. He looked as though he were going to explode. She reached out and touched his arm gently, but he pulled away again.

''Then how . . .''

''Constantine was taken with you. You were only four then, and everything he had hoped Damian would have been. He would spend hours with you, and Melina was relieved, because he seemed happy, truly happy, for the first time since Damian had died. She wished it could go on forever, but she knew as soon as the filming was over, the Ryans would be returning to America. She told me on the telephone that she was sure it had changed his mind about adopting a baby, if only the courts could be persuaded.''

''How did they manage it?'' Alexander asked coldly. ''How did they manage to make my parents believe I was dead?''

''It was not planned,'' Karamanlis said quietly. ''It was during the last week of filming. Madame Ryan's role was completed, but she wanted to stay on in Greece as long as possible. It was a most unfortunate decision for her.''

Alexander nodded. He was trembling dangerously.

"The child—you—wandered away from the set one day, and fell into the old well. Your mother became hysterical when she was told and had to be sedated," Karamanlis remembered. "She was under sedation the entire four days. The rescue teams worked night and day, trying to save you. They finally gave you up for dead at the end of the fourth day. What they didn't know was that Constantine Kirakis had already recovered you from the well."

"And how did he manage that?" Alexander asked bitterly. "Oh, I have forgotten—when Kirakis money talked, *everyone* listened, even God Himself."

"That is not amusing, Alexander."

"*I* am not amused, Doctor," he snapped, his black eyes ablaze with anger. "Go ahead, I want to hear the rest of the story."

Karamanlis nodded. "Yes. Of course." He paused. "The well project had been called off, if you remember, because the men kept drilling into the underground caves. Constantine remembered this and contacted the men who had worked on the well. They went in through one of the caves and found you. He had them take you to the villa he and Melina had rented nearby, and he sent for me."

Meredith's eyes widened in disbelief. So *that* was how he had survived!

"How convenient for them," Alexander said through clenched teeth.

"When I arrived in Ioannina, you were in serious condition. You had slipped into a coma. You were in shock and suffering from a severe case of hypothermia. It was extremely cold in the well, and you had been wearing very little—shorts and a T-shirt. Costa made it clear that no one was to know of your whereabouts, and Melina was quite angry with him. She pleaded with him to go to the Ryans and tell them you were still alive, but he refused. She knew what he was thinking . . . Melina could read his mind. She confided in me. She was afraid he was never going to tell them about you, and let them go on thinking you were dead."

"Obviously," Alexander said.

"You recovered—physically, that is. But you were unable to remember who you were or what had happened to you. In fact, you could not recall anything about your life before the accident.''

"I still do not remember," he admitted, wringing his hands in frustration.

"This was what Constantine had hoped for. He told all of us that we were never to tell anyone who you were or what had happened to you. He planned to take you back to the island. He said you would be safe there, that you were *his* son now, that God had sent you to him. He believed it with all his heart." The doctor paused. "None of us were willing to go up against him, even those of us closest to him. He was a vengeful man when he was betrayed."

"And what about my mother? Melina . . . '' Alexander looked as though he were being tortured.

"Ah . . . Melina was afraid she would lose her mind. She wanted to go to your parents and tell them the truth, but she was as frightened as the rest of us, though for a different reason. Her husband had already lost five children. She feared that it might kill him to lose you as well.''

"And no one seemed to care what it might do to me," Alexander concluded.

"It was not that way at all," Karamanlis insisted. "Costa adored you. He wanted to give you the world. You were his salvation. As for Melina, she worshipped you. You were her perfect child, the son she had dreamed of giving her husband and couldn't. She was a strong lady, but a traditional Greek wife who would never have opposed her husband. After a while, the deception became easier for her. She wanted you to be her child so badly, that after a time, she began to believe that you were.''

Alexander waved the adoption decree furiously, his face contorted with rage. "Tell me, Doctor, if it was as difficult as you say to adopt a child in those days, how did they manage this?" he demanded.

"Well, you were already living with them on the island by then. When they submitted a petition to the courts in Athens, they had a false birth certificate, which I had arranged, indicating that you were the child of a distant relative of Constantine's who had passed away and left you in their custody. Frederick Kazomides worked with the legal department at Athena Maritime to make it look authentic. A blood relative, you see, would encounter no resistance from the courts, and in such a case, the wealth of Constantine Kirakis proved a definite asset.''

Alexander sucked in his breath and nodded slowly.

"So they bought themselves a judge and—''

"I have never known a Greek judge who could be bought," Karamanlis answered flatly.

"Anyone can be bought or sold," Alexander argued.

"Even you?''

"Yes, but I am quite expensive. As I am sure Madame Ryan can tell you . . . or would if she could speak.''

Karamanlis looked puzzled. "You—''

"I know where she is, Doctor," Alexander said, his eyes still blazing. "I know everything." He got to his feet, charging about the room like a wildman.

Meredith hoped Karamanlis would not try to deny it. Alexander was dangerously close to physically assaulting the older man.

Karamanlis nodded. "After they told her you were dead, her mind snapped. Her husband took her to a hospital in Athens. They told him she belonged in a psychiatric hospital, where she would get proper care. He made several discreet inquiries, and found the Clinique de Lausanne, one of the best in Europe. I am told that he chose to leave her in Europe because of the publicity she would receive back in America if he were to take her home. It was the most merciful thing he could have done for her.''

"Merciful?" Alexander asked incredulously. "How can you speak of mercy when you had a hand in destroying her?''

"Alexander—''

"But you were all bought and paid for by Constantine Kirakis and you really had no choice, did you?" Alexander's voice was curt and razor-sharp.

"You must understand—" Karamanlis began helplessly.

"I do *not* understand, Doctor! I don't think I shall ever understand how you—how *all* of you—could have allowed a child to be stolen from his parents, how you could send a woman to her fate like that without a regret!" Alexander stood now at the leaded-glass windows, his back to them.

The doctor shook his head.

"There were regrets. But one learns to live with it after a

time. After it was done, we all knew that we could not go back. We had to live with it.'' Karamanlis's voice was filled with sorrow. ''We have all lived with our guilt for many, many years, though that may be difficult for you to believe now.''

''Difficult? Yes, quite difficult . . .'' Alexander looked out at the peaceful calm of the Aegean.

''Melina was concerned about the fact that your memory had never returned. She was also alarmed about the nightmares. We talked many times, and she told me she wanted to tell you the truth, but Constantine would not allow it. It was the only source of friction between them.'' Karamanlis paused again. ''Even on her deathbed, Melina begged him to tell you the truth—set your soul free, as she put it.''

Alexander thought about it for a moment. ''The night he died he was trying to tell me something. Could he have been trying to let me know the truth?'' He turned and looked at Karamanlis questioningly.

Karamanlis nodded. ''He told me he had not yet kept his promise to Melina, that he had to tell you before it was too late. Unfortunately, he was in a great deal of pain, and I had to keep him heavily drugged. As you well know.''

''Yes, I remember.'' Alexander paused. ''Even after he was dead, no one saw fit to tell me.''

''We had all lived with the lies for so many years, Alexander. We had come to accept it. And once your papa was gone. . . . You had come into power—you were an angry, bitter man then, one to be reckoned with. I had no idea how you might react if I told you. After we had put it off for so long, I realized it was not a good idea to go to you with it.''

''Of course. Tell me, Doctor, how many people who knew the truth are still alive?'' Alexander asked.

Karamanlis hesitated for a moment.

''Only a few. Of the men who were in Ioannina then, only two. George Damos, the foreman. Another man, I think his name was Papersenos. And myself. The attorney who handled the adoption was killed in a plane crash in 1957. The others were very old, most of them just passed away with the usual ailments of aging.''

"This George Damos—where is he now?" Alexander asked.

"I believe he lives in Trikkala. Your personnel manager might be able to locate him for you."

Alexander nodded silently, stuffing the papers back into his attaché case.

"Alexander, may I ask you a personal question?"

He looked up. "You may ask. I may not choose to answer."

Karamanlis understood. "Of course. That is your prerogative," he agreed. "I was only going to ask if you were not happy all those years."

Alexander looked at him oddly. "What do you mean?"

"Were you not happy as the son of Constantine and Melina Kirakis? Were they not good to you? Was there no love between you?"

"They were very good to me, and I loved them more than you will ever know," Alexander admitted.

"Then please, Alexander, do not hate them. They paid for their crimes. You were everything to them. They would have died to protect you. Believe that."

Alexander stared at him for a long moment. "Dr. Karamanlis, at this moment I have no idea what to believe."

"You know the truth now, Alexander," Meredith said as they crossed the airstrip of Hellenikon Airport in Athens to their private jet, her long hair whipping about her face, her cheeks flushed in the cold December air. She turned the collar of her Blackglama mink up about her neck. "Don't you think it's best to leave well enough alone, to just go home and try to come to terms with it?"

He shook his head. "There is one more thing I must do before I can think about the future, about where I am going from here. One more stop has to be made."

"Where?" she asked.

He looked at her. "Lausanne."

The administrator of the Clinique de Lausanne had been surprised by Alexander's sudden interest in Elizabeth Ryan. Though he was aware that Constantine Kirakis had been responsible for her expenses since her admission in 1953, and that the Greek billionaire had made sizable contributions to the clinic over the years, the younger Kirakis had never shown any interest in seeing Mrs. Ryan or even inquired about her. The administrator could not help wondering what had brought about this sudden change of heart.

Now, as he found himself face-to-face with the young Greek, he found himself intrigued. Alexander Kirakis explained that, until recently, he had not been aware of the woman's existence. He seemed genuinely interested in her history, and assured the administrator that the Kirakis Foundation would continue to take full responsibility for her expenses. She was to have the best of everything, of course, and he was not concerned about the cost.

"I have already spoken to her doctor. He said it could be arranged for me to see Madame Ryan," Alexander told him.

"Of course. That would be Dr. Goudron. I believe he is expecting you, no?" He leaned forward and pressed the switch on his intercom. "Solange, page Dr. Goudron and ask him to come to my office."

"*Oui, monsieur.*"

"*Merci.*" He turned back to Alexander. "Dr. Goudron will join us shortly, Monsieur Kirakis. Would you like some coffee?"

Dr. Henri Goudron was a short, dapper man in his mid-fifties, a partially bald, myopic, jovial gentleman who looked more like a banker or a diamond merchant than the highly respected psychiatrist that he was. Unlike the administrator, who seemed somewhat uncomfortable, Dr. Goudron was open and relaxed in Alexander's presence.

"I had just joined the clinic's staff when Madame Ryan was admitted," Dr. Goudron told Alexander as they walked down a long corridor together. "That was in the fall of 1953. She has been here over thirty years now."

"And there has been no improvement since then?" Alexander questioned. "May I ask why not?"

"You may ask, yes, but the answer is not a simple one, I am afraid. Psychiatry, monsieur, unlike other branches of the medical profession, is not an exact science. If one breaks a leg, it will be reset and a cast applied until it heals. If one has cancer, the doctor will consider the options. But in psychiatry—" He took a deep breath. "One cannot heal a mind that cannot be reached, unfortunately."

"I am afraid I do not understand, Doctor," Alexander admitted. "What, exactly, is Madame Ryan's—problem?"

"Emotionally, it boils down to one thing: she was unable to deal with the death of her son," the psychiatrist explained. "The mind is a remarkable and complex instrument, you see. It is virtually impossible to predict how it will respond to extreme stress—shock, if you will. Sometimes, the only acceptable course is to shut out the pain and deny the reality."

"What about drug therapy?" Alexander asked then.

"Drug therapy?" The doctor's expression was one of disapproval. "Ah, that is a question I have considered many times. There is a new breed of psychotherapist, particularly in America, that professes that all—or most—emotional disorders are chemical in origin. They treat depression with antidepressants, anxiety with tranquilizers, and manic depression with lithium carbonate. When all else fails, they will resort to ECT—electroconvulsive therapy, or shock treatments, as they are often called. Do not misunderstand, I am not saying these methods do not work. They do, and sometimes with dramatic results. But I have always felt that to treat emotional disorders with drugs or ECT, without trying to determine the underlying cause, is an oversimplification."

"You have not tried drugs or shock therapy with Madame Ryan?" Alexander asked.

"I have tried *everything,* monsieur," Goudron responded indignantly.

"And you cannot help her?"

"Sadly, no." Dr. Goudron frowned. "As I have already said, once the mind has chosen to shut the rest of the world out, it can be reached only if it chooses to be reached. Alas, all we have been able to do for her is to make her as comfortable as possible, to shelter her from the outside world—where she would be treated as a freak—for the rest of her days on earth. And we can pray for her."

"Then you have stopped trying to help her?"

"Oh, no, I will never stop trying. But I am a psychiatrist

and a logical man. I am also a realist. I do not believe she will ever get better. Thirty-three years is a very long time."

"There was a gentleman who came to visit her many times. A Greek gentleman, no?"

"Ah, yes—he came many times. He seemed to understand her problems so well that I did not turn him away," Goudron recalled. "There was a time I thought he might actually be able to help her."

Karamanlis was telling the truth after all, Alexander thought dismally.

"I see. And did she have any other visitors?"

"Only her husband. He had been careful to make certain that no one ever found out where she was or what condition she was in. Monsieur Ryan loved his wife deeply. There is no doubt in my mind about that. He chose to bring her here, where he knew she could live in seclusion, rather than take her back to America where she would be a defenseless target for the press." Dr. Goudron paused thoughtfully. "It was difficult for him, but he was here once each month, as regular as clockwork, always armed with expensive gifts. He would stay for a few days, and it would always be difficult for him to leave her. Monsieur Ryan had to live with both losses—his wife and the child. But even after he had fallen victim to alcohol, he continued to visit her once a month until he died in 1980."

"I am told he died in an automobile accident," Alexander commented.

"Yes, that is correct."

Alexander studied the doctor for a moment. "I want to see her," he said.

The doctor shrugged. "If you wish. But I must warn you—she may not know you are even there," he cautioned.

"It does not matter. *I* will know," Alexander said promptly.

Alexander had not been prepared for the rush of powerful emotions that overwhelmed him the moment he walked into Elizabeth Ryan's room and saw her for the first time. She was the most breathtakingly beautiful woman he had ever seen. She was almost sixty, he knew, but she could easily pass for thirty-five. It was as if time had stood still for her. Her exquisite oval face was unlined and youthful-looking; her long dark hair shining and luxuriant. Only the eyes, as black as his own, seemed dull and lifeless.

"How are you today, madame?" Dr. Goudron asked, talking to her as if he believed she could hear him and understand him. "You look especially lovely. A new dress, no?" He turned to Alexander. "The women on staff go into town often to buy things for the patients. Sometimes they will lure a hairdresser out here to do the women's hair. It is pleasant for the patients, I think."

Alexander seated himself in the chair the doctor had indicated for him. "Does she understand when you speak, Dr. Goudron? Can she hear you?"

The doctor shrugged. "There is no way of knowing. I take the chance that she does." He turned to the silent, motionless woman. "I have a special treat for you today, madame. You have a visitor." He turned to Alexander again. "She has not had a visitor since the death of her husband," he explained. "I think she misses it."

Alexander wasn't listening now. He was staring at the woman in front of him.

"Elizabeth—this is Monsieur Kirakis," Dr. Goudron told her. She did not acknowledge either of them. "Monsieur, may I present Madame Elizabeth Ryan?"

Alexander reached out and took her hand, bowed his head, and kissed the woman's hand. "I am most happy to meet you, Madame Ryan," he told her in a low, gentle voice.

Elizabeth Ryan gave no response. She stared ahead, focusing on something in the distance that only she could see.

Alexander turned to Dr. Goudron. "She has always been like this?"

The psychiatrist nodded, his expression sad. "Always. It is a sad thing. Sad, and hopeless, I am afraid."

Alexander's eyes met the doctor's, and his face was serious. "I have learned through experience, Doctor, that nothing is hopeless."

"Business is different from medicine, Monsieur Kirakis.

One can extend hope only so far. Patients die, they slip away from us—as Madame Ryan has done—and one comes to expect only so many miracles. God is a busy person.''

"We must not give up on her," Alexander said stubbornly.

Dr. Goudron liked the way Alexander Kirakis had said *we*, but he was afraid the man was expecting the impossible. "I have already told you—"

"And I will tell *you*, Doctor—I am financially responsible for her now. She has no one else," Alexander said sharply, shifting in his chair to face the doctor. "I have already told your administrator that he is to spare no expense, but I expect more for my money than simple maintenance. Genuine effort, at the very least."

The doctor was indignant. "I have always put forth maximum effort, as you say. But I am telling you now, she is never going to get better. She will be exactly as she is now until the day she dies."

Alexander studied Elizabeth for a moment, then shook his head emphatically.

"We shall see, Doctor."

"It was a strange feeling—very odd," Alexander confided to Meredith. "I felt as if I *knew* her, had known her all of my life."

Meredith was visibly worried. "I'm beginning to think it might have been better if we had not come to Lausanne," she said.

"No. I *had* to come." He unbuttoned his shirt. "I'm glad I've seen her. I have so many unanswered questions." He removed the shirt and tossed it over the back of a chair.

"And did seeing her answer your questions, Alexander?" she asked dubiously.

He unzipped his pants and took them off. "In some ways, yes. Dr. Goudron was most helpful." He paused. "I have tried and tried to imagine what it must be like for her, but"—he shrugged hopelessly—"I have had no success."

"What did you expect to find here?" she asked finally.

He shrugged. "I don't know. I know only that I felt this woman knew more about me than I know about myself. I felt she knew the answers to all of my questions about my early childhood.''

New York City.

Alexander tossed and turned violently in his sleep, his urgent protests muffled by the pillow in which his face was buried. ''Don't leave me,'' he pleaded. ''No . . . please . . . don't leave me . . . Mother . . . no . . . *Mother!*'' He sat up in bed suddenly, trembling, his eyes wide with terror. ''Oh, my God . . . Mother!'' he gasped.

Meredith, shaken from a sound sleep by his shouts, sat up and put her arms around him protectively. ''It's all right,'' she told him, stroking his head. ''It was just a dream.''

''It's come back to haunt me,'' he whispered, catching his breath. He was still trembling. ''I haven't had that damned nightmare in so many years . . . I thought I was finally free of it . . .''

Meredith looked at him. ''The same one?''

He nodded. ''I could never remember before—just bits and pieces. This time, I remember everything,'' he told her. He sat up, his expression troubled. He looked up at the painting of Elizabeth. ''I saw her face. I recognized her.''

''Elizabeth?'' Meredith asked.

He nodded, realizing now why the portrait had always disturbed him. ''It was her—but she was dressed strangely, in long flowing robes and gold braid, like something from another era.''

''Her costume from the picture,'' Meredith said. ''What else, Alexander? What else do you remember?''

''Darkness. A small, narrow space, underground—the well, I think. I was trapped. I thought I'd been buried alive,'' he said slowly. ''I kept shouting, but no one could hear me. Then I saw her . . . I don't know where she came from or how she got there, but she was so beautiful, like an angel of light. She beckoned to me, she said she loved me and would show me the way out . . . but when I reached out to her, she just vanished.'' He was still staring up at the painting. ''All these years, I've felt so abandoned, so betrayed . . . without knowing why. I hated all women because of her! I thought she'd left me there to die!'' He sobbed openly for the first time he could remember.

For himself, and for his mother.

Southampton.

Meredith woke during the night to find herself alone in bed. She sat up, looking around for Alexander, but he was not there. She brushed her hair back off her face with one hand and reached for her robe. He had not been himself since their return from Europe, she thought as she slipped on the green fleece robe and tied the sash. He was moody and restless and easily distracted. He spent hours looking at those old photographs, staring at the face of Elizabeth Ryan as if trying to look into her soul. He listened to the tapes Meredith had made of her conversations with Tom Ryan. He read each clipping, each journal entry, each piece in the old scrapbooks until he had memorized every word. He told Meredith more than once that he felt as though he were in limbo, as if he no longer knew who or what he was.

She walked barefoot down the staircase and looked around. He was nowhere to be seen. She spotted a dim light coming from under the door of the projection room. She opened the door slowly. Alexander was slumped over in one of the armchairs, his face in his hands. The film had run through and was flapping wildly against the back of the projector, making a steady clicking sound, the only sound in the room. The harsh white light reflecting off the blank screen bathed the room in an eerie glow. Meredith looked down at the large metal film canisters on the floor by Alexander's feet. He'd undoubtedly been watching Elizabeth's old movies again. She switched on a lamp near the door and crossed the room to switch off the projector. She reached down and touched Alexander's shoulder gently. ''It's two in the morning, darling,'' she said softly. ''Don't you think it's time for bed?''

He shook his head but did not look up. ''I couldn't sleep,'' he said in a tired voice.

She nodded toward the projector. ''Do you really think this is going to help?''

''I don't know,'' he said wearily. ''I know only that I've

got to try—try to help her and help myself.'' He raised his head slowly. ''I can't remember, and she can't forget.''

Meredith knelt down on the carpet beside him. ''Maybe a doctor could help,'' she suggested.

''You're talking about a psychiatrist.'' He looked up at her, reproach in his eyes.

She nodded.

''Meredith, I don't need a psychiatrist,'' he insisted. ''I need to get my memory back!''

''I'm not talking about sending you for fifteen years of analysis,'' she told him. ''I thought perhaps hypnosis—''

He shook his head emphatically. ''If and when my memory returns, it will have to do so on its own,'' he said stubbornly.

She backed off the subject, knowing it would do no good. This was a decision he would have to make on his own. It would do no good to try to pressure him into it.

''I've watched these old movies over and over,'' he said, ''trying to imagine what she must have been like before this happened to her. It's a strange feeling to see one's own mother up on the screen and yet feel as though she is a total stranger.''

''It's going to take time,'' Meredith told him. ''You haven't remembered anything in over thirty years. It's not going to come back overnight.''

His smile was sad. ''She was an incredible woman, wasn't she.''

''A lot of people thought she was a brilliant actress,'' Meredith recalled.

''It is more than mere acting ability that made her a star,'' he said slowly. ''To watch her up there on the screen, there is something about the vitality, the intensity with which she performs—as though she is lit by an inner flame.''

Meredith smiled. ''Tom used to say that when she stepped in front of the cameras, she was not playing a part, but living another life. Becoming another person.''

''She had such a range of expression. It's as if she radiates a force that can be felt, that just reaches out and assaults you as you watch her,'' he said. ''I wish I could remember her. I wish I knew what the real Elizabeth Weldon-Ryan was like.''

''Tom said her son was her whole life,'' Meredith

remembered. "He said she regarded it as the most important role of her life, being a mother. She retired for a while because she didn't want to be separated from you."

"It is ironic, isn't it?" Alexander asked, frowning. "She came out of retirement for one role—and it was that one role that would separate us forever."

"Not forever," Meredith said gently. "You've found her again."

He reached out and touched her hair. "Yes, but will she ever know that? Will she ever know that I am not dead? Will she ever come back to reality long enough to know who I am?"

Meredith touched his cheek. For his sake she had to believe that it would happen.

Zürich.

Julius Hauptmann was alone in his spacious office suite overlooking the Zürichsee. He sat at his desk, reading and rereading the reports he had received that morning. A smile lurked at the corners of his mouth. The Kirakis Corporation was in serious trouble, he decided with a deep sense of satisfaction. Already the corporate giant known as "Alexander's empire" had begun to crumble. It was only a matter of time before its ultimate fall, and the final defeat of Alexander Kirakis himself. Soon the Kirakis Corporation would be ripe for a takeover. Soon he and the consortium would make their move, call in their notes. Kirakis had already been put on notice. Soon, Alexander Kirakis *and* his empire would be destroyed.

TWENTY-EIGHT

꧁꧁꧁꧁꧁꧁꧁꧁꧁꧁

Deauville.

Though Deauville, that timelessly chic resort on the Normandy coast, is every bit as appealing in June, July, and September as it is in August, it is in August that the population invariably escalates to sixty thousand, twelve times the number of permanent residents. In August the resort boasts more personal wealth per square foot than any other town of its size anywhere in the world. Notables from all over the world have been known to leave their yachts, villas, estates, and islands to join the Deauville social scene, a phenomenon that attracts two kinds of people: those who love racing and those who love polo. Rich, influential men and women from all over the world congregate at the 880-acre enclave on France's northern coast every year for the same thing: fast horses, fast money, and a fast crowd.

Meredith had accompanied Alexander to Deauville every year since their marriage, and had become thoroughly familiar with the manner in which business deals were made in the owners' boxes at La Touqes or on the edge of the polo fields. She and Alexander had attended the races and the yearling sales whenever time permitted. They had basked in the hot summer sun by the pool at the Hotel Royale and lunched at Le Bar Soleil and Ciro's, and at night they mingled with some of the most prominent members of the international jet set amidst the black-tie glamour of the Casino d'Été. She had observed, more than once, that every important designer in France was represented in Deauville each August, not only in the various shops on the main shopping street in town, but on the backs of the elegantly turned-out women at the track, the polo matches, the casino, and along the famous boardwalk, the Promenade des Planches. The rule for dressing in Deauville during the polo season, she decided, was quite simple: cottons and linens for day, and the important jewels for evening.

Now, in their suite at the Hotel Normandy, Meredith lay on the bed in a sheer silk nightgown, listening to the sound of running water as Alexander showered. She was worried about him. He had been in a strange mood ever since they left New York. She frowned. He had not been the same since he saw Elizabeth. In his business dealings, he had always been tough and unyielding, but now he was positively ruthless. On the polo fields, he had always been a formidable opponent; now he played the game as though he were waging war. She had also noticed subtle changes in the bedroom. There was an urgency in his lovemaking that had not been there before, an intensity that was a bit frightening at times. It was as if he felt a need, more acutely than ever, to prove himself—as a businessman, as an athlete, even as a man.

He came out of the bathroom, a thick blue towel wrapped around his middle, his thick dark hair damp and curling about his ears. As he stood in front of the mirror, running a comb through his hair, Meredith pulled herself into an upright position and hugged her knees, watching him thoughtfully. He had been unusually quiet throughout dinner, and at the last minute had changed his mind about going to the casino. He looked drawn and tired. "I'm glad you wanted to call it an early night," she said. "I didn't feel like going out either."

He turned to face her. "Do you have to be back in New York right away?"

Meredith shook her head. "I have the rest of the week if I want it," she answered. "Do you have something specific in mind?"

"I was thinking of flying to Lausanne for a day or two before we go home." He tossed the comb onto the dressing table.

She nodded slowly. "All right . . . if you want," she said, resting her chin on her knees.

"You don't seem very enthusiastic," he noticed, crossing the room to the bed.

She reached up and took his hand. "It's not that," she said cautiously. "I just don't want you to be hurt any more than you have already." Her eyes met his. "If she doesn't improve, if there's never any change—"

"I have to believe that there will be." He settled down on the edge of the bed. "I have to believe that I'm going to get through to her, that one day she's going to know who I am and come back to reality."

"She hasn't seen you since you were four years old, darling," Meredith said gently, placing her hands on his shoulders. His deep tan glistened, his skin still moist from the shower. "Even if she can hear you—"

"She will know me," he said with certainty. "The first time I saw her, I felt something—something I am convinced I would have felt even if I had not known the truth. I think she will feel it, too . . . eventually."

"But you did know who she was, darling," Meredith reminded him. "She hasn't changed that much over the years, and you look a great deal like her, but she remembers you only as a small child!"

Alexander's black eyes were filled with determination. "I have to try, *matia mou*," he said in a low, firm voice. "I can never stop trying as long as there is the faintest glimmer of hope. Surely you can understand that."

She studied him for a moment. She started to say something, then abruptly changed her mind and just nodded.

Alexander took her in his arms. "I knew you would," he said softly. His mouth found hers, and he kissed her, gently at first, then hungrily. She clung to him as they fell back on the bed, his kisses increasing in intensity as his lips moved down her neck. He paused just long enough to shed the towel and pull her nightgown over her head, tossing it aside. Meredith began to tremble as his lips moved down over her breast, as he covered her body with his own, the desire rising up within her. As he pressed himself into her, she could feel his male hardness, erect and swollen with longing.

And once again, she was swept away on the torrent of their mingled passions.

Lausanne.

Elizabeth sat near the windows in a large velvet armchair, dressed in a pale yellow silk robe, her thick dark hair hanging loosely about her shoulders. Bathed in the warm, white glow of the brilliant midday sun, her pale, translucent skin seemed youthful, almost flawless.

He held her hand, talking to her as though she could hear him and was able to understand what he was saying to her, just as he had each time he had visited her in the past eight months. He believed that she could hear him, that she knew he was there even if she did not know yet who he was. He believed that he was communicating with her, and that sooner or later he would reach her. He wished that he had brought along the photographs from Meredith's files. Perhaps if she saw those old photos of herself with her husband and son, it might trigger something in her memory. "There has to be something I can do for you, Mother," he said in a low, gentle voice. "Something I can do to free you—free both of us—from the past."

He thought about it for a moment. Something to trigger the memory. Photographs. Familiar places. If he could not bring back his mother's memory, then perhaps he could restore his own. He recalled Meredith's telling him about the Ryan estate in California, about the photographs and the memories Tom Ryan had kept alive in that house. His home. His home for the first four years of his life. There had to be a wealth of memories in that old mansion.

He looked into Elizabeth's dull, lifeless eyes and managed a slight but hopeful smile. "Mother," he said softly. "I may be able to help us—both of us—after all."

"How does she seem to you?" Meredith asked in the car, en route to the airport.

Alexander frowned. "The same," he said sadly. "No matter what I do or how much I talk to her, she just sits there, staring off into space, looking like an elegant statue."

Meredith reached out and took his hand, squeezing it affectionately. "I can imagine how you must feel, darling," she began slowly, "but Dr. Goudron could be right, you know. After so many years—"

"I have finally begun to accept that possibility," he confided, his eyes meeting hers. "I've been thinking . . . if I can't regain my memory through Elizabeth, then perhaps she can regain hers through me."

Meredith looked at him, not sure she understood.

"If I can regain my memory through going back, experiencing familiar places and things from my childhood, then perhaps I can be of more help to her."

"What do you have in mind?" Meredith asked.

"I want to visit the Ryan estate."

"I've decided to scrap the Ryan project," Meredith told Harv Petersen. "I've been beating my head against a stone wall for the better part of three years and I've come up with nothing. I can't see any point in pursuing it any further. I've put in a great deal of time—no, make that *wasted* a great deal of time—that I could have been spending on other projects, and all I have to show for it are a lot of dead ends and a lot of headaches." She took a deep breath. She was giving the performance of her life. She couldn't tell anyone the truth. She had to bury the story, once and for all, for Alexander's sake. He had been through enough. He did not need to be hounded by the press any more than he was now.

"I thought you were finally making some real headway with it," Petersen said, surprised by her sudden decision. "Casey mentioned to me that you were getting an overwhelming response to those ads you placed."

"I was, but they all turned out to be dead ends," Meredith lied. "They were either cranks, or they just didn't know enough to be able to help me."

"I'm sorry you didn't find what you were looking for," he told her, taking a long drag off his cigar as the acrid smoke curled upward. "But I suppose I'm not all that surprised.

Reporters have been trying to crack that one for over thirty years. You came closer than anyone else, I think.''

She nodded. ''I'm sorry, too.''

Schiphol Airport, Amsterdam.

A man sat alone in the lounge, reading the *International Herald Tribune*. Page two carried a story about the death of that Kirakis Corporation secretary in London. More bad press. Excellent, the man thought as he folded the newspaper and tucked it into his attaché case. Everything is moving according to plan. It is only a matter of time. . . .

Brussels.

The body of a man had been found in a hotel room near the flower markets of the Grand'Place. He had been dead approximately seven hours, according to the autopsy. In his suitcase were his passport, a map of London, and an envelope containing several thousand francs. According to the passport, he was forty years of age, born in Torres Vedras, Portugal. He had just arrived in Brussels the day before he was murdered. The cause of death was listed as a gunshot wound.

In his pocket, police had found a photograph of a woman. On the back of it, in a barely legible scrawl, was a name: Carolyn Grayson.

Southampton.

Meredith stared at Alexander for a long time, unobserved, as he piled logs into the fireplace and sprinkled them generously with lighter fluid. He had been so quiet all evening, so preoccupied. Not that she really minded; she'd had a great deal on her mind, too.

Alexander lit a match and tossed it into the fireplace, and immediately the bright orange flames licked across the logs, filling the room with a warm, golden glow. He removed his shirt and dropped to his knees on the floor by the fireplace. He did not realize that she was watching him, trying to read his thoughts.

"How about some wine?" she asked, finally breaking the long silence. "It's from our own vineyards."

He shook his head. "Perhaps later," he said in a tired voice.

Meredith settled down beside him on the floor. "I had a meeting with Harv Petersen today," she told him. "I've dropped the Ryan story. I thought I should let him know."

He looked at her for a moment. "I am sorry," he said quietly. "I know how long you've worked on this, how important it's always been to you."

Her arms encircled his neck. "No story is more important to me than you are," she said softly. "I didn't know what you wanted to do, so I thought it was best just to tell him I hadn't been able to come up with anything."

"And did he believe you?"

She nodded. "After all this time, I think he was probably wondering why I hadn't given up on it a lot sooner," she said. "I just told him everything seemed to lead to a dead end."

He kissed her lightly on the lips. "My father—my natural father, Tom Ryan—went to great lengths to protect Elizabeth from unwanted publicity. I think he would have wanted me to go on protecting her. I owe her that. I owe it to both of them to protect her for the rest of her days," he said, staring into the fire. "If this were to get out, she would not have any real peace. She would become the one thing Tom feared most: a freak. I cannot allow that to happen."

"I had a feeling you wouldn't," she said, her eyes meeting his. "I was sure you would understand why he did as he did."

He studied her with a growing interest. "What was he like?" he asked suddenly.

"He was a good man, but a real loner. He erected an emotional barrier around himself. I don't know if he wanted to shut out the outside world or if he was just trying to shut out his own pain. He came off as hard and abrasive, but I always suspected it was just a front. Actually, he was a man whose feelings ran quite deep. He just died a little inside each day. When I look back on it now, I think the responsibility he felt toward Elizabeth, toward protecting her at all costs, was the one thing that kept him going all those years."

"He must have loved her very much," Alexander said, gazing at the flames once more.

"He loved both of you," Meredith said simply. "But don't ever forget that Constantine and Melina also loved you. They loved you as if you were their own flesh and blood. And whatever else they may have done, they gave you a wonderful life."

Alexander shook his head.

"A life built on lies," he said bitterly.

"A life built on *love*," she maintained, determined to make him see that it had not been a waste. She realized how important it was for Alexander to be able to forgive them for loving him too much, for doing what they did because they desperately wanted a child. "What they did was wrong. But regardless of the image of power, of being larger than life, they were mortals, just like the rest of us. They wanted a child and couldn't have one, after Damian died."

"Damian," Alexander said slowly. "Damian's death determined my destiny."

"You know, darling, you were luckier than most children," she told him. "Look how many kids don't have a home, have never had anyone to love them. And you had two sets of parents who loved you and wanted to give you the world. *Did* give you the world. You had Tom and Elizabeth, who gave you life and shared big dreams for you—and you had Constantine and Melina, who took you as their own and loved you and left you with an empire, as well as a legacy of love."

He smiled wearily. He lay back on the rug, holding her close. She snuggled against him, her face against his chest, taking comfort in the sound of his heartbeat. We're going to get through this, she thought. Somehow, we'll make it. We have to.

The wind blew Meredith's hair into her face as she emerged from the limousine in front of the Olympic Tower. She glanced at the slim platinum watch studded with diamonds that Alexander had given her for her birthday in June. Nine o'clock. She was exhausted and glad to finally be calling it a day. She hadn't been feeling well, but she suspected it was due to the long hours she had been putting in, along with the pressures she and Alexander had been subjected to in the past few months. She had been more tired than usual, and had all but lost her appetite. She was nauseous much of the time, but she had not bothered to consult her doctor because she was certain that it was nothing more than stress. When things settle down, when we find out what's behind this insanity within the corporation and Alexander has come to terms with his past, maybe we'll get away from here for a while, she thought as she crossed the lobby to the elevators. Maybe we'll take a month, like we did on our honeymoon —cruise the Mediterranean, or just visit the island. It would do us a world of good.

Alexander had visited Elizabeth several times in the past six months, and had spoken at length with Dr. Goudron who still felt the visits were a waste of time.

But Meredith had known that it would do no good to try to dissuade Alexander.

Meredith stepped into the elevator. Next week, she was flying to the West Coast with Alexander to visit the Ryan estate. She wasn't sure what good it could possibly do, but he insisted that seeing the house, his home for the first four years of his life, might trigger something in his memory. She hoped he was ready for whatever memories it might actually restore—or for the possibility that it might not make him recall anything at all. After all, in all the times he had visited Elizabeth, nothing had ever come of it.

At least now Alexander understood where his feeling of betrayal came from. As a four-year-old child, trapped and frightened in that old well, his primitive instinct had made him call out for the one person who had always protected him: his mother. Young as he was, he had not been able to understand that she had not been able to reach him, that she had wanted to come to him, to make him safe again. In his mind, he felt that she had betrayed his love for her by abandoning him when he needed her most. That, Meredith reasoned, was why his relationships with women had failed until he met her. In her mind, she pictured all of the women whose pictures had appeared in the gossip columns with his. All of them were dark, sultry women like Elizabeth. Subconsciously, it seemed that he had selected those women for their resemblance to her, then treated them badly as a way of lashing out, punishing them for her betrayal.

Los Angeles.

Meredith paused at the door of the mansion and looked up at Alexander questioningly. "Are you sure you want to go through with this?"

He nodded. "My past is in this house," he said, gazing up at the English Tudor exterior. "If something inside can bring back even a single memory, then it will be a start."

Meredith hesitated a moment, then dug into her coat pocket for the key and unlocked the door. Pushing it open, she went inside. Alexander followed her. "It's incredible," she said, looking around. "They've kept it up exactly as Tom Ryan left it. Everything is just as it was when he lived here."

Alexander nodded but said nothing. He stepped past her and walked around, looking through the rooms, taking in everything as if even the smallest object might bring back a memory of his early childhood. She followed him through the entrance hall to the parlor, the dining room, and the kitchen, waiting for him to say something, to remember something, but he remained silent. They went into Tom Ryan's den. The framed photographs Tom Ryan had kept on the bookshelves were still there, just as he'd left them —photos of himself, his wife, and their son. Alexander, picking one up, studied it intently.

"My mother and myself," he said, staring at the portrait thoughtfully.

Meredith nodded. "Tom told me once that it was taken just before the three of you left for Europe," she said softly.

He smiled. "We must have been happy then," he decided.

"Very happy," Meredith said quietly, putting her arm around him.

He took the glittering gold statue down from the mantel

and looked at it for a long time. "She never knew she finally won the Oscar, did she?" he asked.

Meredith shook her head. "She was at the clinic when the awards were given," she said, lightly stroking his arm.

Alexander's smile was sad. "She wanted it so badly, but she was never to know that she had finally achieved her goal." He paused. "Quite a price to pay for the honor. It makes one stop and think about just how important success really is."

Meredith looked at him. "I think if she had been offered a choice, she would rather have kept her son."

He put his arm around her. "I wish I could reach her. I wish I could tell her I am still alive," he said longingly.

"Maybe someday you will," Meredith said hopefully. For both of you, I hope it happens, she thought.

They went upstairs and looked through the rooms. Elizabeth's dressing room was exactly as Meredith remembered it—right down to the raspberry silk negligee draped across one of the chairs. She had always thought it the most beautiful room in the house. Done in shades of mauve and beige, the carpet was thick and soft, the furniture covered in velveteen and brocade. There was a long dressing table resembling those in the studio dressing rooms, only far more elegant, matched couches and chairs, a wardrobe made of cedar, and bay windows overlooking the grounds in back of the main house. On one wall were several framed photographs, most of them photos of her husband and son. Alexander stared at the wall for a long time, fascinated with one photo in particular, a picture of the child David Ryan with a small mongrel pup on the front lawn of the mansion. "Scruffy," he said suddenly.

Meredith looked at him. "What?"

"The dog's name was Scruffy," he said slowly. "I found him on the beach. It was so long ago. We had gone on a picnic. Mother and I were walking along in the sand, and I found this pup." He smiled. "Actually, the pup found me, I think. He followed me back to the car when we were leaving, and I cried until Father agreed to let me keep him." He turned to look at Meredith, amazed. "I *remembered*," he said incredulously. "I remembered a puppy and a picnic at the beach!"

Meredith nodded, smiling.

"It's a start," she said encouragingly.

"I want to see David's—my old bedroom," he insisted.

"Okay," she said hesitantly.

"You have the key."

She nodded. "This way," she said softly.

"It's funny," she said, taking one last look around Elizabeth's room, "that this room could be closed up for so many years and everything is still intact, as if Tom and Elizabeth and their son still lived here, were still a part of it."

As they started to walk out the door, one of the perfume bottles on Elizabeth's dressing table, untouched and undisturbed for so many years, exploded.

Meredith paused outside David's bedroom, the key in one hand, padlock in the other, looking up at Alexander questioningly. "Maybe we should wait until tomorrow," she said gently. "This could be too much for you for one day—"

Alexander shook his head. "We've come this far," he said grimly. "There can be no turning back now."

Reluctantly, she put the key in the lock and turned it. The lock popped open in her hand. She removed it, then opened the door. As they entered, she found the switch on the wall and turned on the overhead light.

Alexander stepped ahead of her and looked around, his face drained of color. The room, untouched for almost thirty-five years, was dusty and had a musty smell about it, but it also gave him a strange feeling of familiarity. It was more than the knowledge that his past was tied to this room: he actually remembered this room and the objects in it. He had seen it briefly, in fragments of dreams and flashes of memory that came to him at unexpected times but always escaped before he could capture them. This room held the secrets of the first four years of his life.

He sank down onto the bed and drew in his breath, running his hand over the soft blue bedspread. The teddy bear on the bed, the catcher's mitt and baseball that still looked new, if a bit dusty, because they'd never been used, the toys in the large toy chest, the child's clothes in the closets, they were all familiar in an eerie kind of way. They were all a part of the past he could not remember.

Zürich.

Herr Hauptmann was curious. Why did the investigator from Interpol want to see him? He had been quite busy and had little time to spare, but he decided to see Inspector Dessain anyway.

"I can think of no reason why you would want to see me, Inspector," he said slowly. "Perhaps you can explain?"

Dessain smiled, a warm, friendly smile that made Hauptmann feel as if he were the Frenchman's best friend. "You are aware, of course, that the Kirakis Corporation has been facing serious financial problems, are you not?" he asked.

"Of course, but I wasn't aware that Interpol involved itself in that sort of thing," Hauptmann said, pressing his fingertips together.

"Normally, Herr Hauptmann, Interpol would not get involved," Dessain admitted. "But it would appear that there have been a number of accidents—somewhat questionable accidents—involving persons who have been connected in one way or another with the Kirakis Corporation. You are already aware of this, no?"

"To be quite honest, I do not concern myself with such things," the Swiss banker told him.

Dessain grinned. "Oh, come now, Herr Hauptmann," he chided him, "a man in your position—"

"Exactly. A man in my position would not concern himself with those things—at least not on a professional level—" Hauptmann started.

"But you *are* the primary financier for the Kirakis Corporation, are you not?" Dessain asked pleasantly.

"That is confidential," Hauptmann pointed out.

"Yes, it is," Dessain agreed. "But it is a well-known fact that bankers are naturally concerned when adverse publicity threatens the soundness of their investments, correct?"

"Yes, of course. But the Kirakis Corporation is solid and has been for many years," Hauptmann insisted. "Their track record is impeccable. The consortium currently acting as the conglomerate's primary bankers—"

"Of which you are a part," Dessain added helpfully.

Hauptmann shook his head. "No. On that you are mistaken."

"I think not," Dessain responded easily. "My sources, you see, are quite reliable."

The banker hesitated for a moment. "It was necessary for me to keep my participation in the consortium quiet for professional reasons," he said quietly. "My board chose to decline the offer to participate in Herr Kirakis's expansion plans, so I invested with my personal funds. Had I revealed it, it could have been taken as a conflict of interest."

"I see." Dessain leaned back in his chair and took out his pipe. He held it up. "Do you mind?"

Hauptmann shook his head. "Of course not."

Dessain lit the pipe and puffed on it thoughtfully for a while, the sweet-smelling smoke filling the air. Hauptmann was hiding something. "I have a theory," he began, choosing his words carefully. "It is my belief, Herr Hauptmann, that someone would like very much to put Alexander Kirakis out of business."

"That's absurd," Hauptmann said quickly. "Kirakis is a multibillion-dollar operation. It would be difficult to imagine the company in serious trouble."

"Oh?" Dessain looked at him oddly. "Then why is it that you have been trying to persuade your fellow bankers to call in their notes to Kirakis?"

TWENTY-NINE

᠊᠊᠊᠊᠊᠊᠊᠊᠊᠊

Meredith stepped up onto the platform and took hold of a chair to steady herself. She felt slightly dizzy as she crossed the *Manhattan Observer* set and took her seat before the cameras. She scolded herself for having skipped breakfast that morning. After the taping was finished, she would have a Danish and some juice to keep her energy level up until lunch. She and Casey were going to the Italian place. I should have talked to Harv about that vacation, she thought. Alexander would be furious if he knew she had not even mentioned it to her producer yet. She looked up as a technician adjusted the lighting. They seemed unusually bright for some reason. And hot. Unbearably hot. She felt weak, but she was determined to make it through the taping.

"I think you could use a touch more makeup, Meredith," the director called from beyond the cameras. "You look a little anemic from where I sit."

She forced a smile. "I *feel* a little anemic from where *I* sit," she responded.

"Are you feeling okay?" he asked, concerned.

"I'll live—if we can just get this taping finished," she assured him, looking over the notes in her lap.

"Okay—let's run through it once, just to be sure," he suggested.

"Fine." Meredith looked up into the camera and smiled. "Good evening. I'm Meredith Courtney. Welcome to *Manhattan Observer*. Our guest this evening is a man who . . . a man who has . . . " She stopped, unable to remember the name of her guest. She tried it again and fumbled her lines. "I'm sorry, Dave, I don't know what the problem is . . . " She looked down at her notes. The words typed on the pages were suddenly blurred.

"Let's take a break," the director called out to his crew. "Meredith, I think you'd better forget about taping for today."

She shook her head emphatically. "No, Dave, I'm fine," she insisted. "I just need some water. It's so hot in here . . . " She stood up, wobbled for a moment, then collapsed.

"When was your last menstrual period, Mrs. Kirakis?" Dr. Holland asked as he looked over her file thoughtfully.

Meredith paused. She couldn't remember. So much had happened in the past few months that she had not even thought about it. "I'm not sure," she confessed. "Is it important?"

"Yes," he said, making a notation in the file. "You've been taking your birth control pills faithfully?"

"No," she said, drawing the thin white examining gown around herself tightly as she felt a sudden chill pass through her body. "I stopped taking them several months ago."

"That would explain it, then." He made some notations on her chart.

"Explain what?" Meredith asked anxiously.

"Your symptoms—the fainting, nausea, exhaustion. Not to mention the fact that you've gained a bit of weight." When he turned to face her, he was smiling. "You're pregnant, Mrs. Kirakis."

Lausanne.

Though Alexander had visited the Clinique de Lausanne many times in the past few months, he had failed to take notice of the opulent surroundings. Now, as he crossed the grounds, with Elizabeth walking passively at his side, he decided it did not look like a hospital at all, let alone the finest psychiatric hospital in all of Europe. It could almost be described as elegant; in fact it reminded him of a hotel in which he had once stayed in Dubrovnik.

Though Elizabeth had never spoken to him, or even acknowledged his presence at the clinic in all the times he'd visited her, Alexander stubbornly refused to give up on her. Somehow, he vowed, he was going to find a way to break down that barrier now separating her from the rest of the world. He had to make her realize who he was, that he was still alive and had come back to her. Now, as they walked along, arm in arm, he carried on a long conversation with her, talking to her as if she could actually hear him and understand what he was saying. If there were even an outside chance that she *did* know he was there, that she *could* hear him, then he had to keep trying. Though he realized intellectually that he had had no control over what had happened in Ioannina so many years ago, though he was well aware that he had been as much a victim as his mother had been, he still felt a measure of responsibility for her present condition. He looked at her thoughtfully, and tried to imagine what it must be like for her now. "How could they have done this to you?" he asked aloud.

As they walked along the lake, a group of ducks paddled idly toward the bank on the other side. The bright midday sunlight danced across the surface of the water like a million brilliant diamonds. Alexander looked into his mother's face, into those great, sad eyes, and he searched for a clue, some indication of what she might be thinking or feeling at that moment, but there was nothing. Her face was blank, expressionless. He wished he could remember what she was like before the accident, before they had been separated from one another. He wished he could recall some of the closeness that must have existed between them. She must have been a good mother, he thought sadly.

Sensing that she was beginning to tire, he led her over to a bench in the sun-dappled shade of a large willow tree. Elizabeth sat beside him in silence, gazing off into the distance. He held her hand and tried to talk to her, but he was beginning to feel discouraged. Nothing seemed to touch her.

Spotting a cluster of wildflowers growing near the trunk of the tree, he remembered something Tom Ryan had mentioned on one of those tapes: his son had often picked flowers for his mother in the park. "Most of the time they were nothing more than weeds," Tom had told Meredith, "but Liz treated them as though they were the most expensive roses. She would arrange them in her finest crystal vase, keeping them until they dried up and fell apart." Alexander got to his feet and went over to the tree. He picked the flowers and took them to Elizabeth.

"These are for you, Mother," he said softly. "I hope you like them." He placed them in her hand and pressed her fingers around the stems.

In her mind, an image flashed before her eyes for just a moment—a small child offering her a cluster of dandelions—but then it was gone. A single tear escaped from the corner of her eye and rolled down her cheek, but Alexander did not see it. Feeling defeated by her lack of response, he slumped over beside her, his face in his hands, trying to summon up the strength to go on. He shook his head. "Mother," he said in a voice so low that it was almost inaudible. "What will it take? What must I do to reach you, to make you know me again? How can I make you hear me?" For the first time, he felt as though he might crack under the strain.

Suddenly he felt something brushing lightly against the back of his head. He turned his head slowly. Elizabeth's hand was outstretched, her fingers lightly stroking his hair. She was looking at him, but her stare was still blank, as if she did not really see him. She did not speak. But it was a beginning. It was something. Alexander reached up and took her hand.

"Mother?" he whispered.

Then he saw the tear in her eye. He reached out and held her close. "You *did* hear me," he gasped. "You *do* know! You know that I've come back!"

"In the future," Dr. Goudron began, "I would appreciate it

if you would check with me before taking Elizabeth from her room.''

Alexander paced the psychiatrist's office like a caged animal. ''I cannot believe this,'' he said evenly, trying to control his anger and frustration. ''You have not heard a word I have said.''

''I *have* heard you,'' the doctor said. ''I *do* understand your excitement at this new development. But I am a realist as well as a physician. I have looked after Madame Ryan for thirty-four years now. I am more familiar with her, I think, than you could ever be.''

Alexander swung around to face the psychiatrist, his black eyes blazing. ''Meaning what?'' he shot back.

''Meaning, monsieur, that if you are expecting a miracle, I am afraid you are setting yourself up for a great disappointment,'' Dr. Goudron replied. ''This is hardly a major breakthrough.''

''But she knew me! She knew I was there!'' There was an overwhelming urgency in Alexander's voice.

''Let me try to explain something to you if I can,'' Dr. Goudron said patiently. ''Madame Ryan has been catatonic for a good many years. In such cases of catatonia, we are never certain how much of the outside world reaches her troubled mind. Maybe none. Maybe everything, and she has simply chosen not to acknowledge it. It is impossible to tell with any degree of certainty.'' He pressed his palms together thoughtfully.

''But the flowers—could that not have triggered—'' Alexander started.

''It is possible, yes.'' The doctor paused. ''In psychiatry, there are *always* possibilities.''

''You are telling me that this is nothing, that it was just . . . a fluke?'' There was a look of disbelief on Alexander's face.

''Perhaps not. What I am trying to tell you is that while it happened once, it may never happen again. This is not the first time a patient like Madame Ryan has responded to one isolated incident and never responded again,'' Dr. Goudron said quietly.

Alexander stood at the window, staring out toward the

lake where he had sat with his mother only an hour earlier. "It seems odd that the only breakthrough in all those years came from the time I have spent with her," he said slowly, choosing his words carefully.

Dr. Goudron stared at him for a moment. "You have been quite patient with her," he said. "It surprises me that someone like yourself should take such an interest in a woman like Madame Ryan, who is a stranger to you."

Alexander smiled. "Someone like myself," he repeated wryly. "Now how many times have I heard *that?*"

"No, I meant only that—" the doctor began, slightly embarrassed.

Alexander dismissed it with a wave of his hand. "It is all right," he said indifferently. "I am accustomed to it."

"You must try to understand," Dr. Goudron said, speaking in a low, measured tone. "The mind is a most complex thing. When it suffers a trauma that it finds unbearable, it protects itself in a number of ways: sometimes it blocks out only the unpleasant memory; sometimes it retreats totally, cutting itself off from the external world. It cannot be reached if it does not wish to be. In Madame Ryan's case, the break was complete. After having cared for her as long as I have, I am convinced that only one thing could help her now, and even that might not work. Unfortunately, it is the one thing that will never be possible."

"What is that?" Alexander asked, still staring out at the lake.

"The resurrection of her dead child," the doctor said sadly, drawing in a deep breath.

"Suppose her son were still alive," Alexander said slowly.

Dr. Goudron looked at him, not sure he understood. "But, monsieur, you know that her son died in 1953—"

"Suppose I were to tell you that he is still alive and that I know where he is?" Alexander suggested.

The doctor shrugged. "As I have already told you, there are no guarantees. But if he is alive, if you can prove this—"

"I can."

Dr. Goudron paused, unable to believe what Alexander was telling him. "And where is he now?"

Alexander hesitated for a moment, knowing that by revealing his secret to anyone, there could be serious repercussions. But he also realized that this might be his only hope of helping his mother, that her fate was now in his hands, in his willingness to trust the doctor with his secret. He had a choice to make, and in that moment, he made his decision. He turned to face Dr. Goudron.

"You are looking at him," he said quietly.

The next day, Alexander returned to the clinic. This time, he did not talk with Dr. Goudron, but he was certain there would be no further objections from the psychiatrist concerning the time he spent with Elizabeth. After his startling private confession, he was convinced the doctor would see things his way, even though Gourdon had not believed him at first. Surely the doctor could see that the more time he spent with Elizabeth, the more likely he was to reach her.

Now, as he led Elizabeth along the edge of the lake, he began to hum a tune. It was a melody he'd carried with him since childhood without knowing what it was or who'd taught it to him. Now, as he continued to hum, he noticed an odd expression on Elizabeth's face. On her lips appeared the beginning of a smile. Could the tune have come from her? he wondered. Encouraged, he hummed the melody again. Elizabeth's mouth trembled slightly as a tear escaped from one eye and slid down her cheek.

"Mother," he whispered, clutching her hand. "Mother —you did hear me!"

New York City.

Meredith was having dinner when Joseph came into the dining room. "Telephone for you, Mrs. Kirakis," he announced. "Mr. Kirakis, calling from Switzerland."

Meredith got to her feet. "I'll take it in the study, Joseph," she said. She hurried into the study and closed the door. Settling into Alexander's high-backed executive chair, she picked up the phone. "I have it, Joseph," she told their houseman. Hearing the click as he hung up in the living room, she spoke again. "Alexander?"

"Yes, darling," said the familiar voice on the other end. "I phoned earlier and Joseph told me you were resting, so I told him not to disturb you. Are you all right?"

"Never better. Just tired," she assured him. "He should have told me you were on the phone."

"Joseph knows better than to disobey me."

"How is Elizabeth?" Meredith asked.

"I think she's recognizing me," Alexander said, encouraged. "It wasn't much, she just touched my hair for a moment the other day and today she smiled, but it's a start. She knew I was there."

"That's wonderful!" she said. "What does the doctor say?"

"He feels it's too soon for a celebration." Alexander paused. "I have told him everything."

Meredith hesitated for a moment, surprised. "You told him about Ioannina . . . and who you are?" she asked, clutching the receiver.

"I felt I had to," he said simply. "If telling him the truth could help her, if there was the slightest chance, then I had to do it."

"I understand," she said softly.

"I am sure he can be trusted," Alexander said confidently. "After all, he has kept Elizabeth's secret for all these years."

"I suppose you're right," she said, leaning back as another wave of nausea swept over her.

"I've been thinking," he said. "Perhaps if I were to stay on in Lausanne a few more days . . ."

Meredith's heart sank, but she tried to conceal her disappointment. "Do you think that's wise?" she asked. "With everything that's been happening within the corporation . . ."

"Things have been fairly quiet for the past few weeks."

"Could be the calm before the storm," she mused.

"Is something wrong, darling?" he asked. He could sense her moods, even over the phone.

"No," she assured him. "It's just that I have a surprise for you, and I want to share it with you."

"Can it wait a few more days?" he asked.

"It will, but I don't think *I* can," she confessed. "I went to see Dr. Holland yesterday, Alexander. I'm three months pregnant.'' She hadn't wanted to tell him this way, over the telephone, but she couldn't wait a moment longer.

''Pregnant?'' he asked. ''Are you sure?''

She laughed. ''Absolutely positive, darling.''

Paris.

Adrian Dessain had gone over all the facts at least a dozen times. Now, as he sat before the computer terminal in the basement at Interpol headquarters, scratching his cheek thoughtfully as he studied the data on the screen in front of him, he wondered if he could have made a mistake. It did not make sense, and yet. . . . He keyed in another entry and the screen changed, giving him yet another set of data. Coincidence? No. Dessain did not believe in coincidence. How had he missed this before? he wondered. How had he overlooked anything so significant? The implications were frightening.

If his hunch was correct—and they were seldom wrong —Alexander Kirakis was in a great deal more danger than he had realized. This person wanted to ruin Kirakis, yes, but his motive was such that destroying the Kirakis Corporation would hardly be enough to satisfy his insane need for revenge. If Dessain was right, there was a madman headed for New York City with one objective in mind: to kill Alexander Kirakis and anyone who happened to get in his way. Dessain snatched up the phone next to the terminal and tried to call Kirakis. Unable to locate him, Dessain called Air France, making a reservation on the next flight to New York. He had to find Alexander Kirakis. He could only hope he made it in time.

Southampton.

''There's a storm brewing,'' Alexander told Meredith as they walked together on the beach, a brisk breeze tousling their hair. ''Look—to the south. The dark clouds coming up. It's going to be a rough one.'' He pointed to the forbidding black clouds off in the distance.

She smiled. ''Where did you learn so much about

clouds?'' she asked, drawing her white alpaca sweater around herself against the cool wind.

"When I was growing up—in Greece," he said, still gazing upward thoughtfully. "Father used to take me out on the boats with him. Living on an island, we were always alert to changing weather conditions. He taught me about the different clouds, the different weather patterns. He learned all about them as a stevedore, he said, watching for the tempests that wreaked havoc with the boats at sea and in the harbor."

"Did you hear yourself?" Meredith asked. "You called Constantine Father."

He frowned. "Old habits are hard to break," he said quietly, staring at the southern skies thoughtfully, his dark hair blowing in the wind, his eyes blacker and more threatening than the clouds.

"Are they?" Meredith stopped walking and took his hands in hers. "Will you never be able to forgive them, Alexander?"

"Could you, in my position?" he wanted to know, his face taut with anger.

"I think so, yes," she said truthfully. "Whatever else they did, they loved you more than anything in the world. I never met them, of course, but I came to know them quite well in the course of my research, and I believe they would have died for you."

"Or killed for me, as the case may be," he said coldly.

"Accept it, darling, and put it behind you," she urged him. "To go on like this, you'll only be hurting yourself —and me. I can't stand to see you torment yourself this way."

"How can I simply forgive and forget when my entire life has been pulled apart?" he asked. "The problems within the corporation, and now this . . . I feel as if suddenly the whole world, *my* whole world, is crashing down around me!"

"You know the truth now. You know that your mother —your natural mother—is still alive. You know that Constantine Kirakis tried to make amends, that he and Melina wanted to tell you everything . . . " Meredith told him.

He gazed upward, trembling with rage. "But I do not

know who I am!'' he roared. ''Am I David Ryan—or Alexander Kirakis?''

She stood quietly for a few seconds. ''In a sense, David Ryan did die in Ioannina,'' she said softly. ''David died and was reborn as Alexander—a new identity and a new life. Alexander is the man you became. You couldn't go back now if you wanted to. You can only go forward. You are Alexander Kirakis, as you have been since the day you were found in that cave in 1953. A piece of paper can't change that. But you are going to have to put the past behind you and get on with your life. To do that, you must be able to forgive Constantine and Melina for loving you, for wanting you to be their son so much that they went as far as they did to make it happen. You still care very deeply for them. I can see that, even if you can't. Forgive them and put your own pain behind you.''

He smiled wearily as he took her in his arms. ''What would I do without you?'' he asked.

''I'm not about to give you the opportunity to find out,'' she said matter-of-factly. ''Now . . . why don't we go back to the house and I'll make some hot cocoa? It's getting cold out here.''

''Hurricane Sybil is at this time approximately one hundred miles south of Cape Hatteras, North Carolina,'' the disembodied voice of the radio weathercaster announced. ''It is expected to brush the eastern tip of North Carolina, then move northeast on a course that will put it parallel to the shoreline of Virginia, Maryland, Delaware, and New Jersey, with hurricane conditions expected all the way to New England.''

Meredith, curled up on the couch next to Alexander, was concerned. ''Isn't it headed right for us?'' she asked.

He smiled, stroking her hair. ''Don't worry about it, *matia mou*,'' he told her. ''It is a very long way off right now. Even if it should come this far, it will probably lose strength before it reaches New York.''

''Probably?'' she asked.

''Hurricanes are unpredictable,'' he said. ''Right now, Sybil's winds are assaulting the coast at one hundred fifty miles per hour. But that could easily change long before she travels this far north. The tides are up to twelve feet, but by the time they reach Long Island, they may be ten or less. If it hits Long Island at the right moment—optimum low tide —its force will be weakened a lot.''

''And if it doesn't?''

He kissed her forehead. ''I don't want you to worry about it. I don't want you to worry about anything,'' he said emphatically. ''You are to rest and stay as calm and relaxed as possible. I will keep track of the hurricane warnings. If it appears there may be a genuine threat, we will take appropriate action.''

''How can you be so calm?'' she asked.

He gave a low chuckle. ''I grew up in Greece, darling,'' he reminded her. ''The storms that hit the islands with much regularity are quite similar to the hurricanes here, only much more common. I am accustomed to riding out this kind of weather.''

Meredith looked up at him and smiled. Oddly enough, she felt safe in his arms, hurricane or no hurricane. In spite of everything he had been through himself in the past few months, his first thought was still for her. She wrapped her arms around his neck and kissed him, tenderly at first, then again, lingeringly. She drew back and smiled at him again. ''I love you,'' she said softly.

He smiled, too. ''Tell me, did Dr. Holland place any restrictions on our lovemaking?'' he asked in a low, husky voice.

''Not so far,'' she said, looking at him. ''What do you have in mind?''

''I think I would rather show you than tell you.'' He stood up, and in one swift movement, he scooped her up in his arms and carried her up the stairs to the master bedroom. Depositing her gently onto the bed, he closed the door and removed his shirt. Then he returned to her, stretching out beside her on the bed, and took her in his arms, kissing her long and deep.

''Trying to take my mind off the storm?'' she asked when he finally released her.

''What do you think?'' he asked with a suggestive smile.

''I think you'd better finish what you started.'' She pulled him down to her again, kissing him hungrily as she unbuckled his belt. She fumbled with his zipper for only a moment, then her hands found him and began caressing him.

He unbuttoned her blouse. "Not so concerned about the hurricane now, I see," he teased.

"What hurricane?" She kissed him again as his hands moved over her breasts, squeezing them gently. He unzipped her gray wool slacks and pulled them off, casting them aside carelessly. When they were both nude, he took her into his arms again as he pressed himself against her, kissing her with a gentleness that caught her by surprise.

They were oblivious of the hard rain, now beating steadily against the bay windows. They kissed long and hard with a renewed urgency, a renewed longing that had all but disappeared from their lovemaking in the wake of the pressures of the past six months. They took their time, arousing passions that had been ignored for too long. "Already, you're a bit rounder than usual," Alexander commented as his hand lingered on her lower abdomen. "It won't be long before you begin to show, will it?"

"Possibly as early as next month," she said, running her fingers through his hair. "How will you feel, being seen in public with the fat lady from the circus?"

"Proud," he answered without hesitation. "You will always be the most beautiful woman in the world as far as I am concerned—pregnant or not." He kissed her again.

"What do you want—a boy or a girl?" She fondled a lock of hair at the nape of his neck as she gazed up at him in the darkness.

"I want you," he said. "Boy, girl, it doesn't matter. As long as I have you."

At two in the morning, Alexander was downstairs again, listening to hurricane updates on the special weather band on the radio, while Meredith slept peacefully upstairs. "It is most likely that Sybil's center will be staying close to the coast, with hurricane conditions existing all the way to the New England states," said a spokesman for the National Hurricane Center in Florida.

". . . Expected to reach Long Island by Friday afternoon,'' said another, speaking from the National Weather Service in Rhode Island. ''She's comin'—it's going to be a day of reckoning.''

''Winds of one hundred thirty miles per hour . . . scaffolding at the Jefferson Memorial in Washington, D.C., has been secured to protect the marble . . . the Pentagon has ordered warships out to sea to ride out the storm, while fighter planes have been sent inland to avoid the hurricane's destructive attack . . . Fire Island evacuated . . .''

Alexander stood at the French doors leading to the terrace, pondering the southern skies. The hurricane was definitely coming. On its present course, it would hit Manhattan around noon on Friday, and Long Island sometime thereafter. He should have taken Meredith back to Manhattan last night, when the warnings were first issued. If anything were to go wrong now, she was much too far from her doctors. But they couldn't even attempt to get back to Manhattan. It was too risky. Already, the skies were restless. By morning, the situation could easily change. Sybil could pick up speed overnight. No, they would have to stay.

As the hurricane continued on a collision course with Manhattan, the city prepared itself for the full onslaught of nature's fury. The World Trade Center was ordered closed. Businesses were shut down for the day in anticipation of the 150-mile-an-hour winds expected. The normally crowded, bustling streets of Manhattan were empty as the city came to a standstill. Publicly, Mayor Koch stated that ''anyone driving into Manhattan Friday should have their heads examined.'' Ships in New York Harbor were moved to safety upriver. City crews removed twenty-five thousand trash cans from city streets so they would not become ''unguided missiles'' in the gale-force winds. All incoming and outgoing flights were canceled at Kennedy, La Guardia, and Newark airports.

At Kennedy Airport, Inspector Adrian Dessain had been trying to reach Alexander Kirakis by telephone. When he finally got through to their apartment, he was informed that Mr. and Mrs. Kirakis had gone to their home at Southampton for the week. Trying to get the address of their Long

Island home out of their houseman had been like trying to get government secrets out of a captured agent, but Dessain had finally persuaded the man to tell him, convincing Joseph that he really was with Interpol and that this really was an emergency. He could only hope that he was not already too late.

He met with further resistance when he attempted to hire a pilot to take him to Southampton by helicopter. "No pilot in his right mind would go up now," the owner of one charter service told him. "Don't you know there's a hurricane coming, mister? It could hit at any time!"

"But you do not understand, monsieur," Dessain said urgently in his heavily accented English. "This is an emergency! It could very well be a question of life or death!"

"So is this, buddy," the man told him. "That god-damned hurricane's expected to hit New York with the force of an atomic bomb. To go up in a chopper in that kind of wind would be suicide!"

Finally, Dessain had given up hope of getting a private pilot to make the flight. He had taken the only course of action remaining.

He went to the New York Highway Patrol.

"Don't worry, everything is going to be all right," Alexander assured Meredith as he sat on the edge of the bed beside her.

He stayed with her until she finally drifted off to sleep, then left the room quietly and returned to his post downstairs. Standing at the French doors, his gaze fixed on the skies to the south, he glanced at his watch. Eleven-thirty.

The storm would hit Manhattan any time now.

At that moment, Dessain and two Highway Patrol officers were in a patrol car ten miles south of Bellport, racing against time. If Dessain's hunch was correct, the man who was out to destroy Alexander Kirakis would make an appearance very soon.

He could only pray that he got there first.

* * *

As Alexander monitored the increased velocity of the winds ripping across the beach, sending debris and tree branches soaring through the air, he listened to updated reports on the hurricane on the radio, still tuned to the special weather band. It appeared that the storm's fury had weakened considerably by the time it reached Manhattan, shortly after noon. The winds were reported to be much weaker than predicted, only forty miles per hour. Minimal damage had been reported. It now appeared that the storm would hit Long Island at low tide, which meant it would be weaker still. He was relieved. While there was bound to be some damage from the winds, the threat was lessened. He decided not to wake Meredith. She had had a somewhat restless night and needed to rest as much as possible. He had tried to call their apartment but was unable to get through. Telephone lines had been knocked out all over Long Island by the storm, and the phone was dead.

The sound of the doorbell took him by surprise. He had not expected anyone to be out on a day such as this. He opened it, but he did not recognize the man who stood before him. "Yes?" he asked.

"Mr. Kirakis," the man said quietly, obviously having recognized him.

"Yes?" Alexander repeated, puzzled.

"You do not recognize me, do you?" the man asked with a strange smile.

"No. I cannot say that I do," Alexander admitted, puzzled and somewhat uncomfortable. He had an odd feeling about this man, though he was not sure why.

"My name is Julius Hauptmann." He spoke English with a heavy German accent. "I am the sixth member of the banking consortium in Zürich. I must speak with you. It is very important. May I come in?"

Alexander hesitated for a moment, still brushed by a sense of unease. "Of course, Herr Hauptmann. Do come in," he said finally, stepping aside to allow the other man to pass.

As he closed the door, his uneasiness increased.

Inspector Dessain attempted to telephone Alexander from an outdoor phone booth in West Hampton, but he discovered the lines were down. He ran back to the police car, the belt of his trench coat flapping wildly behind him, twigs and other debris whirling about him in the fierce winds. "We must get to Southampton as quickly as possible," he told the two patrolmen. "We do not have a moment to spare!"

"We may have to pull over and wait it out," one of the officers told him. "It would be dangerous to try to drive if the winds become much stronger. Anything can happen —falling trees, power lines brought down in the storm—"

"If we do not make it, they may be dead by the time we do get there," he responded gravely.

"You do not know who I am, do you?" Hauptmann asked as he stood by the fireplace.

Alexander, seated on the couch, looked up, puzzlement on his face. "Of course," he answered. "You have already told me. You are Herr Julius Hauptmann, and you are the only member of the consortium I have never met in all my dealings with them." The man was behaving strangely, and Alexander was concerned. Why had he come here? What did he want? Certainly this was not an official visit.

Hauptmann's eyes met Alexander's, and his stare was deadly cold. "It is just as I thought," he said. "You do not even remember Marianne—do you?"

"Marianne?" Alexander asked. Then it hit him. "Marianne Hauptmann . . . oh, my God . . . " He shook his head slowly.

Hauptmann glared at him. "Marianne was my daughter, Mr. Kirakis," he said, thrusting a yellowed clipping from a Geneva newspaper down in front of Alexander. "She died seven years ago. Shall I tell you how she died?"

"I already know how she died," Alexander said, his mind racing. Of all the people he had suspected of trying to destroy him, it had never once occurred to him that Marianne's father could have been the one. His eyes shot to the top of the stairs, and he silently prayed that Meredith would not awaken.

Hauptmann's face was a mask of rage. "She hanged herself in that miserable hotel room because of you!" he roared. "She took her own life because she loved you and you turned your back on her! You seduced my daughter and used her for your own pleasure, then discarded her when you tired of her!'' His laugh was mirthless. ''Marianne was such a lovely, innocent girl. So naïve. She actually believed you were in love with her and wanted to marry her!''

''I never meant to hurt Marianne—'' Alexander began in an attempt to pacify Hauptmann. The man was clearly deranged and Alexander was determined to get him away from the house before Meredith awakened.

''Silence!'' Hauptmann shouted angrily. ''You never cared about my daughter's feelings—you who were so notorious for discarding women as easily as you discarded your clothes! I know all about you, about the trail of destruction you left in your wake. How many women tried to kill themselves over you? Were you proud of that?''

''Listen to me, I—'' As Alexander stood up, he froze. It was at that moment that he saw the gun in Hauptmann's hand.

Dessain and the patrolmen were delayed just outside Southampton by a fallen tree blocking the road. As they struggled to move it enough to allow them to pass, Dessain looked up at the gray, threatening sky.

Are we already too late? he asked himself.

Meredith was roused from a sound sleep by the sound of men's voices raised in anger. She recognized one of the voices as Alexander's, but the other was not familiar to her. She sat up on the edge of the bed, trying to determine what was happening downstairs. Unable to hear them clearly, she slipped into her robe and crept quietly to the top of the stairs, sensing that something was terribly wrong. She could see Alexander, but she was unable to see the other man's face clearly. Neither of them saw her.

''I have waited a long time for this moment.'' He paused, breathing hard, obviously agitated. ''Seven long years of pain, of building a weapon with which I could destroy you. A long time, but worth the pain and the waiting, for your day of reckoning.''

''Listen to me, man!'' Alexander's tone was urgent, and Meredith could see the look of alarm on his face, even from that distance. She could feel her own heart beating wildly in her throat.

"Nothing you could say now could possibly be of any interest to me," the other man snapped, quivering with rage. "Do you have any idea how it feels to lose someone who has been your main reason for living? I doubt it. I doubt you have ever cared enough for *anyone* to feel the kind of pain I have lived with since that morning in Geneva!"

"I *do* know how you feel—" Alexander began.

"No, you don't!" Hauptmann roared. "How could you? You . . . a man who has always used others for his own ends!"

"You know nothing about me except what you may have read," Alexander said carefully, trying to get through to him without antagonizing him.

"I know what kind of man would use an innocent, vulnerable young woman for his own selfish pleasure—what kind of man drives a woman to take her own life!" Hauptmann's troubled voice took on a razor-sharp edge, sending a chill down Meredith's spine as she listened in the shadows. "The day I buried my daughter, Herr Kirakis," the man continued in low, measured tones, "I vowed to devote my life to making you pay for your sins. It has taken time, longer than I would have liked, but this moment has made it all worthwhile."

Alexander stared at him incredulously. "It was you—"

The other man's laugh was hollow. "Over the years, I have amassed enough money and enough power to destroy you," he gloated. "I have orchestrated your final defeat very carefully, attacking the weakest points in your all-powerful empire. It was I, Herr Kirakis, who arranged for the fire in Montreal, but that was only the beginning, as you well know."

Alexander stared at him, saying nothing.

"My people—they are very efficient, no?—were behind the legal problems plaguing your nuclear research facility," Hauptmann declared triumphantly. "It was not easy, swaying your American politicians. But as you yourself have said on many occasions, everyone has a price." He paused. "Including your man in Turkey."

"Kafir?" Alexander asked. "What has Kafir to do with this?"

"Actually, he proved quite useful to me," Hauptmann

revealed, his thin lips twisting into an evil smile. "Once I discovered the skeleton in his closet, persuading him to do my bidding was a relatively simple matter."

"Skeleton?" Alexander didn't understand.

"Your man Kafir had a terrible gambling addiction," Hauptmann said with a smirk. "I am surprised you were never aware of that fact." He chuckled softly, mockingly. "I bought all of his markers, and so he became my property."

"I knew it," Alexander said under his breath, remembering Kafir's odd behavior that morning in Istanbul.

"My people set Kurt Badrutt up as well," Hauptmann went on, savoring the fear in Alexander's eyes, unaware that Alexander's fear was not for himself but for his pregnant wife. "We would have succeeded in blackmailing your man in England as well, had that woman not stumbled onto the information we had used against him. If only she had not discovered what was taking place. . . . It was a most unfortunate turn of events—for her."

"You had Carolyn Grayson killed?"

Hauptmann smiled icily. "Let us just say I arranged an accident for her."

Alexander looked at him. The man was nothing more than a cold-blooded murderer. And he was condemning Alexander for Marianne's death! "What about Carlo Manetti?" he asked carefully. "Were you behind that as well?"

"Of course," Hauptmann admitted without hesitation. "Manetti suited my needs perfectly. When his company was forced into receivership, everyone—including Manetti himself—was quick to believe that you had been behind it. It was the perfect setup." He paused. "When the fool decided to kill himself, it came as an unexpected bonus. His daughter *did* make you look very bad in the press, do you not agree?"

"My God, you're insane!" Alexander rasped.

"I was behind all of your troubles, Herr Kirakis," Hauptmann continued. "The pharmaceutical company, the bad press concerning the instability of your empire—but I think my finest hour came when I finally uncovered the truth about *you*."

Alexander stared at him, suddenly hit by the certainty that Hauptmann knew about Elizabeth, about Ioannina.

"I had been following your wife's investigation, and was

so intrigued that I decided to conduct a bit of research on my own,'' Hauptmann said. "I dispatched people to Athens, to Ioannina, even to Los Angeles. It was I, Herr Kirakis, who sent your wife the proof she sought.''

"You!'' Alexander looked stunned. At the top of the stairs, Meredith's heart stopped for a moment.

"I considered taking everything to the press,'' Hauptmann went on. *"Everything,* Herr Kirakis—the truth about the accident in Ioannina, the truth about who you really are and where your mother is now, the truth about how far Constantine Kirakis had been willing to go to insure the future of his empire. It would appear that you are not really a Kirakis at all!'' His smile was pure evil. "But then I decided I would much rather have you continue to live with the knowledge that someone else knew the truth about you —someone whose identity you did not know—and that it could all blow up in your face at any time. Unfortunately, I had to change my original plan. That man, that Interpol inspector, was getting too close. Too close to the truth.'' As he changed position, Meredith saw the gun. Quickly, silently, she crept back to the bedroom to call the police, but she discovered the phone was dead. She looked around the room wildly, then suddenly remembered the shotgun Alexander kept in the bedroom closet. As she took it out, her fingers trembling, she prayed it was loaded. She checked and saw that it was, then went back to the top of the stairs. They were still arguing. The man with Alexander still held the gun on him. He was saying things that made no sense to Meredith. She crept down the stairs. Alexander, facing the staircase, looked up just as she reached the landing. "Meredith!'' he called out to her. "Go back upstairs—quickly!''

Startled, Hauptmann pulled the trigger. A single shot rang out, and Alexander fell back onto the couch. Reacting instinctively to protect her husband, Meredith raised the shotgun and fired once. Hauptmann fell to the floor, blood spurting from the back of his head. Meredith fell back on the stairs, trembling uncontrollably, her heart pounding violently, as Alexander, gripping his left shoulder, got to his feet slowly and approached the still figure lying at the bottom of the stairs. Not taking any chances, he kicked the gun away from the body, out of Hauptmann's reach. He noticed a shiny object lying next to him. He bent down and picked it up gingerly. It had been a long time, but he still remembered it: the bracelet he'd given Marianne at Gstaad.

He looked up at Meredith, who lay back against the railing, still trembling. "Are you all right, *matia mou?*" he asked as he started toward her.

She nodded. "Is he dead?" she asked in an unsteady voice.

"Yes," he assured her.

"Who was he, Alexander?" she asked as she pulled herself up. "Why did he want to kill you?"

His smile was weak. "It is a very long story, darling. I—"

The sound of someone pounding furiously at the front door interrupted him. He went to open it, still clutching his shoulder, the light gray wool of his sweater now soaked with his blood. As he pulled the door open, he saw Dessain and the two policemen and was flooded with relief. Dessain looked at him and turned to the two officers. "Call for an ambulance," he said, turning back to Alexander. "Hauptmann?" he asked.

Alexander nodded. "In the living room."

He rushed past Alexander and bent over the still figure of Julius Hauptmann, checking the pulse in his neck. "We will also need the coroner," he said quietly. "This man is dead."

THIRTY

᠎᠎᠎᠎᠎᠎᠎᠎᠎᠎

New York City, June 1988.

The financial world was buzzing with excitement. The *Wall Street Journal*'s headlines proclaimed one of the largest corporate mergers of all time: the Kirakis Corporation was merging with Hammond Transcon, the third largest conglomerate in the world. After a year of setbacks and serious reverses, a year in which it was rumored that the Kirakis Corporation was cursed, that Alexander Kirakis was facing the final defeat, Kirakis had bounced back, bigger and better than ever. There was also a footnote to the story: in Los Angeles, the Kirakis nuclear research facility was about to reopen.

Athens.

The museum opened only weeks earlier by Alexander Kirakis and his lovely wife had been dedicated to the memory of his late parents, Constantine and Melina Kirakis. It was drawing large crowds with its exhibits, most notably a collection of Impressionist paintings by Monet, Renoir, and Manet. Everyone was still talking about the moving and poignant speech Alexander Kirakis had delivered at the dedication ceremonies, and the strong devotion he displayed toward his late parents.

Lausanne.

Though Dr. Goudron had never been a believer in miracles, he felt as though he were actually witnessing one. In the year that had passed since Alexander Kirakis's startling confession, there had been a subtle but definite improvement in Madame Ryan's condition. After thirty-five years of silence, of no response whatsoever, Goudron actually felt as though a breakthrough had been achieved. Alexander Kirakis visited his mother regularly, and it seemed to the trained eye of the psychiatrist that he was actually able to communicate with her. She did not speak yet, but the doctor was certain now that it was only a matter of time. It made him wonder if there were indeed some inborn instinct that gave one the ability to recognize one's offspring, even under the most difficult of circumstances.

Paris.

As Alexander and Meredith emerged from their private jet with their infant daughter, reporters and photographers gathered at the fence several yards away, clamoring for the first photographs of the newest addition to the Kirakis dynasty. Though the child was now six months old, she had never been photographed by the press. Everyone guessed that, after all Alexander and Meredith Kirakis had been through in the past two years, they were afraid someone might try to kidnap the infant. It had been rumored that Meredith Kirakis's pregnancy had been a difficult one, and that she had come dangerously close to losing the baby twice, the first time following the shooting at their Southampton home.

Now, as they reached the bottom of the ramp, Alexander put one arm around Meredith, who carried the baby in her arms. The press called out to the couple, pleading with them for a picture or at least a comment. Meredith looked at her husband, smiling. "Shall we?" she asked.

He smiled too. "Why not?"

They walked, together, over to the fence. Meredith reached over and removed the child's lace bonnet to reveal a face strikingly like her father's, with a mop of thick dark hair and the same black, flashing eyes that had been his trademark. "Ladies and gentlemen," Alexander said proudly, "our daughter—Alexis Elizabeth Kirakis."

216